GW01112098

Richard Ryan has spent his working life as a writer and director in film and television. Recently he has concentrated on writing, resulting in this, his first novel.

He lives in Sydney with his wife and three sons.

RICHARD RYAN

funnelweb

MACMILLAN
Pan Macmillan Australia

All characters in this publication are fictitious and any resemblance to real persons, living or dead, is purely coincidental.

The story of Arachne is adapted from the prologue of Keith C. McKeown's *Australian Spiders: Their Lives and Habits* (Angus & Robertson, 1952).

First published 1997 in Macmillan by Pan Macmillan Australia Pty Limited
St Martins Tower, 31 Market Street, Sydney

Reprinted 1997

National Library of Australia
cataloguing-in-publication data:

Ryan, Richard, 1948– .
Funnelweb.

ISBN 0 7329 0888 4.

I. Title.

A823.3

Typeset in 12.5/15pt Sabon by Post Typesetters
Printed in Australia by McPherson's Printing Group
Maps by Robert Parkinson

For Rita

I am become death, the destroyer of worlds.

BHAGAVAD GITA
c. 200 BC

1

In a dark and secret place, the spider stirred. He was safe here, damp and warm. A perfect lair, an impregnable fortress, the place had served him well.

But now, the noise had come – the piercing metallic jangle, the raucous cackling jabber – noise that had raged all day and throughout the night before.

The spider was distressed. His cycle of rest and activity had been broken. And he was hungry. No light penetrated these depths but instincts of three hundred million years told him that the day was ending. It was time to leave and forage for food. He crept forward.

Slowly, precisely, the spider picked his way up out of the blackness, ascending the widening silken tube of his funnel-shaped web. Finally he came to its entrance, a fissure in a vertical face of rock. Below, murky water lapped onto a muddy shore. Across the water, a sky thick with heat hung magenta over a shimmering city. But the spider's attention was not on these things. His gaze was fixed on the cause of his annoyance, the source of that interminable, unnatural noise – a group of humans. They were cavorting and bellowing nearby outside one of their habitations. From the shadows of the fissure, the spider watched them.

At a place called Mosman Bay on the North Shore of Australia's Sydney Harbour, a raunchy New Year party was hitting its stride with a thousand watts of Led Zeppelin's 'Black Dog'. Beautiful young women frolicked with drunken, ageing ravers. Others bathed naked in the pool. Beneath the pergola, a fat man fornicated with a silicone-breasted blonde whilst on the sun terrace a man snorted cocaine as he watched his wife take the virginity of a youth. French champagne and mescal flowed freely, and the scent of marijuana smoke drifted on the hot breeze.

The spider watched it all, and as he watched, hormones seeped from his cerebral glands and triggered a primeval urge – the urge of the predator to prey on the weak and debilitated. For the spider's every instinct told him that these humans were sick. But he did not attack, because the instinct to survive was paramount, and he knew above all else that to attack any human meant death. So the spider moved off, picking his way stealthily down the rock face, and disappearing quickly into the gathering darkness.

Not far away, another deadly creature prowled in the gloom, but the catastrophe within its body was of a different order to that of the funnelweb spider. Off Bondi Beach, beneath the swell of the Pacific Ocean, the US nuclear submarine *Montana* nosed northward, unseen and unheard.

The patrol had been painfully routine, so the hundred and fifty-five men cooped up for two months in the cramped steel hull were getting touchy. It hadn't taken much twisting of the captain's arm to allow this minor, unauthorised deviation from the *Montana's* course, for some harmless New Year's Eve distraction.

Barely twelve inches of the *Montana's* periscope broke the ocean surface. A black carbon-fibre tube less than an inch in diameter, it had several times the tensile strength of steel and was hydrodynamically shaped to leave no telltale wake. A miniature digital camera mounted on a tiny gyroscope at the tip was sending pictures down into the *Montana's* belly, where a computer enhanced the images to the standard of broadcast television before feeding them to the boat's forty-seven TV screens.

And what images they were, custom made to lift the spirits of any lonely submariner. Australia's finest swarmed along Bondi that night, flitting like insects in the firelight of a dozen beach parties – hundreds of girls, all fit and tanned, parading and petting, pouting and preening, kissing and cuddling and coupling in the shadows with their boyfriends.

The fresh American faces gazed in painful appreciation at the delights before them. And with many of the *Montana's* crew hailing from Southern California, lust was not the only emotion prompted by the glow of the cathode ray tubes. As The Beach Boys' 'Still Cruisin' played softly over the boat's PA, many eyes moistened with bittersweet pangs of homesickness.

Perhaps that was why it happened. Maybe the launcher manning the weapons conn was thinking about what his fiancée was up to back home in San Diego. Or maybe the officer of the deck's concentration on his readouts was distracted by some irresistible image of Australian womanhood. Whatever, it was more than eight seconds before the watch reacted to the coolant servo failure in the

Montana's number 41 warhead, one of ninety-six hydrogen bombs mounted atop the submarine's complement of twenty-four Trident IIa (E6) ballistic missiles, each armed with four W101(APA) 345 kiloton thermonuclear warheads individually encased in Mk 9 Manoeuvrable Reentry Vehicles, or MARVs.

The servo failure itself need not have been disastrous. Every aspect of the *Montana's* weapons system had multiple backups. Under normal circumstances, one of the three backup servos installed in each warhead to counter just such a failure would have switched in automatically to stabilise the flow of coolant around the warhead's antimony-plutonium core.

But no system devised could beat evil fortune. Zero point three seconds into 41 warhead's primary servo failure, there was a glitch in the response to the event by the warhead's on-board computer. The glitch came from a bug which had been introduced into the system's self maintenance package by a defect in the Read Only Memory chip in which the software had been embedded for delivery. The sub-contracted programmers had saved three dollars a unit on ROM blanks by purchasing clones manufactured offshore. To all intents and purposes the quality of the substitutes was identical with that of the domestic brand. Except, unfortunately, in the case of that one chip. Subsequently, the bug had lain in the warhead's brain like a banana skin under a rug in a dark corner of a half-remembered room, as it had in every one of the other two hundred and eighty-seven W101(APA) warheads deployed with the US Navy.

Under normal circumstances, the bug would eventually have been detected by the routine sweeping of all active service Defense Department software designed to identify just such one-in-a-million problems. But on this occasion, it came to light in a manner that was somewhat more dramatic, when it changed the warhead computer's comprehension of the situation from:

> *failure of primary coolant servo has occurred –*
> *switch in first backup and activate audio alarm*

to:

> *failure of primary coolant servo is anticipated –*
> *route printer alert via central computer to conn.*

By the time the officer of the deck glanced down at the humming printer at his elbow, then looked across to check the readouts on the weapons status panel, the incident had a history of eight point three seconds and the coolant temperature reading for 41 warhead was already into the red.

The officer of the deck's bowels was just registering the impact of a sledgehammer, and his left hand was halfway to the oversized red button marked General Alarm, when the *Montana's* central computer beat him to it. The boat's big brain, which as well as having recorded the printer alert was receiving unusual data from the electronic thermometers in number 11 missile tube, computed the probability of a serious situation and blew the whistle.

All hell broke loose! Lights flashed – horns sounded – white-faced crewmen raced urgently to their battle stations. Within seconds, the captain and the executive officer were in the conn, listening to the officer of the deck's report. They were trying to piece together what had happened when the intercom speaker crackled with a tinny version of the weapons officer's voice, speaking directly from the weapons conn. Yes, he confirmed, there had been a total failure of 41 warhead's primary coolant servo, and no, he had no idea why the on-board computer had got it wrong. The backup servo had now been switched in manually and was functioning correctly but there was still a problem. When the coolant fluid became overheated, a seal in the coolant pump housing must have swollen and leaked. Sensors indicated that about a millilitre of radioactive fluid had seeped outside the radiation containment circuit and was free inside the MARV casing.

The captain, who was a stoic man, muttered what the others took to be a blasphemy but which was in fact a prayer. He knew that his exemplary nineteen-year career in the service would be on the line when it came out that the *Montana* had ventured into Australian territorial waters, even though it was widely known in the Pentagon that American submarines constantly broke international maritime law by straying into foreign national territory. Traditionally it had been a way of keeping the other side guessing and an expression of the submariner's buccaneer spirit – a cavalier gesture in the great game.

Now the game was up, and everyone knew it. But that was not the captain's main concern of the moment. Antimony-plutonium alloy, or APA, was a new development only recently introduced into fusion bombs. Its function was to be the spark plug, or igniter, which detonated the chain reactions in the secondary and tertiary stages of the weapon, giving rise to the main explosion. APA produced a more complete reaction than the older plutonium-239 or uranium-235 Oak Ridge alloy spark plugs, resulting in a more efficient burn with minimal 'dirt'. But APA emitted radiation in a wider spectrum than the traditional materials, and the effects of that radiation, in low dosages and at close quarters, were still relatively unknown.

The weapons officer, who even from the weapons conn knew exactly what was going through the captain's mind, broke the silence. 'Sir, I can go in there and swab that stuff up. If you can hold station for ten minutes – rock steady – I'm sure I can get it all.'

Grim faced, the captain looked at the executive officer for an opinion.

The executive officer looked optimistic. 'Should be no problem right here, Captain.'

The captain turned away. 'Do it, gentlemen,' he said quietly, '. . . and good luck.'

When his subordinates had gone, the captain dropped heavily into the commander's seat. And from the loneliest place aboard, he reflected on how the events of the past two minutes would probably ruin his life.

The figure that entered the upper-level missile compartment a few minutes later looked more like an alien astronaut than a submariner. The oversized radiation-proof suit had mirror metallic surfaces, designed to show up even the most minute speck of contaminated dust. And its power-assisted limbs only added to the impression of otherworldliness.

The weapons officer inside the suit moved cautiously along until he came to the tube with the number 11 painted on its side. Working quickly, with the confidence of endless drills, he soon had the tube's access hatch open and Trident 11's nose cone released and hoisted clear. Revealed within, four five-foot high cone-shaped MARVs, each containing one warhead, gleamed silver in the harsh work lights. At the base of one designated 41, the weapons officer located a nine-inch square hatch labelled Coolant Circuit Access, and marked with the Radioactive warning symbol.

Despite his cumbersome gloves, the weapons officer deftly flipped up two flush-fitting catches and opened the hatch wide. Inside, at the junction of a black metal box and a chrome pipe, he found what he was looking for – a tiny drop of viscous yellow fluid seeping from a hairline joint so fine as to be barely perceptible.

Perspiration forming on his face beneath the radiation suit's thick glass visor, the weapons officer began to wipe the liquid up with a three-inch square of white cotton gauze. The gauze had been specially prepared for the purpose, hemmed with plastic to stop stray threads, and impregnated with a synthetic solvent to prevent the viscous coolant from smearing. Working with intense concentration, the weapons officer noted that the executive officer was being good to his word – the massive submarine was holding perfect station in the current almost as if it were in dry dock.

The weapons officer finally removed the last radioactive traces from the joint with the fifth square of gauze. Each soiled piece had been carefully placed into a lead-lined steel container the size of an attache case which the weapons officer had carried in with him.

Just as he was placing the last piece of gauze into the container, the weapons officer's earpiece exploded. 'Phil! Secure for evasive action – then get the fuck outta there!' The voice belonged to the officer of the deck and was accompanied by the general alarm – the second time it had sounded in ten minutes.

But before the words were out, the boat's twin turbines were already racing to full revolutions, and under the impulse of forty-five megawatts, nineteen thousand tons of submarine leapt forward like a Ferrari off the starting grid.

The weapons officer had no chance. Half crouched, he was thrown completely off balance. He tumbled across the radioactive material container and sprawled like a turned turtle against the missile tube.

With huge effort, he rolled himself over and got back onto his feet. Hurriedly, and in a filthy mood, he slammed the container shut and resecured the missile. Then, grabbing up the heavy box by its handles and moving off quickly, he clicked on his helmet's jaw switch and spat into the microphone, 'What the fuck is going on, George?'

The weapons officer burst through a radiation-proof door marked Decontamination, and as it swung closed behind him with a loud clang, his earpiece crackled again.

'Sorry, Phil – the local posse got a sniff of our ass. We give you a little heartburn down there?'

Stepping forward into the decontamination shower, the weapons officer snapped, 'I got bowled over like a hooker on pay night – take a look at 41's sensors for me, will you?'

Amused at his colleague's wrath, the officer of the deck replied, 'Sure, be right back,' and the earpiece clicked off.

The weapons officer turned a lever marked Scrub, and the radiation suit was hit from all directions by a dozen high-pressure jets of sea water. A non-foaming alkaline detergent broke down nearly all of the water's surface tension, making the solution a more effective cleansing agent than caustic soda.

The officer of the deck's voice cut back into the earpiece. 'Great job, Phil! Not enough Rads in there for a suntan. Daiquiris on me.'

The weapons officer breathed a sigh of relief. Despite the gymnastics, his efforts had been successful. Now he looked forward to a cold drink, even if the daiquiri would be no more than iced mango juice – like all US Navy ships, the *Montana* carried no recreational liquor.

The weapons officer turned off the Scrub lever, walked out of the shower and moved into a cubicle marked Radiac Check. There was a hum as the device switched on automatically and the weapons officer noted from readouts that there was, as he had expected, no residual radioactive contamination on his suit.

Suddenly exhausted, he stepped through a watertight door marked Locker Room, then slammed it shut and sealed it tightly behind him.

The waste sea water and detergent solution from the Scrub shower passed along a vacuum disposal pipe and was vented directly into the ocean. Since the *Montana* was at sea, no other precautions were considered necessary. The purpose of the Scrub was to remove only the most minute of irradiated particles which in the vastness of the ocean presented no measurable risk.

On this occasion, the Scrub effluent had contained nineteen radioactive particles. Eighteen of them had been airborne fragments of human skin, each with a mass of less than a milligram and so small as to be invisible. But the nineteenth particle was bigger. It was something which had stuck, unnoticed, to the underarm of the weapons officer's radiation suit when he had fallen over in the missile compartment – a three-inch square of cotton gauze, hemmed with plastic, and impregnated with radioactive coolant fluid.

The gauze rose up through the still, dark water until finally it reached the ocean surface. And there, beneath a star-filled sky, it caught an inshore current and began drifting towards the heads of Sydney Harbour.

In the *Montana's* conn, the mood was elated. Tension had evaporated with the successful evasion of a patrolling

Australian destroyer which had picked up the big submarine on sonar. Had the American warship been identified by the Australians, there would have been a hell of a row. As it was, the *Montana's* formidable acceleration meant that by the time the destroyer had approached, there was no trace of anything.

His heart still pounding, the captain gave orders to set course for mid ocean, back to the security of the Central Pacific depths. Then he remembered the weapons officer, and threw an inquiry at the officer of the deck.

'All okay, Captain,' came the reply. 'Trident 11's down but clean. Phil's out of Decontamination and back in the wardroom.'

The captain said 'Very well,' then turned away, musing on the situation. Maybe it wasn't so bad. If any of this got out, his superiors stood to lose as much as he did, so it was equally in their interests to fudge the whole thing over. And no harm had been done. No – there really was nothing to worry about.

Comforted, the captain called up his navigation charts and settled into the commander's seat for the long and tedious journey back to nowhere.

By six-thirty the next morning, the sun was blazing over Sydney in a painfully bright blue sky. With the temperature rising fast and the humidity suffocating, the day already threatened to blister.

Along a rocky harbour shoreline, the funnelweb spider was making his way back to his nest. The night's hunting had been fruitless, mainly because the spider's reflexes had been so dulled by tiredness. And now what equated in his psyche with mood was cantankerous.

The spider rounded a bend and ascended a black,

oily boulder at the water's edge. Beyond, there was a hidden stretch of sand no more than ten-metres long at a place where two currents met. As a result, the little beach was always covered in debris and scavenging insects. The spider was starving and had come this way hoping to find an easy meal. But what he actually found was untypical, and caused him to scamper down to the water in a frenzy.

Dozens of fish were strewn along the beach, all either dead or dying. And seagulls and magpies which had feasted on the carnage were fluttering around in agonised death throes. The spider darted up and down, so crazed with hunger that he could not decide where to start. Finally, he picked a baby shark already ripped open by seagulls, and ravenously began to feast on its guts.

The spider was so intent on his feeding that he did not notice others of his species approaching from the surrounding rocks. First a few, then a dozen, then a hundred – the sun was beating down now and the stench of rotting fish carrying far.

The funnelwebs were predators, not carrion feeders, and usually would not have taken dead flesh. But today, as never before, they acted against their nature, and gorged upon this carrion with mounting ferocity.

It was not until the first spider had eaten through the baby shark's intestine that he began to feel something. At first, it was just a throbbing, like something ominous approaching from the distance. But then the pain came – a searing pain that lanced into him like white hot needles, bringing agonising but strangely pleasurable feelings, of power, and of awesome aggression. The feelings pulsed through him like a thousand drums beating, growing and growing until he felt that he would explode. It was then at the very core of him that something unhooked . . . and a deluge of acrid force erupted and flowed in him like lava.

The spider darted and froze, he reared back and trembled, he spun and leapt and quivered in a crazed dance. And the force incinerated his pain as it cauterised his every nerve, and overwhelmed him with urges that were black, and irresistible.

As the other spiders watched, they were disarmed – none of their kind had ever acted this way before. But then they heard the drumbeats, and one by one the pain came to them too. They darted and froze, they reared back and trembled, they spun and leapt and quivered in a crazed dance. And when the acrid force erupted in each and every one of them, the gathering on the little beach was visited by pandemonium.

The madness went on and on and on. For what seemed like an age, the funnelweb spiders ran amok. They strutted and postured over the mound of rancid carrion like a deranged army crazed with the stench of death. Then, as if at some secret signal, they scattered and dispersed in every direction from which they had come.

The first spider reared back and shook. Then taken with some all-consuming purpose, he rushed off across the sand towards his nest. As he passed the baby shark on which he had first gorged he paid no attention to its intestines, now gaping wide from the ravaging of many funnelwebs. Spilled out of it, mixed in with the bile and gore, was something unusual – a three-inch square of cotton gauze, hemmed with plastic, and impregnated with viscous yellow fluid.

At seven fifteen, the Mosman Bay New Year party was on its last legs. Robert Plant and Jimmy Page had given way to Tony Bennett, and coffee and croissants had replaced less nutritious consumables.

But one couple soldiered on. To the strains of 'San Francisco', the fat man and the silicone-breasted blonde who had earlier occupied the pergola clung to each other, hung over but happily satiated. Feeling no pain, they shuffled past debris and comatose bodies, whilst a handful of other late stayers watched amused from the verandah.

The funnelweb spider glared at them from the entrance to his lair. His body throbbed with hatred. No caution remained in him. And no instinct either, save one – an all pervading lust to kill.

The silicone-breasted blonde was feeling sexy. To further amuse her friends, she ran her hands over the fat man's buttocks and around into the front of his jeans. Then when she took out his penis and caressed it to an admirable erection, the verandah came to life with hoots of approval. Encouraged, the blonde slid down and took the fat man's member into her mouth, at the same time teasing his scrotum with elegant, crimson fingernails.

The verandah erupted. Someone predictably changed the record to Donna Summer's 'Love to Love You', and people gathered round to enjoy the impromptu sex show. Before long, the silicone-breasted blonde was naked and straddling the fat man. She impaled herself on him furiously, provocatively exaggerating the rhythmic bouncing of her breasts. Soon all inhibitions were swept aside, and as the audience clapped wildly, the first of them began to join in.

The spider seethed. As the sexual activity escalated and the noise level rose, the urge to destroy these foul humans overtook him. He darted and froze, he reared back and shook, he spun and leapt and quivered in a crazed fury. Then every filament in him snapped and he shot out of his hiding place with the impetus of a bolt from a crossbow.

Surrounded by debauchery, the silicone-breasted blonde was close to orgasm. As her ecstasy mounted, she knew she was having the best sex of her life. Which was as well – for it was to be her last.

The spider charged at her. She saw him coming just as her climax peaked. Through a haze of bliss, she realised what was happening – and the exhalation of rapture that was exploding in her belly twisted in her throat and came out as a horror-stricken scream.

The spider leapt at her. He buried his long black fangs deep in her face and, surging with malevolence, pumped every drop of venom he had into her. The silicone-breasted blonde flailed screaming in hysteria. Then she fainted, and collapsed to the ground.

Torn from their lechery, the others looked around to see the big black spider spring from his victim's cheek. Some ran off screaming. Others passed out with fright. The fat man scrambled aside and vomited uncontrollably into the pool.

The spider scurried off and made good his escape to safety beneath the house. And from there, turning back, he saw that his victim was starting to convulse. Increasingly she trembled until her whole body was in seizure, and as the other humans fell over each other, an unearthly rasping emitted from her throat. Then her limbs contorted and stiffened, and her last twitching quivers gave way to the rigidity of death.

The spider watched in fascination, mesmerised by the effect of his action, until slowly he became filled with a realisation of victory. He reared back in triumph. He trembled with elation. He strutted and postured and posed in grim celebration. Then in a hideous reflex, his genitals throbbed and discharged, and he was overcome by an urge to descend into the earth, and copulate.

2

Saint Valentine's Day in New York was cold as sin. A late snowfall and snap freeze had virtually brought the city to a standstill. The sidewalks were deserted.

Helen Parkes looked out at the desolate landscape from the back of a speeding Yellow Cab. As she was driven north along Broadway, she wondered if the great metropolis, which had been home for all of her twenty-eight years, would be anything like this after a nuclear attack. Shivering, she put the unthinkable from her mind.

Helen was what a pulp writer might describe as 'a looker'. She was five-feet seven-inches tall with long legs, a slender figure and startling, mystical green eyes. She wore her honey blonde hair off the shoulder and was dressed in a calf-length navy trench coat over a stylish blue business suit. The overall effect resonated with the forties, which may have been associated with the fact that her favourite movie was *To Have And Have Not*. Whatever, Helen was pleased that she was far enough past teen age to affect her chosen style with conviction.

Passing the Lincoln Center, she pondered that she rarely ventured far uptown any more, not since her student days. Then, hanging out in Morningside Heights had been as obligatory as experimenting with sex and drugs – a part of the process of cutting her umbilical cord with rich but indifferent parents. During her four years majoring in journalism at Columbia University, Helen had done it the hard way. And she had survived – but not without scars.

Getting off heroin after a six-month dalliance had left her with recurring nightmares. And the great love of her life had ended badly. At twenty-two, in her last year at Columbia, she had fallen head over heels for a man twelve years her senior. He was the antithesis of her conservative upbringing, an aspirant writer burdened with a heavy social conscience and possessed of a melancholy charm that she had found irresistible.

But beneath his attractive exterior, he had been woefully corruptible. He increasingly had found his way into the beds of other women, especially those with money. And the materialistic good life which he had so despised when Helen had first met him seemed to offend him less and less the more he tasted it. She finally kicked him out at five o'clock one morning when he rolled home stoned and stinking of sex, and she never saw him again.

Since then, she'd kept men strictly at arm's length. She usually had one around for socialising, and occasionally for something more on lonely nights. But she always made sure they weren't too interesting, and she never kept the same one for too long.

She'd thrown herself into building a career, or to be exact, two careers – one which had begun shortly after the end of her relationship, which was private, and the other, which was very public, as a freelance journalist. She had worked as a newspaper reporter since graduating from Columbia but now, six years on, things were happening for her. Her reputation had been boosted by a series of features on New York – the writing had been intelligent and provocative, and her phone had rung steadily ever since.

It had rung last night, in fact, which was why she was heading now through a grey and frozen Manhattan. The features editor of the *New York Times* had picked up on a bizarre story coming out of Australia which he felt merited a background piece, and he'd asked Helen to write it.

She opened her briefcase and took out a crumpled fax which had arrived on her machine earlier that morning. It was from page one of the previous day's *Sydney Morning Herald*, and now, for the third time, she read the two-column article circled in highlighter. It was headed, *Two more killed by funnelwebs*, and it read:

> *Two more people died from funnelweb spider bites in Sydney yesterday, bringing the death toll this year to five and causing consternation among scientists and doctors who had previously thought the funnelweb antivenom to be 100 per cent effective.*
>
> *Ms Eileen Singleton, 52, of Lennox Avenue, Willoughby, died before reaching the Royal North Shore Hospital late last night after telling neighbours that a large spider had attacked her as she was gathering laundry in her garden.*
>
> *Pathology tests confirmed that Ms Singleton's blood contained a high dose of funnelweb venom, among the most toxic known to science.*
>
> *Earlier yesterday, Mr Paul Henderson, 19, of Wicks Road, Denistone, died 10 minutes after receiving funnelweb antivenom at Ryde Hospital.*
>
> *Mr Henderson, a contract gardener with the State Rail Authority, had been bitten by a spider while working in flower beds at Eastwood Station.*
>
> *Mr Henderson killed the spider and took it to hospital with him. It was later confirmed to be a Sydney funnelweb.*

Mr Henderson's case is the second this year of a victim dying despite receiving antivenom. In January, Mr Georgiou Stavros, 31, of Chatswood, died an hour after being bitten and 40 minutes after receiving antivenom.

Doctors and toxicologists had previously believed the antivenom, perfected in 1980 at the Commonwealth Serum Laboratories, to be totally effective.

Dr Graham Barnes, the laboratories' research director, declined to comment until after a full investigation.

The NSW Health Department confirmed yesterday that Sydney hospitals generally treat fewer than five funnelweb bites in a year. A spokeswoman said that no fatalities had been recorded since the introduction of the antivenom but could offer no explanation as to the dramatic rise in cases this year.

Also of concern is the reported ferocity of the spiders and their apparent lack of provocation, as in the now notorious 'Happy New Year' incident in which 25-year-old American screen actress Ms Frances Fullerton died after being bitten on the face.

Ms Fullerton was at a film industry New Year party with Australian film producer, Mr Gerald Heinemann, and the couple were reportedly nowhere near any funnelweb nest sites.

The spider would have had to cross several metres of open ground and jump to a height of up to a metre to bite Ms Fullerton.

Experts agree that, despite the funnelweb's aggressive reputation, such behaviour is unknown.

Helen put the article down on the empty seat beside her and glanced out the window. It certainly was a curious story – killer spiders? – baffled authorities? – fatal attack at a film party? – it sounded like an old Roger Corman movie.

Helen had never really thought much about Australia and now that she was being paid to, she realised she actually knew very little about the place. She was familiar with the clichés, of course – kangaroos, koalas, Aborigines with boomerangs, rough sunburned men drinking cold beer – but that didn't add up to much of a picture. What about the people, the industry, the economy, the politics? And what about the dark side? It was rule one for a journalist that the best insight into any country came through a knowledge of its underbelly – its crime and corruption. But as far as Australia was concerned, she couldn't recall very much at all.

What contact had she had lately with anything Australian? She'd seen an Australian movie recently and found it okay in a quirky sort of way. Australian soaps ran on cable TV but she'd never watched them. She'd read somewhere that they'd taken Britain by storm. She made a mental note to catch one.

None of this gave her much to go on. She opened her briefcase again and took out a copy of the text file she'd downloaded earlier from the Australian Zoological Society's Website. It was entitled *Dangerous Australians*, and she scanned through it.

Whatever else could be said about it, Australia certainly had its fair share of nasty animals. Many kinds of spiders, including the black widow, or redback as they called it. Many species of poisonous snakes – tiger snakes, brown snakes, diamondbacks – one called the dugite snake that was even supposed to come looking for you if you got on its wrong side.

And Australian beaches sounded interesting – there were sea wasps which could put you in hospital for weeks, stonefish which killed you stone dead if you stood on one, blue-ringed octopuses which had the most poisonous venom in the natural world, and sharks – sharks everywhere, even in Sydney Harbour.

And, of course, the Sydney funnelweb spider – aggressive, lethal, and living in your own backyard – literally.

Perhaps the surprising thing about Australia was not that it was a vast country with such a small population, but that it had any population at all! Helen mused on what kind of people the Australians must be – fatalistic presumably.

Anyway, she was on her way to meet one now – Doctor John Fitzgerald, a zoologist. More specifically, he was an arachnologist, an expert on arachnids, which meant spiders, scorpions, mites, and most other things which were unpleasant and had eight legs. And he was an Australian, a visiting associate professor of biology at Columbia. Helen had called the Department of Biological Sciences for a lead on the funnelweb story and had been told that Fitzgerald was the man. She'd called his office and they'd said he was working at home. She'd called his apartment and reached an answering machine. She'd left a message but he hadn't returned her call. So she'd decided to track him down before the competition beat her to it.

Putting her papers away, she settled back into her seat and tried to enjoy what was left of the gloomy journey.

The cab pulled up outside Fitzgerald's apartment block at the corner of 116th Street and Amsterdam Avenue, which was directly opposite Columbia's East Main Gate. Helen knew the building – she had sometimes eaten at the tiny subterranean Viennese restaurant on the corner. The place should have been open for lunch but as she paid the driver, Helen noticed it was closed because of the weather.

Let into the building's overheated lobby by an outgoing resident, she took the elevator to the second floor where she found Fitzgerald's apartment. She pressed the buzzer and got no response. She pressed it again but still there was no sign of life. After the third press, she was about to make inquiries at the next apartment when she heard the latches being turned inside.

The door opened three inches and a man looked out. He was around forty, tall and slim, and might have been quite good looking. It was hard to tell at that moment because he looked so ill. He was pale and red eyed, with tousled, greasy brown hair and three days growth of beard. He wore a stained T-shirt, crumpled jeans and was barefoot.

Helen said 'Doctor Fitzgerald?' and the man nodded.

'I'm Helen Parkes from the *New York Times*, Doctor Fitzgerald.' She pushed a business card through the door into his hand. 'I'm sorry to drop in on you like this, unannounced – I did call but I could only get your answering machine. I'd really appreciate it if I could talk to you for a few minutes about the funnelweb spider problem in Australia.'

Fitzgerald looked vacant for a moment, then puzzled. 'Funnelweb . . . problem?' he half whispered, in a thick, sticky voice.

'The funnelweb spiders, Doctor Fitzgerald,' Helen repeated. 'They're killing people – in Sydney.'

Fitzgerald looked blank again, then irritated. 'Didn't occur to you, Miss . . .' he consulted the business card, '. . . Miss Parkes, that someone might leave their answering machine on because they didn't want callers?'

Helen suddenly caught the sour smell of whisky on his breath which instantly accounted for the way he looked. She felt immediately dispirited – her spider expert was a drunk. Just at that moment, however, he was the only one she had. She persevered.

'You obviously haven't heard, Doctor Fitzgerald, that the funnelweb spiders in Sydney are behaving very strangely.' She took the newspaper fax from her briefcase and offered it to him. 'I think you'll find this interesting.'

Fitzgerald considered, then opened the door fully. He took the paper from Helen and started to read the circled article. A moment later, he looked up at her.

'You'd better come in,' he said, then turned and walked back into the apartment. Helen followed him inside.

The apartment's living room was a tip. The place was strewn with full ashtrays, squashed beer cans and discarded junk food wrappers. There was a half full J&B bottle on the table and an empty one lying on the floor. The air stank of stale tobacco and spilled booze, and even though it was past 1pm, the blinds were closed.

Fitzgerald threw them open and squinted in the cold grey light. He fumbled around in the cushions of a couch until he found a pack of cigarettes. Then, lighting one with a zippo, he returned his attention to the newspaper and was instantly engrossed.

Helen stood in the middle of the floor, amazed that anyone could live like this. Her first impression was of dirt and she instinctively avoided contact with everything. However looking past the mess, she could see that the room was quite pleasant. The furniture was good, the decor tasteful and the atmosphere enhanced by interesting prints and well-stocked bookshelves. But there was something wrong, as if none of it had anything to do with the man who lived here.

Fitzgerald looked up from the paper. 'You know anything more about this?' he asked.

She shook her head. 'No, I don't. I was hoping you could throw some light on it for me.'

Fitzgerald considered, then said, 'Who d'you say you were with?'

'I'm freelance,' said Helen, 'I'm covering this story for the *New York Times* – if there is a story?'

Fitzgerald looked back at the newspaper, and murmured, 'There could be.'

Suddenly, he seemed conscious of the condition of the apartment and of himself, and of the glamorous woman who was standing there taking it all in. 'Look, er . . . excuse the state of the place,' he said awkwardly, 'I had a bit of a party. Come through to the kitchen and we can talk.'

With such grace as he could muster, Fitzgerald indicated an open door on the far side of the room. Helen nodded and walked through, and Fitzgerald followed her.

The kitchen was small but by contrast with the living room, clean and tidy. The only blemish was an open dishwasher crammed with dirty dishes. Fitzgerald closed it quickly and switched it on.

'Er . . . how about some coffee?' he asked, struggling to appear normal despite what was plainly a fuzzy head.

Helen knew exactly how he was feeling, and not just from memory of her youth. She seldom drank too much any more but when she did, it left her feeling like hell. 'That'd be fine,' she said, in a more friendly tone.

She watched him as he filled the percolator with

water and measured in some fresh ground coffee. Despite his wretched condition, he was an attractive man, with good strong hands and fine features. And he moved well, with natural poise and precision. But the thing which intrigued her was his voice – not so much the tone of it, although that was pleasant enough, but his accent. It was basically Australian with some educated American creeping in. But there was something else in there too, something underlying that she couldn't quite place. Was it British – an English accent maybe? She couldn't tell. Whatever, the effect was unusual, and a little mysterious.

As the coffee began to bubble, Fitzgerald scanned back through the newspaper article. 'The background stuff in this is sound enough,' he observed. 'Funnelwebs are nasty bastards – they'll go for you if you corner them, or disturb their nests, especially in the breeding season. And their venom is wicked, especially the male's.' He scanned further, concentrating. 'But if all this is true . . .' he looked up, 'then it's very strange.'

Helen looked quizzical. 'Any ideas?' she asked.

'Not a one,' he answered frankly.

Helen smiled. An expert who admitted to not having all the answers was rare. 'So where do I go from here?' she asked.

Fitzgerald scratched his head. 'Well . . . what I need to make any kind of guess about this is more information.' He stroked the stubble on his upper lip thoughtfully. 'The best place to get information is in the field . . . and in this case, the best source in Sydney . . .' Fitzgerald looked pleased with himself, 'is a friend of mine.'

Helen perked up. 'Who's that?'

'Bill Reid . . .' said Fitzgerald, standing, 'Doctor Bill Reid, at Macquarie University.'

As Helen took a notebook and pencil from her

briefcase and scribbled down the name, Fitzgerald crossed to a wall phone, found an address book next to it and looked up a number. Lighting another cigarette, he lifted the receiver and punched out the digits. 'Help yourself to coffee,' he said, then returned his attention to the phone as somebody answered.

'How are ya, you old bastard?' Fitzgerald cracked into the mouthpiece, his accent suddenly broad Australian Strine.

Immediately, he grinned at the response which Helen took to be in the same vernacular as the greeting.

Fitzgerald continued, 'Who else would spend good money phoning you from halfway round the world?'

Again, the unheard response provoked a warm grin, and Fitzgerald turned to Helen and winked. But then, grin fading, he turned away and responded quietly, 'Good to hear your voice too, mate. Sorry I left it so long . . . no, everything's fine . . . yeah, really . . . anyway, look, what's all this about the funnelwebs?'

Helen didn't make much sense of the conversation which followed. There seemed to be a lot of talk about 'fractured response patterns' and 'chromosomal abnormality' and 'modified growth inhibitors' and 'hedgehog genes', none of which meant a thing to her. But what she did pick up was Fitzgerald's growing concern. Within a few minutes, he seemed intensely puzzled. Whatever was going on in Australia, it sounded more serious than half a dozen unfortunate deaths.

By the end of the conversation, at least one thing was clear – Fitzgerald was going to Sydney. He assured Reid he would have no problem covering his next two weeks commitments and promised to let him know when he would arrive. Then, after subdued 'goodbyes', Fitzgerald hung up.

Helen was bursting. 'So what's the story, Doctor Fitzgerald?'

Fitzgerald was miles away. He looked like he had almost forgotten she was there. Snapping out of it, he shook his head in mock offence.

'Nobody calls me "Doctor Fitzgerald" out of school, especially when I'm this hung over. It's Jack.'

Helen smiled, pleased that she no longer had to pretend she hadn't noticed. 'Okay, Jack. I'm Helen.'

Fitzgerald looked awkward again. He picked up the coffee cup which she had filled for him ten minutes earlier and emptied it down in two swallows.

Then he said, 'Look, er . . . Helen. I've been on a bit of a bender . . . and I need to clean up.' He refilled their cups. 'I'll make you a deal. You help me get my trip organised with some calls while I get showered and packed – and I'll give you everything I can on the funnelweb story, including a guided tour of Columbia's arachnid lab. What do you say?'

Helen didn't think about it. She simply said, 'Deal!'

The travel arrangements Helen made were inconvenient but workable. Kennedy was a graveyard but she managed to find Fitzgerald a seat on a Qantas flight to Sydney out of Dulles International the next day.

She also recommended a cleaning service to give the apartment the deluxe treatment, which would keep the owners happy as Fitzgerald had only rented the place from them for a few months whilst they were away in Europe.

That accounted for Helen's feeling that he had been out of place there, but at the same time opened up other questions. And she found there was something increasingly attractive about him, particularly now that he was shaved and dressed in a stylish Swiss ski jacket and slacks. However as they crossed Amsterdam Avenue and passed through Columbia's East Main Gate, those thoughts receded when her mind was invaded by memories.

New York's Columbia University is one of the world's great centres of scholarship, and for those who have studied there it is an evocative place. To Helen, it had been home, the place of nurturing she had always longed for, a sanctuary among her peers after the loneliness and ill-treatment of childhood. Now crunching again across the frozen campus, Helen remembered earlier, more carefree times – studying and sunbathing through warm spring days on manicured greens, laughter and friendship at the seemingly endless round of parties, deliciously forbidden lovemaking in the secret niches of undergraduate fraternity houses. Helen hadn't expected it, but being back gave her quite a jolt.

'This is it,' Jack said, as he pushed open a painted metal door and led Helen into a concrete building that could only be described as utilitarian. Columbia's Department of Biological Sciences was housed in the Fairchild Building, and crossing its tiled hall, Helen was instantly transported by the smells – wet wool, coffee, fast food – on days like this, all of Columbia's buildings smelled the same. Except here there was something else in the mix – formaldehyde, wafting up from the laboratories below. Surfacing from reminiscence, Helen followed Jack past the bulletin board and down the well-trodden staircase to the basement.

The arachnid laboratory was at the far end of the lower corridor and unusually, due to the weather, was unoccupied. The fluorescents were switched off and the only illumination was from incandescents which ran down the centre of the room. One wall was taken up with glass cases displaying close to a thousand formalin jars, each containing a different species of arachnid. Equipment ranged from Bunsen burners to a scanning electron microscope and a dozen computers were linked in a local area network.

Fitzgerald unlocked the laboratory's double doors and led Helen in. As she looked around, he moved to the far end of the room, put down the suitcase he was carrying, unlocked a tiny office with his name on the door and went inside. A moment later, he emerged with a thick cardboard file. He flicked on a workbench lamp, opened the file and looked through the dozens of photographs inside. Soon, he found what he was looking for.

'Take a look,' he called.

By the time Helen reached him, there were six eight-by-ten glossy colour prints laid out on the workbench. The quality of the photographs was superb but their subject sent a cold shiver through her.

'Oh, my God!' Helen felt reluctant even to touch the pictures.

'That's him,' Fitzgerald said. 'Atrax robustus – the Sydney funnelweb. Ugly son of a bitch.'

For Helen, that was an understatement. The funnelweb was just about the most repellent looking thing she'd ever seen. She didn't care greatly for spiders at the best of times. As a six year old she'd been petrified by a big garden spider that had run across her bedroom wall one night, and she'd screamed the house down. She remembered that her parents had been annoyed because she'd disturbed a dinner party. Her mother had smacked her and told her not to be stupid.

But that garden spider was a teddy bear compared

to what she was looking at now. The funnelweb was everything nightmares were made of – big, black, with a hard shiny body and skeletal, hair-covered legs. Its eyes, all eight of them, were dead and lifeless black beads. But worst of all were its fangs, which looked utterly fearsome. Some of the pictures showed the funnelweb rearing back in a stance of attack, fangs poised to strike and dripping venom. Helen had never seen anything so creepy. When she spoke, she found that her mouth was dry.

'It looks like it's going to jump . . . that's what happened to the woman in the news story.'

Fitzgerald looked at the picture. 'Spiders are generally more scared of you than you are of them. Even a black widow or a tarantula will run away if they can. But this one won't – he'll go for you.'

Fitzgerald passed across some other photos. 'The first thing you have to understand about the funnelweb is that he's very primitive . . . much more than other spiders even. He's part of a group called the mygalomorphs which evolved on the floors of primordial rainforests three hundred million years ago. And they haven't changed much since.'

When Jack saw Helen taking out her notebook, he uncovered one of the computers and switched it on. 'Rather than trotting out all the basics, I'll give you the first year notes on mygalomorphs – that'll give you the background.' When the computer finished booting, Jack punched in a few commands and a printer began spitting out the data. Then he turned and headed for the display cases, saying, 'Come and see a real one.'

Helen did not relish the prospect but followed anyway, and as she approached, Jack switched on the display case's internal illumination. Then he grinned and pointed to an exhibit at eye level.

And there it was – the Sydney funnelweb spider. The cold shiver Helen had felt from the photographs now ran all the way down her spine. Even though the creature was dead and behind two layers of glass, Helen still recoiled. The funnelweb's body was less than two-inches long but the wide span of its legs and its aggressive stance combined to make it seem bigger. And its fangs – thrusting down from its head like precision instruments of death.

'How do the fangs work?' said Helen, trying to sound as if her interest was purely academic.

'Like hypodermic syringes,' Fitzgerald replied. 'There's a needle-fine capillary from the venom gland inside the spider's jaw which comes out in a tiny hole just to the side of the fang's point. The hole isn't exactly at the point so that it won't get blocked with the victim's flesh as the fang goes in, which would stop the poison flowing.'

Something turned in Helen's stomach. 'Isn't nature wonderful,' she murmured.

'Have you ever looked at a bayonet?'

Helen thought, then answered, 'Not really.'

'It has channels down the side . . . to let the blood flow out and release the pressure so the blade goes in easily.'

'Is that what they're for?' Helen felt queasy.

Fitzgerald indicated the spider. 'The funnelweb's fangs are channelled in the same way . . . only he figured it out three hundred million years ago – and we think we're clever.' He was clearly enjoying himself.

'You actually like them, don't you.' Helen looked bemused.

Fitzgerald thought about it. 'I find them fascinating . . . and admirable really, when you get to understand more about them . . . otherwise I wouldn't do what I do, I suppose.' He considered it further, then said, 'If you treat them with respect, they leave you alone – which is more than you can say for people.'

His last remark had an edge to it, and could have been an opening. But it was not the time or the place to pursue it, and there was another question that had been forming in Helen's mind.

'Jack . . . why do they scare us so much . . . I mean, spiders . . . all spiders. Most of them are harmless, as far as I've read, but so many people are terrified of them – more than of snakes or sharks, for instance.' Helen paused a moment, reaching down to where her deepest fears lay. Then she said 'It's not just about getting bitten . . . or even eaten, like with sharks or big cats. With spiders, it's something else, something illogical, something . . . unnatural.'

Jack was silent for a moment. Then he said 'It's really a question for a psychologist . . . but I know what you mean. Even I get twinges of it, especially if I'm alone in here at night.'

He fell silent again, and in the silence an atmosphere was building which both of them could feel – an atmosphere of foreboding. Jack broke it by moving away, saying 'Let's get some coffee,' and Helen was only too pleased to follow him.

The scalding 'instant' that Jack brewed in the lab microwave was characterless but warming. He sipped on it as he sat behind the desk in his office, scanning through books and periodicals. After a moment, he said 'The fear of spiders is a recognised medical condition . . . called "arachnophobia" . . . and there's been a fair amount written about it over the years.'

Helen sat opposite, her notebook out, looking more comfortable.

Finding something he'd been looking for, Jack

continued, 'The usual explanation for it is also the most predictable . . . and of course, the least interesting.' He read aloud from a medical journal,

> *'No firm evidence exists that arachnophobia is anything other than a combination of primitive revulsions and fears which are already well documented and found in the human psyche universally. These may include the standard "fight or flight" response to the physical appearance of non-mammalian forms (including insects and reptiles as well as arachnids), an instinctive fear of small, scampering creatures, particularly nocturnals which may venture into places of human habitation (common examples being spiders, cockroaches and mice), and a natural revulsion at the spider's feeding method, entailing the pre-digestion of prey by enzymes contained in the venom and regurgitated stomach juices, resulting in the flesh of the victim being partially liquefied prior to ingestion.'*

Helen's eyes narrowed, as she said, 'Yuch!'

Jack mused, then shook his head. 'I've never found the obvious explanations very convincing, even though my scientific training makes me want to.' He put the journal aside.

Helen finished scribbling a note and looked up. 'So what else is there?'

'Well . . .' Jack opened a weighty academic volume, looked something up in the index, then leafed back. 'There's an ancient Greek myth concerning the origin of spiders . . . which in fact is where the word "arachnid" comes from. You interested?'

'Sure.' Helen sipped her coffee then picked up her pencil.

'Okay. The story of Arachne . . .' Jack found the place, and read,

'Long ago, when the gods of ancient Greece still dwelt upon the heights of Olympus, there lived in a village in the plains below a beautiful maiden whose name was Arachne. She spent her days weaving and embroidering, arts at which she excelled above all others. Not only her fellow villagers gathered to watch her as she worked, but the nymphs of the woodland and water crept out from their secret places to gaze in awe at the skill of her nimble fingers, and upon the wondrous pictures she wove.

But Arachne had such a pride in the certainty of her prowess that, although her friends and neighbours marvelled at her genius, she was never loved, for her endless boasting prevented it. She became so enamoured of her own skill with loom and needle that she announced that not even Athene, goddess of wisdom and patroness of the arts, could rival her in her work.

The statement reached the ears of the goddess, who was incredulous that any mortal could be so presumptuous. She left her home on the summit of Olympus and, disguised as an old woman, visited Arachne and warned her against incurring the wrath of the gods. The maiden's response was only to repeat her boast, and she added that if she could but meet her, she would challenge Athene to a contest to prove which of them was superior. Athene was so incensed that she threw off her disguise. Appearing in her own heavenly form, she accepted the challenge.

The goddess and the mortal set up their looms and began to weave. Athene chose for the subject of

her tapestry her own contest with Neptune and the origin of the olive tree. Arachne chose for her subject the abduction of Europa. As Arachne and the goddess toiled, so both tapestries took magnificent form.

At length the labour was finished, and each turned to see the result of her rival's effort. Wonderful as Arachne's depiction was, one glance sufficed to show that she was beaten. In her despair, she tried to hang herself, but Athene was unwilling that her rival should escape her anger so easily. The goddess changed her dangling body into the misshapen form of a spider, and Arachne was condemned to spin and weave without rest throughout all time. And the silk that she wove would be drawn from her own agonised body, once so beautiful, but now repulsive and frightful.'

Jack looked up, and quipped, 'Not many laughs.'

Helen smiled. 'But interesting. It makes the spider a tortured creature . . . that would be full of bitterness and hate, and motivated to get revenge. I mean, the function of mythology in pre-modern society was to explain the world, to give some sense to the harshness of it, and make life easier to cope with. It's interesting how the story gives the spider a reason for being frightening and dangerous.'

Fitzgerald looked blank. 'And I thought it was just an old yarn.'

Helen looked embarrassed. 'Sorry – comes from too many literary lunches. I'll get over it.'

Fitzgerald smiled easily. 'No, don't. If the world was full of scientists, we'd all die of boredom.' He tapped the text with his finger. 'You want a copy of this?'

Helen said, 'Thanks, that would be good.'

As they waited for the Xerox to warm up, Helen asked, 'Any other gems?'

Jack put the textbook into the copier and pressed the Print button. As the machine whirred and lit up, he thought about it. 'The fact is that nobody really knows what causes arachnophobia. One explanation is as good as another . . . and some of them are pretty off-the-wall.' He reflected. 'There's one that's interesting.'

Helen looked quizzical. 'Let's hear it.'

Jack opened the Xerox, replaced the textbook with the medical journal, then pressed the Print button again. 'Well . . . there is a theory . . . which used to be considered crackpot, but is now being taken more seriously . . . that arachnids have evolved from organisms which did not originate on this planet.'

Helen looked vacant for a second, then incredulous. 'You mean . . . spiders are from outer space?'

Jack grinned. 'Well, not exactly – but, in a way, yes. The idea is that at the time the first life forms were developing in the primeval oceans, some other primitive organisms, which originated somewhere else in the universe, may have been brought here by a meteor. Then as time progressed, the vast majority of life on Earth as we now know it evolved from the terrestrial material. But a few forms, including the creatures we call spiders, evolved from the material which came from space.'

Helen's incredulity gave way quickly to scepticism. 'So . . . the funnelweb is actually ET!'

Fitzgerald looked philosophical. 'I told you it was pretty off-the-wall. But what is interesting is that the more we understand about molecular biology, the more the theory seems to hold water. There are things in the genetic chemistry of arachnids that are, well . . . odd . . . subtly unlike the biochemistry of other life forms. And it does provide an intriguing reason for arachnophobia.'

'How?' Helen's scepticism was tempering.

Fitzgerald thought the notion through, then articulated it carefully. 'If it is the case that arachnids derive from genetic material which originated beyond this planet . . . and we're not talking here about little green men in flying saucers – we're talking maybe a few microscopic organisms locked up in the rock of an asteroid for eons, then released into our atmosphere when that asteroid collided with Earth . . . then it is possible that in modern highly evolved forms of terrestrial origin – humans for example – there may be some genetically inherited electrochemical mechanism – what we would call an instinct – which warns us subconsciously that the descendants of those extraterrestrial organisms – spiders for example – are foreigners . . . and therefore, a potential threat. In other words, even after hundreds of millions of years, there may still be a message coming down to us in our DNA – a genetic memory, or echo if you like – which tells us that spiders originate from "out there", and are, biochemically speaking, aliens.'

Even in the dim light, Helen paled a little. All she could say was, 'God.'

Fitzgerald concluded, 'The effect of that genetic memory would be to trigger the response that we call "arachnophobia" whenever we encounter a spider – the closer the encounter, if you'll excuse the phrase, the more extreme the arachnophobic response – death from heart failure has been recorded in some cases.'

'Okay . . .' Helen was getting right into it. 'Okay – that all makes logical sense, as far as it goes. But even if it's true, spiders, whether they're alien or not, are almost all harmless . . . except funnelwebs and one or two others which are only found in certain parts of the world. So it doesn't explain why people everywhere suffer from arachnophobia, even in places where spiders only do useful things like eat flies.'

Jack thought back over his explanation. 'Sure . . . but the point is that at the time the experiences occurred which gave rise to the genetic memory, there were no spiders – and no people. At that time our ancestors might just have been microscopic spirals of DNA floating around in some primordial puddle – and the spiders' ancestors may have been some extraterrestrial DNA floating around in the next puddle. Then one day it rained, and the two puddles flowed into one another – and there was a battle for supremacy of the big puddle, which was the whole world for both sides. And maybe they gave us a good hiding, which through electrochemical printing, alias "genetic memory", we still "remember" the trauma of to this day – hence, "arachnophobia".'

Helen's mind was racing, trying to wrestle with the implications. 'Is it really possible?' she asked, half to herself.

'Maybe it is – as I said, we just don't know enough yet. Every year we get deeper insights into the workings and the origins of life – maybe one day we'll be able to trace these things back to their source, like railroad lines on a map. But it won't be in our lifetime . . . or for a few lifetimes to come.'

Helen felt very small. Pondering the epic scale of the universe and her own insignificance within it always made her uncomfortable, like a feeling of vertigo. It was one of the reasons she could never have been a scientist. She consciously forced her thoughts back to the here and now. 'So has any of this got anything to do with what's been going on in Australia?'

Fitzgerald was amused by the journalist's attempt to tie up disparate fragments of reality into a neat story. 'Absolutely nothing,' he said, with a wry smile.

'So what do you think is happening down there . . . now you've spoken to your colleague in Sydney, er . . .' Helen flipped back through her notebook '. . . Doctor Reid?'

'Hm . . . I hope you don't think I've enlisted your help under false pretences, but I've no idea yet – I seem to be saying that a lot today.'

Helen persisted. 'You seemed worried by what he told you. Can't you give me any idea about what might be going on?'

Fitzgerald picked his words carefully. 'The research they've done so far has turned up one or two minor abnormalities in the physiology of some funnelwebs, which could be due to anything . . . disease, pollution, increased solar radiation from depletion of the ozone layer – at the moment, it's just a grab bag of possibilities. Bill Reid has asked me to go down and give them a hand in the area of genetic analysis, which is my field. But until I get there, and until a lot more work is done, we're not going to know any more.'

Helen gave him the look of a disappointed schoolgirl. 'You're not holding out on me?'

Fitzgerald handed her the photocopies, put away the originals, then led her back out into the lab. 'I promise. There's nothing more I can tell you that I'm sure of. I'd be lying if I said I didn't have a couple of ideas, but that's all they are so far – ideas. If I talked about them now and they got published as "quotes from an expert" or something, then it could do more harm than good . . . because I may be way off target.'

Fitzgerald arrived at the computer printer he'd set

going earlier, tore off the fan-folded print-out and handed it to Helen. 'Anyway, I hope you can get enough of a story from what I've given you.'

Helen glanced through the print-out, then folded it around the photocopies and her notebook. 'You've given me a wealth of stuff, Jack . . . far more than I could have hoped for. There's enough here for three articles – maybe I can sell them a series!'

Fitzgerald was pleased. 'Well . . . as long as you got what you needed.' Again, he smiled easily, but there was something about his eyes which gave nothing away, something guarded.

Helen was in no doubt that she liked him, because in the back of her mind a bell was ringing. It told her that the man she was looking at could mean something to her. It was something that hadn't happened for a long time, something that usually made her instantly turn around and walk away. But this time she didn't want to walk away – and it worried her.

She realised that she'd been looking into Fitzgerald's eyes for an age. She covered her embarrassment by looking at her watch. 'Hey, look at the time. You need to get to the station.'

Jack nodded, then paused. For a moment, he seemed about to say something. But he didn't. Instead he turned away, and said only, 'I'll call a cab.'

An hour out of Pennsylvania Station, the Amtrak Metroliner sped south towards Washington DC through a landscape that was black and icebound. In the club car, Jack Fitzgerald toyed with the cocktail stick in his Bloody Mary. The roast beef sandwich had been just what he'd needed but now he'd overdone the Worcestershire and

Tabasco in his nightcap and he was waiting for the ice to cool them down.

It was his first drink of the day and would be his last, just a cure to soothe the hangover that had been punishing his head since he got up. It also might help him to rest when he returned to his seat, and maybe even to sleep, which most often eluded him when he was sober.

He was thinking about Helen. She was the most attractive woman he'd met for a long time – for longer than he cared to remember. She had shared the cab with him to Madison Square Garden, then had gone downstairs with him to Penn Station to see him off. It was then, as they'd shaken hands and said goodbye, that she'd given him that look again – the same look that he'd seen in her eyes just before they'd left the lab. It told him that she found him attractive too, though God only knew why, given the state he'd been in when she'd first laid eyes on him.

Ten years ago, a single man then as now, he wouldn't have thought twice about it. He'd have put off his trip, laid on the charm he'd inherited in cartloads from his forebears, and swept Helen off for an intimate supper.

But not any more. All that was over for him now. Because for the past four years, he had been fighting an all out war. It was a war fought one day at a time in the battlefield of his mind, and his enemies were grief, loneliness and despair.

It was in fact four years and three days since the war had started. February 11th – a warm and sunny Friday in the green Sydney suburb of Narrabeen, which boasted the longest of the city's beautiful northern beaches, and where Jack had lived in a comfortable cottage overlooking the ocean. It was a place and a day that he would not forget – partly because it was his son, Kieran's, second birthday – but mainly because it was the day that Kieran and his mother, Colleen, had died.

The driver of the battered Ford utility had died too. Which was as well, since had he lived, Jack would surely have killed him. The man had been drinking heavily for hours at a nearby hotel before the accident – the Coroner had said his blood alcohol level was three times the legal limit – and the vehicle's brakes and steering had been criminally faulty. All of which had contributed to the man losing control and colliding with Colleen's Toyota, as she was driving their little boy to his birthday party at the local McDonald's.

Jack had spent the morning on a field trip with his students from Macquarie University, and had gone directly to the restaurant. When he'd arrived twenty minutes late, the police were waiting – and the war had started.

At first, he just drank heavily. But his drinking developed into eighteen-hour binges which put him out of action for three days at a time. Then the abuse began. He abused strangers in bars and in the street. Then he abused his friends and lost most of them. But when he started to abuse his students, his closest and most loyal friend took positive action.

Bill Reid, professor of zoology at Macquarie, persuaded the faculty to give Fitzgerald a year's leave of absence to sort out his problems. But when they agreed, Jack's emotional dam finally gave way, and he suffered a complete nervous breakdown.

Weeks of purgatory followed. But Jack's treatment worked, and after four months convalescence, on the advice of his doctors to make a fresh start, he applied for the job at Columbia. And he walked it.

That had been three years ago, and he hadn't been back to Australia since. He liked America – it had been good to him and he'd seen no reason to leave. But there hadn't been a day or an hour in those three years that he hadn't thought about Colleen and Kieran . . . hadn't seen their faces looming up in distracted moments. And the only nights he hadn't lain awake longing to be with them were the nights that he'd been too drunk to care.

He had his drinking down to a fine art now. He seldom if ever appeared drunk even when he was, and he never allowed it to interfere with his work. He knew just how much to drink to take the edge off his pain, but not so much as to lose control. Only when he was alone at night, when sometimes the pain welled up in him like molten steel – then, if he knew he could go to ground without arousing suspicion – then, he would drink. He would drink and drink until every trace of feeling was scoured from the inside of his skull, until every sense he possessed was obliterated. Then, and only then, would he sleep. He would sleep the perfect dreamless sleep known only to the unborn and to alcoholics – that blissful, peaceful, beautiful oblivion – that rapturous living death.

Three days ago – February 11th – the pain had come to him. Had Kieran lived, it would have been his sixth birthday. He would have been at school for a year and the garden at Narrabeen would have been alive with the sound of his voice and the voices of his friends. And maybe one of those voices would have belonged to Kieran's little brother or sister – Colleen had been talking of a second child.

Colleen. He had waited all his life for her. There had been others before – many others. But she was the only woman who had gone to the core of him. He'd always thought that it was a tribal thing. He'd been uprooted from his home in Ireland at the age of seven, after his mother had died and the three hundred acres in the Wicklow Mountains which the family had farmed for generations were reduced to forty. His broken father had increasingly neglected his work in favour of drink, and had sold off the land, field by field, to pay for it. Eventually John, the youngest, had been sent to Australia to be raised by his father's cousin and her husband who'd lived in Brisbane. They were childless and well off, but unfortunately, they had not been loving people.

Despite his misery, or perhaps because of it, John had been an outstanding student, and at twenty-three he had won a postgraduate scholarship to Trinity College, Dublin. For sixteen years he had dreamt of going home to Ireland – the idea had sustained him through his worst times. But by then his father had been dead for ten years and his two brothers had long gone to England, and at the end of the twenty months that it took him to get his doctorate, John knew he no longer belonged there.

The day he sailed out of Dun Laoghaire on the car ferry to Britain, to catch his flight back to Australia from Heathrow, he stood alone on the ship's aft passenger deck with tears streaming freely down his face. He watched Howth and Bray Head and the Sugarloaf, all precious memories from childhood, fade slowly into the descending mist. And as he shivered in the freezing wind, he knew that he would not see Ireland again. He had joined the ranks of the Wild Geese – those who had left never to return – and in that moment he swore to himself that he would never again be possessed by ghosts of the past.

He took up a research fellowship in Sydney and, renaming himself Jack, settled in to enjoy all the social and sexual benefits of a successful academic career. But there was always something missing, some void deep inside him that would not be filled. It had been there since he'd left

Ireland and try as he would to deny it, the Celt in him still yearned for the company and comfort of his own.

That was when he met Colleen. Her people were Irish, from Connemara in the far west, and she had the dark, smouldering beauty so typical of that part, due some said to the blood of Spanish seafarers who'd traded along Ireland's west coast for a thousand years. Colleen had been born and raised in Australia but throughout her childhood she had known that same void – a void that could only be filled by someone of her own Gaelic tribe.

Within minutes of meeting him, she knew that Jack Fitzgerald was that someone. If ever there was love at first sight, this was it. Three hours after laying eyes on each other they were together in Colleen's bed making the most intensely passionate love of their lives. They devoured each other's bodies as they inhabited each other's souls, and each found in the other a fulfilment neither had previously known.

And so it continued through their marriage, which they made official eighteen months later, and the birth of Kieran thirteen months after that – until February 11th two years on, when a man with a badly maintained car and a gutful of sour beer switched out the lights, and started Fitzgerald's war.

Jack drained the last of his Bloody Mary and went to the counter. The cocktail had still been red hot. He signalled the attendant.

'Club soda, please – hold the ice and lemon.'

As the attendant poured the soda, he looked at Jack curiously, then asked in a broad Brooklyn accent, 'Do I detect some Irish in your voice, sir?'

Jack looked surprised. 'You do. Not many pick it.'

The attendant was pleased with himself. 'Never

miss an Irishman. My own people are from County Kerry.'

Jack smiled. 'Ah – "The Kingdom" – a land apart.'

'As you say, sir. And yourself?'

' "The Garden of Ireland" – County Wicklow – but more recently of Sydney, Australia.'

The attendant looked impressed. 'An Irish-Australian then – you'd be a good man in a fight.'

Jack was amused by the man's unintended irony. 'Sometimes you have to be.' He swallowed his soda, then stood to leave, and said 'Good night.'

The attendant took Jack's glass and said 'Good night to you, sir – and good luck!'

As he left the club car to return to his seat, Jack found himself wondering just how much luck he might be needing in the days and weeks that were to come.

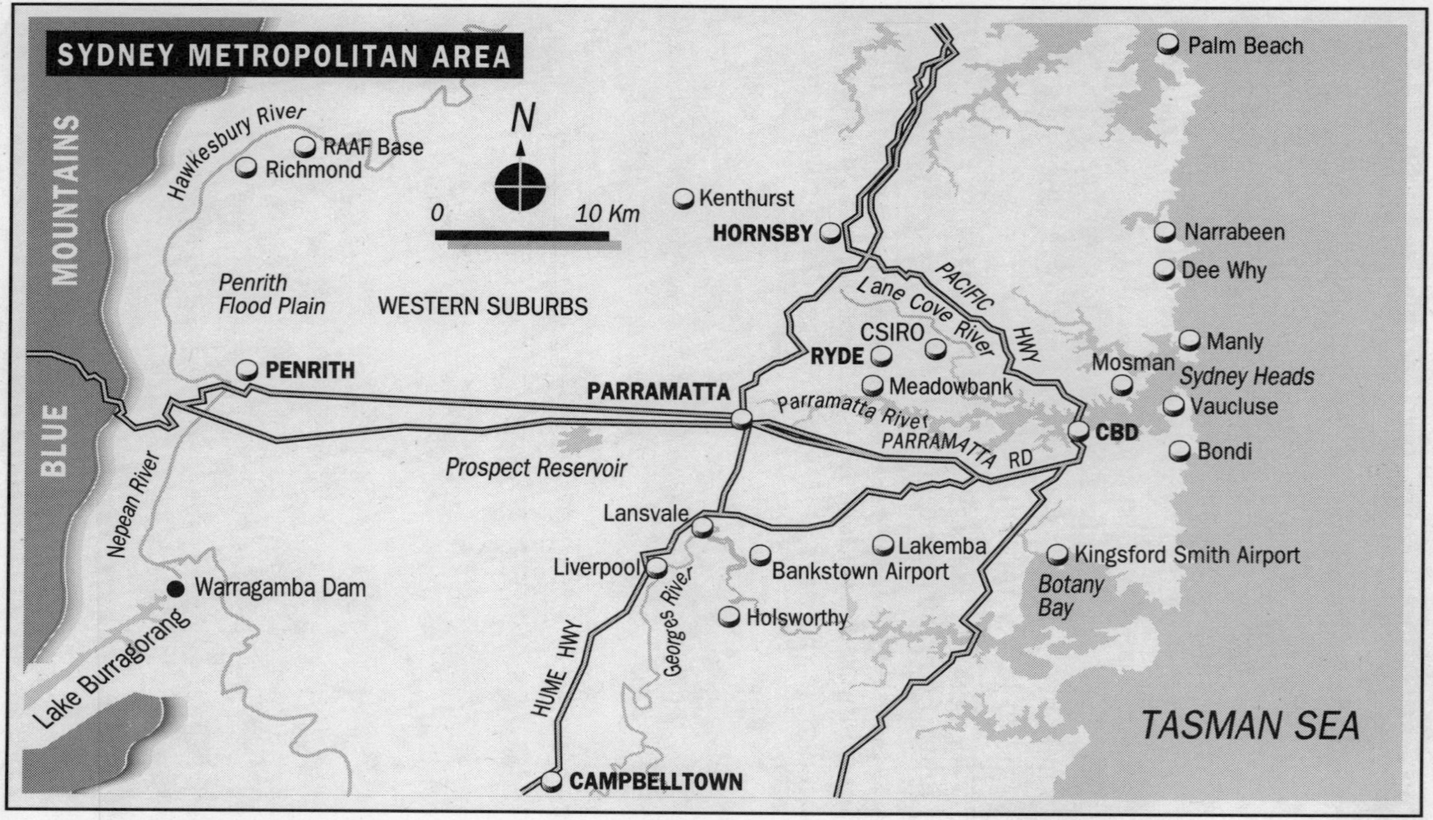
SYDNEY METROPOLITAN AREA
N
0
10 Km
BLUE
MOUNTAINS
Hawkesbury River
RAAF Base
Richmond
Penrith
Flood Plain
WESTERN SUBURBS
PENRITH
Nepean River
Warragamba Dam
Lake Burragorang
Kenthurst
HORNSBY
PACIFIC
HWY
Lane Cove River
CSIRO
RYDE
Meadowbank
PARRAMATTA
Parramatta River
PARRAMATTA
RD
Prospect Reservoir
Lansvale
Liverpool
Georges River
HUME
HWY
CAMPBELLTOWN
Lakemba
Bankstown Airport
Holsworthy
Palm Beach
Narrabeen
Dee Why
Manly
Mosman
Sydney Heads
Vaucluse
CBD
Bondi
Kingsford Smith Airport
Botany
Bay
TASMAN SEA

3

The funnelwebs responsible for the spate of deaths in Sydney had been the majority of those that gathered at the little beach on the morning of January 1, and been exposed to radioactive contaminant from the USS *Montana*. The majority, but not all.

Those irradiated most extremely, perhaps twenty of each sex, had been driven to go deep underground. And there, in a dank and airless cavern, they had copulated wildly. They had copulated and copulated until the males, including the spider that killed Frances Fullerton, had all died of total exhaustion, and in the process furnished nourishment for the females in their periods of gestation.

But as the gestations advanced, things happened inside the females which at first agonised, then crippled, then killed them. Their bodies literally burst from the prodigious growth of their eggs. The eggs had swollen to many times their normal size because the offspring they contained were creatures of a different order.

Days passed, and the eggs matured until finally they ruptured. And a vile abomination spilled out into an oblivious world.

Even taking into account that it was only 7am, the international arrivals hall at Sydney's Kingsford Smith Airport was quiet. Jack Fitzgerald came through the sliding doors from customs and looked around. There was no sign of Bill Reid, even though the flight from Washington was over an hour late. He went to the information desk and asked if there was a message. There was. Reid apologised for not being there and asked Fitzgerald to take a taxi and meet him at a place he knew well, the North Ryde laboratories of the Commonwealth Scientific and Industrial Research Organisation, more commonly known as the CSIRO.

As he passed the terminal escalators on his way to the cab rank, Fitzgerald saw that the departure lounge upstairs was bustling. It seemed no-one was coming to Sydney, but a lot of people were leaving in a hurry.

The CSIRO's main laboratory complex in New South Wales is ten kilometres north-west of central Sydney, in the hi-tech industrial suburb of North Ryde. The complex occupies 30 hectares of native bushland on the north side of the Lane Cove River valley, and is a conglomeration of huts, sheds, brick buildings and concrete constructions dotted seemingly at random down the steep wooded slope to the river. Here the CSIRO conducts advanced research in a myriad of fields, including energy, minerals, biology, agriculture, and engineering.

But as his taxi cruised around the perimeter, the complex, despite its recent corporatisation, still reminded Fitzgerald of a World War II army camp. In the Antipodean sunshine, amidst the ancient rocks and eucalypts, it all appeared to be somehow out of place. To Fitzgerald, with the perception of a jet-lagged returning expatriate, it seemed a symbol that the Australian nation's hold on this secret continent remained precarious.

With emergency funding from the New South Wales Government, Bill Reid had set up a research unit at North Ryde using the facilities of the Biomolecular Engineering Division, to investigate what had come to be termed simply 'the funnelweb problem'. Reid had recruited a formidable team of people from all over the country and had just about covered all the disciplines involved in the fields of zoology, biology and biochemistry. What he needed to tie the whole thing together was a top arachnological geneticist – Jack Fitzgerald.

When Fitzgerald was escorted by a security officer into Room B9, which was in one of the complex's newer buildings, Reid was concentrating so intently on the screen of a scanning electron microscope that he didn't look up.

Fitzgerald motioned to the guard that he was fine. Then he quietly walked up behind Reid, peered over his shoulder at the glowing screen, and inquired, 'Good movie?'

Impassive, Reid replied, 'Nah . . . too slow.' Then he turned to Fitzgerald, and chided, 'You took your bloody time!'

'Just putting off seeing your ugly face,' Fitzgerald retorted.

Reid laughed and grasped Fitzgerald's hand in a generous grip. 'Welcome home, mate,' he said warmly.

'Thanks, Bill. It's good to be back,' Fitzgerald replied truthfully, and was amazed to feel tears welling in his eyes. He repressed them, and returned Reid's solid handshake.

Reid looked the same as ever, big and tanned with just the trace of a paunch, but still youthful for his fifty-three years. There was the unmistakable stamp of the bushman about him, and despite the fact that he had a string of degrees to his name, including a PhD from Cambridge, he could more easily have passed for a Queensland stock foreman than for one of the most prominent research scientists in Australia. Just at that moment however, he looked tired and harassed.

'Sorry I couldn't get to the airport,' Reid said, 'but I've been trying to make sense of this shit for days.' He indicated the electron microscope's screen which glowed with a convoluted tangle of spirals and loops. Fitzgerald peered in at the maze.

'Forget it,' said Reid, taking Fitzgerald by the arm, 'first I'm dropping you home to get some sleep.' Then easing Fitzgerald into the corridor, he went on, 'Marilyn can't wait to see you. She's made a bloody great pile of those potato cakes you like for your breakfast.'

Fitzgerald was instantly unsettled. Irish potato cakes. He hadn't tasted anything like them since he'd gone away. Marilyn, Bill's wife, made them perfectly. Colleen had taught her how. The apprehension he'd been suppressing since he'd walked out of the arrivals hall surged up. He stopped in his tracks and looked straight into Reid's face. 'I can't, Bill . . . not yet.' Fitzgerald was shaky. 'I need a day or two . . . before I see anybody. Can you explain to Marilyn?'

Reid had been worried about how returning to Sydney might affect his friend. He smiled sympathetically, and said, 'Sure, Jack, no problem. Take all the time you need.' Then he led off in another direction, saying, 'We'll just have to make do with the wombat piss they still serve up as coffee round here.'

For the next two hours, Reid briefed Fitzgerald on the work the team had done so far, and brought him up to date with what had happened since they'd spoken on the phone. What was clear by the end of it was that things were getting worse by the hour. During the past two days, the attacks had intensified and three more people were dead.

Reid introduced Fitzgerald to the other members of the team. All ten of them were known to Jack, four of them personally, and each in their field was world class. Jack was also impressed by the facilities the CSIRO had put together. They weren't quite the Rolls Royce standard he'd become used to at Columbia but they were well in the Mercedes league. The main laboratory, which was in the same building as the electron microscope, was spacious and well fitted. And it had the unheard luxury of duplicated equipment, raided from universities throughout New South Wales and beyond. Even so, the facilities were over stretched. Everybody had started putting in long hours as the situation had worsened, and every bench was covered with spider specimens in various stages of dissection. However despite all their efforts, no-one yet had a clue about what was going on with the funnelwebs.

At 10.30am, Bill and Jack sat down with everybody else in the hut which served as the team's common room to catch the mid morning news on TV. And it was all bad. There had been no fewer than five attacks by funnelwebs that morning, all of them fatal. Sydney was very jumpy. The roads out of town were congested. There were long queues at Central Station for all country and interstate destinations. And, as Fitzgerald had seen for himself, there were crowds at the airport clamouring for plane seats to anywhere.

The Police Minister was interviewed and appealed to people not to overreact, saying road accidents were currently causing more fatalities than the funnelwebs. And the Health Minister tried to sound reassuring when he reported that everything possible was being done at the CSIRO to identify the cause of the problem, and that he was hopeful of an early breakthrough. That prompted a few derisive remarks from the assembled company. By the end of the bulletin, there were a lot of gloomy faces in the common room, and people drifted back to work in an atmosphere of tension.

Jack was suddenly exhausted. The journey, the concentration of the morning and the remains of his epic hangover all caught up with him at once and he could barely get up from his chair. Bill carried Jack's suitcase to the makeshift dormitory in the building next door, where Jack collapsed instantly into one of the six iron-framed bunks. And there he slept, dreamlessly and undisturbed, for nine and a half hours.

When Jack eventually awoke at eight-forty that evening, the last light of dusk was fading in a turquoise sky. The bush outside was alive with cicadas and a hot breeze scented with eucalypt was drifting up from the river. It was a typically perfect Sydney summer evening, and to Jack its atmosphere was a familiar and welcoming blanket. He just lay there quietly, savouring the textures of it. Then, after an age, his mind finally caught up with his body, and he felt as well as knew that he was back. He got up and took a lingering shower in the adjoining bathroom. Then he dressed in fresh clothes and headed back over to the laboratory.

What he found when he got there was a group of very unnerved people. Seeing Fitzgerald, Reid approached from their midst. 'How you feeling, Jack?' he inquired, without a trace of a smile.

'Fine thanks, Bill, much better,' Fitzgerald replied. 'What's up?'

Reid looked back over his shoulder and called to one of the others. 'Alistair, come and meet Jack Fitzgerald.'

A tall, thin young man with a shock of red hair approached. Reid introduced him. 'Jack, this is Alistair MacKenzie, one of the CSIRO's postgraduates assigned to us as a researcher.' MacKenzie looked drawn but managed a polite smile. He shook Fitzgerald's hand, saying 'How do you do, Doctor Fitzgerald,' in a cultured Scottish accent.

Reid went on, 'Alistair's been running around all day collecting funnelwebs and he's come back with something that's a bit of a worry. You'd better take a look.'

Reid led Fitzgerald to the rest of the group which comprised most of the research team. They were gathered around a workbench, staring down at something. Then as Reid cleared a path, Fitzgerald saw what they were looking at, and his heart missed a beat. On the table were two dead funnelwebs, both of them normal in every respect, bar one.

'Jesus!' Fitzgerald breathed, as he stepped forward and carefully picked up the specimen nearest to him. It was a male, intact, and perfectly formed. But it was getting on for three times its normal size.

Jack turned the spider over, and what he saw made him shiver. The funnelweb's fangs were almost two centimetres long, and caked with blood.

'I netted him on the back of a cat he'd just killed – he wasn't at all pleased.' Alistair's droll Scottish manner was somehow reassuring.

But Fitzgerald looked puzzled. 'Cats are immune to funnelweb venom.'

Alistair raised his eyebrows, and said, 'Not any more, it seems.'

Fitzgerald put the spider down, then asked, 'Did you see any others this size?'

Alistair nodded, 'Plenty – and I got a glimpse of one in Neutral Bay that was quite a lot bigger. He was too quick for me, unfortunately.'

Fitzgerald looked over at Bill Reid. Reid grimaced, and said, 'Looks like you've arrived in time for the main event, Jack. Your corner's ready.'

Reid led Fitzgerald to an area which had been partitioned off at one end of the laboratory. It was virtually a mini-lab in itself, stacked with an array of equipment both electronic and conventional. Reid inquired, 'You want to pick up on anything you've seen or start a tunnel of your own?'

Fitzgerald tossed something onto the specimen bench. It was the big funnelweb he'd just been looking at. 'I'll start with a look around this bloke's brain . . . then take it from there,' Fitzgerald replied.

Grinning for the first time, Bill slapped Jack's arm and walked off, saying, 'Good luck.'

Remembering his musings on the Metroliner, but putting them instantly from his mind, Fitzgerald picked up a scalpel and sliced deep into the funnelweb's skull.

Father Edwin Hilary SJ, headmaster of Saint Francis Xavier College, Hunters Hill, had taken careful measures to safeguard the twenty-seven boarders who remained in his charge, most of them boys whose parents were overseas. They had been moved into one residential block in which every window had been covered with fine wire mesh and the edges of every door sealed with strip rubber.

Despite reports that funnelwebs no longer seemed affected by fumigation, Father Hilary had had the entire school sprayed by pest exterminators. He had also initiated a night patrol roster for his staff in residence, comprising himself and another eight members of the Society of Jesus, otherwise known as the Jesuits.

At 10.35pm, an hour after the last of the boys had retired to their bunks, Father Hilary completed his evening's paperwork and correspondence, and adjourned from his spartan office to the comforting solitude of the school chapel. After twenty minutes spent in prayer, he made his way to the residential block where he was due to take over the dormitory night patrol from his bursar, Father Peter Clements.

Father Clements reported that all was well. One boy, Kevin McMahon, had been crying in his sleep with nightmares but seemed settled now. Only twelve years old, Kevin had a vivid imagination and had been more disturbed by the stories of killer funnelwebs than most of the boys.

The two men bade each other goodnight and Father Hilary set off for his first patrol of the upstairs dormitory. As he ascended the creaking wooden staircase two steps at a time, he unconsciously slid his hand into the deep pocket of his cassock. There, he felt the reassuring form of the stout leather paddle he had recently resurrected from the depths of an ancient cupboard. It was a relic of the days of corporal punishment, now abolished by the Jesuits. But tonight what Father Hilary had in mind for the instrument was not its application to the rumps of errant schoolboys.

All the boys in the top dormitory were sleeping soundly, for which Father Hilary was thankful. The only positive benefit he was personally deriving from the extra duty was that for the first time in years, he was able to indulge in his great secular enthusiasm, which was for classic American crime fiction. Having already revisited the shadowy netherworlds of Messrs Spade and Marlowe, tonight he was looking forward to journeying again the dark and dangerous streets of the 87th Precinct.

When he arrived at Kevin McMahon's bunk, Father Hilary paused a moment. The boy was sleeping quietly but his breathing was shallow, and the muscles of his face were tense.

It was then, as he was moving to the side of the bunk to adjust Kevin's tangled covers, that Father Hilary saw the spider. How it got into the dormitory no-one would ever know. But it had gotten in – a male funnelweb with a leg span of fifteen centimetres, and looking bigger in the gloomy yellow night light. It stood motionless, staring at Father Hilary from the bedside locker, only half a metre from the sleeping boy's head.

Even at the age of forty-nine, the tough priest's reflexes were razor sharp, the legacy of years as an accomplished amateur tennis player. In a millisecond, the leather paddle was out and raised. And before the spider could move, Father Hilary had splattered it into a mess of red and yellow goo.

Kevin sat bolt upright, eyes wide. For a second, he looked confused, not knowing if he was awake or dreaming. Instantly, Father Hilary dropped the paddle and grabbed the boy, lifting him carefully so that he would not see the dead spider.

Other boys were already out of their bunks and approaching in a buzz of excited chatter. Father Hilary addressed them with calm authority, 'Two lines down the centre, boys, quick smart! Collins and Murray – switch on the lights.'

The second funnelweb must have been on one of the crossbeams that supported the vaulted ceiling. Perhaps that's how the spiders had gained entry, through a dislodged roof tile, or a gap in the timbers under the eaves. Whatever, as Father Hilary turned to move off, the second funnelweb dropped onto his shoulder and sank its fangs deep into the fibrous tissue of his neck.

Father Hilary arched back. He dropped Kevin and fumbled at the back of his head. Then when he managed to dislodge the second spider, which was fully as big as the first, it jumped to the floor and scampered down the length of the room.

The boys fled in panic. Two of them were stomped on and badly hurt. One of them suffered an instant asthma attack. But none of them looked back as Father Hilary was seized with convulsions, and flailed and thrashed around in agony on the dormitory floor. It took almost three minutes for him to drown in the fluid which secreted into his lungs, and then, at last, to fall still.

Only one boy saw all this happen. He sat on the floor where he had been dropped and watched Father Hilary die. He remained quite motionless and his face remained blank. But until the paramedics arrived twenty minutes later and injected him with a heavy dose of sedative, Kevin McMahon's screams could be heard three streets away.

On the other side of the harbour, a child just a little older than Kevin had been having a good day. In the early hours, Rosie Pentangeli had turned a lucky trick with two Lithuanian seamen in the dockland backstreets of Woolloomooloo. The sailors had been blind drunk and for no more than a grope and a torn blouse, Rosie had relieved them both of fat wallets. She had gone straight to the private hotel in Potts Point where she knew she could get the only thing she now cared about – the only thing which had mattered to her since soon after she'd arrived in Sydney just nineteen months before.

Then, at the age of thirteen, she had run away from the sexual abuse and beatings of a drunken stepfather.

After evading the police and starving for a week around Hyde Park, she had drifted with the other homeless children to Kings Cross, the city's red-light district, and had sold herself for the price of a hamburger.

But Rosie had been a pretty child, with the long dark hair and big brown eyes typical of her Italian ancestry, and she had found that the men who came to the Cross to look for children were prepared to pay well for her. Before long she was making a thousand dollars a day. But the money had done her no good. Partly because three-quarters of it now went to the pimp who had picked her out of the gutter the night she had been beaten senseless by a senior public servant. And partly because whatever she had left for herself, she invariably spent at the private hotel in Potts Point, on heroin and crack cocaine. Now, lying in the filthy squalor of her Darlinghurst room, Rosie had satiated herself with a cocktail of the two drugs, and she was feeling no pain.

In her beautiful delirium, Rosie chuckled at the memory of her stepfather, screaming after her that she'd either be back within three months or dead before she was fifteen. Although he'd been wrong on the first count, she mused that he would probably be right on the second. But it didn't bother her. Most of the kids she had known when she first came to the Cross were dead already, some from overdoses, some murdered – she had done well to survive for so long.

But her looks were going fast. She already appeared more than twice her age and the sunken red-ringed eyes and facial sores which betrayed hard drug abuse and chronic malnutrition were well advanced. Rosie's takings were down to four hundred dollars a day now, which was barely enough to support her habit even when she held back a hundred or so from her pimp. And that she did often, despite the fact that on the two occasions he'd caught her out, he'd tried to dissuade her from doing it again by applying a glowing cigarette end to her armpits, where the burns would not show and so not further compromise her waning profitability. But today, Rosie didn't care . . . about any of it. She had enough dope to keep her high for days. And after that, well . . . what the hell.

Suddenly, surprisingly, she felt ravenous. It was true that she'd barely eaten in a week. She didn't have much appetite these days and would usually just force down some junk food when she started to faint more than two or three times in an hour. As often as not she would throw it all up again anyway.

But this was different. This was a delicious craving for something wonderful to eat – a craving she knew was not the result of a healthy appetite but rather was narcotically induced. That didn't matter. She would indulge herself anyway. And maybe she could turn a trick into the bargain to pay for it.

Half an hour later, in heavy make-up and a satin dress slashed to the waist, Rosie strutted confidently down Darlinghurst Road heading to The Bourbon and Beefsteak. A famous Kings Cross restaurant and hang-out for Sydney night owls, the B&B was also popular with tourists. Rosie had often taken middle-aged Americans, who had lost their wives for the evening, from outside the B&B to a nearby flophouse, and emerged after twenty minutes or so two hundred dollars the richer.

But tonight, that was not to be. Nor any other night. For as Rosie came to the corner of Darlinghurst Road and Roslyn Street, she found herself face to face with a funnelweb spider. The creature was just standing there, in the middle of the footpath, unnoticed by the other people passing by. Which struck Rosie as strange, as the spider's legs spanned at least twenty centimetres.

Rosie stopped in her tracks and looked at the funnelweb, and the funnelweb looked back at her. And through her gorgeous chemical haze, she had the strangest feeling that the creature had been waiting for her.

She did not have long to ponder the idea. The spider scampered straight at her, sprang into the air, and thrust its fangs deep into her exposed right thigh. As if on cue, at that moment, a dozen other people saw the funnelweb. And after three seconds of hysteria, Rosie was alone, bemusedly looking down at the chilling black form on her leg.

Slowly, a dark curtain descended around Rosie's mind. She felt no pain, and no fear. Just the sense of an approaching abyss – an enveloping, comforting, peaceful, absolute nothingness.

The funnelweb did not move. It clung to Rosie's leg even as she sagged and crumpled to the pavement. It stayed with her until after the smile of death had parted her lips, and was trapped in the stiffening muscles of her lower jaw. Then, and only then, did the funnelweb withdraw its fangs, and prowl silently away into the night.

Perhaps Rosie's death grin was a bizarre effect of rigor mortis, or perhaps it was an expression of relief at her escape from a living hell. Or perhaps it was a dying realisation of a final, meaningless triumph over her stepfather. For it was now nine minutes past midnight on the morning of the eighteenth of February, which was Rosie's birthday. She had made it to fifteen after all.

Two kilometres away, Glen Petersen was a very relieved man. The event he had been working towards for six ulcer-making weeks was as good as over. And it had gone wonderfully well.

In the sumptuous private function room of the Sydney Opera House, wild animals of all kinds had prowled, growled, cavorted and leapt from Glen's giant video projection screen, all many times larger than life and made even more spectacular by two thousand watts of full surround audio. The fund raising video for the New South Wales Zoological Parks Board had enthralled the invited audience of potential corporate sponsors, and they had queued afterwards to pledge money for the State's zoos.

Glen had only completed the video at four o'clock that afternoon following a forty-hour straight on-line edit and audio mix. At seven that morning, when the computerised Edit Decision List had crashed, the whole thing had seemed headed for disaster. But as always, somehow, the show was finished on time. And now, at a quarter past midnight, at the request of hangers-on still quaffing gratis champagne, the video was running again.

Despite total exhaustion, Glen was basking in his success. And he was confident that his client's press officer, a stunning brunette who had not left his side for an hour, had the same thing in mind for later as he did.

But then, something curious happened. As the video image dissolved to a gloomy jungle scene, a shape appeared in the frame which Glen had not seen before. The shot was dark and he peered to make out what it was. But when the shape began to move in from the edge of the screen, Glen was left in no doubt whatsoever, and he was utterly astonished. There was a spider in the shot which he had never seen before.

No sooner had the absolute impossibility of that happening occurred to him than his whole body froze.

Because the shot had changed to a bright day scene of blue sky and ocean, and the spider was still there.

Like an automaton, Glen moved to his control console. He faded up the houselights and switched the projector off. Then, forcing himself to look back down the room, he saw what he had most dreaded. The spider on the screen was real – a funnelweb, with a leg span of almost thirty centimetres.

The audience of forty people, most of them well oiled, slowly comprehended what they were looking at. But there was no immediate panic. Rather a chilled sobriety moved through the room as if someone had opened a freezer door. People just began to stand and silently edge towards the exit.

Perhaps they all would have gotten out alive if it hadn't been for Glen Petersen. The sight of the funnelweb had fixed him to the floor. The more the press officer tried to urge him away, the more impossible it was for him to move. Because Glen Petersen was a chronic arachnophobe. Which was why when all but a dozen of the audience had filed out safely, his eyes were still glued to the screen, and he became aware of the thirty or so funnelwebs, all bigger than the first, clinging to the velvet drapes beyond.

The coronary Glen suffered instantly was massive and killed him in three seconds. But as he died, he emitted a scream of such piercing intensity that it antagonised the funnelwebs, causing them to scatter, and attack.

For the next six minutes, the room was visited by bedlam. At the end of it, ten corpses were littered around the exit door and two were lying at the back of the room behind the video console. Glen Petersen's eyes were wide and staring, but thankfully for him, they saw nothing. Because immediately in front of them, a huge funnelweb was feeding – on the enzyme-dissolved tissue of the brunette press officer's face.

But whilst at street level Sydney reeled from the funnelweb horror, underground, neonate leviathans were prowling in the dark. Ravenous, groping blind, the infant monsters had at first cannibalised each other, the strong consuming the weak in a ruthless *danse macabre* of survival.

But then they had found an alternative source of sustenance – a river flowing past full of nourishment that was sweet and rich. They gorged on it, their appetites insatiable from the imperative of accelerated growth. And they thrived on it, and grew bigger . . . and bigger.

4

John Czarnecki was a worried man. His first ten months as the youngest premier in New South Wales' history had been a dream time, and up to a few weeks ago his honeymoon with the electorate had continued without a glitch. Now, a general swing to the right in the political mood of the country as well as the funnelweb problem had soured the honeymoon with a tirade of disaffection and criticism.

That was not why Czarnecki was worried. He was no wimp. His upbringing as the son of a Polish immigrant coalminer in the tough Central Coast town of Newcastle had seen to that. At the age of five, by the end of his first week at school, he had already lost teeth in fights with dinky-di Aussie kids who'd made the mistake of calling him a Polack. And Czarnecki had been fighting ever since – to study for his school exams despite sharing a room in the family's Housing Commission fibro with two of his five brothers, to win a scholarship to the University of Sydney where he'd achieved honours in law, and to claw his way through the perilous Right Wing faction of the New South Wales Labor Party, first to become leader, then after just thirteen months in opposition, to win victory at the polls.

So Czarnecki was not afraid of confrontation, nor

of tough decisions. What worried him about the funnel-web problem was that for the first time in his life, he felt that he was not in control. He was having to rely totally on the opinions of experts, all of whose views seemed entirely at odds with each other. Now, after weeks of this inexplicable phenomenon which was fast escalating out of control, Czarnecki found himself chairing a highly charged emergency meeting of those who were embroiled in the affair. The New South Wales Parliament House main committee room was packed with doctors, academics, police, military and bureaucrats. And it was clear that still not one of them had any idea about why the funnelwebs were killing people.

Czarnecki was finally losing patience with his Deputy Police Commissioner and the General Officer Commanding, Land Command, who were having an aggressive difference of opinion over interpretation of the Commonwealth's Emergency Powers Act. Just then, the door opened and Bill Reid walked in followed by Jack Fitzgerald. Czarnecki was relieved. He'd sent for Reid earlier to get an update on the research team's progress, and even a scientist's report would be more interesting than this contest of machismos between two menopausal men.

Czarnecki rapped his pen on the expansive oval table in front of him. 'Gentlemen, we'll pick this up again later. Doctor Reid of the CSIRO team has just come in and I'm sure we're all anxious to hear from him. Come to the front, Bill.'

Reid made his way forward. Arriving at a lectern, he turned to look back at the surly faces around the table, and wondered how they might look in a few minutes time.

'Thank you, Premier. Ladies and gentlemen, in the past twenty-four hours, we've made some significant discoveries, principally through the work of my colleague here, Doctor John Fitzgerald.' Reid indicated Fitzgerald who had followed him to the lectern. 'I think it would be best if Doctor Fitzgerald tells you about it himself. Jack . . .'

As all eyes turned to Fitzgerald, his mind went completely blank. Employing a trick he'd learned as a young lecturer, he took a deep breath and addressed a series of points between and behind his listeners' heads.

'This is a little hard to explain in non-technical terms, but basically . . .'

Fitzgerald raced over what he was going to say in his mind. It was hopelessly inadequate to convey the shattering enormity of what he had found in the oversized funnelweb's brain. But to an audience of non-scientists, it would have to do.

'Basically, we've identified an alteration in the molecular structure of the funnelweb's growth-governing gene . . . sometimes referred to as the "hedgehog" gene – the mechanism that among other things controls the animal's cell reproduction. The altered "hedgehog" seems to be countermanding the funnelweb's normal growth controls, meaning that its cells are reproducing at an accelerated rate.'

Having started, Fitzgerald relaxed a little, and ventured a look into some of the faces in front of him. They were blank.

He went on, 'Now normally, we would expect that to lead to malady, probably to a carcinoma of some kind . . . and the animal would die. But in this case, the alteration in the "hedgehog" is symmetrical. And because of that, cell reproduction is increased proportionally in all parts of the animal's body. So the funnelwebs are staying healthy . . . but growing bigger.'

A murmur of puzzled apprehension went around the table, and a voice came from the back, 'How much bigger?'

Jack shook his head. 'We're trying to answer that question now, but at the moment, we don't know.'

The murmur rose to a buzz. The Minister for Education, an over-coiffed, impatient-looking woman, asked challengingly, 'Aren't spiders like insects, with their skeletons on the outside – I thought that restricted their size?'

Fitzgerald had thought this might come up. 'Yes, it's true that spiders have exoskeletons. But their unique physiology allows them to grow much bigger than insects. In theory, with altered growth inhibition, there's no reason why they can't grow . . . considerably bigger still.'

Reactions varied from sarcastic jokes to escalating alarm.

Czarnecki pulled in the reins. 'Two questions, Doctor Fitzgerald. First, does this explain why the funnelwebs are killing people? And second, can it help us to stop them?'

The room went quiet again. Jack had everyone's attention. 'In response to your first question, Premier, we now know that one effect of this . . . condition . . . is imbalanced hormone production, which seems to be making the funnelwebs behave in a way which in human terms we would call psychotic. In response to your second question, the answer at this time is no.'

The room droned. A tall, smartly suited man spoke above it. 'A question, Premier.'

Czarnecki pointed, 'Yes, Doctor Barnes?'

The man turned to Fitzgerald. 'Graham Barnes, Doctor Fitzgerald, Research Director of the Commonwealth Serum Laboratories. We've been trying to find out why the funnelweb antivenom has been ineffective in these recent cases and we've discovered that the atraxotoxin component of the funnelwebs' venom has become more concentrated. Is that consistent with your findings?'

Fitzgerald thought about it, then nodded. 'Yes, Doctor Barnes, it could be. Venom secretion like all the animal's other physiological functions would be modified. What you've described could well be explained by the altered "hedgehog".'

As the message sank in, Jack noted reactions around the table were shifting from unease to resentment. He recalled the fate of the Roman messenger who brought bad news.

The Premier seemed particularly antagonised. 'Let's get this straight, Doctor Fitzgerald. What you're telling us is that something has happened to the funnelwebs which is making them bigger, making their venom stronger, and making them kill people for no reason – is that right?'

Fitzgerald looked at Czarnecki. 'Yes, Premier.'

'But so far you've no idea how to reverse this . . . phenomenon?'

Fitzgerald shook his head. 'No, we don't. But we do have an idea about what may have caused it.'

The room fell quiet again as Jack turned to Bill Reid. Reid addressed Czarnecki. 'Premier, the odds against something like this happening in nature are so long that our computers can't even calculate them. So we're as sure as we can be that this has been caused by some unnatural influence. And although there is no corroborating evidence, we believe the most likely explanation is that the funnelwebs have been exposed to some kind of ionising radiation.'

The silence could have been cut. After a few seconds, it was – by the voice of the Minister for Health. 'If you have no corroborating evidence, Doctor Reid, why do you think that?'

Reid and Fitzgerald exchanged looks, knowing they were about to trigger an explosion. Addressing the table,

Reid said, 'From the limited research we've been able to do overnight, what's happening to the funnelwebs looks like it might be consistent with results from recent American studies into the radiation emitted by the new generation of weapons grade fissile materials.'

The explosion came. People were on their feet, protesting, accusing, denying. The Minister for Education's outrage peaked through the din, 'Premier, if the military have been illegally experimenting with nuclear weapons in this State, we have a constitutional crisis on our hands!'

Incensed, the Land Commander retorted, 'The Defence Force is fully accountable for its activities to the Commonwealth. The lady would be better advised to seek out the culprits in her own universities, who appear to be accountable to no-one!'

As the uproar escalated, Czarnecki finally snapped. He leapt to his feet and bellowed with a fury owing less to his upbringing than to his Cossack ancestry, 'For Christ's sake, this is not a fucking high school debate. Shut up, all of you!'

The room hushed instantly. Then people shuffled back into their seats, muttering embarrassed apologies. Czarnecki recomposed himself, and spoke again to Bill Reid. 'Bill, are you optimistic that you can find a way to counteract this . . . thing?'

Reid considered, then said, 'Not optimistic, Premier – but hopeful.'

Czarnecki looked fateful. 'All right, that'll have to do. From now on I want you to stay on this twenty-four hours a day. Anything you need – people, facilities, money – you've got it. Any bullshit, contact me personally, day or night, clear?'

'Okay, Premier, thank you,' Reid said, as a weight of responsibility fell on him which he'd not previously known.

Czarnecki turned down the table and addressed the Minister for Health. 'Harry, get all the manpower and facilities you can lay your hands on working for Doctor Barnes – we've got to come up with a new antivenom then produce it in bucketfuls. And on the quiet, tee up every hospital in the State for more casualties.'

The minister looked sceptical. 'I don't want to sound negative, John, but it took fourteen years to develop the original funnelweb vaccine.'

Czarnecki's face remained impassive but his voice was steel. 'You *are* sounding negative, Harry. Just do it!'

The minister looked admonished, and said only, 'Yes, Premier.'

Czarnecki turned to the Land Commander. 'General Lawrie, as soon as this meeting is finished, I'll be speaking to the Prime Minister to advise him that I may soon be forced to declare a State of Emergency in New South Wales and to request the Federal Government to make a Defence Force commitment for the duration. In the interim, I'd greatly appreciate your active co-operation with the New South Wales Police Force. I want plans prepared for controlling any civil disturbances and, if it should come to it, a total evacuation of the Sydney metropolitan area.'

The Land Commander was taken aback even at the mention of such possibilities. But he recovered quickly and said, 'The civil authorities will have our full co-operation, Premier.'

The gravity of Czarnecki's request had shaken everyone. The Minister for Education was horrified. 'John, surely you don't really believe that . . .'

'I hope to God that it doesn't come to it,' Czarnecki interrupted impatiently, 'but yes, I do really think, on today's evidence, that it could. So we'd better be ready.'

Then before anyone had time to respond, Czarnecki stood brusquely saying, 'I'll go on TV tonight and make a statement, before the press gets a chance to speculate too much, so no-one say anything before then. Meantime, we've all got work to do. Good morning.'

With that, Czarnecki strode from the room, followed by an entourage of assistants. Once he had gone, the rest of the gathering dispersed quickly in a mix of depression and urgency.

Outside Parliament House, Macquarie Street was mayhem. Dozens of journalists and TV crews clamoured for good positions behind lines of burly policemen. Behind the media, several hundred people were packed along the pavement – some anxious for news of developments, some to protest at what they felt was government inaction, but most out of idle curiosity.

As Reid and Fitzgerald came out of the building with others from the meeting, reporters surged forward and launched a barrage of questions. What was the government doing about the funnelweb killings? Was the government aware that there'd been another three deaths that morning? Was the Premier intending to declare a State of Emergency?

The experts and officials ducked their heads and called 'No comment!' as they bustled into the convoy of waiting cars and sped mercifully away. Jack was just following Bill into the government LTD which had brought them from North Ryde, when somewhere behind him a woman's voice called, 'Doctor Fitzgerald!'

Jack turned and scanned the sea of faces. At first, he saw no-one he knew. Then, from much closer, the same voice called 'Jack!' and he recognised it. Five paces away, Helen Parkes was trying to persuade a policeman who was twice her size to let her through. But he was having none of it.

Fitzgerald felt instantly better. He moved quickly to the policeman and spoke loudly above the din. 'It's okay, officer, this lady's with us.' The policeman looked annoyed but allowed Helen through, only just relinking arms with the officer next to him in time to prevent a full-scale breakthrough.

In contrast to the last time Fitzgerald had seen her, Helen was dressed in sneakers and jeans, and looked hot and bothered. But she was still stunning. 'Small world,' she said with a pixie grin.

'Long way to come for more spider stories, Miss Parkes,' Fitzgerald said, trying to conceal his obvious pleasure.

'Funnelwebs are page one all round the world, Doctor Fitzgerald. I had a head start so the *New York Times* thought I'd better stay on it.' Helen smiled with the look of a schoolgirl who was pleased with herself.

Jack glanced around, considering. 'Well, since you've come all this way, I suppose the least I can do is buy you lunch – CSIRO canteen sound okay?'

Helen grinned. 'Like more fun than Tiffany's.'

Jack picked up the bag which Helen had manoeuvred past the policeman and showed her into the back of the LTD. Then, as he introduced Helen to Bill Reid, the limousine made a fast U-turn and headed north for the Harbour Bridge.

Throughout the afternoon, reports flooded into the city's newsrooms of continuing attacks by funnelwebs, and by evening the death toll for the day had reached nine. In an interview following the ABC's evening news, the Premier did his best to be reassuring. But how did you tell four million people that their worst nightmares were coming true and sound positive. Czarnecki had a stab at it, but even under the make-up and lights, he looked grey. The bottom line was that Sydney was infested with killer spiders. And as yet there was no way known to get rid of them.

So as darkness fell, the city was gripped with fear. Its people cowered in barred and bolted rooms, and the streets were deserted.

But as the hours passed, and midnight came and went, something was happening that would change the very nature of the funnelweb problem. For weeks, monsters had been growing underground, in an old and forgotten backwater of Sydney's sewers. They had nourished themselves on the abundance of human faecal matter which flowed down to them from every part of the city. And they had flourished on it, and grown to enormous size.

But now they had reached a stage where they needed more substantial sustenance. So they began to move out from their nurturing cradle and foray in search of living, breathing prey. They broke through into the city's railway tunnels where all they found was a meagre population of rats. Still ravenous, they were forced to go further afield. And the only way left to go was up.

Centimetre by centimetre, with meticulous care, they ascended the filth-encrusted walls of the tunnels' ventilation shafts. Until finally when they reached ground level, they scattered in every direction, and voraciously began to forage for anything and everything alive.

In company with ninety per cent of Sydneysiders that evening, Khoeung Seng had been glued to the Premier's broadcast. Now, at a little after 1am, he and his wife, Rami, were efficiently packing as much as they could into their twelve-year-old station wagon, aiming to be many kilometres down the Hume Highway towards Melbourne by dawn. Rami's sister, who lived in Springvale, had been pleading with them for days to come and stay with her family until the funnelweb problem was resolved. Until now, Seng had resisted, not wanting to burden his in-laws. But tonight, John Czarnecki had changed his mind.

Seng was a Cambodian refugee, one of the fourteen thousand survivors of Pol Pot's Democratic Kampuchea who had found sanctuary in Australia. As a child, he had lost his parents to the torturers of Tuol Sleng, and later he had watched his older brother bludgeoned to death in the 'killing fields' by two Khmer Rouge guards. Both had been thirteen-year-old girls.

One night, when he could no longer stand the screams of his countrymen as they were taken out of their beds and murdered, Seng had crawled past the sentries and escaped into the countryside. He had survived in the rainforest for weeks, living off the land, until finally he'd crossed into Thailand and reached safety in an Australian Carmelite mission. That had been in 1978, when he had been eleven years old. Now as a married man with a young son of his own, it seemed fate had once more picked him to live in 'interesting times'.

Rami had also lost her father and sisters to the Khmer Rouge. Her experiences had left her with a permanent nervous disability, a raw rash which appeared all over her legs and body whenever she became stressed or frightened. That was why, as she rushed around the house on this warm summer's night, she was dressed in a long-sleeved blouse.

Seng knew exactly what that meant but he did not remark on it. Instead, his mind was racing through everything that would have to be done to get his family away from the city to safety. The small house in Meadowbank which had taken them years to save for would have to be abandoned. But if Seng had learnt anything in the course of his remarkable life, it was to seize the chance of survival before it was too late.

Seng's son, Peter, or Pete as he was known to everyone except his mother, was sprawled on the carpet in the lounge room, disinterestedly toying with the Transformer he had been given for his sixth birthday two weeks before. Pete didn't really understand why his mother and father had seemed increasingly worried over the past days, nor was he especially troubled by it. Like all young children he accepted his parents' idiosyncrasies as given – his mother's frequent fits of tears and his father's anguished cries in his sleep had always been a part of Pete's life – they were things he didn't question, or even think about. So his parents' recently acquired obsession with keeping all outside doors and windows closed, and their new rituals of pulling furniture apart, cleaning the house several times a day and moving his bed into their room, seemed only more examples of the unfathomable behaviour of adults.

But now Pete was looking forward to a terrific treat. He was tingling with excitement as only a six-year-old can at the prospect of driving through the night for a holiday with his cousins in Melbourne. In fact he was so excited that he was finding it difficult to stay amused whilst his parents took such an interminable time to get ready.

The only member of the family indifferent to it all was snoozing peacefully under a lounge room chair. His name was Snowy, and he was a spirited three-year-old white Scotch terrier. As an only child, Pete had invested all the affection normally reserved for siblings into his dog. He had named him after the companion of his favourite cartoon character, Tin Tin, and the inseparable pair spent many hours lost in Pete's imagination, re-enacting the adventures created by the genius Hergé.

Suddenly, and for no apparent reason, Snowy's eyes snapped open. He laid there for a time, perfectly still, listening to something that humans could not hear. Then, he got up and walked quietly out into the hallway, uncharacteristically passing Pete without even a look.

Pete glanced up and saw Snowy disappear into the kitchen. Pleased with an alternative distraction, he discarded his toy and followed. But when he looked in through the kitchen door, he saw Snowy behaving very strangely. The dog was standing stock still, staring intently at the foot of the back door. He wasn't barking as when he was excited, nor growling as when he sensed an intruder, such as the postie or the neighbour's ginger tom. Snowy was rigid, as if frozen with anticipation, or alarm.

Pete crouched down, ruffled his dog's pointed ears, and said, 'What's up, Snowy? Want to go out for a pee?'

Still Snowy didn't react. He remained motionless, mesmerised by whatever it was outside that he was listening to.

Pete started to worry. He had owned Snowy since he'd been an eight-week puppy and he'd never behaved like this. Maybe he was feeling sick. That must be it. He'd eaten something bad and wanted to go out to be sick. Snowy was the cleverest dog in the world and would never get sick in the house. Pete looked up at the back door. As well as the spring latch at his head height, there was a brand new heavy-duty bolt which his father had fitted only the day before.

Pete pulled over a chair and stood on it. The bolt was stiff but after a bit of working, it slid back. He climbed down, pushed the chair aside and turned the latch handle. Then, as he opened the door wide, Snowy darted out.

Pete peered through into the darkness. The muted wailing of an ambulance drifted across the Parramatta River, but otherwise the night was still.

Snowy had gone directly to the shed at the back of the carport. Seng had moved the car into the street for packing and Rami had left the shed door open when she had gone in to get their raincoats. Again, Snowy was standing motionless, glaring into the black interior, his white coat the only thing visible in the gloom.

Intrigued, Pete went out and walked up to the shed, and only then did he hear what Snowy had heard – there was something moving around inside. That was the moment when Snowy started to bark, and instantly, the movement stopped.

Passing each other on the front path, Seng and Rami froze in their tracks. Rami dropped the groceries she was carrying and was halfway to the gate by the time the glass jars shattered on the concrete. Seng was just ahead of her and turned the corner of the house in time to see Snowy darting into the shed. He was growling so ferociously that Pete looked too frightened to move.

As Seng reached Pete, a melee was raging. Snowy was snarling and snapping and the contents of the shed were crashing around violently. But then Snowy yelped and gave out an agonised howl, and everything fell silent.

Seng grabbed Pete and passed him back to his mother. Then he reached around inside the door and switched on the light. In the glare of the naked bulb, the place was chaos. Hardware and bric-a-brac were scattered everywhere. In the middle of it all, Snowy was lying motionless, soaking in the blood still oozing from punctures all over his body.

Seng gazed at the scene in horror. Because standing over Snowy were two creatures like giant spiders, but grotesquely distorted and with legs spanning over a metre. Both had their fangs buried deep in Snowy's carcass, and were pumping him full of fluid that was dissolving him into stinking black goo.

Seng grabbed the door and slammed it hard. But as he turned and eased his family away, Pete started screaming for Snowy. Seng grabbed his son and embraced him very tightly, trying to smother his anguish and to protect him. Having slammed the steel door shut, he gave no more thought to the monsters. But he'd forgotten the shed window which Pete had broken with his soccer ball three days earlier.

Looking over his father's shoulder, Pete saw two shadows drop from the window and scamper towards him at terrifying speed. There and then, in his father's arms, he died of fright, his heart, weakened by infant rheumatic fever, unable to cope.

An instant later, as he registered that his son had gone limp, Seng was visited by the most excruciating agony – his back was impaled by two white hot spears which flooded him with molten lead.

It was only two seconds before Seng was dead on the ground. But in that time, the images of his entire life flowed in front of his eyes – his loving mother looking down at him as he suckled on her breast . . . his brother telling him that their parents had been tortured to death . . . his brother's head imploding like a coconut beneath the cudgels of children . . . the first glimpse of Pete's face at the instant he was born, the first instant that Seng could remember being in love with life.

Now father and son lay embracing in death, and Seng's back was already liquefying into a feast for the two gorging monsters. Nearby, Rami stared down at the obscenity. But she made no sound. She just looked, with eyes glazed, expressionless – watching, but not seeing.

In the house, the phone rang. Mechanically, Rami turned and walked in, her gait strangely fluid, almost as if she was floating. Like an automaton, she went to the phone and picked it up. The anxious voice at the other end was her sister's, and spoke in Khmer.

'Hello . . . hello, Rami, is that you? Hello! Is that you, Pete? It's your Aunt Vannak, in Melbourne . . . hello . . . who's there . . . HELLO!'

Rami did not reply. She could hear the voice at first, but it wafted away as she floated ever deeper into a darkening well. Down and down she went, until at last she was in a place with no name, no light, no sound . . . and no pain.

Rami had still not spoken when her sister hung up a minute later. And when the police arrived ten minutes after that, and found Rami still standing there, she did not speak to them either. And despite the fact that, as fate would have it, Rami would live for many years to come, she would never again say a single word to anyone.

At 2.20am, only a few kilometres but a whole world away, in the blue-ribbon eastern suburb of Vaucluse, Agnes Weaver was alone in her bed. She was wide awake, staring at the ceiling, and irritated by the night sounds that were wafting across the harbour from the city.

Agnes had lived in the ramshackle three-storey house all her life, and had owned it since the death of her father forty years earlier. Currently, despite its deteriorated condition, the property was conservatively worth eight million dollars. That anyway was the price Agnes had been offered for the place twice during the past twelve months, but on both occasions she had gracelessly declined. She certainly didn't need the money, having inherited the fortune her father had made in mining along with the house. But even though she rattled around in the old pile and had been under increasing pressure from her doctor to move into something more sensible, she had doggedly refused. This was her home -- she would die in it, and that was that.

But there was more to Agnes's refusal to give up the house than the foibles of a cranky old lady. The fact of the matter was that Agnes was extraordinarily mean, and knowing as she did that the property was appreciating in value, she would not part with it as a matter of financial principle. At the same time, she would no more pay out good money to have the house maintained than fly in the air. She loathed and distrusted all tradesmen, and baulked at the thought of paying their scandalous charges. In fact, she regarded anyone who had to work for a living as her inferior, along with people who used public transport, or who did their own shopping and housework, or, iniquity of iniquities, found themselves in any way dependant on welfare. Agnes regarded all of these things as the traits of lesser stock, and consequently had never done anything remotely philanthropic in her life.

Now, a childless spinster in her sixty-seventh year, and friendless save for the occasional gold-digger who would not be seen for dust as soon as they realised they'd never see a cent for their trouble, Agnes Weaver laid wide awake in the middle of the night in the cold comfort of her living mausoleum, nervous for her safety because of the funnelweb problem, but fretting more about the effect it might have on the value of her property.

There was a noise downstairs. Not a loud noise, but an unfamiliar one. The house made many noises at night, mostly the creaking of ageing materials contracting. But Agnes knew the sound of every timber and every slate, and she knew this noise had been made by none of them.

In her apprehension, she cursed the builder she had been forced to engage a month earlier to fix a leaky roof. The impertinent man had advised her to upgrade her security, insisting that she should have refitted window frames and new locks throughout. But he had quoted a ridiculous price and she had sent him packing with a flea in his ear.

If the man had not so obviously been trying to take advantage, perhaps she would have agreed to his proposal and whatever it may be that had made the noise downstairs could not have gotten in. She took comfort from the fact that she had refused to pay the builder's account for the roof. As was her habit with creditors, she would wait until the very last minute before he took legal action, then settle out of court for a reduced amount. Yes, it was that awful builder's fault that she may now be in danger of her life.

But whatever Agnes Weaver's failings, cowardice was not one of them. Or perhaps she was just so mean that she valued her property more than her physical safety. Whatever, she got up, pulled on the threadbare dressing gown that been a present from her long-dead mother, groped under the bed for the ancient Webley revolver which her father had brought home from the First World War and stepped as quietly as she could to the bedroom door.

Agnes listened intently, not daring to breathe. Now she heard only the familiar sounds of the house – the creak of a loose floorboard, the click of a warped bannister – perhaps what may have been there had gone, or perhaps it had just been the wind. Agnes had always been obsessive about her pre-bed locking up routine but she knew that her memory and concentration were not what they were. She comforted herself that she must have forgotten to close a window, and that the wind had blown something over. Despite the fact that the night was as still as the grave, she felt better.

Agnes opened the door and peered out over the landing. The entrance hall below was illuminated with a drab yellow light, which was all that emanated from the three low-wattage globes remaining in the hallway chandelier.

Nothing moved. Agnes summoned her courage and edged out of the bedroom. Then, with her heart in her mouth and the corroded old pistol proffered, she haltingly began to descend the rickety stairs.

Somehow, Agnes got down to the entrance hall without fainting. Still there was no sign of anything, and no recurrence of the noise she had heard. She crept on past the closed double doors to the sitting room, past the bolted and chained front door, and round the hallway corner into the library passageway. It was then that she saw it, through the open library door – a door she was positive she had closed on her rounds. As she peered through the door, something big and black moved soundlessly across in the shadows.

Agnes was cemented to the floor, her stomach in the jaws of a vice. With a supreme effort, she edged along the passageway, just a few short paces which felt more like a thousand. Then, trembling, pointing the heavy gun into the dark, Agnes reached inside the doorjamb – and switched on the light.

On the opposite side of the room, standing on a table against one of the floor-to-ceiling bookshelves, there was a man. He spun around and glowered at Agnes, his eyes full of fear. He was a young man, twenty at most, short and wiry, and dressed in black. And at his feet there was a backpack half full of the old dusty volumes which occupied the library's top shelves.

There was a frozen moment as the two frightened people just stared at each other. And in that moment, Agnes realised that she knew the young man. He had been to the house, with the builder who had repaired the roof – he was the builder's labourer.

Ken Collins was nineteen, and had laboured for a few builders over the past three years since his release from the last of his spells in Juvenile Justice Centre. He had managed to go straight for most of that time, trying to do the right thing by his eighteen-year-old wife, Loren, and their twin baby daughters, Kylie and Dani.

But now Loren was pregnant again, and labouring work was increasingly hard to come by. And because he could not bear to see his family wanting, sometimes Ken would go out at night and practise the one remarkable talent he possessed, which with his boyish good looks had won him the almost affectionate nickname among the Newtown police of 'the baby burglar'.

Four weeks ago, during a break from hauling tiles up to Agnes's roof, Ken had started chatting to the daily domestic, a kindly woman called Marjorie. She hadn't found his questions about the contents of the house suspicious, assuming them to be the innocent fascination of the poor for abundant wealth. And she had unwittingly given Ken a perfect opportunity to case the place when on three separate occasions she had brought him into the kitchen for coffee.

So when the builder had laid Ken off only a week later, blaming cash flow problems arising from bad debts, Ken had thought instantly of those 'rare books' on the top shelves of Agnes's library which, according to Marjorie, '. . . must be worth thousands and thousands'. He also thought of the fence in Newtown who would give him a few hundred dollars for them. And he thought of the antiquated kitchen windows, which he knew he could open quickly with nothing more elaborate than a penknife.

It had, as it turned out, been almost that easy. Ken

had opened one of the windows in only a few seconds, but it had not been touched for years and had made a sharp crack when it shifted. He had waited for an age in case he'd been heard. But finally, when no-one had appeared, desperation had overtaken him and he had climbed carefully and soundlessly inside.

He had stolen through to the library and, being the professional he was, the first thing he had done there was to open the window for a quick line of escape. Then he had moved the reading table from the centre of the floor to the place where the oldest looking, and presumably the most valuable, books were shelved.

He was about to climb up to them when he thought he heard somebody moving upstairs. He had gone stiff, and had listened without breathing for a full half minute. But then, when the noise had not come again, he had crossed to the door and ventured a look outside. When he'd seen no-one, he had still waited a full two minutes before deciding the coast was clear and crossing back to the table. That had been the instant when Agnes had turned into the passageway, and seen Ken's black figure moving past the doorway in the shadows.

Now, as she realised what was happening, Agnes became bitter. 'How did you know?' she spat accusingly.

Ken looked from Agnes's beady eyes to the big black gun she was pointing. But he said nothing.

Agnes felt panicky. 'How did you know where to look, you bastard! How did you know!'

Ken's mind was racing, weighing up the odds of making the window without getting shot.

Agnes's fear was being overtaken by anger. 'You vile little bastard! If you don't tell me how you knew, I'll shoot you right now!'

There was something in Agnes's voice that made

Ken believe she would do it. His spine turned to ice. 'It was Marjorie,' he blurted, 'your woman, Marjorie . . . she told me. I swear!'

Agnes's face went momentarily blank, then flooded with confusion. 'Marjorie? But . . . how did Marjorie know? How did she know?'

In his trepidation, Ken thought his eyes must be playing tricks on him. He thought for an instant that what he saw behind Agnes must be a hallucination. But as it came closer, and the light from the library fell fully onto it, Ken grappled with the realisation that the horror he was seeing was real.

At first, Agnes felt rather than heard the presence behind her. Or perhaps she detected a shift in the order of Ken's fear. Whatever, she knew before she looked what she was going to see, but what did take her by surprise when she turned was the funnelweb's size.

It was a female, bigger than the male even under normal circumstances. But the creature looking at Agnes from eight paces away was not normal. Her grotesque, armoured body was a metre in length, and her contorted hair-covered legs spanned over two metres.

For a moment, the funnelweb regarded Agnes with its eight dead, black eyes. Then abruptly it reared back into a stance of attack, and rose fully to Agnes's head height.

Agnes went into a trance. Her mind simply refused to accept what it was that she was seeing. So as the funnelweb sprang at her and impaled her on its fangs, she felt nothing. She just stood there, with her face and mind totally blank, and died.

Ken couldn't remember what happened next. But what he did in that instant saved his life. Grabbing his pack, he leapt to the window and with the power in his legs doubled by terror, he bounded straight through. Then he crossed the expansive lawn and was over the garden wall before the funnelweb had time to shake Agnes Weaver from its fangs.

Marjorie had been wrong about the old books on the top shelves of the library. They were worthless, being mostly turn of the century anthologies of dreary Victorian fiction. Worthless, and unreadable. Unreadable not because of talent lacking in their authors, but because they had been carefully hollowed out to be used as secret containers.

What they contained, or five of them anyway, was cash – two hundred and twelve thousand dollars in used twenties and fifties, unmarked, and untraceable. It was part of nine hundred thousand dollars in notes, bonds and gold hidden on the top shelf of Agnes's library, amassed over the years because of Agnes's fear of a stock-market crash.

When Ken got home and rummaged through his pack, it took him several minutes to realise that he wasn't dreaming. It was like winning the lottery. And almost instantly, he knew exactly what he would do with the money. He would buy a hardware store, just like the one his father had worked in before he'd died of cancer when Ken was only nine. He and Loren would live in comfort, and grow old happily together, and never again have to worry about where the next dollar was coming from. Kylie and Dani, and their new brother or sister, would not know how the family fortune was made. But now they would grow up with every advantage that money could buy – thanks to the unwitting philanthropy of Agnes Weaver.

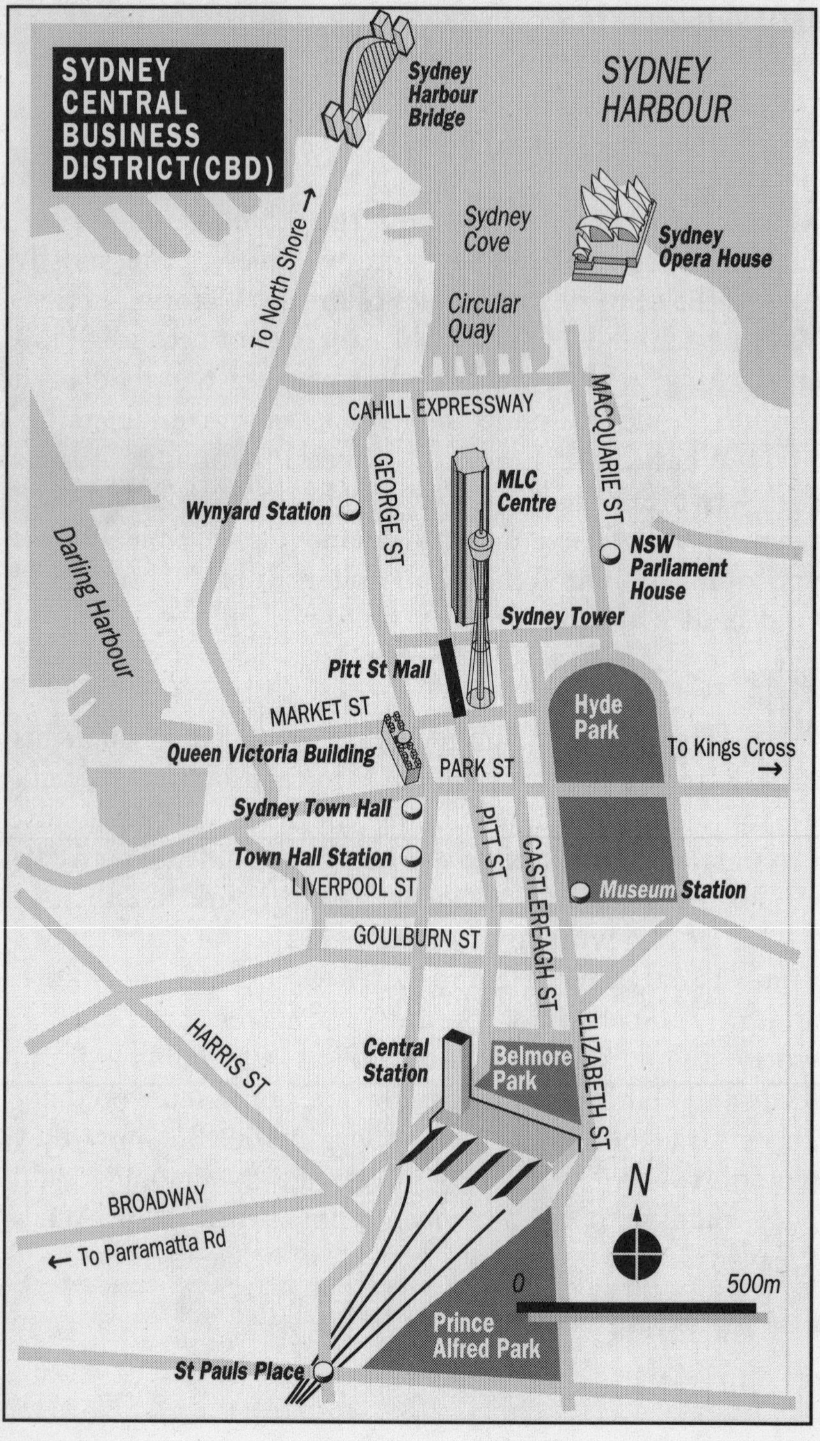
SYDNEY CENTRAL BUSINESS DISTRICT(CBD)
Sydney Harbour Bridge
SYDNEY HARBOUR
Sydney Cove
Sydney Opera House
To North Shore →
Circular Quay
CAHILL EXPRESSWAY
MACQUARIE ST
GEORGE ST
MLC Centre
Wynyard Station
NSW Parliament House
Darling Harbour
Sydney Tower
Pitt St Mall
Hyde Park
MARKET ST
Queen Victoria Building
To Kings Cross →
PARK ST
Sydney Town Hall
PITT ST
CASTLEREAGH ST
Town Hall Station
LIVERPOOL ST
Museum Station
GOULBURN ST
ELIZABETH ST
HARRIS ST
Central Station
Belmore Park
N
BROADWAY
← To Parramatta Rd
0
500m
Prince Alfred Park
St Pauls Place

5

The Premier was wakened at his home in Killarney Heights at 2.50am with first reports of the obscenity spewing up from Sydney's sewers. It sounded like something out of a horror video. But right here and now, it was real. Dozens of monster funnelwebs had emerged north of the harbour as far west as Ryde. And more than twenty had been reported in the Eastern Suburbs, at Double Bay and Vaucluse. However a veritable plague had erupted in the heart of the Central Business District, from the underground railway stations at Wynyard and Sydney Town Hall. They had materialised out of the tunnels then crept along deserted platforms and ascended silent stairways and escalators. And it was there, at Wynyard, that they had first tasted human blood.

At 1am, nine members of a railway cleaning crew had been returning to work from their meal break. When they reached the head of the stairwell leading down to Platform Five, they found themselves face to face with three monster funnelwebs. One of the cleaners, a woman in her fifties, died immediately from an epileptic seizure. Two others, both men, fainted. The rest scattered screaming and ran headlong into a mob of monsters spilling up into the concourse from another stairwell.

Those nine railway workers, all from the former Yugoslavia and only three of them fluent in English, had a dubious double distinction. They were the first human beings to see the monster funnelwebs, and also the first to be eaten by them.

The monsters fought furiously over them, scampering across each other to get at them, impaling them and frenziedly ripping them apart. The cleaners' terrible screams pierced up through the Wynyard Arcade and out into George Street. There they froze the blood of two passing state police officers who leapt from their patrol car and pulled back the folding gates just as the first of the funnelwebs appeared in the subway below.

What made the two veteran policemen panic was not so much the sight of the giant misshapen spider, although that would have been unnerving enough. What got to them was the object impaled on the monster's fangs – the legless but living torso of an eighteen-year-old woman, arms flailing and still burbling from the mouth of her half-severed head.

The policemen ran in terror, leaving the arcade gates wide open. Within minutes, the monster funnelwebs were cavorting up and down George Street – darting and freezing, rearing back and trembling, spinning and leaping and quivering in a crazed dance. And what would come to be known as 'the funnelweb war' had started.

As well as Wynyard, fatalities were reported at Meadowbank, Vaucluse and a dozen other suburbs. And the list was growing by the minute.

At 2.59am, from the study of his home, Czarnecki declared a State of Emergency. Then he put a call through to The Lodge in Canberra and formally requested the support of the Commonwealth from the Prime Minister. After thirty seconds to come to terms with what he was hearing, the Prime Minister assented, and before the receiver was back on its cradle, he had instructed his aides to call an immediate meeting of Federal Cabinet.

At a little after three o'clock, Czarnecki was speeding across the Roseville Bridge with a heavily armed police escort. Nine minutes later he was standing next to Jack Fitzgerald and Bill Reid, gazing at a nightmare materialised. The specimen had been collected from the roadside at Gladesville by Alistair MacKenzie after he had received a call from a very shaky Station Sergeant at Ryde. A long-distance trucker starting out early for Broken Hill had been heading west on Victoria Road when he'd ploughed into the giant funnelweb. The driver hadn't stopped until he'd reached Ryde Police Station, where the constable on the desk had assumed the man was high on amphetamines.

But he hadn't been, and the proof of his story was now laid out in the CSIRO laboratory across three workbenches. Three benches were necessary because the body of the dead mutant funnelweb was just under two metres long, and its legs in their standing position would have spanned something closer to four.

Not only its size was remarkable. The creature still resembled a funnelweb, retaining the distinguishing characteristics of its normally sized antecedent. But in mutating, its build had been distorted – its abdomen and thorax were more compressed, and its legs, whilst still long, were sturdier and more powerful. However by far the most disconcerting thing about it was its fangs – smooth, jet black, delicately curved like twin sabres, and fully half a metre long. The thick spiky hairs bristling all over its body only underpinned the impression of a being conceived in hell.

Untypically, John Czarnecki was speechless. His lower jaw just hung limply beneath his blood-drained face. If the carcass was not horrible enough, the sixteen-tonne semitrailer had burst the monster's abdomen, and its guts were spread over the floor.

Eventually, Czarnecki found words. 'How is it possible?'

'We've only had it for an hour,' Fitzgerald said, struggling to maintain his scientific detachment, 'but it's already clear that this is . . . something different . . . to what we've seen before.'

Czarnecki looked baffled. 'I'd have thought that was obvious to anyone, Doctor Fitzgerald.'

Reid interjected. 'What Jack means, Premier, is that this is not just more of the same but bigger. Apart from their size, the funnelwebs we've been looking at up to now were all normally formed mature adults. I have to tell you that this . . .' Reid swallowed hard, 'this . . . specimen . . . has all the characteristics of a juvenile.'

There was a tangible silence, as in a moment following the passing of a death sentence.

Czarnecki turned slowly to Reid. 'A juvenile?'

Reid simply shook his head, the strain of being face to face with the impossible showing clearly in his eyes.

Fitzgerald stared intently into the creature's open skull. 'We think that whatever started this . . . exposure to radiation, or whatever it was . . . has had some kind of escalating effect on the funnelwebs' genes.'

Czarnecki turned to Fitzgerald. Fitzgerald looked up at him, and explained, 'What we've encountered so far . . . the aggression, the excessive growth . . . may have been the effect on the original funnelwebs that were exposed to the triggering influence.' Fitzgerald looked down again. 'But when those original spiders reproduced, and their altered DNA was passed on to their progeny, the effect of it was multiplied exponentially . . . my guess is with every embryonic cell division.'

Czarnecki's mind was trying to catch up when Fitzgerald laid it out for him. 'What we think, Premier,' he said, 'is that this is the progeny of the originally affected funnelwebs, but mutated to such an extent that it is, for all practical purposes, a new species.'

Czarnecki looked around the room. The members of the research team gazed past him at the monster, their faces filled with apprehension. He looked again at Fitzgerald, then at Reid, and asked, 'If this is only a juvenile . . . how big will they get?'

Reid and Fitzgerald regarded each other. Then Reid said, 'Anything we say now would only be a guess, Premier.'

'For fuck's sake, Bill,' Czarnecki snapped, 'how big will the bastards get – what's your best guess?'

Reid shrugged, then hazarded, 'Size of a truck, maybe.'

Fitzgerald spoke almost to himself. 'Not a truck – a battle tank – armoured . . . weaponed . . . and fast.'

The temperature in the room dropped, and Czarnecki asked, 'How fast?'

Fitzgerald surveyed one of the funnelweb's stiffened legs. 'Forty . . . fifty kilometres an hour . . . maybe more.'

As the Premier's insides knotted, all he could say was, 'Shit!'

Then Reid stepped forward, and said, 'Let's leave the team to it, Premier – there's a lot to do.'

Czarnecki looked again at all the faces, and said quietly, 'Please find a way to kill this thing, ladies and gentlemen.' And with that, he walked out to the helicopter which had just landed noisily nearby.

Jack ambled to the far end of the room where Helen

was typing feverishly into a laptop. 'How's the story?' he asked.

'Like you said – not many laughs,' Helen muttered absently, as she finished her dispatch and hit the Save key.

Fitzgerald reflected, then said, 'If you've got any sense, you'll get out of here . . . while you can.'

Helen looked up, amazed. 'Leave here? Now? Are you crazy? This is the biggest story since Pearl Harbor!'

Fitzgerald looked preoccupied. 'What Czarnecki said was right. If we don't come up with something soon . . .'

Helen interrupted, 'Jack, do you really think I'm about to walk away from the best break I've ever had?'

It was perfectly clear from her expression that she was not. Standing, she smiled and said, 'You need an eye opener. C'mon . . . I'll buy you a cup of coffee.'

Helen led Jack out of the laboratory and into the building's entrance hall. But as they approached the doors, their way was barred by a burly policeman in dark blue fatigues. 'Sorry, folks, we're all staying in tonight,' he said, his authority underpinned by the Self-Loading Rifle slung over his shoulder.

Helen looked affronted. 'We're going to the canteen for supper, officer,' she said, with New York assertiveness.

'I'm sorry, Ma'am,' the policemen said more insistently, '*nobody* goes outside – there's hot food and bedding coming in.'

Then through the glass entrance doors, they saw other policemen outside with automatic weapons, and the gravity of their situation was frighteningly apparent.

Jack said calmly, 'Bill keeps a plunge in his office.' Then he took Helen's arm and led her back into the safety of the laboratory.

Two minutes after the army Black Hawk had left the CSIRO, it was already halfway to Holsworthy Barracks in Sydney's south-west – the designated location for a crisis meeting of the New South Wales Government.

Slumped in an uncomfortable seat at the back of the helicopter's cabin, the Premier paid no attention when his personal bodyguard, a useful-looking detective sergeant, inquired of the Premier's senior press aide, 'Who was the blonde you were perving, Steve?'

The press aide grinned. 'Yank journo – great tits.'

Snoozing next to Czarnecki, the Premier's private secretary grunted from behind closed lids, 'In your dreams, sonny!'

The press aide grinned wider. 'Lady journos love me, George – they sense I've got my finger on the pulse of power.'

'Only pulse your finger's on's in your dick,' the private secretary retorted, his eyes opening to slits.

'Can't get at it past the lady journos, George,' the press aide boasted, looking pleased with himself.

The private secretary muttered with finality, 'Get fucked,' and reclosed his eyes.

'Shut the fuck up!' Czarnecki snapped at them all, 'I can't think through this bullshit!'

The banter stopped, and the Premier gazed out through the window onto the lights of Parramatta. He was worried, although not, as might have been expected, about what he'd seen at North Ryde.

A few minutes after he'd been wakened with news of the monster funnelwebs, he'd received another phone call. It was from a man he knew well, but who was not a public official, nor anyone personally involved with the funnelweb crisis. The man was a lawyer, and he had called to invite Czarnecki to meet urgently with certain of his clients, who were aware of what was happening and were concerned.

Czarnecki knew the lawyer's clients also, and well enough to know that their concerns would not be for the community. Rather, they would be for their own, very particular, interests. Since becoming Premier, Czarnecki had profited personally from his association with these people. But that meant that they were able to apply pressure on him – and they were applying it now.

Everyone was puzzled when Czarnecki barked instructions to detour to the rural suburb of Kenthurst, and even more puzzled when the Black Hawk landed in the grounds of an elegant but isolated country house. However the Premier's staff knew when and when not to ask questions, and his mood at that moment signalled this was decidedly 'when not'.

An immaculate Range Rover collected the Premier from the landing site and he was gone for more than forty minutes. But when he returned, and barked, 'All right, Holsworthy, quick-smart . . . and get me the PM on the Bat phone,' everyone was relieved that his mood seemed completely reversed.

The emergency meeting of Federal Cabinet had already been in session for several minutes when the scramble telephone rang in the Cabinet Room and the Prime Minister took his second call that morning from John Czarnecki.

Richard Bartlett was, in fact, Prime Minister of Australia only by default. He had ascended to the top job when his predecessor had resigned under a cloud of alleged financial impropriety. Until then, Bartlett had been dismissed as something of a joke, having been seen as a token 'dry' in what was, on the whole, a moderate if not particularly effective Liberal Government. When younger, he had been a favoured son of Melbourne silver-spoon society. But his family wealth had been all but lost in the crash of '89, and his political star had subsequently waned with a series of fumbles and petty embarrassments.

He had been dropped from the cabinet but kept on as a junior minister, mainly to appease the drawing room matrons of Vaucluse and Toorak. But when faith in the government had been dangerously rocked by scandal, Bartlett was dragged out of stagnation and unceremoniously shoved into The Lodge.

He was put there only as a caretaker, to be replaced as soon as things had settled down. But Bartlett surprised everybody, particularly the Centre-Right powerbrokers of his own party, whom by stealth he effectively marginalised. Once in power, he moved quickly to erode his predecessor's policies to a degree that they were practically unworkable. At the same time he beat the Labor Party at its own game by reclaiming the populist spotlight with a latent gift for performance on television.

The quality press, the opposition and many of his own party reviled him as a 'Right Wing simpleton'. But the silent majority – those suburban Anglo-Celtic Australians fretful about declines in their real incomes, worried by mounting urban violence, resentful of 'dole-bludgers' and Aboriginal welfare, and fearful of Asian immigration – went along with him.

Richard Bartlett cut taxes and undermined the unions. He introduced draconian sentencing and put capital punishment back on the agenda. He established work-for-the-dole programs and reduced Aboriginal funding. He froze non-European immigration quotas and reversed the trend of integration into the Asia-Pacific region in favour of renewed economic ties with America and Europe. Accordingly, despite never having won an election, Richard Bartlett soon emerged as the most popular Australian prime minister since Menzies.

But as he put down the telephone from talking to the New South Wales Premier, the last thing on Richard Bartlett's mind was savouring his success. He didn't like John Czarnecki – he found his migrant working-class hero routine a bit thick for a self-made millionaire with a taste for good clothes and fine wine. And like most Victorian conservatives, he had a knee-jerk distaste for any product of the New South Wales Labor Right. But he knew Czarnecki was not a hysterical man, nor one to exaggerate when it came to non-political matters. And so he believed every word of the report that the Premier had just given him. The problem was, what should he do about it?

The first thing was to deal with the immediate crisis, and it was unanimously agreed to commit the military to whatever extent may be necessary to contain the problem. The newly appointed Chief of the Defence Force, Air Chief Marshal Edward McGovern, had been summoned and was seated at the Cabinet Room table. Listening with astonishment to the Prime Minister's directive, McGovern's mind raced, trying to comprehend the situation and at the same time juggle a thousand military variables.

At 4.35am, back at his desk in Russell Offices, McGovern placed a call to the GOC, Land Command, in Sydney. General Andrew Lawrie had already been at his headquarters in Victoria Barracks, Paddington, for twenty minutes, alerted to what was happening by an unofficial call from the Premier's Department. The two senior officers knew each other well, Lawrie having been one of McGovern's earliest personal appointments. Their conversation commenced with an expression of mutual disregard for politicians in language both unmilitary and unprintable. Then they got down to business and sketched out a preliminary Plan of Operations.

Within an hour, as the eastern sky was lightening to overcast grey, an observer on the Hume Highway could have been forgiven for thinking that Australia had gone to war. Seventy-six M113 Armoured Personnel Carriers (APCs) of 5/7 Battalion, the Royal Australian Regiment – the Australian Army's mechanised infantry – thundered towards Sydney's Central Business District from their base at Holsworthy in the city's south-west. Most of the fully tracked vehicles contained an infantry section of nine men, comprising a section commander and four riflemen armed with the Steyr automatic rifle, two machine-gunners each armed with a Minimi light machine-gun, plus a vehicle commander and driver. Additionally, most vehicles were armed with turret mounted .50 calibre and .30 calibre machine-guns, and specialised vehicles carried mortar, demolitions, signals, intelligence and reconnaissance teams.

Despite post-Cold War budget cuts, an Australian infantry battalion in full war paint remains a formidable proposition. But now, as the Diggers saw it, they were being sent in to be pest exterminators, and they were not impressed. One of their number was already locked up in the Holsworthy guardroom for breaking the nose of a RAEME corporal who had unwisely referred to 5/7 Battalion as 'Rentokil'. But bravado aside, more than a few men that morning were wrestling with a secret revulsion – arachnophobia was as prevalent among combat troops as it was in the community at large. Except that soldiers had not the luxury of betraying even a suggestion of such fears.

Warrant Officer Class 2 James 'Jimmy' O'Rourke,

Company Sergeant-Major, 'Bravo' Company, had seen it before. Some of the young soldiers he had served with in the jungles of Vietnam had been more frightened of the massive swamp spiders than of the NVA. That morning after briefing, he'd scrutinised the faces of every man in each of the three platoons in his charge, and he'd picked out around twenty he thought had a problem. He'd called his three platoon sergeants together, all good NCOs but with no combat experience outside UN peacekeeping duties, and he'd told them which of their soldiers they should keep an eye on.

O'Rourke then did a wise and clever thing – the kind of thing sergeant-majors have been doing since the time of Alexander. There is a tradition among soldiers of giving their enemies irreverent nicknames, to make them less forbidding – there were the Froggys at Waterloo, the Jerrys in the two World Wars, Charley in Vietnam, and the Argies in the Falklands. Without comment, O'Rourke began referring to the Funnys, and a new institution was born. Every man fighting a secret and irrational fear that morning felt just a little better when he heard it, and Funny jokes were instantly outpouring from the battalion comedians.

'Bravo' Company had been detailed to seal off and secure Central Station, and were point company. So it was that the company commander, Major Pat Howard, was among the first of the troops to catch sight of what they were up against. The commander's vehicle was the third from the head of the column and as it turned east into Parramatta Road at Haberfield, the driver yelled out in alarm. Three monster funnelwebs had scattered across the road in front of him and were quickly disappearing between the old and closely packed buildings.

Howard had just gotten his head out of the turret in

time to see them. Unlike his CSM, he had been too young for Vietnam. But he had served with the UN in Somalia and had seen more action than he cared to admit when as a young lieutenant he'd spent six months in Northern Ireland on an exchange attachment with the British SAS. He had also been prominent in Adventurous Training, and had only been denied the summit during a Defence Force expedition to Everest by a freak blizzard which had bailed him up in a tent for six days above eight thousand metres.

Pat Howard's courage and military capabilities were beyond question. But this was something no soldier had faced before. The monster funnelwebs were awesome – their chitinoid bodies sprouting arthritic-looking legs which were not arthritic at all but intricately and powerfully articulated. And their fangs, looking longer than the half metre that they were and continually dribbling glutinous venom. Howard guessed their standing height was something between two and three metres. And they moved with incredible speed, many times faster than a man could run, with that characteristic scampering gait that sent any arachnophobe into a fit of blind panic.

But Pat Howard was not any arachnophobe. He was an Australian front-line infantry officer with personal responsibility for the lives of one hundred and five men. Before ducking back inside he took three deep breaths, and tried to suppress the dread that was churning around in his guts.

'They're ugly bastards, Warrant Officer O'Rourke,' Howard called with as much bravado as he could muster to his CSM, who was sitting at the back of the vehicle.

O'Rourke responded with characteristic irreverence. 'With respect, sir, I don't give a flying fuck – I won't be dancing with 'em!'

The other passengers, members of the Company Headquarters, laughed nervously, releasing some of the tension that had been building throughout the journey. Howard grinned at the man he felt closer to at this moment than even his wife or infant son. In combat, the company sergeant-major is the company commander's best friend, and Howard trusted and respected O'Rourke absolutely.

O'Rourke regarded Howard steadily, then looked back to the street directory page he had been committing to memory. At this moment, however, his mind was elsewhere. He was thinking about the man in whose eyes he had seen the most terror that morning, the only man of concern in the company whom he had not mentioned to any of his platoon sergeants. Major Howard was as bad a case of arachnophobia as O'Rourke had ever seen – and that was the very last thing he needed to deal with today.

Little more than ninety minutes after 5/7 Battalion's Commanding Officer had received a signal containing operational orders from General Lawrie, the sixteen APCs of 'Bravo' Company peeled off from the battalion column at the corner of Broadway and Harris Street, and within two minutes were deploying at each of Central Station's three main entrances.

What the troops found at every one of them was bloody mayhem. Massive crowds thronged at every arch and doorway in a state of hysteria – people were screaming and shouting, and trampling and crushing each other without regard. The reason for their panic was plain. Dozens of monster funnelwebs were herding the crowds against the station facades. Periodically one would scamper in and strike, impaling a victim on its fangs then dragging them off to be devoured. In the streets all around, the monsters were gorging on partly liquefied cadavers.

The crowd's sole protectors were a few brave state policemen armed with a hotch-potch of firearms, mostly just standard issue revolvers. They were managing to dissuade some attacks, although their .38 ammunition seemed to be inflaming the funnelwebs' tempers more than slowing them down. One good marksman had sent spiders scurrying with direct hits to their eyes, and two others firing ex-service Self-Loading Rifles had notched up half a dozen cripplings. But on the whole, it was clear that they were fighting a losing battle.

'Bravo' Company fanned out and let fly at the funnelwebs with everything they had. Within seconds the giant spiders were scattering all over the road and the crowds erupted in wild jubilation.

A thought which had occurred to O'Rourke as they were leaving Holsworthy was paying dividends. He had remembered a pile of flame-throwers rusting in a corner of the armoury, disused since they had been proscribed in 1983 as 'inhumane weaponry' by the Geneva Conventions. O'Rourke had taken it upon himself to designate the Funnys as unprotected by international law, and he'd had the flame-throwers brought along.

They were proving to be appallingly effective. Where the funnelwebs seemed able to absorb an incredible number of bullet hits, blazing petroleum was a different matter. The flame-throwers transformed the monsters into screaming, scampering fireballs which within moments were reduced to charred mounds of smouldering flesh.

Holding himself together with brute will, Pat Howard soon had the crowds protected on all sides and organised into lines filing steadily into the station. With crowd control methods which were effective if not always gentle, the lines were directed into carriages at every platform, and before long trainloads of refugees were speeding out of the metropolis.

But the battle was not all one way. As well as their fangs, the monsters had developed a longer-range weapon. They had learned to rear back and spurt their venom, its atrax-otoxin now so concentrated that it literally dissolved skin on contact.

1 Section, 3 Platoon learned how deadly the venom was when they attempted to scale the ten metre wall to the elevated section of track running parallel with Elizabeth Street. Howard had detailed them to seal off the tunnel from the city centre. But when the first four climbers were halfway up, two monster funnelwebs appeared on the parapet and hosed them with venom. Even in the din of battle, the entire company heard their screams as they fell and lay convulsing in dying agony. When Howard arrived and saw the bodies, he immediately ordered the company into their nuclear-biological-chemical warfare suits. The inert plastic NBC suits, which with their 'Darth Vader' helmets made the wearers resemble alien invaders, were impervious to corrosives and proved good protection against the venom. But they were cumbersome, and slowed the soldiers down.

That reduction in mobility was a factor in the company's worst loss of the morning. After their initial dispersal, the funnelwebs began to regroup south of the station in the flat open expanse of Prince Alfred Park. Howard detailed 2 Platoon to clear the park and set up a fire control point at Saint Pauls Place, which crossed the railway lines where they converged beyond the station to the south-west. The platoon commander, Lieutenant George Fisher, a bright but somewhat flash twenty-three-year-old less than a year out of the Royal Military College, was thrilled with his first chance of combat even if it was to be against a swarm of overgrown garden pests. Fisher put his three sections into 'arrowhead', and 2 Platoon commenced to torch and blast its way across the park like a scythe. The young infantrymen resembled kids in a video arcade, yelling wildly as they obliterated the Funnys with flame-throwers and grenades, until the field was ablaze and scattered with incinerated spider flesh.

But what no-one had seen before was the speed of the monsters in open ground. Taken with blood lust, the members of 3 Section on the left flank momentarily dropped their rearward observation, and by the time they became aware of the six funnelwebs rushing at them from the backstreets, they were so slowed by their NBC suits that they were unable to regroup in time to counter attack. They had barely begun to wheel when the funnel-webs were on them and instantly ripped into them with blind savagery.

All of the section were either dead or fatally dismembered when George Fisher gave the order to open fire. Corporal Alan Thomas, Section Commander, 1 Section, refused, and railed that Fisher was a murderer for ordering the Diggers to fire on their mates. But the platoon sergeant, Colin Coombs, a hard arse from the caves of Coober Pedy and a man to brook no dissent, laid Thomas out with a single right hook. Then he pulled his Steyr into his shoulder and snapped off ten rounds rapid, killing outright the four vilely mutilated soldiers that remained alive.

That was the prompt for the rest of the platoon to go berserk. They just let fly, and burned and blasted until long after their comrades' bodies and the remains of the funnelwebs were indistinguishable.

Jimmy O'Rourke arrived and re-established control. George Fisher was in shock so O'Rourke had him escorted to Company HQ and took command himself. Within a few minutes, what remained of 2 Platoon was in a textbook defensive position around Saint Pauls Place and was setting up its machine-guns on fixed lines. Training was telling and most of the troops had quickly recovered from their experience, on the surface at least. O'Rourke was soon confident to leave them in the capable care of Colin Coombs, and he quickly returned to company headquarters.

As O'Rourke arrived back at Central, panic erupted again among the refugees as three funnelwebs forayed under the canopy from behind the station parcels office on Railway Square. But they were quickly dispatched in a crossfire of Minimis, which tore them to pieces and splattered the tracks with their gore.

In front of the station, along Pitt Street and in Belmore Park, the funnelwebs were hanging back now. This had been their first taste of opposition and they had learnt to keep their distance from these spiky green-and-ginger-suited humans. They prowled the backstreets, looking for another approach to the tempting food source. But any that advanced felt the sting of a Steyr, and they soon drifted off in search of less difficult prey.

Pat Howard had his phobia completely under control now and was ensconced in the station supervisor's office, briefing his platoon commanders on revised defensive positions. O'Rourke looked in and was reassured enough to slip away and do rounds.

Crossing the concourse at a little after 8am, he was relieved to see that the crowds were reduced to only a few hundred. Morale among the Diggers was good, most of them having found this pest control to their liking. Even the arachnophobes seemed okay, buoyed by adrenaline, and victory.

O'Rourke moved quickly among the men, snapping orders, offering encouragement, bestowing praise. But within himself, he was worried. He'd seen how quickly the funnelwebs had learnt to retreat, how they'd measured the power and range of the soldiers' weapons, and, most disturbingly, their awesome speed. These were no mindless, freak-sized bugs. The funnelwebs displayed intelligence, although to what extent he still had no way of knowing.

What he did know was that the company was getting through its ammunition fast. Even with the extra they'd stacked into the APCs, they'd already expended nearly half their total supply. He'd been assured that resupply would soon be on its way from the Ordnance Depot at Moorebank, but he suspected the Hume Highway would be getting pretty congested by now.

Suddenly tired, he dropped down beside a friendly face. It belonged to Andy Shute, the massive half-Fijian, half-Maori platoon sergeant of 1 Platoon, who was tucked behind a Minimi at the end of Platform 6.

'G'day, sir,' Shute grinned, 'come for a shooting lesson?'

'Fuck off, you cheeky black bastard,' O'Rourke chided, 'just flash the ash!'

Shute was delighted – a smoke with one of the best blokes in the army would be just the thing after the morning's excitement. He took cigarettes from his tunic and passed one to O'Rourke, then gave them both lights with a battle-scarred Bic.

O'Rourke inhaled deeply, but then as he exhaled he realised how tense he was. Anxiety was not an emotion he'd known lately but the truth was that the funnelwebs unnerved him. Only half listening to Shute's yarns of *derring-do*, O'Rourke found himself wondering for just how long they could contain this abomination.

It was 9.55am when the order came over the Battle Group Command Net to evacuate Sydney. But by that time, the city had already been emptying for hours. The plans drawn up by the authorities on the orders of the Premier had not taken into account the outbreak of full-scale panic, but that is exactly what the monster funnelwebs had caused. Official estimates were that five hundred people had been killed in the previous twelve hours, but unofficially the word was that deaths were doubling every ninety minutes.

Certainly Central Station and Circular Quay had been slaughterhouses. And all roads out were jammed because the highways they led to were blocked by breakdowns and crashes. Terrifyingly, the monsters had seemed to sense the easy pickings, and had started foraying along the traffic queues and cracking people out of their cars like oysters from their shells. What it meant was that since sunrise, tens of thousands of people had been fleeing the city on foot.

By 10.05am, Lieutenant Damien Mitchell had been at the controls of his Kiowa helicopter for almost four hours, having been turned out of his bed at 5.40am in the Officers' Mess at Holsworthy, which as well as housing 5/7 RAR was also home to Army Aviation's 161 Recce Squadron.

After such an extended sortie, Mitchell would normally have been looking forward to lunch in the mess followed by three hours study for his mathematics Master's and a late afternoon game of basketball. But today, he had other things on his mind.

Mitchell had spent most of the morning darting around over Circular Quay, Sydney's city centre ferry terminal and anchorage for international ocean liners. Built on the 250 metre southern shore of Sydney Cove, where the First Fleet landed in 1788 to establish a penal colony and unwittingly seeded a nation, Circular Quay was one of the most historically celebrated as well as picturesque spots in Australia. Framed as it now was by the Sydney Opera House and the Harbour Bridge, it was a magnet for tourists and Sydneysiders alike.

But that morning, Mitchell had witnessed a new and bizarre chapter in the history of Circular Quay. Over a hundred people had been massacred and twice that number injured when dozens of monster funnelwebs had swarmed out of the railway tunnels from Wynyard. The spiders had emerged at dawn, when the first ferries were arriving with early commuters.

Caught between the monsters and the water, the first passengers to disembark had no chance. Those behind pushed back onto the boats as the pilots reversed to the safety of the open harbour. Many tried to re-board too late, and jumped or fell or were pushed into the deep, oily water. A few managed to swim out to the ferries, or to hang on to lifebelts until they were rescued. But many, perhaps another hundred, were drowned.

Mitchell had risked his own life many times, flying down to hover centimetres above the swell so that flounderers could grab onto the Kiowa's skids. Then he'd lifted them gently and carried them to the boats, where passengers and crews had tried to catch them in tightly stretched tarpaulins.

Sometimes it had worked, sometimes not. An exhausted man was killed when he slipped from the skids and broke his back across a ferry's deck railing. And a pregnant woman and her unborn child died instantly from the impact of a fall.

Every so often, Mitchell broke off from the rescue to overfly the Quay, trying to frighten the funnelwebs off.

But the spiders quickly realised the noisy little flying machine was harmless, and ignored it.

Now the only people left in the water were dead, and the ferries had been ordered to leave the harbour and steam to Gosford, north of the Hawkesbury River. When the last of them had gone, Mitchell banked away and headed south for Holsworthy. But as he climbed above the city, his adrenaline dispersed, and he had to work hard to steady his hands on the Kiowa's controls.

At debriefing, it was obvious to his squadron commander that Mitchell had been disturbed by what he'd seen. But the army had no guidelines for dealing with the effects of combat with mutant spiders and today, helicopter pilots were at a premium. Incredibly, armed gangs had been spotted looting in the city by 5/7 RAR's patrols, and they had requested air support. So at 10.40am, Mitchell took off again for the Central Business District with a two-man gun team and a Browning .50 calibre machine-gun.

The only gunships operated by the Australian Army were two squadrons of Hueys, helicopters dating back to the Vietnam War and based two thousand kilometres away at Townsville on the North Queensland coast. So the Kiowas of 161 Squadron with bungy mounted .50 cals were that morning in Sydney the army's state-of-the-art ground support aerial weapons system.

The Kiowa is the military version of the Bell Jet Ranger, a well-tried and tested but far from young design. With only a two-blade rotor and sixties avionics, it is a good workhorse for reconnaissance and light liaison but was never intended for combat. So Damien Mitchell was acutely aware of his limitations as he turned hard to the right over Darling Harbour, and nosed down into the glass and concrete canyon of Pitt Street Mall.

Despite sixteen hundred hours piloting helicopters, Mitchell never tired of the thrill of flying tactically in restricted airspace. Now with buildings flashing past three metres either side of his rotor disc, he felt better. It was the greatest video arcade game, but for real – no roller-coaster ride on Earth could come close to it. Being airborne troops, the corporal and private manning the Browning in the rear would have thought nothing of jumping from an aircraft at ten thousand feet. But at this moment, they were experiencing difficulty in keeping down their breakfasts.

Mitchell spotted looters – about ten of them, armed with hunting rifles and shotguns, moving in and out of the David Jones department store at the corner of Market and Castlereagh Streets. They were loading everything they could into a three-tonne hire truck with firing portals hacked into its sides.

Several of the looters immediately raised their weapons and fired at the Kiowa. Mitchell pulled back hard on the collective and the helicopter went straight up like an express elevator. The gun crew were too excited to worry about the stomachs they'd left behind and quickly readied the Browning for use.

Mitchell slipped sideways over the buildings and spun the aircraft through ninety degrees, then he slammed the cyclic forward and the Kiowa shot across the rooftops like an arrow. Suddenly the roofs were gone and Mitchell dropped like a stone to just two metres above the tarmac of Elizabeth Street. Hovering, he switched on the intercom in his face mask and snapped, 'I'll slide onto the corner, and you take out the truck.'

The helicopter floated forward and eased past the corner just as the last looter was clambering into the vehicle. The corporal on the Browning opened fire and the Kiowa's airframe, not intended as a gun platform, shook violently. But the heavy bullets found their mark and smashed into the sump of the accelerating truck's engine.

The truck stopped dead in a cloud of steam. The driver and front passenger knew nothing of it – they had been torn to shreds by flying shards of metal and glass. But the rest of the looters bailed out and took to their heels along Castlereagh Street, loosing shots off wildly as they went.

Mitchell climbed to clear the truck and followed at three hundred metres, which he judged to be a reasonably safe distance from men turning and firing on the run. Which was how he lost sight of the looters as they turned west into Park Street, heading, Mitchell presumed, for the refuge of Town Hall Station.

But when in pursuit the Kiowa darted out into George Street, Mitchell was so startled and jerked the cyclic back so hard that the Browning smashed into the airframe's central superstructure, and in the process opened the private's face from the temple to the lower jaw. What had startled Mitchell was the most chilling thing he'd ever seen, and prompted him to switch on the Kiowa's video camera. Because without hard evidence, he thought no-one might ever believe him.

In both directions, as far as the eye could see, George Street was draped with gargantuan funnel-shaped spiders' webs. They were suspended from buildings, lamp posts, vehicles – everything and anything solid enough to support them. And the Kiowa was hovering directly in front of the biggest one. It was a gossamer tube gaping ten metres across at its mouth, strung diagonally between the Town Hall building and the north-western corner of Woolworths. Trailing back across the intersection, the tube then narrowed and disappeared into the grandiose main entrance of the Queen Victoria Building.

But what chilled Mitchell most was the scene just fifty metres ahead of him. In their haste, six of the looters had run smack bang into funnelweb 'trip wires', snare threads of spider's silk trailing out in all directions from the giant web mouth. Stuck fast, they struggled desperately in the strong sticky fibres, their screaming drowned by the din of the Kiowa's turbine. But the more that they struggled the more entangled they became, and the more their vibrations were carried up the web to its source.

At first Mitchell and the gun crew could only gaze in mute amazement at the sight. But then a primeval howl of horror issued from deep in the corporal's belly as the utterly unthinkable – the unimaginable – materialised in front of them.

An enormous female monster funnelweb emerged from the Queen Victoria Building and picked her way down the inside of her web towards the looters. When they saw her coming, the men thrashed and grappled for their lives, one wrestling so hard that he dislocated his arms. Mitchell screamed for the corporal to open fire on the funnelweb but the impact with the Kiowa's superstructure had completely jammed the Browning's mechanism. The corporal bellowed in frustration, tears streaming down his face, as he fumbled with bloodied fingers to free the breech block. But all his best efforts, like those of the luckless looters, were in vain.

The funnelweb fell upon her first victim, grasped him with her forelegs and carefully lifted him into the mouth of her web. But she did not kill him. Instead she deftly cocooned him, spinning him around and around in her silk until he was so tightly bound that he could not move. Then as the soldiers watched aghast, she carefully rolled him back up inside her web, and down into her nest buried deep in the bowels of the building.

She did the same with each of the looters until eventually, only one remained. He was a young man, in his late teens, and remarkably strong despite his slight build – strong enough, and determined enough, to dislocate both of his arms. For several minutes Mitchell and the corporal were almost mesmerised by his eyes, so filled with terror that even at fifty metres they were burningly intense.

When the monster came for the last looter, Mitchell made a rush at her in a desperate attempt to frighten her off. But she reared back and spurted venom which only missed the Kiowa by centimetres and burned a deep smoking scar in the road.

Then when the funnelweb had cocooned the last looter and was rolling him away to her nest, Mitchell could have sworn he heard his screams above the whine of the engine. But in seconds it was over, and the funnelweb and the last looter were gone.

Mitchell remained there for several minutes, his head exploding from the rage he felt at his own impotence. The corporal was sobbing freely, long past the stage of worrying about what anybody thought of him. Meanwhile the private was bleeding all over the cockpit floor, almost thankful for the distraction of the searing pain in his face.

Eventually, when it felt as if his anger would overwhelm him, Mitchell forced himself to accept that there was nothing more he could do. So switching off the video camera, he eased back on the collective and the Kiowa climbed away into the suffocating noonday sky.

It was some small mercy that by the time they reached the funnelweb's nest most of the looters were unconscious, and so were spared immediate knowledge of what their fate was to be. But the last looter was wide awake when he arrived, his mind penetratingly alert from a cocktail of fear and unspeakable pain. Ken Collins, the baby burglar, had only come out that morning to look after his younger brother, Tony. Having faced a monster funnelweb already, he had not been keen when Tony had phoned at 5am, saying the city was wide open and that everything was theirs for the taking. The Marrickville gang Tony ran with already had things organised – they'd stolen a truck, retrieved their cache of firearms from beneath the floor of a rented garage, and were raring to foray into the city and get rich quick.

Ken had tried to talk Tony out of it, saying that he'd made a big score that night and would cut his brother in. But Tony, being a wild eighteen-year-old, was motivated as much by machismo as by greed, and would have none of it. Even Ken's tale of the monster funnelweb that had killed Agnes Weaver only boosted his brother's determination.

So after burying his two hundred thousand dollars, Ken had written a note for his sleeping wife, Loren, saying that he wouldn't be long and telling her to get ready to drive up to Brisbane. Then he'd gone around to Tony's for one last little outing with the lads.

Now, in the murky, foul-smelling basement of the Queen Victoria Building, Ken Collins had descended into hell. The place was a charnel house. People were hanging all around the walls, bound up in spider's silk like chickens awaiting the spit. Some were already dead, dismembered or part eaten, but most were alive and fully conscious of what was going on.

Ken desperately looked for Tony, but could not see him. Then he contemplated escape, his mind focused with that clarity induced only by imminent death.

But there was no escape.

In the hours that followed, Ken passed through

torment, then anguish, then fury, then despair, then finally into tranquil resignation. He began hallucinating, and no longer heard the wailing of his fellow looters, as one by one they awoke to discover their predicament.

Ken hung on that wall for a day and a night, and by the time the funnelweb came for him, he was already close to death. As she lifted him down and carried him into the chamber where she ate, in Ken's mind he was being carried by his mother into a sun-filled garden. Loren was there, and Kylie and Dani, and his father – his wonderful father whom Ken had so longed for throughout his painfully empty childhood.

And everyone was smiling, and so delighted to see him, and so warm and so loving that he felt like crying. He was safe now – safe in the bosom of his family – so safe and so happy that he quietly . . . dropped off to sleep.

6

At 8pm that evening, for no reason, it occurred to Jack Fitzgerald that he hadn't had a drink since he'd arrived in Sydney two days earlier. Probably for the first time since his wife and son had died, he was totally sober. Exploring the unfamiliar sensation, he was surprised that he felt so calm, particularly under the circumstances.

He was, to all intents and purposes, besieged in a military fort. The CSIRO complex at North Ryde had been abandoned except for the Biomolecular Engineering building occupied by Bill Reid's team. That building was now ringed by a company of airborne troops, who had parachuted in at midday to relieve the state police.

And they'd arrived none too soon. Shortly after 1pm, monster funnelwebs were spotted moving up through the Lane Cove River National Park. Thirty minutes later, the valley was a shooting gallery. The monsters had attacked the CSIRO for almost an hour, scampering and spurting venom and making lightning forays at the defenders. The troops had repelled them until they'd retreated to the river, there to regroup and lick their wounds. The perimeter was left strewn with the remains of fifty funnelwebs, and the smell of gasoline and cordite had hung in the air all afternoon.

Through it all, the scientists had worked on inside, desperately trying to find answers. But they had known that the odds were against them and that soon, inevitably, their task would have to be abandoned.

His mind returning to the job, Jack forced himself to face bitter disappointment. For the third time that day he'd performed a critical and complex experiment on the DNA of a specimen monster funnelweb, and for the third time the results were inconclusive. Dejected, he strolled next door to the electron microscope room and gave the bad news to Bill Reid. Reid listened closely, putting on a brave face, but it was plain to Fitzgerald that his friend was close to collapse.

All the research team were chronically tired. Everyone was making mistakes and real progress had slowed to a crawl. As a result, everyone was getting on each other's nerves and tempers were frayed – there'd been two screaming matches that day and Reid had insisted that one team member get some sleep after she'd erupted into floods of tears.

Now, as they regarded each other in the glow of the microscope's screen, Fitzgerald and Reid knew well that the game was over. There was nothing to discuss, nothing to ponder – time and opportunities had just run out. They weren't going to crack the funnelweb problem, not here and now.

Bill sat for a while, saying nothing. Then he just switched off the equipment, slapped Jack on the shoulder, and shambled away to his little office and the folding cot he'd not been near for seventy-two hours.

Alone in the dead room, Fitzgerald felt the need for some air. He wandered up the three flights of stairs to the roof where earlier, in a shadecloth-screened corner which had formerly served as a rest area, he had laid out his mattress and a blanket.

Strolling around the parapet to clear his head, he was disturbed at the sight of the troops and the carnage below. He'd heard the fighting, but he'd been engrossed in his work and had not allowed it to distract him. Now his own words of warning to the Premier came back at him. The remains of the monster funnelwebs really did look like the wreckage of armoured vehicles – bizarre engines of war whose only purpose was the wreaking of havoc. But these were not machines. They were living, breathing mutations of one of the deadliest creatures on Earth. And Fitzgerald knew well that they were edging ahead in the battle.

'Penny for them,' a voice said softly behind him, and Jack turned to see Helen watching him from the shadows.

'How long have you been here?' he asked, pleased to see her.

'About ten minutes,' she said, 'since the phone lines went dead as I was downloading today's stories to the paper.' Plainly annoyed about it, she approached to stand next to him, and looked up.

The night was clear as crystal, the southern stars so bright that they looked unreal. Before long, the ambience had soothed her. 'I can't believe this place,' she murmured. 'Even with all this going on, it's still . . . extraordinary.'

And it was. The cicadas were singing. The hot breeze was stirring the treetops. The battle stench had given way to the scent of frangipani. And the presence of the river could be felt more than seen, flowing silent and deep in the darkness beyond the perimeter.

Up here, Jack could almost forget the funnelwebs. In his years away, he'd missed this country, the sounds and the smells of it. It was like nowhere else, intoxicatingly beautiful, and yet at the same time remote, and secret. Maybe it was because it was secret that Australia did not intrude on him – it left him alone. And despite the loss he had suffered here, it still felt like home.

Gazing out over the encircling eucalypt forest, Jack said, 'We're losing it.'

Helen looked questioning. 'Losing it?'

Jack turned to her. 'The funnelweb war. It'll take months, maybe years for us to turn this around. And by the time we do . . . who knows what might have happened?'

Helen studied Jack closely. Then she said, 'And what about your war, Doctor Fitzgerald?'

Fitzgerald was caught off guard. '*My* war?' he said ingenuously, but knowing exactly what she meant.

Helen looked away again. 'She must have been quite a woman . . . for you to still be so hung up on her.'

Jack was jolted – jolted enough to look into the void that had consumed him for so long. And impelled by what he saw there, he decided it was time to switch the lights back on.

'My wife – Colleen – died.'

Helen felt a kick in her stomach. 'Oh, Jack, I'm sorry, I . . .'

Fitzgerald interjected, 'Four years ago . . . in a car crash.'

Realisation overflowed in Helen Parkes. The questions that had perplexed her, tantalised her since the moment she'd first met him, had now all been answered in that one statement.

Jack felt light-headed, as if something had lifted from his shoulders and floated away. He took a deep breath, and for the first time in a long time, savoured the textures of the night.

Helen could not look at him when finally she said, 'Jack, I really am sorry. I feel like a fool.'

He regarded her openly. 'No, you're right. I *am* still

hung up on her.' Then he gazed back out over the trees, and said, 'And I'll never forget her . . . but it's time I got past it.' Then he added, 'She would have wanted me to.'

For the next moments, neither of them said anything. But then there were four heavy thumps, and the ground all around was flooded in a harsh, white light. The glare from the parachute flares penetrated deep into the bush and illuminated an approaching mob of funnelwebs. The soldiers immediately opened fire with triangulated machine-guns and the monsters were soon scuttling for the safety of more distant cover.

When everything fell silent, Helen was shaking.

Seeing her, Jack exclaimed, 'Jesus Christ! This all makes it a little fucking ridiculous, doesn't it?'

Helen grabbed his arm, and said challengingly, 'No, it doesn't – but it should make your way ahead easier to see.'

Jack was shaking also, and in her eyes he saw again the look he'd seen earlier. Only here, now, surrounded by madness, it was unqualified. She wanted him. He had known it since New York. And he'd also known, since the moment he'd laid eyes on her, that he wanted her too.

He took her hand and led her to his bed beneath the shadecloth. And there, in the heat and the darkness, something re-awoke in him. The women he had been with, had paid for, in recent years had brought relief but not satisfaction. This was different. As Helen kissed him, caressed him, explored his most intimate senses, Jack experienced an intensity of passion he had all but forgotten. She teased pleasure from every pore of him, and their pleasure went on and on for what seemed like a blissful age. Until finally when their fires rose, their muscles tightened, their backs arched, and every nerve in them screamed for release – gripping each other wildly, they exploded in ecstatic orgasm.

After, they lay quietly, drained and soaked in sweat, and clinging to each other like children in a forest. And for a few precious moments, until he fell into a dreamless sleep, for the first time in more than four years, Jack Fitzgerald was happy.

Throughout the day, Sydney's radio and television stations, transmitting from hastily fortified studios, had been relaying instructions to the city's depleting populace about the evacuation. Key exit points, including Central Station, Circular Quay, Manly Quay, Sydney and Bankstown Airports, Richmond RAAF Base, and the beaches at Bondi and Dee Why, had been secured by troops. People had been entreated not to drive out of the city but instead to get to their closest exit point and be evacuated from there. The instructions had also been displayed on banners trailing behind light aircraft which had buzzed in the sky over the suburbs all afternoon.

Unfortunately many people had persisted in trying to escape by car, often with dire consequences. Some had failed to run the gauntlet of funnelwebs prowling the main roads, and had met horrible deaths. Of those who had gotten through, most had been forced to abandon their vehicles within the metropolitan boundaries and join the tens of thousands of refugees fleeing on foot. By day's end, the footsore columns stretched for more than fifty kilometres in every direction.

But the wise had followed instructions and by mid evening, incredibly, over a million people had somehow managed to escape. The beaches and quays had been like a re-run of Dunkirk, but on a much bigger scale. Everything that floated – and in Sydney the number of boats was into six figures – had steamed, sailed, and even rowed back and forth, time after time, between the exit points and the safety of Gosford and Wollongong. Vast transit camps had been thrown up on the outskirts of those towns and refugees were being assisted to travel on to family or friends in other parts of Australia. The plan was to assign those with nowhere to go to local councils throughout the country, then make them as comfortable as possible whilst they waited for transport. But as the day wore on and the numbers of refugees multiplied, the situation worsened. Until by nightfall, the exit points and transit camps were descending into chaos.

Typically, by 10pm, Central Station was Armageddon. The condition of those arriving had degenerated to such an extent that the scene on the concourse resembled a staging of the *Marat/Sade*. Everywhere, people were wailing, screaming, fighting, bleeding and dying. There were the appallingly injured, the mentally unhinged, the emotionally shattered and, worst of all, the psychopaths, given freer rein in the midst of escalating anarchy. As darkness had fallen, incidences of robbery and rape had multiplied and the men of 'Bravo' Company had been decreasingly inclined to treat the perpetrators kindly. So when Colin Coombs and 2 Platoon's 1 Section found three men sexually assaulting a nine-year-old girl in a service tunnel beneath the concourse, they reacted extremely. The soldiers turned their backs as Coombs, the hard arse from the caves of Coober Pedy, forced the offenders to lie face down on the floor, then slipped the safety off his Steyr and casually blew all of their brains out.

More generally, 'Bravo' Company, exhausted from fourteen hours of fighting funnelwebs and controlling crowds, had finally just about run out of ammunition. As Jimmy O'Rourke had feared, no resupply had gotten through. Pat Howard had called Battalion to request an air drop but had been told there was no chance – everything flyable was airlifting people interstate. He was ordered to carry on as best he could until relieved by 5/7's 'Charlie' Company, and then to proceed directly to Holsworthy.

It was at 11.04pm, as the last Minimi belts were being broken up to be passed around the riflemen, that 'Charlie' Company breezed into Central off George Street, pennants waving and all swagger and bullshit. Relieved, Howard and O'Rourke went to brief their opposite numbers. Then as 'C' Company's officers deployed their troops, the men of 'B' Company gratefully mounted vehicles and started engines.

Heading at a snail's pace through the unlit backstreets of Camperdown, the APC drivers were many times forced to barge aside abandoned vehicles, and often to run over human corpses. Horror had visited every street and there were bodies everywhere. Some were funnelweb victims, torn apart or dissolved and part eaten. Some were road crash victims, left in their vehicles to die. And some were suicides, mostly jumpers, at one place in Lewisham what looked to be a family of five. But what shook Pat Howard most, surveying from the turret of the commander's vehicle, was the sheer scale of the devastation.

Every metre of the way, along parallel streets, the funnelwebs shadowed the column, hanging back out of range but staying close enough to spook the entire company. Ammo was low but gasoline was not, so O'Rourke had flame-throwers rigged up to every turret. And occasionally he would order them fired, to remind the Funnys to stay at a respectful distance. Despite that, the soldiers often glimpsed them in their spotlights, foraging and feeding on human remains. And it made every last one of them sick to the pit of their stomachs.

It may have been that eighteen hours of extreme physical and mental effort had exhausted him, or perhaps it was the partial release of pressure. But as Pat Howard caught just such a glimpse of three funnelwebs ripping into a mound of bodies on the northern bank of the Cooks River, he panicked. He started shaking uncontrollably, and was flooded with the urge to leap from the vehicle and run for his life.

Inside, Jimmy O'Rourke sensed as much as saw that his OC was in trouble, and correctly guessed the reason. He sprang up, gripped Howard tightly by the arms and shouted above the din, 'Time for a brew, sir. Let me take the turret for a while.'

Howard was rigid, his knuckles white from his grip on the machine-gun mount, his eyes popping out of their sockets in terror. Somehow he managed to gasp, 'Warrant Officer O'Rourke . . . I can't fucking move!'

O'Rourke tightened his hold, put his face next to his OC's ear, and said with that authority unique to sergeant-majors, 'Yes you can, sir – you're just tired. Come down into the bucket for a brew.'

Through a chink in the blanket of dread suffocating him, Howard gleaned an insight. He stared into O'Rourke's eyes, and said, 'You know . . . don't you, Jimmy . . . you know.'

O'Rourke just said, 'Yes, sir. Come on now, let's get inside.'

Something in Howard gave way. His stomach churned and erupted and he vomited violently all down the side of the vehicle. O'Rourke held Howard's head down until he'd spat out the last of it, then he eased him back through the hatch, calling, 'The boss is crook – get him a strong one.'

The signaller grabbed a vacuum flask, half filled a mug with thick, scalding coffee laced with sugar, and handed it to Howard as O'Rourke steered him down into his seat. Then O'Rourke looked around the worried faces of the Company Headquarters staff, and for the sake of clarification, announced, 'Fresh must have had a wog in it – I'll flay the fucking caterer alive when I get hold of him!'

As everybody looked away, grinning inwardly, Howard and O'Rourke regarded each other. Each knew what the other was thinking – Howard had taken care of business and now O'Rourke was taking care of him.

O'Rourke said, 'Get a nap, sir,' then turned and stood up into the turret, and immediately loosed off a fireball at an unfortunate funnelweb.

Howard's stomach churned again as he felt the tracks crunch the monster's bones. But he steadied himself with a gulp of air and took a deep swallow of coffee. Then closing his eyes and forcing himself to relax, he mused on how fortunate he was to be serving with a man like Jimmy O'Rourke.

Just at that moment, however, O'Rourke himself was not feeling particularly flash. As the column meandered out of Canterbury and on through Belmore, he was witness to desolation and death on an extraordinary scale. And for the first time that day, it seemed that what he was seeing could not possibly be real, and he recognised the early symptoms of battle fatigue.

He knew the feeling of old – remembered it from the night he'd been point man on patrol and so had been first into a Vietnamese village where the population had been butchered – Charley had tied, gagged and disembowelled every man, woman and child. O'Rourke had been only eighteen and he had nearly gone under. But he had coped with it. And because of that, and because of his training and his maturity, he knew now that he could cope with this too. But tonight, the memory of that earlier night was close, like the ghost of an old friend travelling along in the darkness beside him.

Spooked, he thought at first the voice he heard must have been in his head. But when it came again, and again, O'Rourke snapped out of his trance, and listened intently. It was a wailing chant, distorted, and foreign, yet somehow familiar. And it was loud – loud enough to be heard over the clatter of an armoured column. Then O'Rourke realised where they were, and it clicked with him what it was. The company was passing through Lakemba, a centre of Sydney's Muslim community, and the sound was the chant of the muezzin calling the faithful to prayer.

Even in ordinary times, the Lakemba Mosque was a remarkable building, its dome and minaret transforming the Sydney skyline into a vision of the Middle East. But that morning, in the moonlight, towering high over ruination, it appeared more as a symbol of resistance.

O'Rourke barked into the radio for the lead vehicle to swing left, then he ducked inside, and called, 'Major Howard, I think we've found survivors!'

Howard approached the mosque tactically and positioned the APCs all around it in a defensive ring. Volleys of fireballs from the flame-throwers held back a growing mob of intensely aggressive funnelwebs, which for no apparent reason began arriving from everywhere.

Howard felt the panic rising again. O'Rourke saw his commander was in difficulty and considered suggesting the 2IC should take over. But he decided against it as

Howard battled to stay on top, and when the position was secured the OC led a patrol on reconnaissance into the building.

Of all the horrors they'd seen that day, and were to see in days to come, what 'Bravo' Company found in the Lakemba Mosque would be amongst the worst. The cavernous building was transformed into a vile mausoleum. A thousand human bodies were piled up on the floor, and like so much rotting meat the stinking midden was alive with maggots. But the worst was hanging from the walls – perhaps eighty or a hundred people, their bodies twisted and dismembered, trussed up in spider's silk and strung around like sausages. And many were still alive, and wailing dreadfully in a soul-rending dirge.

For an eternity, or perhaps for less than half a minute, the men of 'Bravo' Company stood and stared, transfixed by suffering so terrible that it paralysed them. In the end, Andy Shute was the first to react. As ever toting a Minimi as a personal weapon, he raised the gun to his hip and mechanically raked the walls until every living soul was released from torment.

When the gun finally stopped, nobody spoke. Only the muezzin's call, still chanting from the loudspeakers, continued to echo down like a ghostly requiem. Shute lowered the Minimi's bipod and laid the gun on the ground. Then he turned to face his commander, fully expecting to be placed under arrest.

Howard glared at him harshly, and said, 'Sergeant Shute, if you ever again fire on a non-lethal target without an order, I'll have you court-martialled. Now – pick up your weapon.' Then turning to his radio operator, he snapped, 'Ask the CSM to join us with a section of flame-throwers.' And the incident was never again mentioned.

It was then, with Shute torn between relief and

distress, that the Call to Prayer abruptly stopped and the soldiers heard another voice. It was muffled, but was unmistakably an anxious cry for help, and it was coming through a massive wooden door to the base of the minaret.

Howard arrived at the door a pace ahead of Shute. He tried the iron handle but it was locked. So he put his face to the timber, and shouted loudly, 'Who's there?'

Beyond, high-pitched and frantic, the voice called back, 'Please help us! In God's name, help us! I can't unlock the door!'

Howard shouted again, 'Get back and take cover. We'll blow it open. Do you understand?'

The voice said, 'Yes! I understand! Thank God! God bless you,' and then was silent.

Howard called up the demolitions team who arrived a minute later with O'Rourke and the flame-thrower section. And even though the radio operator had warned them what to expect, some of the younger soldiers had to be sent back outside.

The explosives specialists soon had their PE4 wired and ready to go. Howard called again, 'We're firing now. Stand clear of the door! Answer if you hear me!' But no answer came.

Howard went for cover with the rest behind the midden, and shouted, 'Detonate!' The subsequent explosion from the charge was muted, but the powerful *plastiche* opened the door as neatly as you please and Howard, Shute and six others rushed straight through into the smoking chasm.

Beyond, a spiral staircase led up inside the minaret. Shute dashed to the base of the stairs and covering the advance, signalled the others to come ahead. Howard hit the treads on the tail of his point man and they ascended like mountain goats. Until at balcony level, ten metres up, the stairs opened out onto a landing, and there the soldiers found the owner of the voice that had called to them.

She was a Catholic nun, around forty, her clothing stained and torn, and the only adult with a group of maybe fifteen children. She rushed straight to the biggest man and embraced him, crying, 'Thank God, I knew you would come, I knew He would send you. Are the fathers alive? Are any of their fathers still alive?'

Andy Shute gazed down at the nun, but he could not speak. Then, as he turned away, his commander saw the tears in his eyes. So Howard moved past him, and said gently, 'Everything's fine now, Sister. We've come to take you away.'

Apart from dehydration and hunger the children were physically well, but all of them were traumatised and suffering the effects of severe shock. When the medics arrived, they sedated and carefully blindfolded them. Then, with each grasping the one in front's waistband, like a file of baby elephants, they were led down the stairs and out to the waiting APCs.

Outside, a battle royal had been raging. The remains of a hundred funnelwebs ringed the company in a smouldering circle. But despite their losses, the monsters had continued to press home a determined attack. Howard understood why – the mosque was a food cache, presumably in preparation for a new aggregation of nests. Now he would take satisfaction in denying the funnelwebs the fruits of their labour.

He'd been petrified of spiders since the day, when he was four, that he'd walked into a huge orb weaver's web in his garden. The sense of being trapped in those sticky fibres had paralysed him, and he'd watched close to fainting as the enormous spider had picked its way down towards his face. His two older brothers had heard his screams and had rescued him, but for weeks after they'd taunted him that if he didn't do what they said, they would feed him to the spider.

That child's fear had stayed with Pat Howard, and rather than easing as he'd grown, it had intensified. Until that very morning on Parramatta Road, when he'd first laid eyes on the monster funnelwebs, and he'd realised that confronting them would be the great defining test of his life.

Contrarily, what he had seen inside the mosque had fortified him. Howard was not an overly religious man but if ever there was a creation of Satan, the funnelwebs were it. Glancing up, he saw the Crescent of Islam in silhouette against the sky, and in his exhaustion, an idea came to him with the clarity of a revelation: the fight against the funnelwebs was to be his holy war – his *jihad* – against a dark and ungodly aberration. He was filled with a clear sense of what had fired the Crusaders and the Saracens to fight over Jerusalem. Now he saw his destiny was to crusade for this, his own Jerusalem, and it was a notion so potent that it steeled him, and exorcised his fear.

When all the children were in the vehicles, Howard gave the order to cremate the dead and the flame-thrower section torched the midden. The bodies caught light quickly and soon blazed up into a fat-spattering inferno. Then three minutes later, as the company were pulling out, the domed roof collapsed and the entire building went up. And for the rest of the night, the fire continued to burn so brightly that it could be seen in every direction for thirty kilometres.

The column rumbled through Punchbowl and on into Milperra as in the commander's vehicle, Sister Matthew of the Sisters of Mercy told her story for the benefit of the Operational Log. She recounted that the children had been in the minaret without food or water for twenty hours, since the funnelwebs had first appeared on the streets of Lakemba. She had been driving past very early on her way to a nearby Catholic hospital when she had first seen the monsters, and she had rushed to the mosque for sanctuary. The rudely awoken sheikh had at first thought she was mad, but when he'd looked for himself, he had acted decisively and with courage. Annexed to the mosque was a hostel for Muslim children. At the time there had been three families in residence. All their mothers were in hospital and at night their fathers took over from the women who looked after the children during the day.

The sheikh had dragged them all from their beds and had bundled the children into the minaret with Sister Matthew, instructing her to remain there until he returned. But he had not returned. The last she had seen of him was when he had locked them inside, as behind him the children's fathers had gone to repel the funnelwebs crashing in through the windows.

Sister Matthew had led the children up to the *almedne* – the balcony – and there they had cowered as the din of the fighting had given way to terrible screams. Sister Matthew had tried to cover the smaller children's ears, but nothing could have shielded the older ones from the sound of their fathers' agony.

At dawn, Sister Matthew had ventured to look down over the balustrade and had barely been able to believe what she'd seen. Monster funnelwebs were everywhere, busily coming and going, bringing human bodies into the mosque then scampering away again to collect and return with more.

Only that door of Lebanese cedar had stood between the funnelwebs and the children. Time and again, they'd heard the monsters banging it or scratching it or jabbing at it frustratedly with their fangs. But the timber which for centuries had made the ships of the Phoenicians indestructible had now proved its worth against the funnelwebs, and they had not gotten through.

All day long Sister Matthew had tried to lift the children's spirits with songs and stories and guessing games, and to comfort them with readings from the Koran. On at least ten occasions, she had tried to attract the attention of a passing aircraft, but without success. When darkness had returned, the children had despaired and her own spirit had sunk to an all-time low. It was then, when she'd noticed the small electric generator, that Sister Matthew had received divine inspiration.

Five times each day, the muezzin, or singer of the Koran, calls the Muslim faithful to prayer from the minaret, and his voice has evoked Islam universally for fifteen hundred years. But recently, as in most things, technology has overtaken tradition – in mosques everywhere, the muezzin's call is now often a recording amplified through powerful loudspeakers. And because the call to prayer must never be missed, minarets are often equipped with generators in case of power cuts.

In her youth an enthusiastic amateur stage manager, Sister Matthew had a fair working knowledge of PA systems. Fumbling in the moonlight, she had found the cassette player with the 'call to prayer' cued up and ready to go. So when the generator had fired on her first pull and she had switched on the amplifier, the voice of the muezzin had poured forth and filled the night air. And so it had continued, replayed again and again as a gloriously inspired SOS, until finally it had been heard in the early hours of the morning by a tired old soldier preoccupied with phantoms of his past.

During the remainder of the journey, the column came upon another forty survivors. They were people who had barricaded themselves into their homes and had managed to repulse the monster funnelwebs, or had mercifully been overlooked by them. Against all odds, they had been found and were now on their way to safety. But they raised a question which troubled Pat Howard. If the company had come upon fifty-six people along a narrow ribbon of back-streets, how many others were still alive in the city, sitting it out and hoping beyond hope for rescue. Howard got O'Rourke to do some rough calculations on the premise that what they'd found was average, and he came up with a figure of seventy thousand. If he was anywhere near right, it was a situation too horrible to contemplate.

In the end, it took them most of the night to reach Holsworthy. And when finally at 5.11am they rumbled in through the heavily fortified gates, they found that their base too was being evacuated. They delivered the survivors to the camp hospital, and as the last of the children were taken in, Sister Matthew broke down and gave Pat Howard and Andy Shute unconstrained hugs. Everybody was moved by it, and even Colin Coombs had to swallow a lump.

At last the company rolled around to 5/7 Battalion's lines, and had no sooner parked up than O'Rourke swung them into the well-drilled routine of maintenance, resupply and rest. Howard gladly left them to it and grabbed a shower and change of clothes in the Officers' Mess. Then following the order that was awaiting him in the Company Office, he went straight to the gymnasium for an unusually well-attended debriefing.

7

That morning, the Holsworthy gym was arranged with concentric semicircles of chairs facing in towards a trestle table. Seated at the table were the Prime Minister, the New South Wales Premier and the Chief of the Defence Force, each with their aides and assistants. At one end of the table, there was a lectern with a microphone.

The chairs were occupied by other principals in the funnelweb war including all Defence Force Chiefs of Staff and General Officers Commanding, the Commissioners of the New South Wales and Federal Police forces, and a varied collection of state and federal government ministers and senior public servants. Sitting in their midst were Bill Reid and Jack Fitzgerald, who had been airlifted from North Ryde at 3am when the CSIRO had finally been abandoned. Helen Parkes had been evacuated with the research team but on arrival at Holsworthy she had been taken to the AFCANS canteen, there to wait with the rest of the press corps for official announcements. Post-Vietnam, the first casualty of war was not truth, but media access.

Now, at 6.10am, in the securely sealed gymnasium, all attention was on the speaker at the lectern. Pat Howard had finished his report of the day's events at Central and was recounting what had occurred during 'Bravo'

Company's journey through the suburbs. His story of the corpse midden at Lakemba, which carefully omitted reference to Sergeant Shute's euthanasia, was received with shock. But when he closed with the news of the fifty-six survivors, pointing to the possibility of tens of thousands more, the room became animated.

Richard Bartlett, who was chairing the meeting, said, 'Thank you, Major Howard. And please convey my personal thanks to your men for their courageous work – I hope you all manage to get some sleep this morning.'

Howard replied, 'Thank you, sir, the men will appreciate it.' Then he saluted, turned about and marched out.

Nobody wanted to speak. Finally, Bartlett said, 'I think we've heard enough to have formed a picture of the situation on the ground, so perhaps it would be valuable to take some preliminary summations.' Heads nodded as Bartlett looked to the desks in front of him, and called, 'Doctor Reid?'

When Reid got to his feet and moved to the lectern, Fitzgerald noted that his shoulders were rounded and his head was down. But when he turned to his audience, Reid looked straight into their faces, and said clearly, 'The CSIRO team was evacuated from North Ryde earlier this morning and, as of now, our work is on hold. Regrettably, the bulk of our research on the originally mutated funnel-webs has been made redundant by the events of the past forty-eight hours. The new monster mutations appear to have a significantly different biochemistry to their progenitors, which basically means that we'll have to start again from scratch.'

The listeners exchanged looks of despair. Undeterred, Reid continued, 'The monsters seem immune to all standard insecticide chemicals. We believe we could develop a compound, a hybrid of tetrachlorodibenzo-para-dioxin, which would be lethal to the monsters. But if it were used in large enough quantities to eradicate them, it could render the Sydney region uninhabitable for decades. So we don't believe it's worth pursuing.'

A frustrated murmur arose. The New South Wales Premier spoke up. 'If I may, Prime Minister,' then to Reid, 'Bill, if we can't poison the bastards, can we get at them genetically – that's mainly what you've been looking at, isn't it?'

Reid nodded, 'Yes, Premier, it is. But as I explained, most of what we've done doesn't apply to the monsters. Jack Fitzgerald has been going flat out since we got the first one in the lab but what we're asking him to do could take months, maybe years, of work.'

The Prime Minister turned to Fitzgerald. 'Can you give us no glimmer of hope for an early breakthrough, Doctor Fitzgerald?'

Jack's heart sank. There was only one true answer, so he stood and gave it. 'No, Prime Minister, at least not without a miraculous stroke of luck – they do happen in science, but to hope for one in this case would be . . . unrealistic.'

Grey, the Prime Minister remarked as much to himself as to the gathering, 'So we can rule out any early scientific solution.' Then looking at the scientists, he said, 'However, I thank you and your colleagues for your dedicated efforts and I'd appreciate it if you would stay until the end of the meeting, for your information and for any feedback you might be able to give us.'

Reid nodded sombrely, and muttered, 'Of course, Prime Minister,' then shambled back to his seat and slumped down.

Bartlett gathered his thoughts, then said, 'General

Lawrie, would you now give us your assessment of the military situation?'

Andrew Lawrie, General Officer Commanding, Land Command, strode forward from the back of the room. He'd been an officer in the Australian Regular Army for thirty years, and in the tradition of his Scottish forebears he'd honed his soldierly trade and done his duty. When Jimmy O'Rourke had been a teenager in Vietnam, Lawrie had been there as a platoon commander, and he'd been a good one.

But since then, he'd seen no action, and he had soured. And until the appointment of a Defence Chief who valued a 'soldier's soldier', he had seemed fated for obscurity in early retirement. Now, at the eleventh hour, in a way he could never have imagined, he again had been given the chance to show his mettle. And, secretly, he was loving it.

At the lectern, General Lawrie adjusted the microphone, and announced, 'Prime Minister, the city has been evacuated from the Georges River in the south, to Hornsby in the north, and as far west as Blacktown. Beyond that, the population is fleeing of its own accord and at the present rate, we anticipate the Western Suburbs will be deserted by 6pm today. In the past twelve hours, we've had to withdraw from Circular Quay and Central Station, and the situation at Bankstown Airport is deteriorating. But we still control the exit points at Manly and Dee Why beaches. Also the First Armoured Regiment will soon arrive from Puckapunyal and deploy its Leopard tanks at Sydney Airport, and the Second Cavalry Regiment, equipped with LAV 25 light-armoured vehicles, have been airlifted overnight from Darwin to defend RAAF, Richmond. We're confident therefore that we can keep both the airport and the RAAF base open for some time. However, I'm pleased to report that as of 05.30, all exit points are clearing and the flow of refugees is drying up.'

Lawrie paused to let congratulatory mumblings roll around him. Then he said, 'Because of that, we're going to release two squadrons of Leopards to patrol the perimeters of the water catchments south of the city. If the funnelwebs get into the catchments it'll be a hell of a job to stop them spreading into the Southern Highlands. So we're putting a major effort into that area.'

Lawrie consulted notes, again allowing the sounds of approval to run their course. As they faded, he continued, 'Latest intelligence indicates that the funnelwebs are now as far west as Parramatta. To the south, they haven't crossed the Georges River yet and all its bridges are sealed. But it's only a matter of time before they wheel around the bend in the river at Lansvale.'

Czarnecki interjected, 'General Lawrie, what is your information about these people still inside the evacuated area?'

With practised ease, Lawrie evaded the question, saying, 'I have no figures on that, Premier, but my civil colleagues may have something.'

The Commissioner of the New South Wales Police quickly took whispered advice from a subordinate. Then he stood up, and said uneasily, 'Premier, we estimate that a quarter of a million people are unaccounted for in the metropolitan area.'

There was a collective gasp. Over the hubbub, the Commissioner declared, 'How many are still alive we simply don't know.'

As the noise subsided, the Prime Minister said, 'Thank you, Commissioner,' then, 'Please carry on, General Lawrie.'

Drawn, the Commissioner sat down as Lawrie

continued, 'What we do know is that the funnelwebs are nesting in the Central Business District – one of our reconnaissance helicopters brought back video footage which we passed to the CSIRO.' Then turning to Reid and Fitzgerald, he said, 'Gentlemen, could you give us your interpretation of the pictures?'

Reid indicated to Jack that he should reply. So he stood, and said, 'The army's video shows the funnelwebs are establishing a nesting colony along George Street. It's exactly to the pattern we would expect of the unmutated species only on an enormous scale. And given the accelerated rate of maturing we've observed, we believe they may have started breeding in there already.'

Bartlett observed hopefully, 'But presumably now the city has been evacuated, the monsters will soon begin to starve.'

Fitzgerald considered, then said, 'If the figure we've just heard is anywhere near right, then there may be enough food left in the city to supply the funnelwebs for months yet. And the army video shows they're not only stockpiling dead humans, but live ones too . . . to keep them fresh.'

Stomachs churned as Czarnecki jumped to his feet. 'Jesus Christ, why weren't we told about this? We can't just leave those people in there to die like that! What is the army doing, General Lawrie?'

Lawrie took a deep breath, then stated, 'Premier, to meaningfully sweep the city for survivors and bring them out, I'd need an armoured division plus two divisions of infantry. I don't have that. What I have is eighty Leopard tanks and a battalion of mechanised infantry. I regret that as much as I would like to, I do not have the means to mount a rescue in the metropolitan area.'

Czarnecki growled, 'So we leave God knows how

many innocent people to be eaten alive, General Lawrie! For Christ's sake, surely we can get some of them out?'

Lawrie went back at him, 'Yes, sir, I believe we could, but on the off-chance of saving a few dozen lives we may throw away the best opportunity we have of stopping this disaster in its tracks!'

All eyes turned to him as the Prime Minister queried, 'You have a proposal, General Lawrie?'

Lawrie said, 'Yes, Prime Minister, I do.'

The Chief of the Defence Force, Air Chief Marshal Edward McGovern, shifted uneasily in his seat. He knew what was coming because he and Lawrie had devised the plan together in the early hours. And he was not looking forward to the reaction.

But Reid and Fitzgerald were intrigued. Lawrie had commandeered them into the planning meeting with the CDF the moment they'd arrived, and he'd picked their brains about the funnelwebs for over an hour. Now they were curious to see how their input had been applied.

The GOC snapped his fingers and two junior staff officers wheeled a covered whiteboard to the lectern. As they withdrew, Lawrie turned to the meeting, and said, 'There are two aims we must immediately achieve. The first is to halt the funnelwebs' advance and deny them more ground. The second is to destroy them and reclaim the ground they now hold, namely the Sydney metropolitan area. As I've pointed out, we do not have the military means to mount what we might call a surgical operation. And so, our only remaining option is a sledgehammer.'

Lawrie threw back the cover of the whiteboard and revealed a map of metropolitan Sydney. It was covered in a complex pattern of coloured lines and arrows.

He continued, 'Operation Sledgehammer is a plan

in three phases. The first phase, to be executed by the RAAF, is the levelling of the Sydney Central Business District by saturation air strike.'

Lawrie got the response that McGovern had expected. Every government minister in the room, both state and federal, was on his or her feet, proclaiming outrage and clamouring for their objections to be heard. The most vocal of them was the New South Wales Premier. John Czarnecki looked as if he wanted to strangle Andrew Lawrie with his bare hands.

Bartlett leapt up, and shouted, 'Order! Order! Ladies and gentlemen, please, resume your seats – immediately!'

The armed military policemen who were positioned around the room looked concernedly to their sergeant, who in turn was watching the Chief of the Defence Force for instructions. When he saw the look in the man's eyes, McGovern waved for him to take no action, and the row gradually subsided to the point where Bartlett could again be heard.

'Thank you, ladies and gentlemen. Let's all just stay calm. It's a trying time and everyone is tired. But we must retain order or we will achieve nothing.'

Seconds later, a weighty silence had fallen. In the midst of it, John Czarnecki was fuming.

Bartlett motioned to Lawrie to continue.

Unshaken, Lawrie went on, 'We estimate that the air strike, utilising deep penetration earthquake bombs, will kill between fifty and eighty per cent of the funnelwebs, including most of those still in the sewers and the railway tunnels. It will also, of course, destroy their nests and their food stores. Phase two will then be the deployment of the First Armoured Regiment, with support from Two Cav. and Five/Seven RAR, who will mop up the surviving funnelwebs above ground. We understand from the

CSIRO that if the roaming males are denied their nesting base, they can be systematically picked off quite quickly, working in from the outer suburbs.'

Everyone turned to Reid and Fitzgerald. As Reid was clearly off form, Jack confirmed, 'We believe individual males might continue to forage beyond the destroyed nesting area for several days, but denied their central food store and any replacement supply, we anticipate they would soon weaken and make increasingly easy targets.'

Bullish, Lawrie concluded. 'Finally, phase three will be the insertion into the CBD of Three RAR, One Commando and the Special Air Service Regiment, to comb the ruins and any surviving underground infrastructure, and destroy nests or individual funnelwebs which may have survived phases one and two. And that will conclude the operation.'

The only person not lost for words was John Czarnecki. He stood up, fixed Lawrie in his gaze, and said, 'General Lawrie, it would not only be the conclusion of your operation – it would also be the conclusion of this city, and very probably of Australia as we know it. Have you any idea what effect the destruction of Sydney would have on the national economy – it would mean total financial ruin. What you are proposing is outright madness!'

Controversy buzzed like a swarm of wasps. Bartlett spoke above it. 'All right, thank you, Premier, thank you, everybody . . .'

The buzz receded. Bartlett paused to think, then entreated, 'General Lawrie, Air Chief Marshal McGovern – I agree with Premier Czarnecki. What you are proposing could reduce this country to a Third World economy. In God's name, is there no less destructive way to kill these things?'

For the first time, McGovern spoke up in support of his Land Commander. 'Prime Minister, the resources of the Defence Force have been totally given over to finding an effective response to this emergency, but what is now clear is that our worst enemy is time. After talking to Doctor Fitzgerald this morning, I'm confirmed in the view that if we do not act boldly – and now – we stand to lose a great deal more than this city.'

Czarnecki shook his head in despair, but before he could speak, Bartlett said crisply, 'Doctor Fitzgerald, perhaps you would come to the lectern and share with us whatever it is that the Chief of the Defence Force is referring to?'

Jack was tired, and irritated by the Prime Minister's tone. He decided it was time to stop pulling punches. So he moved to the microphone, and said, 'Prime Minister, what we can see of the funnelweb colony in the army video is probably just the tip of the iceberg. We know the monsters came up out of the sewers and railway tunnels all over the city, so it's likely that the colony extends throughout the subterranean network. If it does, that means there are dozens of females down there, each one of them getting ready to give birth to hundreds, maybe thousands, of young.'

The implications of Fitzgerald's words took a second or two to sink in, but as a hum of alarm arose, he cut in, 'Now . . . given the monsters' accelerated growth, it may only be a matter of weeks, or even days, before the next generation leaves the nests. And when they do, this country is going to be up to its neck in funnelwebs, ranging out from Sydney in all directions and establishing new colonies. If that happens, I believe there will be no stopping them, which means there will be no national economy, and very soon no nation, left worth the name.'

Openly hostile, Czarnecki interjected, 'How do you know this, Doctor Fitzgerald – how do *you* know this? I should remind this meeting that you and your colleagues have singularly failed to solve this problem. Do you expect us now to ravage this city on the basis of your "probablys" and "maybes"?'

For the first time in a long time, Fitzgerald lost his temper. He railed, 'Premier, I know nothing for certain, and I don't expect *you* to do anything. What I *do* expect is that in three weeks time, people all over this state will be dying in their hundreds of thousands!'

The silence crackled. No-one breathed. Which is why the next words spoken, in a quiet, unprepossessing voice, resonated so clearly through the room.

'If I may suggest, Prime Minister, there may be an alternative . . .'

Everybody looked around at the owner of the voice, who was standing at the back near the door. He was a short, middle-aged man, balding and bespectacled. Bartlett did not recognise him, as he added, '. . . at least, a way of achieving General Lawrie's aims with less collateral damage.'

Bartlett said, 'I apologise, sir, but I don't believe I know you. Would you introduce yourself, please.'

The speaker was suddenly aware that he was the focus of attention, and replied self-consciously, 'Yes, of course. My name is Forrest, Prime Minister . . . Geoffrey Forrest. I'm head of Strategic Studies at the Royal Military College, but presently attached to the CDF's personal staff as an adviser.'

McGovern leant across to Bartlett and said quietly, 'Professor Forrest is one of our best academics, Prime Minister – he's a smart man.'

Bartlett nodded, then looked up again and said, 'Thank you, Professor Forrest. What is your suggestion?'

Forrest pondered, then looked awkward as he said, 'This may seem a bit far-fetched at first sight, but given everything we've heard, I believe it may be worth considering . . . the ERW.'

Most of the faces in the room remained blank. But every person in uniform looked astounded, not least the Defence Chief. McGovern's astonishment was quickly overcome by his instinct to save face, since the man he had endorsed had just made what he judged to be an outrageous suggestion. Feigning reasonableness, he broke in, 'It's an interesting thought, Geoffrey, but unfortunately quite impractical, so let's get back to the GOC's . . .'

'Just a second, Air Chief Marshal,' Czarnecki interrupted, still smarting from Fitzgerald's rebuke, 'Professor Forrest, you said less collateral damage. Can you elaborate?'

Forrest looked like a man who had taken the lid off a bucket of worms. But he was committed, so went on, 'As many here already know, during the Reagan administration, the Americans developed and manufactured a tactical nuclear weapon called the Enhanced Radiation Weapon, otherwise known as "the neutron bomb".'

Lawrie looked as if his brain was going into overdrive, as Forrest continued, 'Basically, it's a small nuclear device which produces relatively little blast but gives off extremely high levels of initial radiation. So damage to structures is minimal but living organisms inside the weapon's effective radius are neutralised. It seems to me that it could be an answer to our problem.'

Forrest's understatement intensified the impact of his proposal. Fitzgerald could barely believe his ears, but Czarnecki looked like a drowning man who'd been thrown a lifebelt. Suppressing eagerness, he turned to McGovern, and said, 'Well, Air Chief Marshal?'

Subdued, McGovern responded, 'Professor Forrest is quite right in what he says, Premier, but we do not have the neutron bomb, nor any other nuclear weapon for that matter, which makes the proposition academic, not to mention somewhat surprising from such a source.'

McGovern's tone was clear indication to Forrest of his superior's disapproval, a disapproval echoed in the Prime Minister's voice when he responded, 'Indeed, that would seem to be the salient point, Air Chief Marshal, in which case we appear to have no alternative to General Lawrie's proposed . . .'

But Bartlett stopped midstream as Czarnecki leant close to him, and whispered urgently, 'Before you say any more, Prime Minister, there are some relevant facts . . . sensitive facts . . . that you should be aware of. It's imperative that we talk privately – right away.'

And from Czarnecki's forcefulness, Bartlett was left in no doubt that they should. So he announced, 'I think we could use some refreshment at this point, so we'll take a short break.'

And as everyone stretched their legs and went for beverages, Bartlett and Czarnecki left the room.

Three hundred metres from the gymnasium, in a deserted rugby field, Czarnecki turned to the Prime Minister and said, 'We don't have time for niceties, Richard, so I'll get right to it. We're not friends and we never will be but at this very moment we are the two people with the power to determine what happens around here. Tomorrow or even tonight circumstances may have overtaken us and that may no longer be the case. But right now, it is, so it makes sense to me that we should get together on this.'

Bartlett's poker face belied the fact that his mind

was racing, as he tried to work out what exactly Czarnecki was up to. But he gave no indication of it when he answered quietly, 'I agree.'

Czarnecki examined Bartlett for a clue as to what he might be expecting. When he saw none, he decided that he had to play his hand. So leading Bartlett in a stroll against the morning chill, he continued, 'Last night I met with a very concerned group of people. They asked to speak to me in confidence to express their interests in this situation, and to make me fully aware of the value they place on those interests.'

Czarnecki glanced at Bartlett to gauge if anything was registering. If it was, there was no sign of it, so he went on, 'Their concerns are for the well-being and preservation of the Sydney inner city, and their interests in it are diverse – philanthropic, cultural . . . and financial.'

'Financial.' Bartlett's word was neither statement nor question. It was a selection.

Czarnecki was encouraged. 'Yes . . . in fact, it was their financial interests which they represented with the greatest conviction . . . and were most specific – and quantitative – about the value they place on them.'

Now Bartlett knew exactly what this was about, and he had to make an immediate decision. He could walk away now and turn his back on temptation. Or he could stay, and face what could be the most defining moment of his life. Confronted with such a rare choice, he was intrigued to know what people thought he might be bought for. So he said, 'Go on.'

Czarnecki ventured, 'If the Sydney Central Business District is flattened by blanket air strike, conservatively its real estate value would be reduced by eighty-five per cent. We may kill the funnelwebs but New South Wales will go broke and foreign interests will buy the state from under us for a pittance. If, on the other hand, the funnelwebs are not eradicated immediately, the businesses and investments of the people I spoke with will decline in value to such an extent that between them they will lose many billions of dollars anyway. Understandably, they would be grateful to us if we were able to protect their interests, which self-evidently are also the interests of the state, and of the country as a whole.'

Bartlett could feel it coming, like an imminent sunrise. He clasped hands behind his back, and said, 'How grateful?'

Czarnecki drew a deep intake of breath. Then he said, 'One hundred million US dollars for each of us, half deposited in a European numbered account today, the other half when the funnelweb situation has been quickly resolved with the CBD substantially still intact.'

Bartlett took himself by surprise. From the instant Czarnecki uttered the amount, there was simply no question about it – he was bought, body and soul. Rationalisations flashed into his mind but he was too intelligent to entertain them. In that instant, he knew that he had become someone else. And to as shrewd a judge of character as John Czarnecki, it was immediately apparent.

Dispensing with platitudes, Bartlett began his new life with the words, 'It appears our only chance of both preserving the city and destroying the funnelwebs quickly is the neutron bomb. And the only way we can get it is by me grovelling to the President of the United States. But if I *can* elicit his help then at least we'll still have a country to live in . . . which will of course be my principal argument to Federal Parliament.'

Every muscle in Czarnecki relaxed. He floated an inch above the ground, and just let Richard Bartlett talk.

'I don't have enough to suspend Parliament and declare martial law yet, and by the time I do it will probably be too late. So if we are going to succeed, we will need, in the national interest and especially in the interest of New South Wales, to take short cuts. And if we're going to do that then we'll need to support each other – in whatever may be necessary.' Bartlett stopped and looked Czarnecki in the eye. Then he said, 'How do you feel about that?'

Czarnecki knew exactly what Bartlett meant. From now on, they would need to work outside the obtrusive niceties of the democratic system. Dissent, whatever its source, would need to be circumvented, or contained.

Czarnecki replied, 'Clearly we must do *whatever* may be necessary by way of mutual support, Prime Minister.'

They understood each other. What they had agreed to was an unconstitutional, and illegal, corruption of Australia's governmental process. The deed was done. They were partners in crime.

Bartlett said simply, 'Good,' and they walked back to the gymnasium.

When everyone had retaken their seats, the Prime Minister said, 'It is the responsibility of all of us to achieve the best possible outcome of this terrible problem for the country as a whole. It is incumbent upon us then to examine any possible way, no matter how unlikely or problematic, of destroying the funnelwebs whilst preserving the value of Sydney's infrastructure.' Then he turned to McGovern, and asked, 'Air Chief Marshal, is there someone who can provide us with specific information about the neutron bomb option?'

McGovern, along with others in the room, felt acutely uncomfortable. It was plain that Czarnecki had somehow persuaded Bartlett to pursue this idiocy. But as a military man, it was not his place to question the Prime Minister. And so, angered by the waste of precious time but confident that the idea would soon self-destruct, he growled, 'Brigadier Christian Phelps of my staff is our foremost authority on nuclear weapons.' Then turning to an intense and scholarly looking officer, McGovern instructed, 'Go to the podium, Christian.'

Swallowing, 'Yes, sir,' Christian Phelps stood and went to the lectern, where Andrew Lawrie made way for him.

Bartlett said, 'Brigadier, assuming for the moment that we could get one of these devices, just answer this one question for me: could we kill the funnelwebs in Sydney with a neutron bomb without destroying the city, or making it uninhabitable – yes or no?'

Phelps reflected that the rest of his career may hang on his answer, but decided anyway to say what he thought, which was, 'Yes, sir, I believe that we could.'

The mood of the meeting transformed as on the turn of a card. But the Defence Chief was dumbfounded, as was Jack Fitzgerald, who felt suddenly frightened.

Bartlett spoke carefully, so as not to betray the excitement building in him. 'Brigadier – now tell us, in plain English please, what would actually happen if we were to do this?'

Phelps had to put the circumstances from his mind in order to think clearly. Holding eye contact with Bartlett, he intoned, 'Prime Minister, a two-kiloton ERW airburst at five hundred metres altitude would have an effective radius of two kilometres. The Sydney Central Business District is a rectangle roughly three kilometres north-south by two kilometres east-west, so it would fit comfortably inside that four kilometre circle. The ERW is designed to give off high levels of neutron radiation to penetrate armour and concrete of considerable thickness, so living organisms in tanks or buildings, or even underground, can be killed by it.'

Hope flourished. But Phelps remained cool, determined not to get swept up in the mood. He went on, 'Now . . . even at only two kilotons, it's still like detonating two thousand tons of TNT right over the city centre, so there would be significant damage to buildings at short range. But I would suggest that if such a device were detonated over Hyde Park, collateral damage would be minimised, as Professor Forrest has said.'

Czarnecki interjected, 'How minimised, compared to General Lawrie's blanket air strike?'

Phelps glanced at Lawrie, anticipating displeasure, but was surprised to receive a nod of encouragement. He thought aloud, 'Maybe . . . all the buildings immediately surrounding the park totally destroyed, plus serious but repairable damage to twice as many more. There would be minor damage to the whole city, of course – there wouldn't be a pane of glass intact for ten kilometres.'

Czarnecki could not help himself beaming, as he muttered, 'Bingo!'

Bartlett, who had been scribbling, looked up. 'Now . . . Brigadier Phelps . . . residual radiation – how long before the CBD could be reoccupied?'

That was basic doctrine. 'Hardened-armoured vehicles could go in as soon as the dust settles, Prime Minister, say within twenty-four hours. Then infantry and sappers in NBC suits in another seventy-two.'

Conscious that those estimates fitted Lawrie's timetable exactly, Phelps could almost feel the Land Commander's glow of approval. He concluded, 'It should be safe for unprotected troops to enter the area in six to eight weeks, and civilian clean-up and reconstruction teams could start work inside three months.'

Half the room was frantically making notes, and consulting reference documents to deduce implications for their various departments. Then everyone looked up, alarmed by nearby gunfire.

Bartlett asked, 'Brigadier, how would this device be, em . . . delivered?'

Phelps replied, 'The most suitable ERW is probably the W-82 artillery shell, Prime Minister, so either by land-based or naval artillery fire, or, suitably modified, as a retarded free fall bomb dropped from an aircraft. In this case, accuracy to within a few metres is essential so the bomb option would be my first choice.'

As the shooting outside intensified, McGovern looked utterly shattered. When Phelps shot a glance at him, he could see *'et tu, Brute'* written all over his commander's face.

The Prime Minister finished dashing off notes. Then looking up, he announced, 'We'll examine this proposal in depth.'

Shaking, Jack Fitzgerald jumped to his feet, and called out, 'Prime Minister, before this goes any further, I really must . . .'

But he stopped when McGovern, who was glaring at Richard Bartlett, said, 'Prime Minister, are you seriously envisaging that Sydney be the first city since Nagasaki to be bombed with a nuclear weapon, and that the perpetrator of that attack be the Australian Federal Government? What about the quarter million civilians we think may still be in there – for some reason we seem far less concerned about them than we were thirty minutes ago!'

Bartlett patently did not appreciate the remarks of his CDF, nor the undiluted vitriol with which they were delivered. Hackles raised, he responded with barely disguised antagonism, 'I am afraid, Air Chief Marshal, that *I* cannot allow myself the luxury of injudicious moralising.'

McGovern regarded Bartlett with contempt, but was saved from responding by a lieutenant-colonel of the Military Police who entered the room brusquely, crossed to McGovern and handed him a note.

When he'd read it, the CDF passed the note to Bartlett, who scanned it quickly then announced, 'It appears there have been developments which make it necessary for us to leave immediately. Transport is standing by apparently, so if we could all move outside . . .'

Repressing his building anger, Fitzgerald called again, 'Prime Minister, before we go, I have to make a point!'

Irritated, Bartlett snapped, 'Very quickly, please.'

Across people gathering their things, Fitzgerald spoke up, 'You know from our reports that we believe this situation may have come about because the funnelwebs were exposed to ionising radiation. So we can't just take it for granted that the neutron bomb would be effective against the funnelwebs . . . at least, not in any predictable way.'

Bartlett didn't want to know. Distracted, he said only, 'I agree, Doctor Fitzgerald, which is why we will conduct an exhaustive investigation before proceeding with anything.' Then pointedly he ended it with, 'But now, I am informed that in the last few minutes the funnelwebs have circumvented the Georges River, so it is time we were not here. Thank you, and good luck to you all.'

And with that, the meeting dispersed.

Unlike most in attendance that morning, Richard Bartlett and John Czarnecki did not leave Holsworthy immediately. Rather, they adjourned to the privacy of the Officers' Mess committee room.

When the Military Police sergeant who had escorted them went out and closed the door behind him, Bartlett stood up and turned away for a moment. Then, turning back, he regarded the man they had invited to join them, and asked soberly, 'Could phases two and three of Operation Sledgehammer be successfully executed if phase one were a neutron bomb detonation instead of a high-explosive air strike?'

Andrew Lawrie answered without pause, 'Yes, Prime Minister. The neutron bomb would actually be better for the purpose because it should kill more funnelwebs – maybe all of them.'

It was what his listeners had hoped for. Reflecting, Bartlett paced. Eventually, he said, 'General Lawrie, it is clear that Air Chief Marshal McGovern is unsupportive of the neutron bomb option. In my view, that makes it unworkable for him to continue as Chief of the Defence Force.' Then he stopped, and looking Lawrie in the eye, asked, 'In the national interest, are you able to put your personal loyalty to Air Chief Marshal McGovern aside and accept an appointment as his replacement?'

This was what Lawrie had hoped was the reason he was here. But to hear the words actually spoken by the Prime Minister was still a thrill. Lawrie knew that if not for McGovern, he would be on the scrap heap. But, as the cliché went, this was war. And who was he to deny his country and his commander-in-chief?

He replied with indecent haste, 'Yes, Prime Minister. As much as I regret the necessity, I accept the appointment. Thank you for your confidence.'

Scribbling a note of instruction, Bartlett muttered, 'Thank *you*, General Lawrie. As of this moment, you are acting Chief of the Defence Force, your promotion to be formally confirmed through usual channels. In the meantime, we'll keep it to ourselves . . . until I've spoken to Air Chief Marshal McGovern.'

When the new CDF replied over earnestly, 'Of course, sir, it's a delicate situation,' Czarnecki could not help but smile at Lawrie's poorly disguised exultation.

Bartlett finished writing, sealed the note in an envelope and dropped it into his attache case. Then he said, 'Now we need to tie up some practical matters. General Lawrie, I want a detailed briefing on what it is that we intend, including a comprehensive specification of the bomb we need. Bear in mind that my request will be scrutinised by hostile elements in the Congress and the Pentagon, so I need to know exactly what I'm talking about.'

Lawrie was already making notes as he replied, 'I'll get Brigadier Phelps onto it right away, Prime Minister – you'll have it in an hour.'

Still pacing, Bartlett pondered, 'Now . . . all that still worries me is what the CSIRO man, Fitzgerald, said. If he's right, and this was started by some radiation accident, can we be sure that the neutron bomb will work against the funnelwebs?'

Lawrie was unfazed. 'I have seen the test data on the neutron bomb, Prime Minister, and I can tell you that no living thing could survive it. I don't care what they are or what made them that way – if they live and breathe, the ERW will kill them.'

'In that case,' Bartlett smiled, 'I'll get my cap in my hand and talk to Washington this morning.'

Czarnecki nodded, pleased with the outcome. But he was still troubled. 'Prime Minister, we haven't covered what we do about the poor bastards still in there.'

Bartlett ruminated, grave faced. Eventually, he said, 'Gentlemen, it seems we are confronted with an appalling reality. I believe we have no option but to abandon those poor unfortunates and focus on killing this plague – for the national good.'

The Prime Minister looked into his cohorts' eyes. On the surface, there was remorse and tragic resignation. But beneath, there was relief, and a glimmer of dark exhilaration.

So it was that the co-conspirators parted in accord, and went off in pursuit of their newly interdependent destinities.

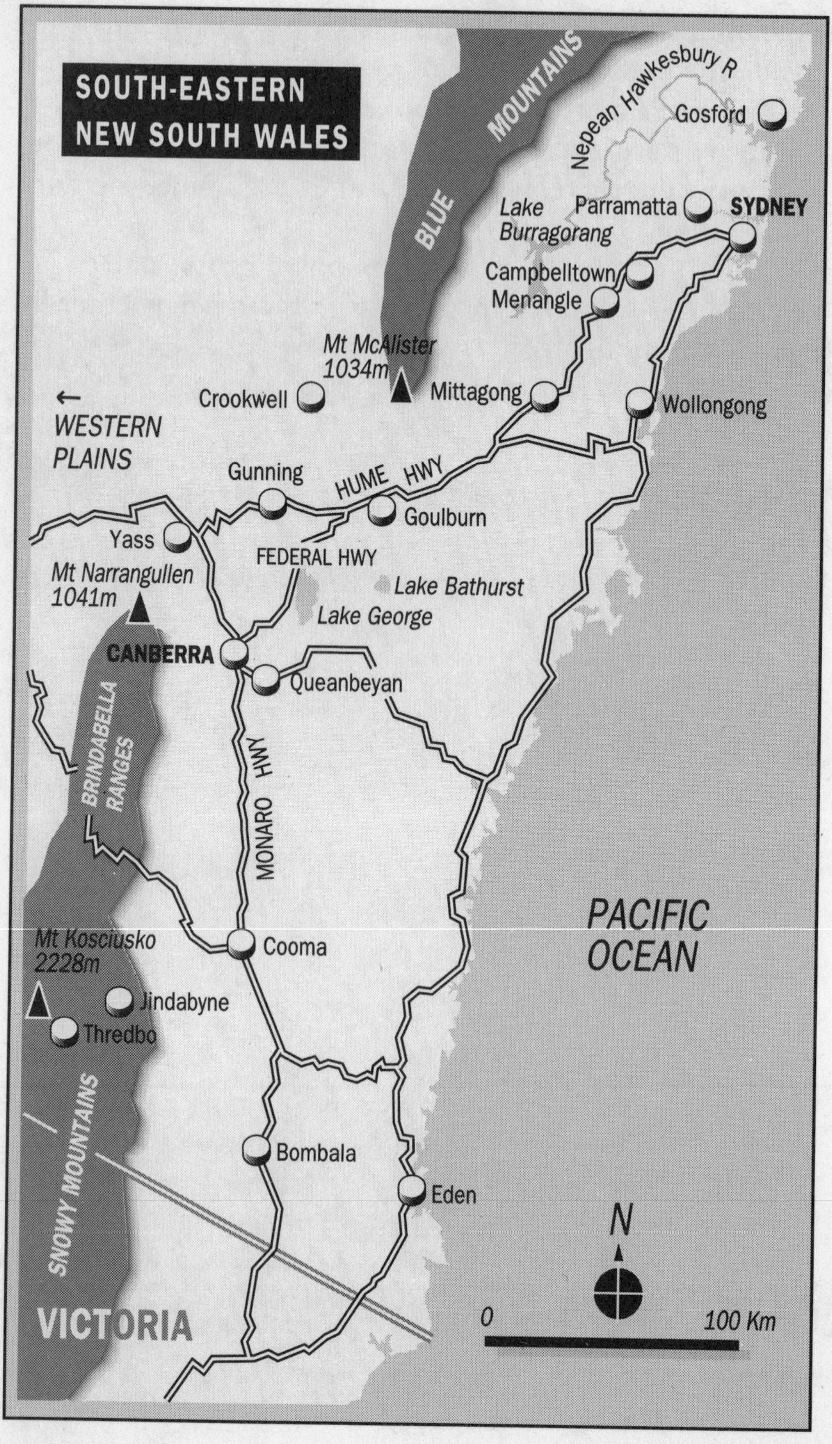
SOUTH-EASTERN
NEW SOUTH WALES
BLUE MOUNTAINS
Nepean Hawkesbury R
Gosford
Lake Burragorang
Parramatta
SYDNEY
Campbelltown
Menangle
Mt McAlister 1034m
Crookwell
Mittagong
Wollongong
← WESTERN PLAINS
Gunning
HUME HWY
Goulburn
Yass
FEDERAL HWY
Mt Narrangullen 1041m
Lake Bathurst
Lake George
CANBERRA
Queanbeyan
BRINDABELLA RANGES
MONARO HWY
PACIFIC OCEAN
Mt Kosciusko 2228m
Cooma
Jindabyne
Thredbo
SNOWY MOUNTAINS
Bombala
Eden
N
VICTORIA
0
100 Km

8

For the biggest city of the driest continent on Earth, water supply had always been a preoccupation. For decades, the soldiers and convicts of the First Fleet had used just one source, the Tank Stream, as drinking fount, bath, laundry, highway and sewer. But now Sydney used two billion litres of water a day, and almost all of it came from the Nepean and Burragorang valleys, extending south and south-west of the city for a hundred kilometres. Reserved exclusively as water catchment for a century, it was beautiful, unspoilt country – a high rolling wilderness thickly carpeted with eucalypts stretching in every direction as far as the eye could see. And dotted within it were the storage dams – concrete leviathans retaining vast reservoirs of water – sentinels against the spectre of drought.

Dating from the 1930s, the dams of the Upper Nepean Scheme – Nepean, Avon, Cataract, Cordeaux and Woronora – were sited in the New South Wales Southern Highlands at intervals along a line running parallel to the coast roughly fifteen kilometres inland, and together they provided up to thirty per cent of Sydney's drinking water. But the remaining seventy per cent came from just one dam, built in the fifties, and situated forty kilometres to the west in the foothills of the Blue Mountains.

Warragamba Dam was the biggest water storage dam in the southern hemisphere, and the reservoir it retained, the seven and a half thousand hectare Lake Burragorang, was anecdotally one of only two man-made things visible from outer space, the other being the Great Wall of China.

But as the summer sun rose over Sydney's catchment areas that morning, four people looking out over them were too preoccupied to appreciate the view. Damien Mitchell had been detailed to fly his three passengers the two hundred and fifty kilometres from Holsworthy to Canberra, the national capital. Two of the passengers, Doctors Reid and Fitzgerald, were VIPs to be delivered to the Australian National University, there to await instructions and further movement orders. The third, Ms Helen Parkes, was an American correspondent travelling with them.

Mitchell had been friendly, particularly since Ms Parkes was the most attractive passenger he'd ever had. But they all seemed despondent, particularly Reid who was sitting up front. And Mitchell guessed that Parkes and Fitzgerald had something going anyway when he'd caught that certain look passing between them. So after a few minutes, he'd given up on small talk and as they crossed the Georges River, the mood in the Kiowa's cockpit was subdued.

But then they overflew Campbelltown, and Mitchell came back to life. Just south of the new suburb, on the perimeter of the catchments, a train had arrived with an interesting load. Twenty-four Leopard Medium Battle Tanks and six Armoured Command Vehicles were being unloaded from their flat-bed trucks, and another twenty box wagons were crammed with enough fuel and ammunition to supply a small war. The men of 'Alpha' and 'Delta' Squadrons, the 1st Royal Australian Armoured Regiment, were swarming over their charges like schoolboys in an arcade, and the tanks would be fuelled, armed and battle ready in under an hour.

Circling the train, Mitchell grinned at the tank jockeys' lewd gestures, graphically suggesting that he might care to go elsewhere. Snapping on the intercom, he observed, 'God help any overgrown spider that shows up here now!'

Reid could only manage a polite nod, but Helen quizzed Mitchell on the tanks, their unit, their weapons and everything else she could think of.

As the words buzzed back and forth, Fitzgerald gazed solemnly around the landscape, and pondered. Lawrie had been right. If the funnelwebs ever got into this vast forest, it would be disaster. There would be no finding them in here, and no way of stopping them from spreading throughout southern New South Wales. Then, if they crossed the Snowy Mountains into Victoria, the worst case scenario he had posed to Czarnecki would no longer be conjecture. He surprised himself by wondering if the idea of the neutron bomb was so crazy after all.

To the north, however, another man was in no doubt that the use of the neutron bomb would not only be crazy, but a criminal act which would lead to his country's international ostracism. And as a true patriot, that was simply not an outcome he could tolerate.

Edward 'Teddy' McGovern was a bomber pilot by trade, and irrepressibly old school. He'd been born too late to remember World War Two but as a boy in the fifties, he'd thrilled to the wartime exploits of Britain's RAF. There'd never been a doubt about where young Teddy's future lay and the very day he'd left school, he'd rushed to the recruiting office and applied to train as a pilot in the Royal Australian Air Force.

He'd been just in time to get his first taste of combat flying Lincoln bombers in Malaya, which had delighted him since the Lincoln was a variant of the Avro Lancaster as flown by the RAF themselves in the latter part of the war. Then he'd been lucky enough to be posted to 2 Squadron in the late sixties and fly Canberra jets against North Vietnam. Promoted to Wing Commander, he'd subsequently been assigned as a RAAF liaison officer to the USAF, and extraordinarily had found himself in 1971 as an unofficial replacement pilot attacking NVA supply lines through Cambodia in a Republic F-105 Thunderchief. Nothing in McGovern's life had matched combat in that brutally powered fighter-bomber, and it had been a fitting if bitterly regretted end to his flying career.

Subsequently, his distinguished active service had stood McGovern in good stead. It had propelled him through the senior ranks of the RAAF until eventually he'd received the ultimate promotion to Chief of the Defence Force. His talents for administration, diplomacy, public relations and picking the right team had all served him well in the top job. But now, in the face of political machination, none of it counted for anything at all.

The Prime Minister's Black Hawk had landed at Richmond twenty minutes after a RAAF Squirrel had delivered McGovern himself. And after a short and intensely unpleasant interview in the Base Commander's office, McGovern found he was not only out of a job but was also to be forcibly retired from the service he loved. The only respite was that he'd persuaded Bartlett he needed the rest of the day as CDF to achieve a smooth transition of authority to the Judas pretender, Andrew Lawrie. Now, ten minutes after the Prime Minister had taken off again for Canberra, McGovern's mind was racing.

As everyone had agreed, if the monsters were

allowed to break out of the city and establish new nesting sites, it would be impossible to stop the entire country becoming infested. So to buy time to get three divisions of troops from the United Nations, as well as to deny the politicians their excuse to use the neutron bomb, the funnelwebs would have to be contained inside the metropolitan area. But how?

McGovern had realised that there may be a very simple way. The monster funnelwebs didn't care for water. On river banks, they'd been observed paddling nervously into the shallows then receding quickly to the safety of dry land. Their conventionally sized antecedents sank to the bottom of swimming pools with tiny bubbles of air to breathe, there to bite the feet of unsuspecting bathers. But the monsters were precluded from that by the physics of surface tension, and seemed reluctant to venture into anything deeper than a puddle.

Lake Burragorang was expansive, and it was also deep. It held two trillion litres of water – four times more than Sydney Harbour – which if released would cause a massive deluge. The possibility of that deluge had plagued the managers and engineers of the Sydney Water Board for decades. Since 1945, Sydney's Western Suburbs had burgeoned below Warragamba Dam across an area known as the Penrith Flood Plain. When the dam had been designed there had been meagre data available on long-term flood patterns. But as knowledge had improved, so had concern about a cataclysm, and accordingly Warragamba had been raised twice since 1987.

All this meant that a vast amount of research had been done on what would happen if Warragamba failed. And inevitably that information had found its way to the Defence Force, as it was they who would have to deal with the disaster if it ever occurred. McGovern had taken a personal interest when for a time he himself had been Base Commander at Richmond, which stood square in the path of the anticipated torrent. So he knew well what would happen if Warragamba was breached, which was that the Nepean-Hawkesbury river system would flood and encircle Sydney to the north and west with a lake ten metres deep and up to fifteen kilometres across.

From memory, McGovern estimated that there would be a thirty-five kilometre corridor of dry land to the south, but that would be a containable front. Moats could be cut using high explosives. Electrified fences could be erected. And the Defence Force had the manpower to effectively seal such a distance. The outer west of the city would be lost but could be rebuilt without bankrupting the nation, and the prize of the metropolis would be preserved until it could be reclaimed. Yes, it was possible. It really was possible!

Warragamba had to go – a three million tonne wall of concrete, a hundred and fifty metres high, three hundred and fifty metres long, and a hundred metres thick at its base. An immovable object? McGovern reflected that the method of breaching it was so simple, and known to anyone with even a passing knowledge of military aviation history.

In World War II, a plan was spawned to boost the British war effort by an eccentric but brilliant engineer, Barnes Wallis. He had previously built airships and designed the Wellington bomber, and he would later invent the variable sweep wing as well as the recently revived 'earthquake' bomb. But in 1942, Wallis was obsessed with a single, fantastic idea. He theorised that if he could find a way to breach the great dams of the Ruhr Valley, German manufacturers would be deprived of hydro-electric power and their war factories would be destroyed by flooding.

Wallis worked tirelessly for months, battling failure and bureaucratic obstruction, until finally he came up with the solution. It was a bomb which, when dropped onto the stored water at an exact height and speed, bounced across the surface like a skipping stone. Then when it impacted with the dam, it sank hard up against the wall until it was detonated at a pre-set depth by hydrostatic pistol. Where dams had previously been protected from bombing by the cushioning effect of water, Wallis's bomb used that effect to concentrate the power of the explosion. In that way, a massive structure could be cracked with a relatively small charge, and once cracked, the pressure of water would cause the entire dam to collapse.

In the event, the dams raid of May 16, 1943, was a strategic failure. Nine out of seventeen aircraft were lost and the damage to German industry was minimal. But two of the three dams targeted, the Moehne and the Eder, were breached, and Wallis, at least technically if not strategically, was vindicated.

As a boy, McGovern had seen the Richard Todd film of the story so often that he could still recite the dialogue. And now, for the second time in his life, the Dam Busters were to be his inspiration. He snapped on the Base Commander's computer and tapped into the ADF Academy's Restricted database. There he accessed Wallis's original figures, and quickly began making calculations. Warragamba was three times bigger than the biggest of the German dams, but the RDX/TNT/aluminium explosive in modern bombs was more powerful than the straight RDX Wallis had used. Allowing for all that, McGovern concluded that 30,000 pounds of bombs would breach Warragamba. The RAAF had high explosive bombs of 500 and 2,000 pounds, but none that would bounce on water and certainly no aircraft capable of dropping such a device. So how to deliver them?

It was a crude solution, and for an old bomber pilot, inelegant. But the obvious way was to drive the bombs onto the dam and roll them over the side into the water. And that's exactly what the Chief of the Defence Force decided to do.

Within minutes, the view from the Kiowa's cockpit had changed. The virgin forest of the catchments had given way to the rolling grasslands of the New South Wales Southern Highlands. It was some of the best beef cattle country in Australia. But this morning the herds trudging the Hume Highway south of Mittagong were not of cattle, but of people. Tens of thousands of refugees, famished and footsore, all non-essential belongings long abandoned, wound from horizon to horizon in a ribbon of misery and despair.

The Kiowa's occupants looked down on the scene, appalled. Fitzgerald was reminded of newsreels of refugee columns winding endlessly through Nazi Europe. Or more recently, of terrified Bosnians escaping the horrors of ethnic cleansing, or emaciated victims fleeing famine and genocide in Africa. But this wasn't the Balkans, or Rwanda – it was Australia, where things like this couldn't happen . . . until now.

For the second time in two days, Damien Mitchell felt enraged at his own impotence. When he could stomach it no longer, he eased his cyclic over and the Kiowa banked away to bypass Goulburn across country to the east.

The mood was sullen. Glancing in the rear-view mirror, Mitchell saw Helen Parkes was struggling to hold back tears. He also saw Fitzgerald was drained. But to his left, he saw that his third passenger was positively ill. The vigour and largesse were all gone from Bill Reid. His ashen face was alive with twitches and he was plainly on the verge of total breakdown.

The landscape beneath became sporadically wooded. Distracted by his own exhaustion, Mitchell did not at first see the ant-like figures darting between the trees. Then he did glimpse them, but he'd barely wondered who they were when a burst of automatic fire slammed into the helicopter and the whine of the engine became a tortured scream.

The Kiowa spun and plunged in a maelstrom of smoke. Mitchell cut the throttle and wrestled with the cyclic, desperately trying to autorotate. But then a second burst of gunfire shattered the tail rotor into fragments, and Mitchell's last thought was the certain realisation that he was dead.

The next Fitzgerald knew, he was pushing Helen into the undergrowth as behind them the Kiowa exploded in a fireball. Some instinct had made him release their seat belts and push Helen from the aircraft before it hit.

His first thought was of Bill Reid, but turning to the conflagration it was obvious that neither Reid nor the pilot had stood a chance. And with that, the full force of their predicament hit Fitzgerald like a train: Reid and Mitchell were dead – he and Helen were unarmed – and whoever had shot them down would soon arrive and do God knows what!

He looked at Helen. She was in shock, staring into space and trembling. Urgently, Jack pulled her to her feet and shoved her ahead into the bush.

Arthur Reynolds was a Pom, marked for life by his immutable Devon accent despite having been an Australian citizen for thirty years. He had spent the past nine of them as head of the Explosives Ordnance Division of the Defence Force's Aeronautical and Maritime Research Laboratory at Maribyrnong, Victoria, and as such was the most knowledgeable person in Australia on the subject of bombs.

Reynolds had known Teddy McGovern for a decade, the two men having survived many a dreary function by sharing a bottle of good claret and talking endlessly of their shared enthusiasm. McGovern was fascinated by anything and everything to do with bombs, and he had soaked up the obscurest technical details from Reynolds like a sponge. For his own part, Reynolds had been pleased to nurture McGovern's interest, and now happily the man who had become his friend had risen to be the nation's Defence Chief, and had been an invaluable ally in the AMRL's eternal bickerings with bureaucrats. So Reynolds had not been surprised when the phone awoke him early that morning with a personal request for help from the CDF. Three hours later he was landing at Richmond in a RAAF VIP jet, only minutes ahead of a squadron of F-111s which flew in deafeningly from Amberley in Queensland with eighty thousand pounds of High Explosive bombs.

Reynolds was the only person McGovern confided in with the details of his plan. And after checking the figures, Reynolds excitedly agreed that it should work. But as he sweated for the next seven hours in a humid hangar secured by the RAAF Police, what he did not know was that the device he was concocting was unapproved – the one lie McGovern had told him was that the plan to breach Warragamba was being executed on the direct personal order of the Prime Minister.

Finally, at 5.11pm, Reynolds tightened the last nut on the lid of his device's main circuit box, and stood back to admire his handiwork. Four olive-drab bomb trailers, each loaded with twenty thousand pounds of High

Explosive blast bombs, were lined up down the centre of the hangar floor. At first sight it looked like a standard bomb load prepared for road transportation. But closer inspection revealed an intricate network of cables and junction boxes, bolted and bracketed and woven between the individual units. For speed and reliability, Reynolds had kept everything as 'low tech' as possible – the first test would be 'showtime' and every sophistication multiplied exponentially the chances of failure.

What he had built from the elements was a single thirty-six ton bomb – almost three times bigger than theoretically needed to do the job. But as McGovern had pointed out, it had taken three of Wallis's bouncing bombs to breach the Eder Dam, and five the Moehne. In 1943, the Dam Busters had had the luxury of several attempts. Today, there would only be one.

An hour later, a mysterious procession roared out through the Richmond gates and sped away into the dusk up the Nepean River valley. Four RAAF prime movers hauling Reynolds' bomb trailers, their loads cloaked with tarpaulins, were escorted by six conventionally wheeled LAV 25 Light Armoured Vehicles of the 2nd Cavalry Regiment, flown in that morning from Darwin by Hercules transports.

Normally each LAV carried six assault troopers but that evening only four of them did. One vehicle was occupied by the CDF plus a RAAF Police sergeant and two riflemen acting as the CDF's personal bodyguard. The fifth passenger was a civilian – Arthur Reynolds.

Another vehicle also had unusual occupants. The five men wore civilian work clothes, addressed each other by first names and for all the world appeared as a gang of unkempt blue-collar workers. They were there as a result of a second interstate phone call McGovern had made that morning, and they had spent the day in comfort on a journey across the continent as the sole passengers in a conscripted Qantas Boeing 767. The only clue to their identity – a somewhat pointed double bluff – was contained in an article of clothing. The wearer was a rough-looking customer with the kind of face that empties bars, and the article in question was his T-shirt. It was a novelty from the Movie World theme park on the Gold Coast, boldly proclaiming the universal sentiment of film special-effects technicians, *Fuck Art – Let's Wreck Something!* The blue-collar workers were in fact a covert tri-service demolition team, unofficially attached to the Special Air Service Regiment based in Perth. The wearer of the T-shirt, a major in the Royal Australian Engineers, was their OC. Now in fine spirits and looking forward to a rare opportunity of plying their trade, the unofficial designation of this unofficial unit which officially did not even exist was, the Wrecking Crew.

After an uneventful fifty minute drive, at a little after 7pm, the column turned off Silverdale Road at Warragamba and meandered down Farnsworth Avenue towards the dam wall. The area was abandoned so no generators were running and the bush on either side was getting murky. The procession snaked past the building housing the dam scale model and into the picnic area with its playground, barbecues and picnic tables. Far from being reassuring, the cosiness of it all was unnerving and only served to heighten the spookiness of the place.

Eventually the crest of the dam itself loomed up. In the dusk, it appeared as no more than a narrow road bridge crossing a placid lake. Except that there was water on only one side of it. On the other there was a void down to the Warragamba River, which emerged at the base of a one hundred and forty metre drop.

The LAVs peeled off into the bush, clearing the way

for the prime movers to back their trailers onto the crest. But first, the crest parapet had to be removed. The Wrecking Crew debussed as the column was still arriving, and were drilling and running cables before their vehicle had even parked up.

Followed by his bodyguards, Teddy McGovern walked to the dam and watched them. After a moment, Arthur Reynolds strolled up to him and was surprised when McGovern asked for a cigarette. Pulling a pack from his pocket, he remarked, 'Thought you quit years ago.'

McGovern quipped, 'I've lived long enough,' as he lit up with satisfaction.

Reynolds absently reflected that it was an uncharacteristic thing for McGovern to say, as the old friends smoked in silence and watched the Wrecking Crew complete their task. They had barely finished their cigarettes when the man with the T-shirt materialised, and said, 'Take cover, sir.'

McGovern led Reynolds and the bodyguards back into the trees. Seconds later, there were three blasts on a whistle followed by a loud 'crump!' which was felt as much as heard. Then shortly afterwards, the man with the T-shirt called out, 'All clear!'

McGovern and Reynolds walked briskly back to the dam. When they got there, they saw that the one and a half metre concrete parapet along the reservoir side of the crest had gone. Reynolds immediately gave instructions for the placing of the bomb and the Wrecking Crew began driving explosive pinions down into the concrete. Meanwhile, strolling off to pace alone in the shadows, McGovern wondered if the opposition would figure out what he was doing in time to stop him.

Throughout the day, foraging funnelwebs had continued their advance into the suburbs and by mid evening were as far west as Prospect Reservoir. That was only twenty kilometres east of the Nepean-Hawkesbury River. Andrew Lawrie chewed over the situation as he perused maps of the Western Suburbs in the comfort of the Prime Minister's Black Hawk. The custom-fitted aircraft had carried the CDF-elect from Canberra to Richmond and now, just after 8pm, was circling to land. Lawrie wasn't looking forward to the next few minutes. Facing McGovern under the circumstances would not be a picnic. But the formal handover of the CDF's authority had to take place, and at least he had spared his former boss some indignity by coming to him. What the hell! It would soon be done, and then he could get on with the business of saving the country. And in that regard, the news was all good.

The Prime Minister's request to the US President had fallen on surprisingly sympathetic ears, and all afternoon encrypted data had been flashing between the ADF HQ at Russell Offices, Canberra, and the Pentagon. Finally, at 5.17pm Canberra time, the urgent approval sought by the White House from Congress had been granted, and a mission order had been routed to Air Combat Command via the US Strategic Command Headquarters at Offut Air Force Base, Nebraska. Fifty minutes later, in a cacophony of reheated turbofans, three speedily prepared Rockwell International B-1B Lancer bombers had taken off into a clear Hawaiian night, and within minutes were overtaking their own pressure waves as they headed west across the Pacific.

Lawrie could hardly wait. As soon as the radiation dropped to safe levels he would enter Sydney at the head of his troops. And with luck there would be a funnelweb or two left alive for him to torch personally. He could see the newspaper headlines now, and not for the first time regretted that his country no longer bestowed knighthoods.

To retain the whip hand, Lawrie had not warned McGovern of his arrival. So the first Richmond knew about it was when the pilot requested permission to land. Nevertheless as he jumped down onto the tarmac, Lawrie was surprised that no-one came out to meet him. Eventually an aide rustled up transport and the CDF-elect was unceremoniously taken to the Base HQ in a maintenance utility.

Preoccupied with the evacuation which had been sprung on him only an hour before, the Richmond CO was irritated by Lawrie's unannounced appearance, and it took a call to the Chief of Air Operations at Glenbrook to persuade him that what he was being told about the change of CDF was true. At that, the CO's irritation turned into embarrassed anger that he had not been informed. However, after bawling out his staff, it became clear that McGovern had said nothing to anyone at Richmond.

Embarrassment was replaced by intrigue and Lawrie was soon interrogating everybody who had been associated with McGovern throughout the day. The delivery of eighty thousand pounds of bombs from Amberley, Arthur Reynolds working on the bombs under guard all day, and the arrival of the Wrecking Crew could only mean that McGovern was planning a major demolition. But of what?

The 2 CAV major who had furnished McGovern with six LAVs was summoned to the CO's office and proffered the operational order signed by McGovern himself. Scanning the paper, Lawrie read, '. . . *to provide escort for delivery of munitions for protection of the metropolitan water supply at Wallacia.*' Lawrie's stomach tightened.

Wallacia was a village on the border between the shires of Liverpool and Wollondilly, and was unremarkable save for one thing – it was the location of Warragamba Dam.

As Land Commander, Lawrie was well aware of the Warragamba flood risk and so deduced instantly what McGovern was up to. Inwardly, he panicked. If the funnelwebs could be sealed inside the city by flooding, the government would be obliged to reassess Sledgehammer, the reoccupation of Sydney would be postponed and he would be denied his opportunity of glory.

He went to the Communications Centre and was connected immediately to the Prime Minister's Canberra residence on a scramble phone. Richard Bartlett had just returned to The Lodge after his triumph with the Americans, but his euphoria was soon dampened.

'In the name of Christ, Lawrie, how could he do this right under your nose?'

'With respect, Prime Minister, I was following your instructions to leave him alone today to get used to the situation. No-one could have guessed that . . . Jesus Christ! Who could have known he'd pull a stunt like this!'

Bartlett considered. 'Will it work?'

Lawrie was subdued. 'The opinions I'm getting say it will.'

Bartlett flared. 'So what do you suggest, General Lawrie? Perhaps I could phone the US President and say, "Thanks but we don't need your neutron bomb after all! The flaky old bastard I just fired has come up with a better idea that's clean and costs us next to nothing so we'll go with that. Oh, by the way can you lend me three divisions of troops instead, to get our city back!"'

Lawrie was silent.

Bartlett railed, 'I'm going to look a complete fucking idiot in front of the entire world, General Lawrie, so you'd better stop him – or I'll nail *your* fucking arse to that dam!' And he slammed down the phone.

Lawrie was shaking. Thinking fast, he could see only one option. He got through again to Glenbrook, but this time to the Air Commander Australia, who was dumbfounded when the new CDF barked at him, 'Scramble the Hornets!'

As the balloon went up, in the night stillness of the Burragorang Valley, the Wrecking Crew were just lowering the last of Albert Reynolds' bomb trailers into position. The trickiest part of the operation had gone without a hitch and all four trailers were now nestling against the base of Warragamba Dam in a hundred and forty metres of water. After a briefing from Reynolds, the Wrecking Crew's navy diver headed down the boat ramp and disappeared beneath the black, glassy swell. His task was to connect umbilical cables between the trailers, then run a detonating lead to a remote triggering device on shore. That would complete the installation, and transform the assembly into a single, remotely controlled, thirty-six ton bomb.

McGovern pulled out a pack of cigarettes donated by the sergeant of his bodyguard and lit up his sixth cigarette of the evening. He had promised his wife that he would quit smoking some years before after a bout of pneumonia. But his wife had died twelve months previously, and tonight he no longer felt bound by his pledge to her. He was standing alone on a ridge overlooking the dam, watching the Wrecking Crew clearing the last of their equipment, when footsteps padded up behind him and an out-of-breath voice gasped, 'Excuse me, sir.'

McGovern turned to discover the Officer Commanding of the escorting 2 CAV detachment, accompanied by a squad of his assault troops. The young lieutenant was not only breathless, but agitated. McGovern guessed correctly what was going on, but gave no indication of it, saying calmly, 'Yes, Lieutenant?'

'With respect, sir, I am informed by my HQ that our mission here is unauthorised . . . and that you are relieved of command.'

McGovern felt his bodyguards tense up. He looked blankly at the lieutenant, and said nothing. After an electric silence, the lieutenant continued, 'Sir, I am ordered to place you and Mister Reynolds under arrest . . . and to proceed immediately to the First Armoured Regiment's Field Headquarters at Menangle.' His voice was wavering and the 2 CAV troopers with him looked jumpy.

McGovern took the bull by the horns. 'What's your name, Lieutenant?'

'Eliot, sir.'

'Given name?'

'Michael . . . Michael, sir.'

'Who gave you these orders, Lieutenant Eliot, and when?'

'My OC, sir, Major Pierce . . . a minute ago, on the radio.'

'What exactly did Major Pierce say to you?'

'He said, sir, that you are replaced as CDF by General Lawrie . . . and that you no longer have any authority . . . and that I was to take all necessary steps to stop you bombing Warragamba Dam . . . sir.'

McGovern fixed the young man in his gaze, and said, 'Major Pierce is mistaken, Michael. The present emergency is being used as a smokescreen by certain interests to undermine the rule of law in this country. Major Pierce has been deceived by those interests. Do you understand?'

'I . . . er . . .' The lieutenant was trembling.

'Do you understand, Michael?' McGovern repeated, with forcefulness.

The lieutenant was almost in tears. He broke. 'Yes, sir, I understand . . . I'm sorry, sir.'

McGovern looked past Eliot to the assault troopers, 'Who's the senior NCO?'

A pockmarked man stepped forward. 'I am, sir. Troop Sergeant Watts.'

McGovern spoke with relaxed authority. 'Lieutenant Eliot is relieved of duty, Sergeant Watts. Place him under arrest and hold him in isolation in one of the vehicles. Then shut down all communications and tell the radio operator to report to me with a portable.'

Even in the dark, Watts was visibly sweating.

McGovern waited a beat, then said quietly, 'Do it now, Sergeant Watts.'

Watts jumped to attention and snapped, 'Yes sir!' Then he barked commands to the rest of the squad, disarmed his demoralised officer, and led him away.

McGovern watched them go, then turned when he heard the clicks of his bodyguards' safety catches. The guard sergeant scrutinised him with a knowing grin, and said, 'With your permission, sir, we'll stick very close to you from now on.'

McGovern replied stolidly, 'Permission granted, Sergeant,' then looked back to the dam.

The diver was emerging from the water with a coil of cable. Reynolds stepped forward and took it from him, then connected it into a junction box located at the bottom of the boat ramp. Another cable ran up from the junction box, snaking past McGovern to disappear into the trees behind.

His task completed, Reynolds ascended the ridge and reported with satisfaction, 'All done.'

McGovern expected that Lawrie would send airborne troops, which he calculated would not arrive for another ten minutes. What he hadn't counted on was a full-scale air strike. His first inkling of it was as they were returning to the vehicle, and distant thunder rolled in across the still water. McGovern knew that the sound didn't come from any storm. He grabbed Reynolds and urged him on, saying, 'Come on, Arthur, the Indians are on the hill. Let's do it!'

For a second, Reynolds was perplexed. But then realisation of what McGovern had done struck him with the force of a thunderbolt. Devastated, he turned to his old friend, and said, almost matter-of-factly, 'Damn you, Teddy. You've gone and killed us all. Damn you, anyway.'

The first F/A-18 Hornet strike fighter screamed over their heads at two hundred feet just as the flares from the PC-9 marker plane burst and the ground lit up like day.

Reynolds stumbled away, shouting, 'No, Teddy, I won't do it! I'm not going to do it!' Then he looked into the sky, and dashed off in terror.

The bodyguards were shaken but when McGovern barked, 'Bring him back!' they tore off after Reynolds like greyhounds. It was then that two more Hornets screamed over and lobbed 500 pounders at the vehicles. The bombs went wide, blowing tonnes of earth and trees into the air, and McGovern dived under a LAV to shelter from the debris. But when he crawled out again, he saw Reynolds and the bodyguards had been blown to bits.

It was then he became aware of movement across the road, and saw Sergeant Watts and other 2 CAV troopers closing in on him. He had earlier watched Reynolds install the bomb's detonating device in the building which housed the dam model, a kilometre back up the road. It was where the cable from the boat ramp led to. Jumping into the LAV, McGovern hit the starter and the engine roared. Then he stamped on the accelerator and the vehicle leapt away just as bullets ricocheted loudly off its armour.

Three hundred metres on, McGovern looked back and saw two LAVs chasing him. Then the second wave of Hornets hit and the ground erupted in a black wall of earth. McGovern swung onto the road but when he looked again, his pursuers had gone. So he turned back into the trees and raced under their canopy to approach the dam model building from behind.

The building was little more than a shed. The Hornets were ignoring it and still plastering the vehicles at the dam site. McGovern slewed up, jumped out and kicked the hut door open. Reynolds' detonating device was there on the floor. It looked simple enough – a metal box with the cable from the bomb attached to red and black terminals, and four switches – Power Off/On, Safety Off/On, Arm/Disarm, and Detonate.

McGovern put the power switch to On and a green light glowed. Then he put the safety to Off and the green light went amber. Then he put the arming switch to Arm, and the light went to red. Finally, with a feeling of light headedness, he threw the Detonate switch . . . and nothing happened. He waited in case there was a delay, but still nothing happened. Panicky, he threw the switch Off and On again, but still nothing. Then his stomach knotted as he realised that the cable must have been cut by the bombs.

McGovern fumbled as he disconnected the terminals. Then he grabbed up the detonator, dashed back out to the vehicle and sped away. More flares lit up as a Hornet put a salvo of rockets into the road. The explosions threw up tonnes of asphalt and McGovern had to swerve violently to avoid being buried.

A hundred metres on there were vehicles on their sides and bodies everywhere. Some were in civilian clothes, one in a T-shirt proclaiming, *Fuck Art – Let's Wreck Something!*

McGovern zigzagged through, trying to stay under the trees, but he was certain that he'd had it when from nowhere a Hornet dived straight at him. He actually saw the 500 pounder dropping but miraculously it skimmed over him and thirty metres back blew the corpses of the Wrecking Crew sky high.

Bursting out of the trees, McGovern saw the boat ramp two hundred metres ahead. At the same time something crossed the moon and he looked up to see a dozen parachutes descending. He slewed to the ramp, grabbed the detonator and jumped out of the vehicle. But he hadn't gone three steps when bullets stitched the ground right next to him, and he dived and rolled the last few metres to the detonator junction box.

The paratroops dropped into the trees as McGovern wrenched the box open and saw it had the same terminals as the detonator. He disconnected the leads and was re-connecting them to the detonator when there were shouts from behind, and his back exploded in searing agony.

The bullet passed through his lung and as he was thrown onto his side, he saw a man staggering towards him, covered in blood, waving a pistol, and hollering, 'You murdering bastard, I'll kill you, I'll fucking kill you!' It was Michael Eliot.

McGovern turned back to the detonator, connected the bomb cable then threw the On switch. The light glowed green. Then he threw the Safety and the light turned amber. Then behind him there was a commotion as the paratroopers arrived, and he heard Eliot screaming, 'There – on the boat ramp – he's got the detonator. Kill him! Kill him *now*!'

McGovern threw the Arm switch and the light turned red. Then bursts from three Steyrs cut him cleanly in half, and threw the top of him forward across the switch marked Detonate.

Like the skin of a gigantic bass drum, the ground quivered . . . and a column of white water arose out of the jet black lake. It rose in slow motion, going up and up and up until it peaked at five hundred metres. And there it seemed to freeze, and hang motionless in the moonlight, like a curtain of the finest shimmering crystal.

From the boat ramp it would have looked spectacular, but there was no-one left alive there to see it. Near McGovern's bisected corpse, Eliot's and the paratroopers' brains had all been literally scrambled by the explosion.

But the Hornet pilots saw it, and so did the crew of the PC-9, who gaped in awe as the lake beneath them boiled like a giant witches' cauldron.

As the water column descended, it atomised into mist and the dam and the lake were enshrouded in cloud. The aircraft climbed above it and circled as they waited, until eventually the moisture precipitated, and the dam wall slowly reappeared.

At first it looked normal, except for the mountainous waves slopping over the crest. But as the lake began to settle, the spill did not quell and it became apparent that the water was no longer washing over the dam, but pouring through it.

Half metre cracks had opened from the crest to the riverbed and were visibly widening by the second. Then the fliers' hearts stopped dead as the entire centre section of the dam lifted, and crumbled like rotten plaster under the weight of two trillion litres of water.

The breach was a hundred metres across. And the water gushing through it in a torrential foaming jet shot horizontally downstream for three hundred metres.

For many minutes, the pilots flew around and

around, looking down on the cataclysm as flitting insects might look down an apocalypse. Until eventually, out of the silence, their commander said, 'Let's go home,' and they left the bones of Warragamba Dam in the care of the dead.

A ten metre wall of water thundered down the Nepean Valley that night, sweeping before it buildings, vehicles and human beings both alive and dead. And when it reached Penrith thirteen minutes after the breach, a lake began to form exactly as had been predicted.

Andrew Lawrie got the news in the Prime Minister's Black Hawk en route to Canberra at 9.02pm. He didn't notice how much later it was that he stepped down onto the roof helipad at Russell Offices. Preoccupied, he went alone to the CDF's suite on the fourth floor which McGovern's staff had vacated some hours earlier. And for the first time as its occupant, Andrew Lawrie entered the inner sanctum that was the private office of the Chief of the Australian Defence Force.

He looked over the vast Jarrah desk with its high leather chair, but did not sit at it. He looked at the imposing glass-doored bookcases housing volumes of military reference, but did not open them. He passed by the hospitality room, and the conference room, and the private bedroom, but without so much as glancing into them. All he did was go to one of the tall, undraped windows, and gaze vacantly out into the night.

9

The Prime Minister heard about Warragamba before Andrew Lawrie did. But he decided to let the new CDF stew. He concluded that the man was incompetent or unlucky, and he didn't want someone who was either around at that moment.

Bartlett deliberated on the situation as he studied the three pages of single-spaced typescript which had been delivered into his hand by a RAAF special messenger at precisely 9pm. The letter, which McGovern had written at Richmond as Arthur Reynolds had laboured in the sealed hangar, outlined the late CDF's reasoning for his actions, and proposed his alternative to the neutron bomb.

But after an uncomfortable hour, the Prime Minister decided that he had nothing to be concerned about. He would argue that it was by no means certain that the flooding of the Nepean-Hawkesbury would cut off the funnelwebs' advance to the north and west. And even if it did, there was no guarantee the southern corridor could be fully secured. More importantly, it could be days or even weeks before a single UN soldier arrived on Australian soil, by which time the floods might have subsided and the funnelwebs have long broken out. In regard to the breaching of Warragamba, history would record it as the deranged act of a man tragically broken by pressure, which is the story he would have disseminated immediately.

So the plan to use the neutron bomb would stand. And Bartlett could not only still look forward to his hundred million dollars from Czarnecki's people, but also to the potential benefits of another relationship. The American President's reaction to the Prime Minister's request had initially been circumspect, and he had taken time to consult with his advisers. However when he had called back, he had been warmly amenable, and taken the line that Uncle Sam was only too pleased to aid its ally in this time of crisis. If his secret terms were taken into account then his benevolence might be somewhat less surprising. However in ceding vast tracts of northern Australia for a new US military base, Richard Bartlett had gained the impression that entering into further such arrangements could result in substantial personal reward.

The Prime Minister looked at his watch. It was 10.10pm. The bombers were less than two hours out now. He had called a cabinet briefing for 10.40 to be followed by an emergency session of the House of Representatives at 11.00. He would have to box cleverly in both sessions to get his way. But he was confident that he would. He needed no stronger argument for extreme and decisive action than the ten thousand refugees that were haemorrhaging into Canberra every hour.

He gathered his papers into his attache case then took out a digital mobile phone and dialled a number in Austria. After an exchange of passwords and the keying of a PIN, the voice at the other end confirmed that fifty million dollars had been deposited into the specified numbered account that day.

Bartlett pressed End and put the mobile back into his attache case. Czarnecki had been good to his word.

However as he walked out to the LTD that was always waiting in the driveway, Bartlett mused that his new fortune may now only be the first blush in an embarrassment of riches.

At twelve minutes to midnight, two hundred kilometres east of Sydney Heads, the three Lancer bombers decelerated to subsonic speed and commenced a descent to five thousand feet. Four hundred and fifty kilometres to the south-west, two dozen pairs of eyes anxiously monitored the bombers' progress on computer displays. The nuclear-hardened operational control centre in the sub-basement of Russell Offices was hushed, making the background hum of the airconditioning unusually noticeable. The only other sound was the monotone mid-west voice of a USAF Air Operations Officer, counting off the time and the distance of the formation to its target.

The visual techno-babble flickering all around Richard Bartlett was Greek to him. But one screen had his rapt attention. It was a real-time transmission from a night-vision camera in the wing tip of the leading aircraft, and across the middle of the picture, distant but discernible, was the thread of the New South Wales coastline.

Since he had arrived at Russell from the Parliament House, Bartlett's feelings had been mixed. The cabinet briefing and the emergency session of the House of Reps had been stormy, but confusion and fear had won the day and Bartlett had extracted acquiescence to the neutron bomb from his harrowed and panicked co-parliamentarians. Despite that, the reality of what it meant had only fully hit him in the control centre and for an uncomfortable fifteen minutes, his feet had felt decidedly chilly. But now, as the coastline loomed up, his reservations were swamped by a sensation he had not previously known –

the rush of the hunter as he relentlessly closes on his kill.

Engrossed, Bartlett was only half listening as the voice of the Air Operations Officer said, 'Southern Star One to Apache Leader – Time On Target, nine minutes – bomb run commencing four minutes thirty – course good – speed good – come ahead, Geronimo.'

The disembodied reply came in a Texas drawl, 'Geronimo to Southern Star One, I thank you, Southern Star – we are over the hill and have visual on the target – looking good.'

For most of the twenty-five people in the room – half of them RAAF and USAF technical staff, the remainder politicians, brass hats and the inevitable 'observers' from the unlisted third-floor offices of the US embassy – the atmosphere was unbearably tense. But the powerfully built man sitting next to Bartlett appeared cool and collected. His uniform bore the insignia of a USAF general, making him the senior American officer present and, as such, the President's personal representative. Finding it difficult to contain himself, Bartlett turned to him and said, 'This is a milestone in the friendship between our two countries, General Coleman. For the United States to expose herself to the criticism which will inevitably follow this operation is an act of great courage. Australia is grateful.'

General Coleman smiled graciously, and responded with Ivy League charm, 'Prime Minister, it is only gratifying to us that we can be of assistance at this time.'

As Bartlett turned back to the video monitor, Coleman smiled inwardly at his own sycophancy. For the military, friendship wasn't in it. He and his Pentagon colleagues could not believe their luck at the chance to test their most reviled weapon on a live target. It was too good to be true.

'Southern Star One to Geronimo – Time On Target, five-oh minutes – bomb run commencing in thirty, that's three-zero, seconds – looking good . . . looking good . . . five, four, three, two, one – commence bomb run – break now.'

'Geronimo to Southern Star One – breaking now, I say breaking now – commencing bomb run.'

A mile above the Tasman Sea, the two trailing Lancers – one an observer plane, the other an electronic warfare aircraft with its belly full of computers and radar equipment – lifted their noses and peeled off to the left and right. The lead aircraft, call sign Geronimo, was the mission plane, and held its course straight and level for the heart of Sydney.

The city was in darkness but through the night-vision cameras it could have been midday. Bartlett's heart pumped so hard he thought Coleman would hear it as the familiar shapes of Sydney Tower and the MLC Centre loomed out of the fuzz. Then three adjacent screens flickered into life as the observer plane's cameras came on line, and the Central Business District was displayed from overhead like a street directory. Coleman watched Bartlett out of the corner of his eye, and wondered what it must feel like to be about to nuke your own largest city.

'Geronimo to Southern Star One – turning onto final approach – fifteen seconds to bomb release . . .'

His every nerve tingling, Bartlett involuntarily sat forward. There, on a monitor relaying a close shot, he clearly saw tiny black dots scurrying to and fro through the streets. The funnelwebs were frantic, perhaps alarmed by the bomber's engines, or perhaps from some intuition of what was about to happen.

'Ten seconds to bomb release.'

Now others noticed the funnelwebs, and a hum of revulsion spread through the room. Soon all eyes were locked on the screens in morbid enthralment.

'Five seconds . . . three, two, one – *bombs away!*'

With his final words, the pilot pushed his throttles through 'the gate' and the Lancer's afterburners punched the big plane away to the horizon.

Alone in the sky, a black canister floated down towards the Pool of Reflection in Hyde Park. The bomber which had dropped it could no longer even be heard, and the only sound was the whisper of the night air through the canister's parachute lines.

The silence at Russell was deafening. Bartlett was on a knife edge. For a moment, time seemed suspended. Then, at a second past midnight, the monitors went white.

There was a collective gasp, then for several seconds, nothing . . . save a crackle of static. But gradually the cameras recovered and as the images reappeared, the scenes they depicted were utterly gut wrenching.

The shots, all close now, showed the monsters vomiting uncontrollably, and the contents of their intestines pouring out of them in jets of bloody excrement.

Bartlett was repulsed by the awfulness of it. But as the funnelwebs collapsed, he could barely contain his mounting elation. Until from the limits of his consciousness there arose a clamour of voices, and he became aware that the room around him had erupted in wild jubilation.

General Coleman was overwhelmed. He pulled Bartlett bodily out of his seat and grasping his hand, exclaimed, 'My God, Mister Prime Minister, we've done it, goddammit! They're all dying!'

Screen after screen of a video wall flickered into life as unmanned camera airships drifted over the city. And everywhere, the story was the same – streets, parks, backyards, rooftops, all littered with the corpses of funnelwebs. Bartlett studied each screen intently, until finally he was sure that there was nothing left alive anywhere.

Fleetingly the unknown number of human beings who had died crossed his mind, but he justified it to himself as a merciful release. In the real world, he rationalised, the end *can* justify the means, and those few lives were a small price to pay for the survival of the nation.

No-one would ever know the actual number of people killed by the neutron bomb. But it had been many more than anyone had dared to estimate. It was true that in the preceding hours there had been thousands of suicides – those for whom the pain and the wretchedness had become intolerable. But those still alive had retained a grain of hope – few would have chosen death at that moment. Indeed many were planning escape, and some, albeit few, could have made it. Now all of them were dead, and one man in the operational control centre that night stood to profit very handsomely because of it.

As far as Richard Bartlett could tell, with the exception of the buildings around Hyde Park, the city was structurally unscathed. It appeared just as Brigadier Phelps had predicted. Inwardly, Bartlett glowed.

Amidst popping corks and gushing congratulations, the Air Operations Officer's speaker crackled, 'Geronimo to Southern Star One – looks like we kicked some serious ass down there.'

The Air Operations Officer sounded almost friendly. 'You sure did, Geronimo. We thank you and say, God speed.'

'Geronimo to Southern Star One – you are most welcome, Australia. Geronimo to War Party – fun's over, boys. Let's go home.'

An aide pushed a champagne glass into Richard Bartlett's hand and suggested he might like to speak to the US President. Finding it impossible to wipe the smile from his face, Bartlett fronted with all the seemliness he could muster, replying, 'Yes, of course. Please arrange a call on a secure phone.'

As the aide disappeared from the room, Bartlett again surveyed the expanse of the video wall. The CBD was certainly tarnished, blackened by the nuclear flash and salted with shattered glass. But in six months it would be as good as new, life would have returned to normal and he would be relishing the benefit.

The celebrations were well under way and everyone else had lost interest in the monitor screens. So Bartlett was alone when he thought he glimpsed movement in the shadows at the entrance to Museum Station. The airship camera platform was drifting, so Bartlett reasoned that it must have been a glint of moonlight. But then he remembered that the moon would be obscured by dust.

He looked again. Nothing. He looked around at all the screens, into the darkest recesses where the shadows were blackest and the night-vision lenses did not reach. Still nothing. Bartlett shrugged to himself. He was getting jumpy. There was so much at stake, it was hardly surprising.

'I have the White House on the scramble phone in the Chief of Staff's office, Prime Minister. The President will take your call immediately.'

Bartlett turned to his aide, and said, 'Okay, thank you. Lead the way.'

Bartlett followed through the bustle, smiling graciously, accepting compliments, and was just going out through the door . . . when somebody screamed.

He knew instantly why. So he had to swallow hard on the football in his throat as he forced himself to turn, and look back at the video wall.

There, on every screen, from every entrance to the railway, dozens of new monster funnelwebs were pouring up into the streets. They darted and froze – they reared back and trembled – they spun and leapt and quivered in a crazed dance. Until in the same instant, they all fell upon their dead progenitors, and ripped them apart and devoured them in a cannibalistic frenzy.

The similarity with the species from which the monsters had derived was fading. This new generation was plainly a different form. They were much more massively powerful, with their eight legs like tree trunks and their fangs now so high on their heads that they almost pointed forwards.

The observers all gawped as the new mutants postured over their carrion like a deranged army crazed with the stench of death. And when as if at some secret signal, they scattered in every direction, the Prime Minister knew that Jack Fitzgerald's worst prediction had come fatefully true.

However at that moment, Richard Bartlett felt no regret, nor any fear. He knew that he would soon be overwhelmed by those feelings but for now he was thankful that the only thing he felt was numb. He nodded for his aide to lead on. And as he walked from the control centre, the Prime Minister focussed his mind exclusively on recomposing his report to the US President.

Bartlett's principal lieutenant in the neutron bomb debacle had already left. Andrew Lawrie had slipped out quietly to return to his suite unnoticed, and it being 12.17am, the fourth floor of Russell Offices was otherwise deserted. So nobody actually heard the single gunshot. In fact it was not until twenty minutes later that the suicide was discovered, when an aide who had been looking for the CDF went into his office.

Lawrie's corpse was seated in the swivelling leather chair and slumped across the massive Jarrah desk. The

9mm bullet had splattered his brains all over the wall and in his shock, the aide's initial reaction was somewhat callous. He thought how inconsiderate the CDF had been not to shoot himself in the bathroom, where the mess would have been much easier to clean up. It seemed in death as in life, Andrew Lawrie's deeds had been characterised by indifference towards the feelings of others.

It was the night that the light came – the cleansing light, the replenishing light – the light that expunged the old and elevated the new. A threat to the nascent form had lain in a potential conflict for ascendancy between the new generation and their antecedents. Now that conflict had been obviated by the portentous deliverance of the light.

Thus unopposed, the new order dispersed in great strength. To the east, west and north, they found their way barred by water, and in those places they prowled the shorelines, devouring whatever sustenance they could find. But to the south their way was clear, and soon they were venturing beyond the terrain that had previously been held by their forebears.

Helen Parkes had never really understood the meaning of the word, fear. But since eight o'clock that morning, she had learnt it. She and Jack Fitzgerald had spent two hours on their bellies in the undergrowth, as time and again they were nearly discovered. The men who'd shot them down knew a man and a woman had escaped the crash – they must have spotted them jumping as the helicopter hit. And now they were everywhere, combing through the undergrowth like jackals.

Helen did not see their faces but the threats they

shouted of what they would do if they found her made her flesh crawl. At one point she thought it was over when one of them stood so close she saw his shoes – they were runners, torn and filthy, and spattered with what looked like blood. The man stopped within a metre of her, poking around with a hunting knife taped to a stick. As he edged nearer, and the blade thrust closer, she felt Fitzgerald lying next to her tensing to leap. But somehow the man missed them, and thankfully went off to search somewhere else.

The ground behind them rose steeply to a rocky overhang. It was a difficult climb and Fitzgerald guessed their pursuers wouldn't go up there. So when he thought it was safe, he indicated to Helen and the two of them scrambled painfully through the brush and up to the hiding place.

No sooner had they got there than they heard voices approaching. Seconds later, thirty metres below, their pursuers emerged from the trees and for the first time Jack and Helen got a look at them. They were a motley mob, like bandits out of an Italian western – ten men dressed in a mixture of jeans and combat clothing, with greasy bandannas and running shoes or Dr Martens boots. They all had firearms, and bandoliers worn criss-crossed Mexican style, and machetes or commando knives in their belts. Their guns were mostly .22 rifles or double-barrelled shotguns, but one had an AK.47, and another, a World War II Sten gun.

As they continued west, two of them guffawed inane obscenities until the Sten gunner barked and shut them up. Fitzgerald looked more closely at the Sten gunner. He was a hundred and ninety centimetres, a muscle-bound thirty and obviously the leader. He sported a 'number one' haircut and, like all of them, a tattoo on his forehead. Fitzgerald tried to make it out but he was too far away, and soon the bandits merged back into the trees, and seconds later, were gone.

'Who the hell *are* they?' Helen rasped, relieved but distressed.

'Human vermin,' Fitzgerald growled. 'This country's got its share.'

He felt suddenly exhausted. He'd barely slept since that first day at North Ryde and now tiredness and dehydration had caught up with him. He thought he would just lie a moment and take a short nap, but no sooner had he closed his eyes than he was totally dead to the world.

When he awoke it was dark, and his every joint ached. The heat of day had given way to the dew of evening and he could feel the dampness deep in his bones. After a moment, he rolled over painfully and edged to the shape of Helen lying ahead in the shadows.

'What time is it?' Jack croaked, his throat the only dry part of him.

Helen whispered, 'Almost nine – you slept for ten hours.'

'Jesus.' He wished he felt rested for it. 'Did you get some sleep?'

'Not really . . . you needed it more than me.'

Fitzgerald felt grateful, if a little foolish. 'Any visitors?'

'No, not human ones, anyway. Some cute little animals checked us out a few times.'

'Possums?'

'Whatever they are, we're hogging their water – take a look.' Helen indicated back into the rocks.

Fitzgerald crawled back in and after a few metres found a trickle of runoff. Helen had cupped some big leaves under it and they contained the best part of two litres. Jack gulped it down, not believing that warm muddy water could taste so good. Feeling better, he returned to Helen, impressed.

'You used to be a girl scout or something?'

'Summer camps in Maine – amazing what you remember. Not so lucky with food though – I couldn't find anything.'

'Raw possum for supper?'

Helen winced. 'No thanks. But ask me later and I might have changed my mind.'

'We may have no choice, if we're still out here in a day or two.'

'But we won't be – the highway can only be thirty miles west of here.'

'Less. But without food and in the heat, we won't move very fast.'

Helen considered. 'We should go now, while it's cool.'

'And easier to hide.' Jack smiled, trying to appear casual. But both of them knew that the elements were the least of their worries.

There was a heavy 'crump', and the earth shook.

'What the hell was that?' Helen snapped.

Fitzgerald jumped up and pulled her out into the open, saying, 'If it's an earthquake, the last place to be is in a cave!' The tremor had unnerved him.

They waited for several minutes, but when no more shaking came, they sorted themselves out and picked their way back down to the foot of the slope. And there they headed west into the inky, tangled bush, still wondering what had caused the violent tremor. They had no way of knowing that what had felt to them like an earthquake had in fact been the death knell of Edward McGovern, and of Warragamba Dam.

For two hours they travelled, guided by Jack's childhood knowledge of the southern sky. Luckily the night was clear, allowing them to navigate and giving more than enough moonlight to see by.

But even with only two short rests, they were making less than three kilometres an hour. The country was not hard, being rolling and sparsely wooded farmland, but to avoid being seen they had to skirt along hedgerows and they stopped constantly to listen out for bandits. At first, the song of crickets covered the sounds they made. But later, when the night fell still, their footfalls seemed amplified, and walking quietly slowed them down to a crawl.

Since leaving the overhang, they'd seen no sign of habitation. So their apprehension was tinged with relief when they came to a farmhouse. The place had been looted then gutted by fire, and as they combed through the debris they saw the looters had indulged in the spoils – the entire area was littered with beer cans and broken wine bottles. Both of them wondered about the fate of the occupants, but neither made any mention of it to the other.

There was no food, but they found some useful things in the yard – a paring knife, three metres of rope and a screw-top milk container. The milk container was gold. It meant they could carry water. They searched for somewhere to fill it but the taps were dry. Then Jack spotted a dam a short distance away and they headed across to it excitedly.

When they got there, the question that had been in their minds was answered. The dam was empty but lying on the bottom were five dead bodies. They'd been in there for days and had blown up like balloons, but were still recognisable as a man, a woman and three young children. All of them were naked and had their hands tied with wire, and all had terrible wounds and missing body parts. In the dark it wasn't apparent how they'd finally been killed but it seemed certain that they'd all died in terrible agony.

Jack and Helen had seen many corpses in the past days, but these were different. These were not the victims of mutant spiders, but of other human beings. Jack recalled a pundit once saying that whether you regarded such people as sick or evil depended on your world view. He found himself trembling as he pondered that for these luckless people, such distinctions were absurdly academic.

The sight of the gruesome family was profoundly shocking, and as they walked away in silence, Jack and Helen were both deeply disturbed.

They pressed on, more mindful than ever of the fate they could expect if they were caught. Then after a long and arduous climb, they found themselves at the crest of an escarpment. The ascent of the dip slope had been exhausting so Helen slumped down to rest against a rock. Meanwhile Jack went to spot the lie of the land beyond the steeper scarp ahead.

Below, it was black as a coal mine. But in the stillness Jack heard a sound drifting up from the valley floor. He listened, and after a couple of seconds, his spirits soared – it was running water, and by the sound of it, not far away. He was turning to tell Helen, to where she was sitting behind the rock, just turning past the black northern sky – when instantaneously the sun rose – and Jack was looking straight at it.

Bathed in an eerie light, Jack groped at his blinded eyes and collapsed to his knees. Helen was stultified but somehow forced herself to stand, and when she did, and looked north, what she saw there was incomprehensible.

A massive fireball was rising over a matchstick city, and increasingly obscuring the stars as it distended into a dull red mushroom cloud.

Jack had told Helen of the proposal to use the neutron bomb but neither of them had believed it could happen. Now, at a minute past midnight, she was looking at the reality of it.

Fitzgerald was on all fours with his eyes wide and staring, and ranting, 'They've done it! Jesus Christ! They've fucking done it!'

Helen waved frantically in his face, and asked, 'Can you see anything, Jack . . . anything at all?'

Fitzgerald raved, 'Not a thing! They've fucked us, Helen! They've fucked us all to hell!'

Helen panicked. 'Oh, God! God Almighty! What do we do?'

Fitzgerald railed, 'We get off this ridge – down into the valley. There's water down there. You'll have to lead me!'

Helen grabbed Jack's arm and led him off, and after a few steps the nuclear day was fading. The fireball rose into the stratosphere where it dissipated quickly, and soon they were stumbling down the slope in unnatural blackness.

The water was further down than it sounded and when eventually they came to it, was little more than a rivulet. But with the thirst of a lifetime they pushed their faces into it, and drank and drank until their bellies were fit to burst.

When she could drink no more, Helen lay back, her head pounding. She knew if they went any longer without food they would make easy prey for the bandits. And now she had to find it alone, and take care of Jack as well. But she had nothing left to give – she was utterly finished – she didn't even have the strength to stand up. Lying there helpless, she started sobbing inconsolably, and had all but resigned to despair . . . when the wind came.

It came with the suddenness of an explosion – a wrathful, howling gale which hit the trees with the impact of a locomotive. Jack and Helen hugged the ground, hardly knowing what was happening but certain that at any second they would be killed.

The nuclear wind passed as quickly as it came.

But no sooner had it gone than they were hit by a flash storm in its wake. The sky was all Gothic thunder and lightning, and as the wind howled and the rain lashed, they again heard the voices of the bandits.

As they scrambled into the undergrowth, a dozen figures emerged onto the opposite bank. The din of the storm made their words impossible to make out but Helen could see in the lightning that a fight was in progress.

Two men were abusing each other as the rest gathered in a semi-circle, swilling wine. Then one of the quarrellers hit the other and sent him sprawling in the mud. The assailant kicked the downed man viciously. Then he dived straight on top of him and they grappled ferociously, punching and kicking and eye-gouging without constraint.

Helen put her lips to Jack's ear and rasped, 'They're trying to kill each other,' when a gunshot exploded.

Her heart in her mouth, Helen looked back to see the assailant pointing a pistol and the other man flailing on the ground. Then the assailant drew a machete and as Helen watched in shock, he viciously cleaved his adversary's skull, over and over again.

Eventually the blows waned, and the assailant stepped back, and looked down.

What had been his victim's head was a bloody mash of brains and skull bone and mud.

With a maniacal grin, the assailant then looked up at the onlookers, and bellowed, 'Anyone else wanna lead?'

Nobody did.

The assailant looked into each of their eyes, but none of them looked back into his. So he laughed, and rubbed at the stubble on his head as a minion stepped forward with his bandoliers, and his Sten gun.

Helen was trying so hard not to retch she almost choked. Then in a lightning flash she noticed one of the onlookers was smaller than the rest. Fighting nausea, she peered into the sheeting rain but at first could not make the figure out. Until a deafening clap of thunder was accompanied by multiple lightning flashes, and Helen saw clearly that the smaller figure was a teenaged girl.

Triumphant, the Sten gunner barked, 'We're outta here,' then strutted off into the bush. The others shambled after him, and as they passed by in a file, Helen got a closer look at the girl. She was seventeen or eighteen, with long dark hair, not pretty but striking, and strong-looking, like she'd been raised on a farm. It struck Helen that she may have been from the family in the dam, or if not, from a family very like it.

Whatever, she was not there by choice. She looked terrified as she was herded along by the bandit with the AK.47. Like the others, he had a tattoo on his forehead. And as he passed close to her, Helen saw it clearly, and she shivered. Because the tattoo was of a spider – a funnelweb spider – and drawn in such a way that it was plainly the sign of a cult.

After the bandits had left, Helen could barely breathe. But eventually, she whispered, 'They're gone,' and buried her face.

Jack's head was thrown back and he was drinking

all the rain he could swallow. He spat out the last of it, and said, 'Okay – give them a minute, then we'll follow.'

Helen thought she couldn't have heard him right. 'Follow . . . the bandits?'

'Yes.'

Her heart skipped. 'What for?' Then she felt frightened, and snapped testily, 'What the hell for?'

'Because they'll have food.'

Helen was suddenly angry with him. 'So how do we get it from them – just ask politely?'

Flat voiced, he said, 'I don't know how we get it. But if we don't eat, we'll get sick. And if we get sick, we can't travel. And if we can't travel, we're finished. This isn't a fucking theme park – it's the New South Wales bush. And if you don't have food and water out here, you die!'

Manic thoughts zapped around Helen's skull. She'd have to be crazy to follow those madmen. She wasn't hungry now anyway, and she wasn't crazy either. Or was she? Was she crazy to think she might wake up and discover this was a nightmare? Or was she crazy to believe something would turn up and everything would be fine . . . like it always did . . . in the real world . . . in civilisation?

She realised she was on the edge. She knew that hunger and shock and fear were getting to her, and that she was close to cracking. It scared her – it scared her half to death – and she was oddly relieved to discover that she was terrified again.

Despite that, or maybe because of it, she said resignedly, 'Okay,' and took Fitzgerald's arm and led him in pursuit of the bandits.

It was dawn when they found them. The storm had passed and the sky was a clear, cobalt blue. The coming of the day had sharpened Helen's mind and in the crisp early light, she could see where the bandits were.

Beyond a slow muddy river at the base of a bushy slope, there was an old stone farm cottage. Oil lights burned inside, three battered utes were outside, and Helen recognised the two men who were pretending to work in the yard. They were the dummies the Sten gunner had bawled out below the overhang, only yesterday morning but more than a lifetime ago.

Whoever lived there had left in a hurry or fallen victim to the bandits – clothes, furniture and household things were scattered everywhere, and in the midst of it, the dummies were making heavy weather of cutting firewood.

For no reason, in her mind, Helen christened them Rosencrantz and Guildenstern, after the characters from *Hamlet* revived in a contemporary play. Rosencrantz had nearly severed Guildenstern's foot with a chainsaw, and Guildenstern had reacted by pulling a Rambo knife and threatening to cut Rosencrantz's balls off and feed them to the chickens.

In other circumstances they might have been amusing. But this morning, Helen didn't appreciate the humour. What she did appreciate, and what had grabbed her attention immediately, were the chickens Guildenstern had referred to in his tirade. The henhouse and chicken run were at the side of the cottage, and as far as she could see held about a dozen birds. Whether it was eggs or a chicken she got she didn't care, but one way or the other she wasn't leaving there without breakfast.

Helen was with Jack a hundred metres up the bushy slope, hidden behind the trunk of a fallen tree. And since they'd arrived twenty minutes earlier, the voices in the cottage had been swelling with drunken arguments.

The door flew open and the Sten gunner stepped

out, the gun trailing limply in his hand. Rosencrantz and Guildenstern immediately busied themselves, like schoolboys caught ducking their chores. The Sten gunner swayed in the doorway, and drained the last drop from a whisky bottle. Then he hurled the bottle at Rosencrantz, and snarled, 'What the fuck are youse doing . . . growin' the fuckin' wood?'

The bottle shattered at Rosencrantz's feet, causing him to jump, and the Sten gunner broke into fits of laughter. Then he staggered into the yard, unzipped his fly and urinated over the meagre woodpile they had stacked.

Rosencrantz and Guildenstern looked affronted, but stood sheepishly, and said nothing. When he'd finished, the Sten gunner glared at them with contempt. Then he zipped up his fly, and slurred, 'Fuck youse anyway – I'm goin' for a swim.'

Slinging the Sten gun, he turned and headed off along the river bank, and no sooner had he disappeared than Rosencrantz and Guildenstern were back inside the cottage.

Helen had been watching around the end of the tree trunk and giving Jack a hushed running commentary. Now ducking back beside him, she said, 'Looks like he's gone for awhile, so now's the best chance . . . before it's too light.'

As Helen loosened her runners and pulled up her socks, Jack worried. Tangling with the bandits didn't seem such a good idea now, and Helen going down there alone was insane.

'Let's wait,' he urged. 'They'll head off later – we can raid the place then.'

Retying her laces, Helen said, 'They could be in there for days. I have to eat *now*.'

She looked again at the cottage. Inside, glass

smashed and there was a peel of laughter, but the yard remained empty. So she said, 'Stay here,' and was gone, leaving Fitzgerald amazed at her audacity. There was clearly a hidden side to Helen Parkes.

The descent to the foot of the slope was through dense bush and it took her a couple of minutes to cover the distance. Then when she arrived at the tree line, between her and the cottage, there was the river.

Hidden in the undergrowth, Helen surveyed it. It was turbid and slow moving – too slow to cover the sound of her crossing. The far bank was twenty metres away and stood a metre and a half above the water. Beyond, the upward-sloping ground was scattered with boulders and elephant grass for another forty metres. Then around the cottage yard there was a low dry stone wall, which at its closest was only ten metres from the front door.

She decided to wade or swim across, then to watch from the far bank until she was sure she hadn't been seen. Then she would dash to the dry stone wall and wait again. If all was still clear, she would crawl around the wall to the closest point to the chicken run. Then it would be luck whether she could get to the chickens, grab one or some eggs, and get back to the river undetected.

She looked again at the cottage. Things seemed quieter. Maybe the bandits had drunk themselves into a stupor. Remembering the Sten gunner, she peered up and down the river, but there was no sign of him. The yard was still empty, so she decided to go for it. She took three deep breaths. Then she crawled fast out of the undergrowth and slid down into the dark brown water.

It was deeper than she expected, and for a moment it took her breath away. But then she was breast-stroking strongly, and before long she grabbed some tree roots and pulled herself into the far bank.

She stayed there gasping, clinging to the wet earth and counting the seconds as she waited for the hue and cry. Ten, twenty, thirty seconds passed, but when finally she reached sixty, she decided that she mustn't have been seen.

She chanced a look over the bank and saw that from this low angle the bottom of the cottage was obscured. So she pulled herself up and crawled fast on all fours until she was close enough to stand and sprint the last fifteen metres to the wall.

She dropped against the flinty stone and sat back with her knees under her chin. Again she started counting but then realised if she'd been spotted, the last thing she should do was stay there. So she moved off, hugging the wall and scampering along like a rodent.

She came to a corner and peeked round it. The coast was clear. She listened, and heard the bandits in the cottage, talking in subdued drunken voices. She moved on, and came to a place which she guessed was near the chickens. There was a gap in the wall with a broken gate. She looked through and sure enough, a few paces off, there was the chicken run.

Helen's heart thumped. She could hardly believe her own boldness. There were no windows on this side so the chicken run was obscured from the bandits. Summoning her resolve, she shot a last look around. Then she sprang up and made it to the chicken run in eight bounds flat.

The hens were scratching at their feed and ignored Helen as she prised open the gate. Then as she stepped in two birds fluttered away, but settled again and continued their pecking, oblivious.

It then occurred to Helen that she had never killed

anything before. Could she really ring a chicken's neck, and so quietly as not to be heard? Queasy, she decided on the soft option and went on into the rusty tin henhouse.

Inside it was dark and clammy, and stank of chicken shit. But there in the laying boxes were nine or ten beautiful fresh eggs. At the sight of them, Helen forgot about danger – she grabbed three of them, cracked them open and swallowed them straight down raw. They hit her stomach like lead and for a second she thought she would puke, but the nausea passed quickly and as her system came back to life, she felt the onset of ravenous hunger.

At that moment, a hapless chicken strutted in. Without a thought, Helen grabbed it and before it could even squawk, she had wrung its neck and was smothering its convulsions.

When the chicken fell still, Helen dropped it. And as she stood gazing down at it, she was so shocked by what she had done that when she first heard the screaming, she thought that somehow it was coming from the chicken. But snapping out of it she realised it was coming from the cottage, and was the sound of a human being in the throes of terrible torment.

Helen forced herself to go to the henhouse door and look outside. The yard was still empty but the screaming went on and on, unending. Helen wanted it to stop. She covered her ears to shut it out. But whatever she did, the screams pierced into her, and tore her apart.

Her mind went numb, and something overtook her. She went out of the henhouse and back into the yard. Then she edged around the corner of the cottage, and up to a window.

Inside, there were bodies everywhere – comatose bandits. But in the midst of them, three men were standing around a table – Rosencrantz and Guildenstern, and the man who'd carried the AK-47. Only now he was holding a bloody commando knife, and tied to the table, naked and mutilated, there was a girl.

Helen spun away. The face had been obscured but she knew it was the same girl she'd seen with the bandits the night before. Her head was swimming and her knees were buckling, but something from inside the cottage loomed up in front of her – on the other side of the room, leaning against the back doorjamb, there was a double-barrelled 12 gauge shotgun.

The crash of the door as it flew open under Helen's kick alarmed even herself, and before anyone could react she had grabbed the shotgun and was pointing it at the mutilator's head. It was then that she saw what had caused those terrible screams – where the girl's eyes should have been, there were now only bloody sockets.

Helen felt herself receding . . . back into the dark . . . until the scene in front of her was like an image on a cinema screen. So when finally she pulled the trigger, she viewed the effect of it with a curious detachment.

The effect was that the mutilator's head exploded. And as his corpse flailed on the floor, Helen was reminded of the chicken in the henhouse.

Rosencrantz and Guildenstern gawped in amazement. Then they threw themselves down and cowered under the table in terror. Helen stood there as if in a trance . . . until the mutilated girl, shocked awake by the blast, screamed, 'Kill me! In God's name, kill me! Please – kill me!'

The second barrel discharged and the mutilated girl was dead. It happened before Helen knew it and in the silence which followed, she stared at the carnage, unable to believe what she had done.

'Fuck me!' The guttural voice was astonished.

Helen spun to see the speaker in the doorway. The water of the river was still glistening on his skin and beading over the tattoo on his forehead. His expression was stunned, but Helen wasn't looking at his face. Her eyes were locked onto the Sten gun he was holding, which was pointing directly at her belly.

'Fuck *me*,' the Sten gunner repeated, 'youse bin 'avin fun?' He paused, and looked down at the headless mutilator. 'An' Wayne . . . Wayne looks like 'e went over the top a bit . . . as fuckin' usual.' He tutted, and admonished, 'Silly cunt.'

Rosencrantz and Guildenstern giggled as they crawled out.

But the Sten gunner ignored them, his attention firmly on Helen as he queried, 'So where did you come from then, darlin'?' Then something flashed into his mind, and he punted, 'From out of the sky?'

Helen's face betrayed her, and the Sten gunner beamed in delight. 'Well now . . . 'ow 'bout that. Fuckin' hours we looked for you . . . an' 'ere you are, pretty as ya please . . .'ow about that.' Then he chortled, 'Fair enough, anyway . . . since it was Wayne what shot youse down . . . wiv 'is AK.'

Helen's insides did somersaults as she turned to the bloody mess that had been the mutilator named Wayne. She had killed the man who had murdered Bill Reid and Damien Mitchell, and God knows how many others. Then something caught her eye – Wayne's blood-spattered runners – the shoes of the man that had come so close to her after the crash. But for luck, it could have been she and not the mutilated girl laid out on that table.

As other bandits surfaced, it struck Helen then that she still had the shotgun, but both barrels were empty.

Then she saw a bandolier of cartridges hanging from a wall hook – three paces from the Sten gunner.

He read her mind. He looked at the bandolier, then back at Helen, and said, 'Go for it.' Then in a tone almost encouraging, he added, 'You got nothin' to lose.'

Helen knew that she was dead. It was just a matter of how. Either riddled with bullets – or like the mutilated girl.

Rosencrantz and Guildenstern were already closing so if it was to be quick, it would have to be now. She was about to crown Rosencrantz with the butt of the shotgun but with no idea of what she would do then . . . when things took a turn.

Blood spurted in a fountain from the Sten gunner's neck. Then the Sten gun fell from his hands to jar heavily on the floor, and bullets ricocheted around inside the cottage like peas in a drum.

Helen was already moving before the gun went off. And as she reached the door and shoved the Sten gunner aside she saw the paring knife buried in his jugular, with its hilt still firmly gripped in Jack Fitzgerald's hand.

When the gun stopped, all the bandits had taken hits and were hollering, as half in shock, half in relief, Helen exclaimed pointlessly, 'You can see!'

Fitzgerald said, 'Well enough,' as he rolled over the still grappling Sten gunner and took his ammunition.

Helen ducked back inside and grabbed the cartridges from the wall hook. Then stepping past Fitzgerald who was retrieving the Sten gun, she slung the bandolier across her shoulder and turned away to start back towards the river.

What she saw in the field behind the cottage stopped her dead in her tracks. And when Fitzgerald stood to follow, and looked where she was looking, he stopped dead too. Because at the tree line beyond the field, at a distance of four hundred metres, there was a line of maybe ten gargantuan mutant funnelweb spiders.

Jack saw right away that these were a new generation. They were at least half as big again as their forerunners – even at this distance, they clearly stood taller than the cottage. And just as he'd feared, despite the dropping of the neutron bomb, here they were – two hundred kilometres from the Sydney CBD.

The funnelwebs stood watching them, stock still, as cats watch their prey. Jack inched to Helen's side, gently tugged at her sleeve, and whispered, 'Across the river and into the trees.'

They edged back around the cottage, half a pace at a time, until they were obscured. Then they dashed to the river and jumped in and thrashed over, swimming faster than either of them ever had.

When they reached the far bank and clambered out onto the mud, their every muscle was screaming from exertion. But they raced on into the bush and straight up the tangled slope without even so much as a backward glance.

Up and up they went until they were high above the river and could finally take not one more step. Only then did they stop to collapse and gasp for breath, and turn to look back down at the cottage now far below.

The funnelwebs had approached and encircled the building, trapping the injured bandits who were hobbling around the yard in hysterics. They limped this way and that, looking for some escape, but each time they tried the spiders sidestepped and cut them off.

They edged closer and closer, ever tightening the circle, and herding the bandits back into the building. Until finally when they were all inside, shrieking to God for salvation, the biggest of the funnelwebs sallied in and ripped off the roof.

Like fish in a net the bandits flopped and fell over each other, until the biggest funnelweb stabbed down into their midst, and impaled Rosencrantz. Pulling him from the building like a mollusc from its shell it took him screaming to the middle of the yard. And there it threw him down and pumped his body full of venom, and sucked out the black, stinking broth that it made of his viscera.

That was the start of a feeding frenzy. The funnelwebs jostled around the cottage, stabbing and impaling, and one by one the bandits died. Until when all those alive had been summarily killed and eaten, the monsters continued to gorge on the dead. Thus in death, the remains of Wayne and the mutilated girl became inseparably married in the bile of the funnelwebs' guts.

Jack and Helen watched speechless as the funnelwebs wolfed down the last of the human flesh. Then the biggest of the monsters – the one that had ripped off the roof – reared back, and tasted the wind.

Fitzgerald froze because he sensed that the monster had remembered them. And when it turned in their direction and its head bobbed excitedly, he knew without doubt that it had found them.

The monster left the pack and went down to the river, but it stopped at the water's edge and hesitantly tested the depth. Then after a moment, it decided not to cross and Jack and Helen breathed sighs of relief. But Jack's heart missed a beat when the monster lifted its head again, and looked up the slope directly into his eyes.

It was the very worst feeling he had ever known – the spider's gaze went to the core of him, and he felt in that instant that he was face to face with evil incarnate.

Helen sensed it too as she recoiled into the trees, and tugged Fitzgerald's arm to urge him away. And when she said, 'Please, Jack . . . let's go . . . I really want to go now,' her voice trembled with a fear that was removed from the horrors of the morning.

10

John Czarnecki had not been entirely open with Richard Bartlett during their talk on the rugby field at Holsworthy. The impression he had given was that he had been acting as an agent for 'the people he had met' the previous evening, who had held out such generous inducements to the preservation of the CBD. That impression was not a true one.

The truth was that John Czarnecki was himself one of 'those people', being up to his neck in a syndicate which for eight months had been manipulating the Sydney real estate market to acquire and artificially inflate the value of CBD properties. Needless to say, the legitimate business enterprises through which the scheme had been operating were facades. The powers behind the syndicate were the Queensland Yamaguchi Gumi, working out of the Gold Coast but controlled from Tokyo, and the New South Wales *'ndrangheta*, or Calabrian Mafia, now moving in on the State Capital after establishing itself in a dozen country towns over thirty years. The two criminal organisations had been headed for a mutually destructive clash as they inevitably expanded into each other's areas of influence. But one man had had the vision to see that if they collaborated in an ostensibly respectable enterprise, untainted by traditional activities in drugs, extortion and prostitution, profits might be forecast not in millions, but billions.

That man was John Czarnecki, who during an earlier incarnation as shadow Police Minister had discreetly befriended the principal identities of organised crime throughout eastern Australia. At first, his worth to them had been limited to providing snippets of political intelligence and some insights into the mechanisms and machinations of legislative government. However when he later became State Labor Leader, and soon afterwards State Premier, his value to the Organisations became incalculable.

Czarnecki was no sop politician to be used and discarded. He was exceptionally intelligent, and his Cossack blood had endowed him with nerves of steel. But the characteristic which marked him above all else was his all-consuming and darkly obsessive ambition. His was not the ambition of a political careerist, to merely jostle to the head of the pack and carve out the biggest slice of wealth and power possible. Czarnecki's ambition was a demon, a locomotive driving force forged in the bitterness of watching his father cough up his lungs night after night. Marek Czarnecki had worked himself to death to save money for his dream that John and his five brothers might serve their apprenticeships to trades, and so not be forced to follow their father into the coalmines of the Hunter Valley.

Children of immigrants are commonly motivated to climb the social and economic ladders of their parents' adopted country. But at the age of thirteen, John Czarnecki had realised that Australia's classless society was a cruel myth. He would always be handicapped in his country of birth by being excluded from its private school old-boy network. However at the same age it had struck him that as recently as the nineteen forties, an absurd-looking, ill-educated and sexually impotent postcard painter had come within a hair's breadth of dragging the civilised world back into the Dark Ages. And from that moment on, young John had known that politics was his way to the stars.

Tragically by the time through sheer brilliance he had won a scholarship to the University of Sydney Law School, his father was already dead and his mother would follow within a year from a broken heart. John was embittered by the deaths of his parents. Nevertheless after four years he graduated with honours, and threw himself with a vengeance into his chosen field.

From the very beginning John Czarnecki had his own agenda, but in the early years chances to advance did not often present themselves. Unlike Adolf Hitler, he had no population seething with resentment to exploit. Nor could he become the symbolic saviour of a nation with its back to the wall, like Winston Churchill. So in the absence of those opportunities he had to content himself with clawing his way up the greasy pole of the New South Wales Labor Right Wing. He soon realised however that Australian politics, federal as well as state, offered too small a stage to satisfy him. He craved to be in the great international game. But to do it, he would first need to accumulate wealth.

Which is exactly what he did, by any and all means available, and with particularly spectacular results since becoming Premier. In the past year, his personal fortune held in secret accounts had risen considerably beyond the one hundred million dollars for which he had bought Richard Bartlett to three-quarters of a billion dollars. And he had aimed within two years to see that figure exceed a billion.

But now, the funnelwebs had spoilt it. And in the wake of the neutron bomb debacle, not only would there be no more profits, but the massive investments his partners had committed to the CBD scheme were also lost. Being the kind of people they were, Czarnecki knew the first thing they would do would be to elect a scapegoat – and the obvious candidate was, of course, himself. Czarnecki was no fool. He'd known the risks of dealing with international criminals from the day he'd become involved. And so, at the outset, he had contrived a contingency plan which tied in neatly with his ultimate goal.

Czarnecki's parents had always immersed their children in the culture of Poland. As a preschooler John had spoken Polish as a first language, and stories of the tragic history of his parents' homeland had been a childhood passion. So when he'd started to make money, Czarnecki had travelled frequently to Poland, mainly to his father's home town of Kraców. And there, over a period, he established himself as an influential expatriate.

At the same time, as in Australia, he secretly courted the leaders of organised crime. He carefully avoided any direct involvement in criminal activity, but through a series of discreet favours, established a network of personal friendships which could be usefully exploited in the future.

Then in the early 1990s, the possibilities of Czarnecki's position flourished with the collapse of the old Soviet Bloc. He immediately saw the situation as the once-in-a-lifetime opportunity he had been waiting for. Because it meant the billion dollars he would soon have could now set him up not only in Poland, but as a dominating player throughout the whole of free market Eastern Europe.

In the meantime, conspiring with Japanese and

Italian mobsters to raise seed money necessitated forethought. Because if something should go wrong, he would need a safe haven. There were few places in the world where an individual could be safe from Mafia and Yakuza vengeance. But one of them was in the bosom of the toughest, most brutal, and most loyal criminal milieu of all – the Slavonic underworld. And because of past favours, the leaders of that underworld had become Czarnecki's avowed friends and protectors.

Now something had indeed gone seriously wrong, and only minutes after receiving word of the failure of the neutron bomb, John Czarnecki decided to cut and run. He had sent his wife and daughters to Kraców a week earlier, ostensibly to be safe from the funnelwebs but in reality to put them out of reach of his partners. Now he would follow by a carefully prearranged escape route.

He left the temporary State Government offices in the Albury Council building at 12.25am with only an attache case, announcing to his shell-shocked staff that he was returning to his suite at the Manor House Hotel for some sleep. But instead, he drove himself in an anonymous State Government car directly to Albury Airport, where a Cessna Citation registered to a company in the Virgin Islands had been fuelled and ready to leave for several hours. The executive jet, owned in fact by Czarnecki, took off with the Premier aboard at 12.50am, the American pilot declaring a routine flight plan to Port Hedland in Western Australia. However several hours later, after failing to arrive or to respond to emergency calls, the aircraft was assumed to have crashed in the outback before the pilot could radio a Mayday. The truth was more sinister.

Ten minutes before its scheduled arrival time, the Citation had crossed the West Australian coast at low altitude a hundred kilometres north of Port Hedland, and set course for the first of its refuelling stops at Jakarta en route to its ultimate destination of Kraców. But the plane never made it out of Australian airspace. Two hundred kilometres out over the Timor Sea, two RAAF F/A-18 interceptors of 75 Squadron from Tindal in the Northern Territory jumped the Citation and shot it down. And everyone aboard, including the New South Wales Premier, was killed.

John Czarnecki was not the first person to have underestimated Richard Bartlett, but he was the first to have died as a direct result of his miscalculation. He had judged the sum of a hundred million dollars to be the optimum to net the Prime Minister – enough to achieve his acquiescence but not so much as to frighten him off. And in that sense, he had read his man well. What he hadn't taken into account was Richard Bartlett's obsessive paranoia.

As soon as he'd returned to Canberra from Holsworthy, the first thing Bartlett had done was to call in one of his oldest personal friends who also happened to be head of the Australian Security Intelligence Organisation. And from that moment on, the spooks had been all over John Czarnecki like a rash. So Bartlett had known about the flight of the Citation from the moment of take-off. The aircraft had been tracked across the continent by ADF radar, and when it became obvious that Czarnecki was jumping the country, Bartlett, now acting CDF himself since Andrew Lawrie's death, had sent in the fighters.

Czarnecki's mysterious disappearance posed considerably less risk to Bartlett than his turning up inexplicably overseas. But the situation would still need to be managed carefully. Happily the funnelwebs afforded good opportunities for a story of tragic demise, so Bartlett would contrive one and have it disseminated.

Because of the failure of the neutron bomb, Bartlett had missed out on the big prize. But half a hundred million dollars was better than none of it, and as the payment had been channelled through Czarnecki, Bartlett guessed that no-one would be coming forward to get their money back.

More significantly, he had been relieved at the attitude of the US President to the failure of the neutron bomb when he had spoken to him earlier from the basement of Russell Offices. Relieved, and taken aback. Because the President had not only been sympathetic but had gone on to moot a new proposal that had confirmed Richard Bartlett's impression of their new relationship – to an extent that he could not have imagined.

So it was that at 8.05am, a mere seven hours and fifty minutes after the greatest disaster in his country's history, the Prime Minister of Australia retired to bed a happier man than might have been expected.

The global reaction to the neutron bombing of Sydney was predictably contentious, and gave rise to a cacophony of pharisaic bleating about 'reckless militarism' and 'environmental vandalism'. But the event finally brought home to an indifferent world that Australia was in real trouble, and sparked an interest in the situation which, despite platitudes to the contrary, was not in the least humanitarian.

Australia is approximately the size of mainland USA. But with its inhabitants numbering less than twenty million and its vast mineral resources still largely untapped, it is per capita a far richer country. In fact, with a wealth per head of $A1.09 million, it has been listed by the World Bank as the richest country on Earth.

Despite that, the desperate ploy of the neutron bomb was clear testimony that the incumbent Australian nation lacked the means to counter the funnelwebs. And that signalled to the wolves of the world that the jewel in the global resources crown might soon be up for grabs.

Only a few hours after the Lancers had taken off, the US 7th Fleet had sailed from Yokosuka, Japan, for some hurriedly concocted 'exercises' in the Coral Sea. At the same time, the Indonesian Eastern Fleet steamed out of Surabaya to assemble east of Timor for 'exercises' in the Arafura Sea. And, most ominously, the Russian Pacific Fleet sailed from Vladivostok only hours before the Red Chinese Qingdao Flotilla headed from Jiazhou Bay into the Yellow Sea. The two light heavyweights of the Western Pacific shadowed each other past the Philippines, then on through the Straits of Moluccas and into the waters south of New Guinea for their hurriedly concocted 'bilateral exercises'.

Though the word was never used, Australia was blockaded. That fact was made clear to the Prime Minister of the United Kingdom when he high-handedly proclaimed to the US President that as Australia's mother country, Britain would quite naturally head up the International Naval Relief Effort. No record of their conversation survived, but in the weeks to come the Royal Navy would get no closer to Australia than Suez.

The hot wind on Jimmy O'Rourke's face was lifting his spirits. It was 8.10am, and the New South Wales Southern Highlands were already baking in twenty-seven degrees of sunshine. Grimy faced and red eyed, O'Rourke had just lived through a night he would prefer to forget. But now he was rumbling across country in the turret of a lone APC, and the sun and fresh air were clearing his head of depression.

Half drunk with fatigue, he looked twice when he saw two civilians breaking from the trees and frantically running down towards him. Their faces were filthy, their hair was thickly matted and their clothes were torn and stained with grass and blood. They were also carrying some serious weaponry. So after ordering the driver to stop, O'Rourke called to the wayfarers, 'Put down your guns!'

Jack Fitzgerald and Helen Parkes were too exhausted to reply. They just threw down their firearms and collapsed with relief against the tracks. They had run out of water an hour before which was why as they'd staggered over their umpteenth ridge that morning, they could have cried when they'd seen the APC.

O'Rourke jumped down and offered Helen his opened water bottle. She grabbed it from him and gulped down the best part of a litre, then passed it to Fitzgerald who drained what was left in four gulps.

O'Rourke regarded them disapprovingly, and chided, 'What the hell are you two doing out here – don't you know there are some bad characters about?'

Fitzgerald could have laughed, but he didn't have the energy. Instead he pulled his wallet from his pocket and took out his CSIRO security pass. Handing it over, he said, 'I'm John Fitzgerald of the CSIRO funnelweb research team. One of your blokes was flying us to Canberra yesterday morning when bandits shot us down. We've been hoofing it ever since.'

When he had examined the pass, O'Rourke said in a modified tone, 'James O'Rourke, Mister Fitzgerald, 'Bravo' Company, Five-Seven RAR. Where's the pilot?'

'Killed in the crash, along with my team leader, Bill Reid.' Jack then turned and said, 'This is Helen Parkes, my associate.'

O'Rourke acknowledged, 'Ms Parkes,' then inquired, 'When did you last eat?'

Jack forced a grin. 'About a hundred years ago.'

O'Rourke nodded, then indicating the battle door at the back of the APC, he said, 'Okay, let's go.'

The half section reconnaissance patrol in the vehicle made Jack and Helen as comfortable as possible, and provided a breakfast of biscuits, tinned jam and lukewarm coffee. It was the best-tasting meal of their lives. They were just finishing when the APC clattered onto a metalled surface, and O'Rourke ducked down from the hatch and said, 'This is it.'

A moment later the APC's ramp was lowered, and Jack and Helen were back in the nightmare. As bad as it had looked from the air, on the ground the plight of the refugees was far worse. They were packed along a highway which could have been the road to Purgatory – filthy, bloody, bedraggled, lame, and blank faced. The smell of them was overpowering – the foul, putrid stink of decay. But worst of all was the sound they made. Not crying nor wailing, but the shuffling of their feet as they shambled on to God knows where.

Jack and Helen followed O'Rourke across the tragic human river, past corpses at the roadside which had been hurriedly wrapped in anything, to another APC on the far side of the road. The front of it was open and two greasy soldiers were immersed, conjuring with tools and pieces of engine.

O'Rourke barked, 'For fuck's sake, Costas, aren't you done yet?'

A corporal mechanic, black to his elbows, called back, 'Be done inside twenty minutes, sir.'

O'Rourke shook his head in mock despair, then

went around to the open ramp and announced inside, 'No Funnys or bandits to the east for five ks, sir, but we picked up a couple of strays.'

Pat Howard stepped out of the disabled commander's vehicle, accepted Fitzgerald's security pass from O'Rourke and examined it. Then he said, 'Okay, CSM. Get a nap. I don't want you falling over on me later.'

O'Rourke replied, 'All right, sir, I'll be in Shute's bucket. But call me when Costas comes good.' Then turning to Jack and Helen, he said, 'This is the OC, Major Howard – he'll look after you. Good luck, so,' and he strode off smartly.

In the back of his mind, Fitzgerald noted O'Rourke's distinctively Irish turn of phrase, as Helen called after him, 'Thank you, Mister O'Rourke.'

Somewhat formally, Howard stepped forward to shake hands, saying, 'Pat Howard, Doctor Fitzgerald.'

Remembering Howard from Holsworthy, Fitzgerald replied in kind, 'Jack Fitzgerald,' then repeated, 'And this is my associate, Helen Parkes.'

Shaking hands with Helen, Howard acknowledged, 'Ms Parkes,' then indicating, said, 'Let's talk in the vehicle.'

'Bravo' Company was positioned along the Federal Highway at the northern end of Lake George, an expansive but shallow natural lake thirty kilometres north-east of Canberra. Lake George is an oddity in that it inexplicably alternates between full and empty, and at that time, its northern quadrant was dry. When exposed, the northern lake bed is a flat and featureless grazing plain four kilometres across, flanked to the east and west by steep escarpments. For fifteen kilometres the highway is sandwiched between the west bank of the lake and a fifty metre cliff which in places is almost vertical. Further south, where the slope is less precipitous, it is thickly wooded.

It was there, a kilometre down the road and twenty metres up in the trees, that O'Rourke found 1 Platoon. Andy Shute was taking the opportunity of the commander's vehicle breakdown for maintenance, and those of his remaining soldiers who were not breakfasting or sleeping were crawling around their APCs. The platoon commander, Simon Forbes, a popular young officer who'd played five-eighth for the battalion, had been killed overnight, and part of Shute's thinking was not to give his men time to dwell on it. But, as O'Rourke realised when he walked into the platoon area, it was as much to keep Shute occupied himself. He'd not been the same since Lakemba two nights before, and on the couple of occasions that he'd slept since, he'd been troubled by nightmares. Now, as he looked up from cleaning his Minimi, his eyes were haunted.

'G'day, Andy. What's cooking?' O'Rourke himself was subdued.

'Not a lot, sir, just tidying up.' Shute snapped the machine-gun together and stood.

Arriving, O'Rourke asked, 'Had some shuteye?'

'Yes, sir,' Shute lied, 'got a good hour on the road.'

O'Rourke knew he was lying, but there was nothing he could do about it, so he said, 'There's no chance of any kip down there with Costas performing, so I'll bunk with you, okay?'

For the first time, Shute smiled as he said, 'We'll have to stop meeting like this, sir, the town's talking.'

O'Rourke spat, 'Fuck off, Andy, you're too ugly for me!' Then enjoining, 'Get the billy on – I'll be looking for a brew in thirty,' he clambered into the Platoon HQ APC, threw down a couple of poncho liners and laid himself out on the floor.

A little cheered, Shute went off chuckling as his CSM drifted instantly into a catnap. Like all seasoned soldiers, O'Rourke could sleep anytime, anywhere. But this morning, his sleep was not restful. His mind was brim full of the previous night's horrors, and no matter how hard he tried, he could not block them out.

It was their eyes that got to him. He knew for others it was their scampering, or their twisted, hair-matted limbs. But for him, it was their eyes . . . cold and soulless . . . all eight of them . . . watching him . . . watching him . . .

He'd not seen their eyes at first, as they'd poured out of the blackness and the tanks had stood their ground, awaiting the order. But then the flame-throwers had opened up and as the first of them were incinerated, he saw a thousand of their piercing black eyes glinting brightly in the firelight.

But the fire did not stop them and they came on and on – wave after wave of them, implacable as an incoming tide. And their dead piled up higher but as they kept coming over them, all he could see were their eyes, coming closer . . . and closer.

Then they loomed over him and deep in their eyes he saw the tragic human river of their victims . . . shambling on interminably and dropping out one by one to die alone and in agony on a mist-enshrouded freezing wet roadside.

Until at last but one remained, trudging on through the mist towards the light of some cruelly imagined sanctuary. Until finally he too collapsed and just lay there in the ditch, too sick to get up and too sick at heart to even try.

And with the last of his strength he plucked a

handful of bog grass and tried to chew on it and swallow it down. But it snagged in his gullet and he retched and spewed violently, and vomited the bloody mucous which was all that remained of his belly.

And as the last breath eked out of him and his bones pierced his skin and his lips parted in a green and black death grin, his eyes bulged with dread as they gazed upon eternity, and he saw that they were – unmistakably – his own . . .

'Wake up, sir! Jimmy, wake up for Christ's sake, you'll raise the dead!'

O'Rourke jarred back to consciousness to see Andy Shute looking down, his face tight. 'You're dreaming about the fuckers, sir. Here . . . drink this.'

O'Rourke sat up and grasped the steaming mug, but after three scalding mouthfuls his hands were still trembling. He seldom felt embarrassed but he did now. He looked at Shute and asked sheepishly, 'Anybody else hear me?'

'Only Col Coombs, sir . . . none of the Diggers.' Then grinning humourlessly, Shute added, 'Glad it's not just me they give the shits to.'

O'Rourke felt like hell. He forced down the rest of the tea and gladly accepted the cigarette Shute offered him. Then, pale and sweating, he went out into the daylight, and tried to purge his mind of the ancient memory that had surfaced to bedevil him.

In the crippled commander's vehicle, Pat Howard had quizzed Helen and Jack about what had happened to them. The story of the bandits interested him – accounts of atrocities committed by a spider cult had been trickling in for thirty-six hours. But what concerned him more was that funnelwebs had been at the bandits' cottage. Tracing back on a topographic map, he saw that the cottage must have been near Lake Bathurst, due east of their present position. Making a quick calculation, he observed, 'That's further south than we thought they were . . . they're travelling fast.'

But when Fitzgerald quizzed back about the flash that had blinded him, Howard clammed up.

Fitzgerald said, 'I know bloody well what it was, Major – I was at Holsworthy when the neutron bomb was proposed.' Then he added, 'But I thought McGovern would stop it – he was the sanest one.'

Howard said, 'You wouldn't know about Air Chief Marshal McGovern,' and he told them the story of Warragamba.

Fitzgerald was astounded. It was an action totally out of keeping with the man he remembered. But he realised instantly what McGovern had been trying to do, and asked eagerly, 'Did the water stop the funnelwebs?'

Howard said, 'Our information is that they reached the Hawkesbury at around four-thirty this morning, and got no further.'

It was brilliant. McGovern had come up with the perfect answer. But it opened a bucket of worms.

Fitzgerald asked the cardinal question, 'What time was Warragamba breached?'

Howard checked the log. 'Report came over at 21.09 hrs – incident occurred . . . at 20.57.'

There was a moment's silence. Then Fitzgerald said, 'And yet Bartlett still dropped the neutron bomb at midnight – without waiting to see if the floods would hold the funnelwebs back.'

The point resounded in Howard's head. If there was an evens chance that the funnelwebs had been contained, surely the ERW should have been postponed until the situation had been reassessed. So why was it used?

Fitzgerald answered the question he saw in Howard's face. 'Bartlett had no interest in the neutron bomb until Czarnecki took him outside for a word. When they came back, Bartlett was a convert – he'd made up his mind. McGovern dissented but Bartlett abused him. Then it seems McGovern succeeded in creating a barrier to the funnelwebs but Bartlett neutron-bombed Sydney anyway. The point of the neutron bomb is to preserve property, so what does that suggest to you, Major?'

Howard wrestled with what Fitzgerald was telling him, until he came to the inescapable conclusion, 'That the Prime Minister and the Premier may have interests in this which are separate from the interests of the rest of us.'

The cornerstone of Pat Howard's adult life had been his loyalty to the elected government of his country. Now he faced the proposition that his commander-in-chief was, to some unknown extent, a traitor. If it was true, it made a fool of every soldier that had died fighting funnelwebs, and a mockery of any such notion as a national crusade. Howard felt like he'd been stabbed in the heart. From the end of a long dark tunnel, he heard Fitzgerald asking, 'What happened after the bomb exploded?'

Subdued, Howard recounted, 'Funnelwebs underground were unaffected, and they came south down the highways like a horde of Mongols. The RAAF bombed the Avon Dam pipeline and flooded the Illawarra which stopped them on the coast. But when we attacked them on the ground at Menangle, there was a hell of a blue. There were hundreds of them – no matter how many we killed, they kept coming. Eventually the First Armoured had to fall back and the Funnys broke through. Couple of hours later they caught up with the refugee stragglers at Mittagong and the dinner bell rang. They hit Goulburn forty kilometres back an hour ago. We reckon there are still twenty thousand residents in there so I don't even want to think about it, except I hope at least the poor bastards will buy us some time.'

It was incomprehensible, the body count starting to mean no more than telephone numbers. Helen had been listening with growing distress. Now she asked, 'But why aren't you back there, Major, trying to save those people?'

Howard had kept the best until last. 'We're ordered to Canberra, Ms Parkes. In the past twenty-four hours it's turned into a massive refugee camp – half a million people, just waiting for somebody to do something. So the army has been ordered to ring the capital and make a last stand of it.'

Jack and Helen looked at each other. Five hundred thousand additional people in a city built for half that number. They were trying to imagine it, when the shuffling outside was rent by screams.

The radio crackled, 'Contact! Contact!' but Howard was already half way out the battle door. Jack and Helen were right behind him, and they all saw the reason for the screams.

Seven or eight giant funnelwebs were bearing down on the highway from across the lake bed. Refugees were shrieking and running everywhere. Taking off, Howard barked, 'Stay inside,' and was gone.

Jack and Helen stared at the advancing monsters. At this distance they appeared even bigger than they had at the cottage. Their legs must have spanned fully eight or nine metres, and they were covered in hair so coarse that it bristled like spikes. And at the front of their heads were their massive black fangs – rapier pointed, and dripping death.

Soldiers in hastily donned NBC suits opened up with flame-throwers and machine-guns, and three or four of the monsters exploded into fireballs or were ripped apart. But two funnelwebs emerged from behind them, reared back into stances of attack and simultaneously shot venom at the troops.

The effect was frightful – the NBC suits dissolved and the flesh of the soldiers was stripped from their bones. Two unlucky men were only partly drenched and thrashed screaming in torment before dying of heart failure. It was then, as a child ran past howling for her mother and one of the funnelwebs started after her, that Fitzgerald moved.

He ran to the dead soldiers and grabbed up a flame-thrower. Then he yanked the trigger and enveloped the advancing funnelweb in an inferno. The creature's shrieks cut the air like a red hot blade and momentarily, Fitzgerald froze. Then from nowhere a stream of venom arced through the air at him, and he threw himself aside to avoid certain death by a hair's breadth.

The funnelweb which had shot at him reared back to shoot again and Fitzgerald was bringing the flame-thrower to bear on it, when in silence and slow motion the creature crumpled in front of him as its legs were severed by a scythe of machine-gun bullets.

From three paces behind, Helen was raking the monster with a Minimi. The fusillade went on and on and fragment by fragment, the mutant spider was shredded into a bloody mulch. The Minimi only stopped when its ammunition was expended, and Jack realised that the silence had in fact been a cacophony of gunfire.

More funnelwebs were coming – twelve or fifteen of them, closing in a crescent from a kilometre across the dry lake bed. The refugees had scattered and were charging around like headless chickens, until the funnelwebs overran them and began impaling them with murderous efficiency.

Helen tossed away the Minimi and moved to help Jack with the flame-thrower. It was a crude weapon – a pipe about the size of a rifle connected by a hose to a pressurised gasoline tank. The tank was strapped to a backpack which in turn was strapped to a dead infantryman. The man's legs and abdomen were a black smoking mess and Fitzgerald was trying to release the backpack without touching the venom.

Helen supported the soldier's torso as Jack released the straps from its shoulders. Then shoving the corpse away, Jack hiked the pack onto his back and set off after Helen at a jog up the slope of the escarpment.

Half way to the trees at the hilltop, Helen looked back to see what was happening. The funnelwebs were everywhere and in a blood-crazed frenzy were gorging their way through the refugees. 'Bravo' Company was rallying doggedly but there were just too many refugees to protect.

Jack arrived gasping and turned to look back also, but when he did, his legs turned to stone. Because from the middle of the battlefield, the biggest funnelweb was staring at him – and he knew it was the spider that had found him on the hillside at the cottage.

The funnelweb started towards them. As it did, Helen saw it too and they turned and dashed up for the tree line. But when they got there and looked back again, the monster was already crossing the road.

They had no chance of outrunning it, so Jack summoned his courage and levelled the flame-thrower. He waited until the funnelweb was thirty metres off, then he pulled the trigger and dispatched a blazing stream. But the flaming jet fell short and Jack realised that the weapon was low on fuel.

The funnelweb stopped when it felt the heat. For a moment, it held back and watched Jack warily. But then, when he did not fire again, the monster came on quickly, and shortened its distance to the hilltop with easy strides.

As Jack grabbed Helen and pulled her back into the trees, she pleaded, 'Torch it! Why don't you torch it, for God's sakes!'

He shouted, 'Tank's empty,' and they blundered on into the brush until fifty metres in they came to a sheer cliff face.

They turned back to see the funnelweb move into the trees and start weaving towards them. Swallowing hard, Jack stepped forward and pulled the trigger again, but the result was a weak dribble which barely ignited the scrub.

Sensing it was safe, the monster continued advancing and was soon so close they could see it in detail – its great fangs smeared with blood, its gaping mouth befouled with flesh, its eight black eyes locked onto them in a diabolical stare. And for the first time they got the stink of it, like a mixture of marsh gas and excrement.

The cliff was barely ten metres away and its base was littered with overgrown boulders. There was nowhere to run – no way to escape – but as fear of death welled up in Jack Fitzgerald, so did his instinct to survive.

He threw off the backpack and scrutinised the flame-thrower's fuel tank. There was a pressure valve with a screw seal where the hose was attached. He closed the valve then unscrewed the hose and, as he'd hoped, there were dregs of petrol left in the pipe.

The funnelweb was less than twenty metres off now, and he was aware in another part of his mind that

Helen was screaming. He leapt forward and ripped a branch from a smouldering bush. Then he jumped back, soaked the fuel tank in petrol and trailed the rest to the base of the cliff wall.

Helen was beside him, scrambling desperately over the rocks and hurting herself. Jack couldn't breathe but he stood his ground and stared fixedly at the funnelweb as it ripped through the trees towards them like a bulldozer. In a moment, the giant spider was almost on them. But then it stepped over the fuel tank, and Jack dropped the smouldering branch.

A flame snaked spiritedly along the petrol-soaked leaf litter to the fuel tank, which burst alight. The funnelweb screeched and jumped as its underbelly was scorched, but it didn't have to suffer for long. Because the tank's neoprene pressure seal quickly ruptured in the heat and when the pressurised fuel vapour hit the air, there was a devastating explosion.

The funnelweb disintegrated – smoking bits of it flew into the sky and scattered over the entire hilltop. But Jack didn't see it, and neither did Helen, because they were burrowed deep down in the undergrowth, hugging boulders.

When eventually they looked, they saw the funnelweb was gone and in its place there was a charred, smoking clearing. Painfully they got up, and for a time they could only stand and stare. Then finally they trudged off, but had only gone ten paces when they stopped at the sound of a deafening boom. And Helen's eyes lit up as she shouted above the din, 'That's a jet!'

They staggered back out of the trees and what they saw on the lake bed below made their spirits soar – the sky was filled with bombers, swooping low over the ground and attacking the funnelwebs with napalm.

'Jesus!' Jack screamed, as the F-111s cut off the highway with a towering wall of fire. There were bodies everywhere, and some unfortunates were still alive on the funnelwebs' side of the flames. But many of those saved were now streaming up the hillside, cheering madly and waving in triumph.

Back in the game, 'Bravo' Company were rallying to the battle. Howard had his APCs on the flanks and his troops were picking off the funnelwebs like wild turkeys. The monsters were scattering everywhere, and those that got away were chased down and destroyed by the bombers.

Soon hundreds of people were on the hill, cheering like some hysterical football crowd. But their mood quickly turned when out of the distant northern haze a crawling black wave materialised. And the hillside fell silent as the black wave transformed into an army of several hundred funnelwebs.

The refugees panicked. They fled away along the hill and to avoid being trampled, Jack and Helen grappled higher into the trees. And from there they first saw there was another army of monsters approaching.

The Leopards of the 1st Armoured Regiment roared out of the north-west and ripped into the funnelwebs with great savagery. Their 105mm guns had been converted into flame-throwers and they engulfed the spiders by the dozen in massive conflagrations. They crushed them with their tracks and they rent them with shrapnel and they cut them down with heavy calibre machine-guns. And inside two minutes, the lake bed was running in blood.

But then another factor came into play. At Menangle the funnelwebs had doused the Leopards with venom, and at first their armour had seemed impervious to it. But in the intervening hours the acid had eaten into the steel, and now in the stress of combat, the tanks began breaking down.

Because of that, 'Bravo' Company suffered its worst casualties to date. What remained of 3 Platoon were wiped out when they went in to rescue a stranded Leopard crew – the monsters surrounded them and drenched their APCs in so much venom that the steel buckled. 2 Section made a run for it but most of them then died when a spurt of venom cut through their vehicle's roof. The driver got back to Company Headquarters but the survivors were all so terribly wounded that Howard had to CASEVAC them immediately.

Before long, there was a standoff, with neither soldiers nor funnelwebs keen to engage. The monsters withdrew to the eastern slopes, the tanks lined up below them, and an eerie calm settled over the battlefield.

Gazing across the carnage, Jack and Helen were transfixed. Everywhere there were dead machines, dead spiders, and dead men, and the only sound heard was the wailing of the wounded and the dying.

Jack's name boomed out. Looking down, he saw an APC on the highway and in its turret, CSM O'Rourke calling through a bullhorn, 'Doctor John Fitzgerald! Come to me!'

Wearily, Jack and Helen made off down the slope. When O'Rourke saw them, he smiled and snapped into his radio, 'He's alive, sir, and Miss Parkes – k and half south of you. I'll bring them up.'

Seconds later, Jack and Helen were holding on like grim death as the APC raced at 40 km/h across country, and soon they clambered out next to the newly repaired commander's vehicle.

Pat Howard was solemn as he walked up to them, saying, 'I told you two to stay inside.' But then his voice was drowned out by the thwack of approaching rotor blades and they all looked up to see a Black Hawk swoop in low over the trees.

As it banked downwind, Howard shouted above it, 'Anyway, somebody knows you're not safe to be out – we've had orders to air evacuate you to Canberra.'

The helicopter dropped like a stone to make a battle landing two hundred metres away, and O'Rourke said, 'If you'll risk Charley's driving again, I'll take you across.'

Pat Howard was standing in his turret as they sped away, a solitary, burdened figure. And perhaps because he knew he was in part responsible for that burden, Jack Fitzgerald thought he saw the clear mark of death on him. He felt the urge to call back to him, to tell him to get away, that if he didn't he would certainly die. But he knew in the same instant that it would of course be a futile thing to do.

Overwhelmed by despair, and by the horrors all around him, Fitzgerald felt the need to grasp onto something familiar. So half way to the helicopter, seemingly apropos of nothing, he called above the clatter, 'So you're an Irishman too then, Mister O'Rourke?'

O'Rourke looked askance, as if surprised by the question. And he considered it carefully before answering. But finally, he replied, 'No, sir. My father was Irish. But I'm an Australian.'

They arrived at the Black Hawk and Jack and Helen clambered aboard as O'Rourke confirmed their identities to the pilot. Then as the APC withdrew, the twin gas turbines powered up and the aircraft lifted off and climbed away.

Now that she was safe, Helen slumped into her seat and everything she had been bottling up erupted, and she cried like a baby. Jack held her hand but said nothing, knowing it was the best thing she could do. And as he looked back down below and saw Jimmy O'Rourke speeding to rejoin 'Bravo' Company, he kept his face turned firmly to the window. Because at that moment, he realised that he was crying too.

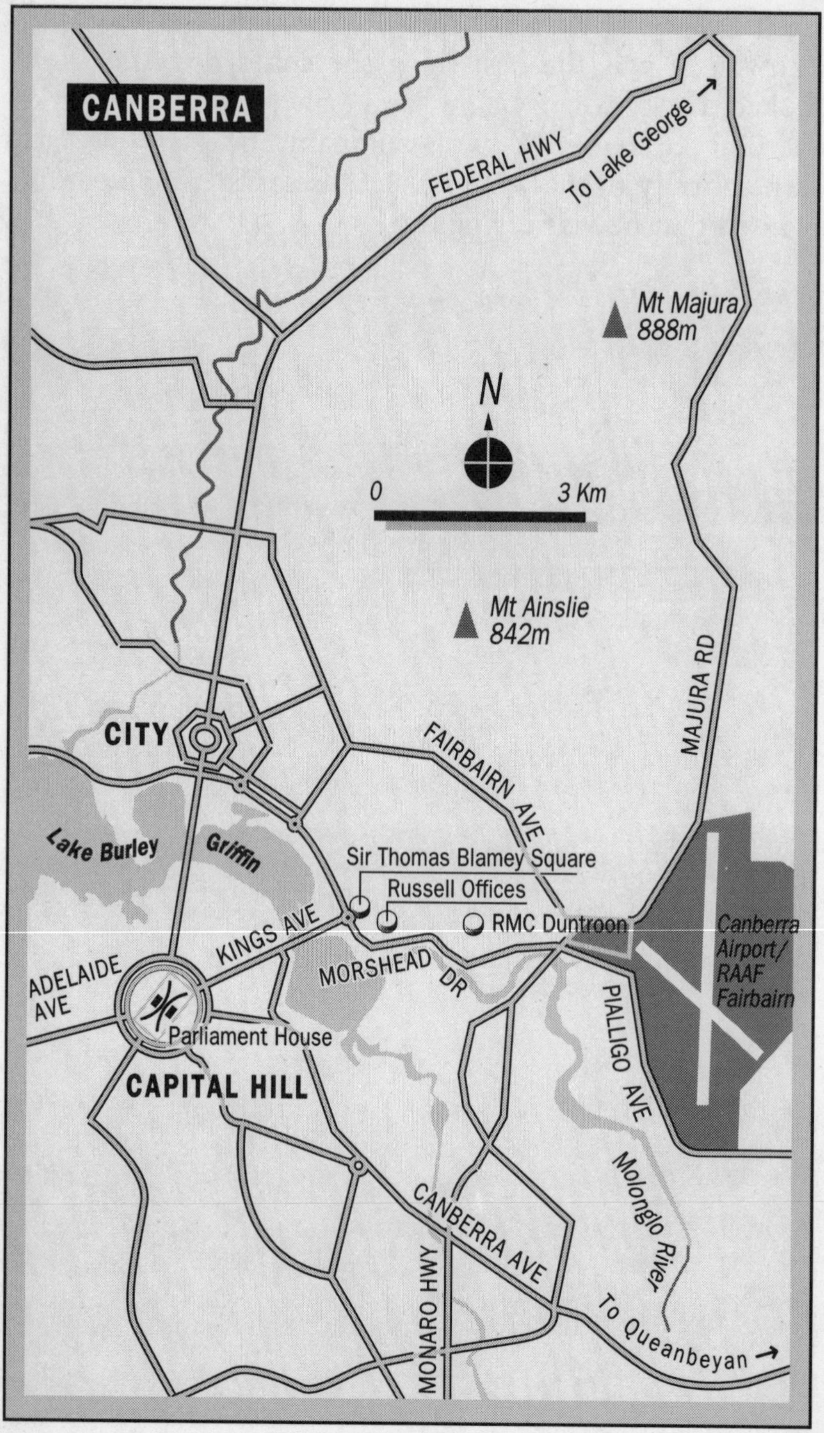
CANBERRA
FEDERAL HWY
To Lake George
Mt Majura
888m
N
0
3 Km
Mt Ainslie
842m
MAJURA RD
CITY
FAIRBAIRN AVE
Lake Burley Griffin
Sir Thomas Blamey Square
Russell Offices
RMC Duntroon
KINGS AVE
Canberra Airport/ RAAF Fairbairn
ADELAIDE AVE
MORSHEAD DR
PIALLIGO AVE
Parliament House
CAPITAL HILL
Molonglo River
CANBERRA AVE
MONARO HWY
To Queanbeyan

11

The new generation, invigorated by the light, was superior not only in size and strength but in intelligence also. As the drumbeats had unhooked a power in their antecedents, so now the light had unhooked a power in them that was greater. It was a power so integral and fundamental to their fabric that it transcended any worldly understanding – a power that had lain dormant for not just three hundred million years, but for the eons before through which their seed had journeyed in suspension.

Now, in an end to this their era of earthly sufferance, the light had unlocked their true potential. And they sensed, as they swarmed instinctively towards the surfeit of living sustenance, that ascendancy over their enemies was no more than a matter of time.

Unusually, the air over Canberra that morning was heavy with smoke. Unlike other cities, the Australian capital had no industry or traffic snarls to pollute its atmosphere. Built on high grazing land from nothing in the early nineteen hundreds, it was a one purpose town – to be the seat of government of the Commonwealth of Australia. And as such, it was a showplace. From the Parliament House on

Capital Hill, wide avenues radiated through green open spaces and forested reserves into pleasant, aseptic suburbs. The Molonglo River had been dammed to form the ornamental Lake Burley Griffin which curved around Capital Hill to the north, and with its fine bridges, dignitaries' residences and lakeside institutions of education and culture, the city consciously echoed the more elegant metropolises of Europe.

But that morning, Canberra echoed more the Zaïrese town of Goma following the Rwandan exodus of 1994. Immediately to the east of the city, beneath the slopes of Mount Ainslie, hundreds of hectares of farmland were covered with what looked from the air to be a seething infestation. Half a million people were huddled around tens of thousands of cooking fires, which were the source of the ever-thickening smoke rising over the city. And now, at 11.20am, with the sun heating the air to 37 degrees, the stench of the putrefying dead was rising with it.

Helen Parkes and Jack Fitzgerald sat mute in the Black Hawk looking down on the wretched scene. No words could convey the immensity of the catastrophe as effectively as a single glimpse of that misery. More and more refugees were flooding in by the minute from the north, and now Fitzgerald could see the entire area was enclosed by barbed wire. Most of the refugees were only too glad to arrive and passively went where they were told. But some were being evicted from the inner city by the army, and in the backstreets running battles were in progress between soldiers and refugee gangs.

Fitzgerald realised that Pat Howard had been misinformed. The refugees were not in the city – they had been excluded from it, and herded into an area where they could be more easily contained. Rather than serving as defenders of the people, here, the army were their warders.

Four kilometres to the south-east, a particularly ugly situation had developed. The residents of the New South Wales town of Queanbeyan had turned their streets into a citadel. All roads in had been barricaded with upturned vehicles and refugees who had tried to enter had been gunned down by vigilantes. The vigilante leader, an ultra right wing car dealer and leading light of the local gun lobby named Ian Worley, had seized the chance to fulfil his fantasy of military command. At the same time he had seized the opportunity to have his main competitor, who happened to be Chinese, beaten up and burned out of business. Worley's troops were the redneck wasters and yahoos of the town's public bars, and they were manning the barricades with automatic weapons from a cache Worley had built up in secret over years. Now his avowed mission was to repel all interlopers, whether two or eight legged, and he had rallied his troops with the cry of his East Belfast forebears, 'No Surrender!' It would end in tragedy.

Jack and Helen were distracted from their gloom by screaming jets, and looked east to see a squadron of F-111s circling to land. The RAAF and Canberra Airport shared Fairbairn airfield, which was encircled by troops and appeared as an oasis of green in the quagmire of humanity. Some bombers were already on the hard standing and the ground crews were refuelling and rearming them to return to Lake George. Helen wondered just how much fuel and ammunition they had down there, and for how long they thought they could keep the funnelwebs away from half a million sitting ducks.

As the Black Hawk flew on over the eastern outskirts of the city, soldiers were in and out of Russell

Offices like a trail of ants. They were loading everything – computers, filing cabinets, documents – into trucks which were ferrying back and forth to the airport. The Defence Force was abandoning its headquarters. It seemed a bad omen.

Then as they crossed Lake Burley Griffin above Kings Avenue Bridge, they saw that the Parliament House itself was transformed into a fortress. The State Circle around Capital Hill was ringed with tanks and field artillery. And for the first time with a view north through the smoke, Fitzgerald could see the streets of the city centre were crawling with troops.

The pilot put the helicopter down on the sports field to the west of the Senate building and a female naval commander rushed across from the stairs to Parliament Drive. She pulled open the door and called in over the din, 'Doctor Fitzgerald?'

Jack shouted, 'Yes, I'm Fitzgerald,' and he jumped out, followed by Helen.

The commander said, 'Judy Swan, Doctor Fitzgerald. Please follow me,' and she led off back towards the stairs. Waving thanks to the pilot, Jack and Helen set off after her.

Inside out of the clamour it was pleasantly cool, and it struck Fitzgerald that they had not been in a building since Holsworthy. They moved along a corridor of what seemed to be an administration area, then passed through double glass doors into a vestibule with lifts. As Commander Swan pressed the Up button, Helen noted how immaculately clean she was, and by contrast how filthy and desperate she and Jack must have looked.

When the lift arrived, they ascended in silence, and unexpectedly emerged into what might have been a four star hotel. They were in a small but tastefully appointed lobby complete with Chesterfields, cut flowers and original bush landscapes, and there was a kindly looking sergeant of the Commonwealth Protective Service behind a desk. The commander approached him and said crisply, 'Doctor Fitzgerald and Ms Parkes – I made arrangements.'

The sergeant punched a computer key, consulted his screen, then handed over two electronic key cards, stating, 'Suites five and eight.' Then, smiling, he said to Helen, 'Buzz me when you're ready and I'll get you something from the kitchen.'

Helen's head started swimming, which worsened as she followed Commander Swan along a corridor and into a small but comfortably appointed sitting room. She took in the deep armchairs and rosewood writing desk, as the commander went on into a connecting dressing room and checked its contents. Draped over a sofa there was an assortment of new clothes – shirts, jeans, sports shoes, and even a skirt. There was a travel bag still in its wrapping, and an en suite bathroom stocked with towels and toiletries.

Satisfied, the commander remarked without humour, 'I got your sizes from the Warrant Officer who found you – he assured me he used to be a quartermaster so everything should fit. Have a shower and something to eat then get some rest. I'll look in on you later when I've arranged your on-travel.' And with that, she turned and went out.

Left alone, Helen felt nauseous. Half an hour ago she'd faced a horrifying death. Now here she was in what could have been the Holiday Inn. She went to the bathroom and tried to throw up, but when nothing came she turned on the shower, stripped off her torn, filthy clothes and stepped in.

The powerful spray was exquisite, and she stood with her eyes closed, soaking up the steam and the heat. Then with shower gel and a loofah, she scrubbed her skin until it hurt, and slowly some of her anguish swirled away with the filthy water. She washed her hair, brushed her teeth and cleaned her nails, and by the time she had finished, she felt almost human again.

Stepping out, she examined herself in the mirror. Cuts and bruises aside, she had come through physically unscathed. Still, she looked changed – leaner, and more aggressive – and the smile in her eyes was replaced by a hunted stare.

As she reached for a towel, she saw Jack watching in through the open door. He too had showered and was wrapped in a bath robe, and he'd shaved and looked fresher and more attractive than ever before.

Helen felt aroused. Dropping the towel, she went out to him, naked and soaking. They looked at each other with deepening intensity, and with the realisation that they were alive, desire surged in them, and overflowed.

She tore off his robe and in carnal celebration, they devoured each other. It was not tender like the first time – now they fucked, like rampant animals – like two dogs fucking wildly in an alleyway. And when soon it was over, the embers rekindled quickly and they coupled again, and again, but with a desperate doom. They were as beasts condemned to die who had nothing left to lose, only frantic to breed because in breeding was their way to immortality.

Until finally they were drained and collapsed completely spent and lay together in a mingling drench of sweat. And with their bodies still entwined they found that deep untroubled sleep which most often is inhabited only by the young and the innocent.

Commander Swan returned to find Jack and Helen still naked and sleeping. She covered them with a sheet before shaking Jack awake, and when he opened his eyes, she said, 'Get dressed, please, I'll be back in ten minutes,' then went out again.

Jack lay there for awhile, just listening to Helen breathing. Then looking at her, he was moved by how beautiful she was, and he knew that there was again a woman in his life.

He got up and went to his own suite, where he re-showered and dressed in the clean shirt and drills draped over his sofa. Then almost to the second, after ten minutes, the commander returned. She gave Fitzgerald a security pass which he clipped to his waistband. Then she led him out through the lobby and down in the lift to the basement.

They walked a long way through a labyrinth of corridors until they reached a heavily guarded security check. The sergeant of the guard eyed Fitzgerald suspiciously, and only consented to let him through after talking to central security. It was there Commander Swan said, 'This is where I leave you, Doctor Fitzgerald,' and walked off.

Fitzgerald was ushered through a heavy steel door and found himself in an anonymous passageway. The lighting was stark and there were no concessions to decor or comfort. He followed a mute CPS officer until they arrived at another heavily guarded door. But this time he was expected, and he was shown directly inside.

The room he entered was small and impersonal, but carpeted and by contrast with the corridor, pleasant enough. Two men were seated at a polished wooden table and one of them, whom Fitzgerald recognised, stepped forward and said, 'Doctor Fitzgerald, thank God you're safe. I'm very sorry about what happened to Doctor Reid.'

Jack shook the man's proffered hand, and said, 'Thank you. Bill Reid was a great man.' Then he asked, 'So what's going on, Prime Minister?'

Richard Bartlett looked tired and had grazed himself shaving, but he was impeccably dressed and seemed perfectly relaxed. As he led Fitzgerald by the arm to the table, he said confidingly, 'I don't know what you've been told since you were picked up, Doctor Fitzgerald, but I'm sorry to tell you that we're in serious trouble. The neutron bomb was a fiasco, the monsters are spreading like wildfire and we've been forced to place New South Wales under martial law.'

At the table, the second man, whom Fitzgerald did not know, stood up and Bartlett said, 'Let me introduce you to Dennis Carson – Dennis, this is Doctor John Fitzgerald.'

The two men shook hands without smiling, and said, 'How do you do.'

Bartlett went on, 'Dennis is a senior public servant attached to my staff, Doctor Fitzgerald, and is familiar with the marvellous work you have been doing at the CSIRO.'

Carson was a thin man, a little over fifty, whose gold-framed spectacles did nothing to soften the ruthlessness in his eyes. He had been busy for the past week, having been exclusively engaged in personal work for the Prime Minister, including the surveillance of John Czarnecki and the tracking of his attempted escape. Dennis Carson was head of ASIO.

As they all sat down, Bartlett opened an attache case on the table and took out a single manila file. Then he said, 'As it turns out, Doctor Fitzgerald, the timing of your arrival in Canberra could not have been better, as only this morning we received information which I am sure will interest you.'

Bartlett took a dozen sheets from the file, then scanning through them, continued, 'This document is a personal dispatch to me from the American President, informing me of an event which occurred on the thirty-first of December last in the Tasman Sea off Sydney Heads. It seems one of their Trident submarines was conducting an unauthorised patrol in our waters when what they describe as an "unscheduled incident" . . . I believe that's American for "accident" . . . occurred.'

The hairs on the back of Fitzgerald's neck stood up as Bartlett slid the document across to him, saying, 'Apparently there was a radioactive leak from one of their warheads which, at the time, the crew believed was contained within the ship. However it was later discovered that a swab used to clean up the leak was nowhere on board. The material involved is a newly developed substance which they have since discovered may give rise to the kind of genetic effects that we are experiencing with the funnelwebs.' Then, with quiet emphasis, Bartlett said, 'Doctor Fitzgerald, you have proposed from the outset that radiation of some kind was probably what caused the funnelwebs to mutate. If this radioactive swab came into contact with the funnelwebs somehow, could it have been what triggered their mutation?'

His stomach knotted, Fitzgerald read the document. And there it all was, chapter and verse. A summary analysis of the radiation emitted by antimony-plutonium alloy, some preliminary results of tests conducted by the Institute for Nuclear Medicine into the effects of APA on genetic structures, and, most tellingly, the specific effects observed in a small group of species including those descended from mygalomorphs, which corresponded exactly with what Fitzgerald had seen in the mutant funnelweb specimens at North Ryde.

Tingling, he looked up, and said, 'In my opinion, Prime Minister, this is almost certainly the cause of the problem.' Then he added, 'And if I can get into a lab with a specimen, I can probably prove it.'

Bartlett and Carson exchanged looks, then Bartlett stood and paced as he said, 'Well, Doctor Fitzgerald, that's exactly what I would like you to do – as head of a new research project we are going to institute, which the Americans have agreed to resource.' Then Bartlett looked steadily at Fitzgerald as he said, 'I'm talking about the most important scientific appointment in the country . . . indeed, under the circumstances, in the world. And the status – and remuneration – attached to it will reflect that importance.'

Fitzgerald felt suddenly off balance. Only hours ago, he'd been dead meat. Now he was being offered the career opportunity of a lifetime. He didn't like Richard Bartlett, or trust him – he knew there'd been something underhand in the decision to use the neutron bomb. But to Fitzgerald, the funnelweb war had become personal. And for the chance to destroy them, he could put all else aside. So when Bartlett pressed, 'What do you say, Doctor Fitzgerald,' he answered, 'I accept.'

Bartlett responded only, 'Good – thank you,' as he retrieved the presidential dispatch and sat down again.

Speaking for the first time, Dennis Carson said in a mild voice, 'It will be necessary then, Doctor Fitzgerald, for you to be privy to top secret information and to be party to decisions of national importance. I'll have the appropriate security documents drawn up for your signature but in the meantime you should understand that everything you hear in connection with the national situation, including what you have learned at this meeting, is confidential, and that any unauthorised disclosure would result in the severest of penalties.'

Fitzgerald felt the hackles rising. He hadn't been spoken to like that since he'd left school. He disliked Carson's manner, and replied in a tone equally clipped, 'I understand.'

Richard Bartlett stood again and closed his attache case. Then saying crisply, 'All right – let's get on,' he turned and led out through a door behind him.

Fitzgerald and Carson followed the Prime Minister into a spartan, bunker-style conference room where perhaps twenty other people were waiting. There were faces familiar from Holsworthy, and Bartlett indicated an empty chair to Fitzgerald next to one of them. It was Christian Phelps, the brigadier who had given credence to the neutron bomb.

As Fitzgerald sat down, Bartlett went to the head of the table and addressed the all-male gathering. 'Gentlemen, I'm delighted to welcome Doctor John Fitzgerald of the CSIRO to this meeting of the Emergency Executive, in an advisory capacity. Doctor Fitzgerald was feared lost in a helicopter accident but thankfully survived it and is here now.'

Murmurs of welcome passed around the table until the Prime Minister cut in, saying, 'Tragically, Doctor Fitzgerald's colleague, Doctor Reid, died in the crash, and I should also announce for those who may not yet know that the Premier of New South Wales was also killed last night.'

The announcement prompted shocked inquiries. Bartlett responded to them collectively, 'After the failure of the neutron bomb, when it became clear that Menangle would be a battleground, John insisted on going there. Tragically the army unit he was with was overrun. It was an act of bravery typical of him. It's a great loss.'

Mournful assent passed around the meeting. But in the back of his mind, Fitzgerald thought it odd that Pat Howard had made no mention of Czarnecki being at Menangle.

He passed over it when Bartlett said, 'However we must move ahead, and in that spirit I have appointed Doctor Fitzgerald as head of our new funnelweb research program – and I have already briefed him on the communication we have received from the Americans.'

Looking around the dutifully approving faces, Fitzgerald got the feeling that Bartlett's Emergency Executive was mainly comprised of toothless public servants, presumably whose purpose was to rubber stamp prime ministerial decisions for the sake of legality under martial law. This was no democratic body – it was a puppet Star Chamber. Fitzgerald noticed the bespectacled stenographer, punctiliously recording every word for the public record. In the future, Bartlett could point to that record as evidence that all his decisions were subject to the processes of legal government. This Emergency Executive was his political laundry, and Fitzgerald was angry with himself that he had so readily been conscripted into it.

Bartlett was continuing, 'Further to that, I can confirm that in the circumstances the President has offered any and all assistance we may need – money no object. As well as resources for the scientific research program, they will provide weaponry and military personnel, and full US protectorate status to safeguard our sovereignty. He has also offered to mount a long-term national rehabilitation plan and provide assistance in its implementation . . . should it become necessary. Needless to say, he has assured me that all warheads armed with this . . .' Bartlett referred to a document on the table, '. . . antimony-plutonium alloy . . . have been withdrawn.'

Most people made a show of scribbling notes, until a man Fitzgerald recognised as the Federal Treasurer stated sourly, 'Well it's good of the Yanks to be so kind to us after they've totally fucked our country – but I'm sorry, I don't believe a word of it. "Protectorate status" and "long-term rehabilitation plan" sound to me like a fast track to becoming the fifty-first state of the Union – at the very least we'll end up in hock to the bastards for half a century, like the Poms did after World War II.'

There was an embarrassed silence as people waited to hear Bartlett's view. But when he said nothing, a senior naval officer queried, 'What intrigues me, Prime Minister, is that all this is so out of character for them . . . I mean, whoever heard of the American President giving top secret information about their nuclear weaponry to the leader of a foreign state?'

Heads nodded as Bartlett said, 'Dennis Carson can give us some insight into that, Admiral Roberts.' Then turning to Carson, who was seated next to him, he said, 'Dennis?'

Carson was known for what he was to everyone in the room apart from Fitzgerald, and feared by most of them. Again in his deceptively mild voice, he reported, 'Our information is that when the funnelweb story broke, the captain of the submarine in question was so guilt ridden that he went to pieces. It seems he went into hiding and was threatening to tell all to the international press unless the US government came clean with us. Two hours ago we complied with their request to confirm to him that they had done so, by the Prime Minister appearing in a satellite interview on US television and answering a particular question with a pre-agreed sentence. We have just heard from our sources in Washington that within the past hour, the officer in question has walked into the FBI office in Albuquerque, New Mexico, and blown his brains out.'

There were muted gasps, and the Federal Treasurer observed, 'Funnelwebs seem to be causing a rash of suicides among senior military.'

Ignoring the snide reference to his last two Defence Chiefs, Bartlett went on, 'As for the President's generous offers of help, it will come as no surprise that they are conditional on our silence – if the radiation leak story gets out, we're on our own.'

Appropriate murmurs arose, and Fitzgerald was just wondering how he could get out of this circus when the telephone at the Prime Minister's elbow warbled. Bartlett picked it up and said, 'Yes.' Then he listened without speaking for a full half minute before he said, 'Give the order,' and hung up.

After a moment, he looked down the silent table, and was genuinely shaken when he said, 'The funnelwebs have started moving south from Lake George towards Canberra.'

Every face paled. Against all logic, people had assumed the capital was somehow sacrosanct. That assumption was now shattered.

Bartlett continued, 'I'm informed that the monsters could be here within two hours. Accordingly . . .' and the Prime Minister cleared his throat, 'accordingly . . . I've given the order for Canberra to be evacuated.'

Heads shook in disbelief as two senior army officers stood, the older one saying, 'If you will excuse us, then, Prime Minister, General Cornish and I have work to do.'

Bartlett dismissed them with an absent wave, saying, 'Yes, of course, General Greenwell. Thank you, and good luck to you both,' and the officers went out.

Fitzgerald was just pondering on how they might

evacuate half a million refugees, when Bartlett said, 'As our time is now limited, we'll cut all other business and I'll invite Brigadier Phelps to outline the proposal he has for us – Brigadier?'

Christian Phelps stood and carried a briefcase to a podium at the table head, as an aide pulled down a roller screen and switched on a slide projector. Phelps took a thin file from his case and opened it. Then, looking every inch the brilliant academic he clearly considered himself, he glanced over his half-frames and in a cut-glass voice, began, 'Thank you, Prime Minister. Gentlemen – the position we face in the current crisis is close to outright disaster. The Defence Force can no longer contain the funnelwebs – they are simply too numerous and too aggressive.'

Looks of apprehension shot around the table, as Phelps continued, 'Since Menangle, we have known that it was only a matter of time before they reached Canberra. We had hoped that it would take them thirty-six hours longer. However, as we have heard, they are already within a few kilometres of this room.'

People scratched involuntarily as Phelps paused to consult his notes. Then he went on, 'I believe that since the CSIRO research operation was suspended there have been no further advancements in the quest for scientific counter measures. But I understand that a new research project is to be initiated on a far bigger scale.' Then turning to the Prime Minister, Phelps queried, 'Have we any indication yet of how long it might take the scientists to come up with something?'

Reseated, Bartlett looked down the table, and inquired, 'Doctor Fitzgerald?'

Fitzgerald was antagonised. What kind of bloody pantomime was this? It was clear Bartlett and Phelps had cooked up some new scheme. And he had been enlisted to promote whatever it was by reaffirming his own ineffectiveness. He said brusquely, 'No,' but expressed considerably more than that in his mien.

Oblivious, Phelps concluded, 'So the position at this time is that we have no means of countering the funnelwebs.'

Nobody said anything. What was there to say? There was a sense that dawn was breaking on the morning of execution.

Contrarily, the lights dimmed. Phelps had done it from the podium. He hit another switch and a slide appeared on the screen. It was a map of south-eastern New South Wales – a black and white map but with areas highlighted in green, blue and yellow.

Picking up a pointer, Phelps said, 'Now . . . this is how things stand,' and he pointed to the yellow areas, which included metropolitan Sydney, the South Coast as far as Wollongong, and a corridor between twenty and forty kilometres across centred on the Hume Highway, encompassing Mittagong, Moss Vale and Goulburn, and ending below Collector immediately north of Lake George.

'The yellow areas show the ground presently occupied by the funnelwebs. As you can see,' and he pointed to the expansive blue areas of the Nepean-Hawkesbury River valley and the Illawarra coastal plain, '. . . they have been stopped by flooding to the north, west and south of Sydney,' then pointing to the yellow corridor, '. . . but they have advanced quickly to the south-west, along the line of the Hume Highway, and for several kilometres on either side of it.'

Despite himself, Fitzgerald was becoming absorbed. He studied the map closely, as something nagged at the back of his mind.

Phelps continued, 'However – if we look at the green areas, here . . .' pointing west-south-west of Sydney to the Blue Mountains, '. . . and here . . .' lowering the pointer to the Snowy Mountains south-west of Canberra, '. . . we see the sections of the Great Dividing Range which lie above the eight hundred and fifty metre contour line,' and turning again to the table, he said '. . . which interestingly corresponds with the extent of the funnelwebs' most westerly advance.'

And Fitzgerald's heart raced as he heard Phelps conclude, 'When we noticed that, we did an analysis of all the intelligence we had. And, sure enough, eight hundred and fifty metres appears to be an altitude above which the funnelwebs will not go.'

The words resounded in Fitzgerald's ears like a clarion. Eight hundred and fifty metres – the Great Dividing Range. Of course! Why the hell had nobody thought of it? Why the hell hadn't *he* thought of it? The mountains of the Great Dividing Range ran the entire length of the Australian east coast, 3,700 kilometres from Cape York peninsula to Bass Strait, and were so named because they divided the narrow eastern coastal plain from the low-lying continental interior. The Great Dividing Range was the reason why pre-mutant funnelwebs, along with other species found exclusively on the east coast, had never migrated inland. And now, in whatever other ways they differed, the monsters seemed to have inherited their forebears' aversion to high altitudes.

One half of Jack's brain was computing implications as with the other, he heard Phelps say, 'If the funnelwebs can be kept east of the mountains, it may buy us time to find a way to destroy them. The problem is . . .' and Phelps pointed again at the screen, '. . . that this section of the Great Dividing Range – between Goulburn and

Canberra – is a depression centring on Lake George which lies below eight hundred and fifty metres.'

Then after a dramatic pause, Phelps observed, 'Unfortunately, like a carrot and a stick, the refugee migration and the flooding have channelled the funnelwebs directly here – to the one place where the mountains are not high enough to stop them infesting the rest of the continent.'

'No! They would have come here anyway. They're going through to the western plains!' Fitzgerald's voice was loaded with authority, and in its wake it would have been possible to have heard a pin drop.

Until out of the silence, Admiral Roberts asked, 'But why? The west is a sparsely populated region?'

Glaring down the table, Fitzgerald replied, 'Sparsely populated with people – but the New South Wales western plains contain forty million sheep.'

Another voice, the Federal Treasurer's, muttered, 'Jesus Christ!' And they were the only words spoken for several moments.

Fitzgerald felt like every kind of a fool. It was so blindingly obvious. Once the human food source dried up, of course the funnelwebs would move on to the next nearest source. And forty million sheep represented enough food for them to become established on the landmass immutably. They could smell all that mutton over the hill. And by instinct they knew that the Lake George depression was their way through to it.

Fitzgerald was so engrossed that he did not notice the excited glances passing between Phelps and Bartlett. But he looked up again when Phelps said, 'Thank you, Doctor Fitzgerald – regrettably what you say only confirms the conclusions we've reached from a purely military assessment.'

Then looking again at the screen, he said, 'So it's clear that what is needed is a way of blocking the funnel-webs' path – of creating a "firebreak" – from the Blue Mountains . . .' and he ran his pointer southwards, '. . . to the Snowies – a ground distance extending safely beyond the eight hundred and fifty metre contour lines of one hundred and twenty kilometres.'

Gaining confidence, and starting to remind Fitzgerald of Andrew Lawrie, Phelps observed, 'In the short time left to us, it looks a hopeless proposition. But in the past eighteen hours, in collaboration with our American colleagues, we have concluded that there is a way it can be done.'

Theatrically, Phelps hit the projector switch and the slide changed. Again, it was a black and white map of eastern New South Wales, and again, the funnelwebs were marked in yellow, the water in blue, and the mountains in green. But there was a new mark – a red line, running more or less south-west from the southern Blue Mountains peak of Mount McAlister, between Goulburn and Crookwell, past Gunning, past Yass, to the northernmost peak of the Brindabella Ranges east of Gundagai. And at the top of the map was the caption, Operation Hot Ditch.

Then Jack Fitzgerald, in company with others in the room, could barely believe his ears when he heard Christian Phelps say, 'Operation Hot Ditch is a plan to block the funnelwebs from passing through the Lake George depression and so deny them access to the rest of the continent. The idea is to create a barrier of radiation so intense – between ten and thirty times more so than the radiation of the neutron bomb – that the funnelwebs cannot cross it. The barrier, or Hot Ditch, will be created by sowing the ground with a latent fissile agent, then radioactivating that agent with high airburst detonations of standard

W-88 thermonuclear warheads, each rated at four hundred and seventy-five kilotons, or thirty-two times the power of the Hiroshima bomb. The W-88s will be delivered in the required pattern by United States Navy submarine-launched ballistic missiles. Each detonation will activate the line sown for a distance of seven and a half kilometres. So it will take a total of sixteen detonations to create the Hot Ditch, an explosive power totalling seven point six megatons – equivalent to seven point six million tons of TNT.'

Engrossed in his monstrous statistics, Phelps seemed unaware of the impact he had made. Most of those present, including Fitzgerald, were gobsmacked. Those who had been party to the plan seemed not to know where to look. However Admiral Roberts, whom Fitzgerald correctly assumed to be the new CDF, had clearly not known of it, and was white. It seemed though that Bartlett had chosen his man more carefully this time, and the Admiral had nothing to say.

The first person to respond was the Federal Treasurer. Incredulous, he said, 'I don't understand, Richard. We know this chain of events was started by a nuclear accident. And we seem to have made it worse with the neutron bomb. Now we're saying we're going to nuke the funnelwebs again. I mean . . .' and he was exasperated, '. . . what's to say this . . . Hot Ditch . . . won't make things even worse?'

Non-committal, Bartlett once more looked to Phelps, and said, 'Brigadier?'

On a roll, Phelps expounded, 'Minister, we must remember that the neutron bomb was a success – it killed all the funnelwebs above ground. Now we don't know if the new generation was saved by the shielding effect of being underground or by some kind of resilience. It's true that some life forms, cockroaches for instance, are resilient to radiation . . . to a degree. The neutron bomb is designed to emit an intense pulse of radiation which lasts for a microsecond, so any life form not directly exposed to it, and particularly one with a degree of resilience, may not be affected. However what we're talking about with Hot Ditch is radiation of a different order, emitted from a permanently emplaced source. It is inconceivable that any living organisms, including the funnelwebs, could survive it.'

Again, the Federal Treasurer could rejoin only, 'Jesus Christ!'

Detecting that shock was working in his favour, Bartlett moved to consolidate. Looking again down the table, he queried, 'Doctor Fitzgerald, from your knowledge of the mutated funnelwebs, what, in your view, would be the effect on them of such high levels of radiation?'

All eyes turned to Fitzgerald, who was simmering. It was plain that he had been brought here expressly to legitimise this abomination. And unwittingly he had done so beyond Phelps' and Bartlett's hopes with his disclosure about the western plains sheep. Now again, he was being cynically used.

Despite that, he could only say what he thought, which was, 'I don't know. By all scientific logic and experience, nothing should have lived through the neutron bomb. But the new generation of monster funnelwebs did. Unlike Brigadier Phelps, in the absence of any scientific evidence, I am not prepared to hypothesise as to why. All I will say is that where the funnelwebs are concerned, we should make no assumptions whatsoever – because, as we've seen with the neutron bomb, assumption is the mother of all fuck-ups!'

The point was lost on no-one. But Bartlett, the consummate politician, rolled with it. Suitably grave, he responded, 'Indeed. Wise council, which we would do well to heed. Thank you, Doctor Fitzgerald.' But then, with quiet finality, he concluded, 'In light of developments in the past hour, however, I can see no other option.'

Admiral Roberts, the conspicuously mute new CDF, then seized the opportunity of non-controversial input by asking, 'What about the Russians, Prime Minister, and the Chinese? How will they react?'

With a nod from Bartlett, Dennis Carson responded, 'The Russians and the Chinese have agreed to Hot Ditch on condition that they are allowed to fully observe the operation. We and the Americans have agreed to that. There are no other international objections that need concern us.'

Fitzgerald was stunned. What an extraordinary remark. Before he had thought about it, he blurted, 'But what about the fallout, for Christ's sake? It'll spread all over the Pacific!'

Carson had been registering Fitzgerald's growing hostility.

But it was Phelps who answered a little nervously, 'The effects of residual radiation from fallout will be mostly confined to the evacuated areas of New South Wales, Doctor Fitzgerald, and will in fact be a bonus because it may kill off funnelwebs that don't approach the Ditch. It is true that the water tables of Sydney and the South Coast will be contaminated for some years, but the funnelwebs will be neutralised and the country as a whole will be saved.'

With those words, it hit Fitzgerald like a ton of bricks what this was really all about. The purpose of Operation Hot Ditch was to contain the funnelwebs all right – but it was also to render eastern New South Wales uninhabitable by humans. Whatever Bartlett and the

Americans were up to, they didn't want the locals coming back to get in the way.

Looking daggers at Phelps, Fitzgerald repeated, 'Contaminated? For how *many* years?'

A crack appeared in Bartlett's veneer. More than a little short, he interjected, 'I think we can safely leave those considerations to our military experts, Doctor Fitzgerald.'

But Fitzgerald wasn't going to leave anything to these people. He probed, 'And what about the residual radiation of your Hot Ditch itself, Brigadier. What is this latent fissile agent you referred to?'

Phelps replied pointedly, 'I'm afraid that's classified.'

Fitzgerald came to the boil. 'Yes . . . it would be. But I'll bet London to a brick it's something we can't clean up for a couple of centuries!'

Phelps swallowed hard, then replied mildly, 'I believe that is a rather pessimistic estimate, Doctor Fitzgerald.'

It was Fitzgerald's opening. He erupted, '*You believe*, Brigadier? *You believe?* You believed the neutron bomb would put an end to this problem. Instead it's escalated it beyond retrieval. Now you believe the funnelwebs can't possibly survive your Hot Ditch. But on what is your belief based. Not on investigative data – because we have none. Not on biological expertise – because *you* have none. Which leads me to suspect, Brigadier . . .' then looking Bartlett directly in the eye, '. . . Prime Minister . . . that the basis of your shared belief is not knowledge of any kind – but the pursuit of some private agenda!'

Around the table, discomfort turned into full-blown fear. The trace of a sickly smile on Bartlett's face did nothing to disguise his antipathy. But most eyes were not on him – they were stealing glances at the head of ASIO, as he passively scribbled a note on a legal pad.

The stenographer stopped typing, and glanced timorously at the Prime Minister. But when his eyes were not met, he looked back down at his machine and recorded what Fitzgerald had said.

Then Fitzgerald stood up, making the two men closest to him start, and glaring down the table, he railed, 'Prime Minister, this Hot Ditch of yours is an obscenity. Even if it destroys the funnelwebs, which is not certain, it will undoubtedly destroy the ecology of south-eastern New South Wales to an extent that it will never recover!'

All eyes turned to Bartlett, who despite the harangue had recomposed himself and looked appropriately grave. Fitzgerald saw hostility wasn't working. So he changed tack.

'Prime Minister, in God's name, don't do this. Let the funnelwebs through. Forty million sheep should keep them inside New South Wales for months. Now we know what caused them to mutate, with the Americans' resources, the odds of our coming up with an answer are good. Give me a chance to save the country without destroying it in the process.'

Bartlett pondered, as the others at the table sat in silence. Eventually, he fixed his gaze on Fitzgerald, and replied. 'Let me assure you, Doctor Fitzgerald, that you are not alone in your concern for this country – all of us share that concern with equal regard. Let me also assure you that the wellbeing of Australia is the *only* concern of everyone here, and that there are no secret deals or smoking guns.'

His tone was admonishing, the principal addressing a recalcitrant pupil, and Fitzgerald knew that his gambit had failed.

Bartlett went on, 'You have already informed us, Doctor Fitzgerald, that you have no idea when, if at all, you will find an answer. As soon as possible, we will set up the new research project and you will have the opportunity to show exactly what you are worth. Meanwhile, please confine yourself to your designated role here as adviser, and resist the temptation to act as an advocate in matters outside your brief.'

It was over, bar the pronouncement. Reviewing notes in front of him, Bartlett asked, 'Are there any more comments?'

There were none. Nevertheless many shivered when they heard Bartlett say, 'Under the circumstances then, and in the absence of any alternative, I must reluctantly order that Operation Hot Ditch will proceed.'

As if on cue, the door burst open and General Greenwell re-entered, accompanied by a sergeant and two corporals of the Military Police. The general was white as he said, 'Prime Minister, I require your order to evacuate Parliament House.' His voice was strained but his tone incontrovertible. Their time was up.

Bartlett said, 'The order is given, General,' and he stood, picked up his attache case and went out without another word. Dennis Carson went out behind him, followed by Phelps and the rest of the military.

When they'd gone, the MP sergeant began calling the civilians' names from a list and each man was given instructions of where to go. When Fitzgerald's name was called, he was told, 'Corporal Woods will escort you back to the ministerial suites, Doctor Fitzgerald – you'll be given further instructions there.'

Fitzgerald was whisked off by one of the tough-looking MP corporals and out through a corridor he had not been in before. As they weaved around corners and through passageways, there was much urgent coming and going – military and civilians, men and women, senior and lowly ranks. But all of them shared the same tautness of fear in their faces.

Eventually they emerged into the carpeted vestibule and the MP corporal pressed the lift's Up call button. Then consulting his clipboard, he said, 'You'll be met in the suites by Commander Swan, sir,' and he turned and went off before Fitzgerald could ask anything more.

The lift arrived and as Fitzgerald got in, his stomach knotted with apprehension – something was wrong.

The lift ascended, the doors opened and he emerged into the lobby of the suites. Everything was as it had been except that the reception desk was unmanned. He walked along the corridor and looked into his room but it was empty. He looked into Helen's room and that was empty too. Then he saw Helen's things were gone, and he felt apprehensive. He looked into every one of the suites and found the place was deserted. So he stood there in the corridor, wondering what to do next, when the lights went out and made up his mind for him.

He strode to the lift and pressed the call button but nothing happened. He pressed again and again but still nothing happened. His fear rising, he turned and moved quickly around the entire area, searching urgently for an emergency exit. And he found one, in a passageway behind the reception desk, but it was barred and bolted.

Fitzgerald put his shoulder into the door but to no effect. He tried again, and again, but after several bruising impacts it was obvious that the door was never going to shift. Then, as his mind raced to the next obvious option, he made the most devastating discovery of all – throughout the entire suites area, there was no window that opened nor any other door which led outside.

The double-glazed windows overlooked a courtyard one floor below. Fitzgerald went to the lobby and grabbed a steel typist's chair. Then he rushed into the nearest of the suites and hurled the chair at the window. It bounced off. He went into every one of the suites and tried the same thing, but with the same result – the area was fully protected with armoured glass.

Standing there alone, looking down into the unreachable courtyard, Fitzgerald felt a suffocating weight descend – the weight of realisation that he was totally and hopelessly trapped.

12

Keegan's Hotel, Main Street, Struggletown, had always been a bloodhouse. The day it opened in 1926, three Aboriginals had been violently evicted by the throng in the public bar. When they'd returned with machetes there'd been a violent fracas, and after six minutes two of the blacks and a white man were dead on the floor. That had set the tone of the place and ever since Keegan's had been a hangout for bruisers, druggies, drunks, Goulburn parolees and, ironically, alcoholic Aboriginals.

Miles French and Johnny O'Carroll were Keegan's regulars. Between the dole, penny-bag drug dealing and petty larceny, they always seemed to be in the bar with plenty of cash to get drunk on. Being permanently shit-faced never impeded their favourite pursuit, however, which they braggingly and inaccurately referred to as the noble art of pugilism. Many's the night they'd stood shoulder to shoulder in Keegan's car park, and extracted retribution from offenders with fists or chains or bottles. Often the offence was no more than an innocent glance down the bar, to which the response was invariably, 'What the fuck you lookin' at?' And whatever the reply, it would inevitably be twisted into justifying a vicious assault.

It was unusual then that for two days straight both

Johnny O and Miles had been sober. And it was even more unusual that despite that they'd had the time of their lives. Kicking the guts out of that flash slope cunt and torching his car yard had been legend. And that had only been the start of it. Right afterwards, Ian Worley had given them all guns, and Miles had got a Sten gun, just like his big brother Denny's. It was a mean-looking mother, all shiny and black, piss easy to shoot and real powerful – the first time Miles sprayed it at the reffos over the Canberra Avenue barricade, it had just about chopped some dumb fucker's legs off.

Pity Denny had missed the fun – he'd gone bush, on a mission, just like the real army. Denny and his mate, Crazy Wayne, had taken some of the Brothers and shot through in their utes to go fossicking up round Lake Bathurst. There was a tart there Wayne wanted to look up – this bitch that prick-teased him all night at the last Goulburn Bachelors and Spinsters then fucked off with some squatter ponce when Wayne was taking a slash. He was really dark about it and Miles didn't fancy her chances if Wayne found her. Wayne was a worry – a full on, solid gold psycho. But he was a top bloke in a knuckle and always stood by his mates, and that was all that counted with the Queanbeyan Brothers.

Now with what was going down in Sydney, Wayne and Denny were rapt. Denny reckoned the funnelwebs were the best thing ever – they'd stopped all the bullshit and now it was down to survival, just like it used to be, like it was in the convict days. In fact Denny and Wayne had got a bit strange about it and reckoned the funnelweb should be their animal, like the coons had in the Dreamtime.

So Wayne made up this ritual . . . the Initiation, he called it . . . where everybody knelt in front of this picture of a funnelweb and said stuff about 'the spirit of the spider' and 'conquest through evil', or some shit like that, then cut themselves and bled a bit. Then Fat Alice, the bikie tat artist from Belconnen, spiked a funnelweb on everyone's forehead, and the boys all got blind and rode the arse off the sluts Johnny O pulled. 'Til one of 'em got the shits when Wayne jobbed her and the three of 'em fucked off.

It was next day, when they sobered up a bit, that Denny said he was leading the first mission of The Sect of the Funnelweb . . . a pillaging, he called it . . . a 'raid for spoils'. Only he wouldn't take Miles or Johnny O 'cause he said they were fuckwits.

Well, fuck him. Now Miles had a Sten gun too. And he'd blown away at least five . . . or maybe eight . . . or even ten reffos. So when Denny got back, he'd *have* to take him on the next mission.

But Miles wasn't thinking about Denny that afternoon, because he was too busy. Himself and Johnny O were back at Canberra Avenue, and since lunchtime they'd chalked up two reffos each.

The mangy bastards were hanging back now, skulking between the railway and the Molonglo, too chickenshit to take on the likes of the Queanbeyan Brothers. There were about twenty of the boys on the barricade that afternoon. And Ian Worley was with them, all tarted up in his flash new uniform that Miles thought made him look like a dickhead but didn't dare say so. Because Ian Worley was right into the *generalissimo* shit . . . and when Stevo and Gra turned up full of piss and bad manners, Worley busted their chops and shot 'em both in the kneecaps.

So no-one else gave Worley any shit that afternoon, as he pranced up and down and barked orders in his funny high voice. He was a weird fucker – there was definitely something wrong about him. There were rumours he was a poofter . . . two or three of the blokes said he'd tried it on when they were pissed. But poofter or not he was a hard case, and nobody argued when he said they had to call him, 'The Colonel'.

Apart from Worley, the rest of the afternoon was quiet, so it must have been about five o'clock when the wind changed. It swung to the north-west and in no time the guardians of Queanbeyan were choking in smoke. Their throats burned, their eyes streamed, they couldn't see the ground in front of them, but worst of all was the putrid stink. It filled their lungs and churned their stomachs, and in seconds most of the Brothers were spewing their rings up in the road.

The Colonel was no help – he just got the shits, running up and down and screaming that he'd shoot any deserters. But then he made his mistake, when Big Mal Seal fronted up to him and told him to go and get fucked.

The Colonel lost it. He pulled out this Magnum and blew a fucking great hole in Mal's chest. No-one could believe it – the Brothers just stood there and stared.

It was Mal's brother, Gerry, made the move. Gerry was a quiet fucker, said nothing most of the time . . . didn't get into blues or drink much either. But when he saw his big brother wasted, a side of him came out no-one had seen before.

Gerry had a Bren gun, a World War II machine-gun – a humungous tool. Its mag held thirty rounds and it must have taken about three seconds for Gerry to put the lot into Worley's guts. It was like one minute he was standing there, pointing his gun and shouting – and the next he was a bloody mess on the floor with this head and legs sticking out.

Gerry said nothing. Not a word. He just looked at Worley, then threw the Bren onto his shoulder and rocked off. It would've been better if he'd screamed or shouted or something. As it was, the effect on the Brothers was dire. They freaked out – threw down their guns and ran back into the town like scared rabbits.

The reffos must have seen it because a minute later a whole mob of them swept into Queanbeyan. And as they caught up with the Brothers and ran them down like dogs, they showed no more mercy than the Brothers had shown to them. Many a slow killing was committed in the alleyways, and screams for mercy pierced the air over the town for nearly an hour.

They caught Miles and Johnny O outside Keegan's, where they'd gone with the idea of breaking in and hiding in the cellar. The reffos hot-wired a couple of cars, tied Johnny O and Miles between them, then inched them apart until their joints popped. Johnny O was shorter so Miles had to listen to him bawling for twenty minutes, and all the time knowing that when it stopped it was his turn next.

Then it finally came, and it turned out Miles had no stomach for pain. In fact he was screaming and shitting himself before the reffos had even taken up the slack. But when they did, Miles couldn't believe just how much trouble there could be in the world. Nothing in his life could have prepared him for that torment, and by the time he slipped from consciousness he'd had a good taste of the grief that he'd always so enjoyed dishing out.

It was as Miles' arms finally separated and the cars jerked and stalled, that in the silence the reffos first sensed the funnelwebs. Against the darkening smoke-filled sky, no-one had noticed them approaching, until now the ominous black shapes were looming in the murk all around them. The humans scattered, leaving their victims' dismembered bodies where they lay, and ran for their lives back to the half million strong encampment from which they'd come.

The sentinels did not chase them. They just stood and watched them go. Because their presence there was part of a wider intention. They were a group that had skirted the battlefield to the east, as others had approached from the north and still others had wheeled to the west and were approaching from there.

They knew that they had far to go before they would reach the abundance beyond the mountains, but they also knew they were surrounding all the sustenance they would need to get there.

So they stood, immobile, like great statues . . . and awaited the coming of darkness in which they would attack.

Pat Howard was a disciplined man, a positive thinker not given to pique or melancholy. But that evening, the Officer Commanding, 'Bravo' Company, 5/7 Battalion, was depressed.

His company had been decimated that day, on a dry lake bed south of Collector, bordering the Federal Highway. 3 Platoon aside, Howard had lost another three soldiers killed and four wounded. Added to those already lost at Central and at Menangle, it meant they were now down to less than half strength – only fifty-one men.

However after Jack Fitzgerald and Helen Parkes had been evacuated, there had been no more fighting that morning on the plain of Lake George. As the hours had passed, the funnelwebs had continued to muster until eventually there had been so many that the troops were completely overwhelmed. So under cover of smoke they had quietly pulled out, until all that faced the funnelwebs was a line of broken down, abandoned tanks.

Now, at 7.05pm, in driving rain, the eight remaining APCs of 'Bravo' Company turned off the Federal Highway and headed south into the dusk towards Canberra Airport. Howard was so tired he could barely stand in his turret, and in his tiredness, the deaths of so many of his men laid heavily upon him. His depression was also intensified by the hell on earth he was travelling through – the Majura Road refugee camp with its half million souls, all suffering and dying in a quagmire of raw sewage and bloating corpses.

It was plain that there was no way to defend these people. But then it was also plain that the army was not there to defend them, but the airport. And to defend it not from the funnelwebs, but from the refugees. For the entire nine kilometres from Mount Majura to Fairbairn, the road was fenced off with razor wire. And the frequent patrols by vehicles bristling with machine-guns could have no other purpose than to dissuade any refugee incursions.

But as bleak as these things were, they were not at the root of Howard's depression. Rather as he stood there, oblivious to the rain, what was eating him was a thought that had been playing on his mind all day. It was an idea he had tried to commit to writing but for which ultimately no words had seemed adequate. And despite his efforts to suppress it the idea had grown in him steadily, until now it was encroaching on his soul like a malignant cancer.

A few kilometres ahead, in the shadow of Mount Ainslie, the airport was bedlam. Lashed by rain, a RAAF C-130 transport was on the hard standing, its turboprops whining. Government officials and senior military were racing out to it and boarding hurriedly as all around the perimeter fence, refugees were rioting and trying to break through. Troops were lined up in front of them, shooting into the air, but the refugees knew that the plane was their last chance and surged ahead even as the soldiers opened fire on them with baton rounds and tear gas.

When the fence finally collapsed, it went in three places at once and the airfield was invaded. The troops fired into the mob but the refugees overran them, took their guns, killed them viciously, then stormed on towards the Hercules.

The pilot saw them coming and immediately started taxiing, leaving passengers on the tarmac. They ran after him, waving frantically and screaming for him to wait, but the refugees arrived and clubbed and shot them mercilessly to death.

The plane reached the runway and was turning onto it when the refugees swarmed up. The loading ramp was closing and the first of them scrambled onto it but were shot from inside or broke their backs as the ramp clamped shut. Others grabbed the undercarriage and tried to climb up into the recesses but all of them slipped and were crushed beneath the rolling wheels.

As soon as he'd lined up, the pilot opened his throttles and the propellers gouged deafeningly into the humid air. Accelerating down the runway, the Herc ran down more refugees. But then its nose lifted sharply, its main wheels came unstuck, and the big aircraft shot skyward in a precipitous tactical climb.

The mob was incensed, and a thousand guns opened up at the climbing plane. Most of them missed wildly, their bullets raining back down to kill dozens more refugees on the ground. But one gun found its mark – slamming a magazine full into the cockpit, and killing the pilot and co-pilot outright. It was the same gun that had killed Ian Worley – a Bren gun – and hitting the Hercules would be the last act of Gerry Seal's life.

In slow motion, the plane yawed wildly, and for a moment seemed to hang in the air. But then as steeply as it had climbed, the plane began to plummet and when the refugees saw it coming back down on top of them, they scattered like ants.

The Hercules hit the ground at 500km/h, its fuel tanks exploded and its airframe crumpled like a beer can. Then with incredible momentum, the white hot wreckage rolled across the airfield and cut a swathe through the mass of fleeing refugees. It went on for two kilometres and left a blazing trail of havoc in which two thousand people died. And by the time it came to rest, along the course of its travel, another five thousand were crippled and hideously burned.

Arriving at the northern perimeter, Pat Howard and his vehicle commanders had seen the C-130 go in. All they could do was to stand there and gape at the aftermath. But then slowly they became aware of a chilling, unearthly clamour, which rose from the blackness like the wail of a banshee and swelled into a din that could have emanated from the abyss of Acheron. At first Howard thought it must be the crying of the injured. But then he discerned that it was coming from all around him, and he realised what he was hearing was the sound of half a million voices screaming.

The funnelwebs were attacking – to the south-east from Queanbeyan, to the north-west from Belconnen, and from the north along Majura Road on the tail of the 'Bravo' Company column. The monsters had the refugees boxed in on three sides, and the company was bang in the middle of them.

Suppressing dread, Pat Howard fell back on his

training and thought fast. There was nothing more they could do here. His responsibility now was to preserve those of his men that were left. Strewn with debris, Fairbairn was finished – there was no way out from there. And in the open country to the north and to the east, the funnelwebs would have all the advantage. The best hope was to head into the city and find a place to hold up – somewhere defendable, where helicopters could land to evacuate them. He knew the funnelwebs wouldn't cross water so a place next to the lake would be best.

Instantly, it was obvious where they should go. Howard grabbed his mike and barked instructions to the company as his vehicle swung a wide turn into the verge. Then the driver slammed his foot down, rocketed back over the road and the APC smashed into the fence with phenomenal force.

The razor wire screeched over the armour and stretched like elastic until it snapped. And the commander's vehicle led the company across the mire of the encampment with refugees scattering in their headlights like startled rodents.

It was a miracle that none of them was killed. But still they were incensed and the soldiers had to lock down under a hail of rocks and shotgun fire. None of which was a problem – until 1 Platoon was hit by Molotov cocktails.

The simple bottle of petrol fused with a flaming rag can be surprisingly effective against armour if concertedly applied. And these were – four of them hit the 1 Platoon HQ APC at the same time and in seconds its interior was like a barbecue oven.

'Bravo' Company had stumbled into a well-organised gang. They had lived high on the hog by terrorising other refugees and were brimming with confidence since they'd butchered the defenders of Queanbeyan. Now they'd set their sights on the 'Bravo' Company APCs as their only chance of escaping from the funnelwebs.

Andy Shute and the 1 Platoon HQ baled out to extinguish the fire as the rest of the column split left and right to encircle them. But as the company were dismounting, more Molotovs rained in and three soldiers were hit and set alight.

Scanning ahead, Howard picked out their attackers – around thirty of them, strung out along a ridge. Then the terrorists opened automatic fire as the sections dropped into cover, and two more soldiers went down.

The Minimis laid down a crossfire and as the terrorists ate dirt, Howard set up his counter attack. He sent O'Rourke with 2 Platoon to skirt the ridge to the east and dispersed 1 Platoon to provide covering fire from the vehicles. Then as soon as they opened up, O'Rourke quickly found the high ground and within seconds the terrorists were under fire from three directions simultaneously.

As Howard had hoped, they panicked and tried to blast their way out. But as they stood against the skyline, they were cut down by the Minimis and neatly rolled up by 2 Platoon attacking from the flank.

The ambush was neutralised. But the company had sustained several more casualties. By the time O'Rourke returned, the medics had the wounded dosed with morphine and because 1 Platoon's replacement lieutenant was among the dead, Andy Shute had taken command. Shute covered 2 Platoon's return watchfully. And when a mob of crazed refugees milled up yelling their lungs out, he dissuaded them from lobbing rocks with a couple of high spurts from a .30 cal.

That aside, the action was over, and as soon as 2 Platoon was tucked away, 1 Platoon withdrew to their vehicles and remounted. Howard ordered, 'Start engines,' and the APCs growled back into life. But it was then, as the first of the vehicles started rolling, that the funnelwebs hit.

The company was only metres from the Royal Military College, Duntroon, and in the heat of the skirmish the monsters had approached through its unlit grounds. There were ten, maybe twelve of them, and before anyone knew, they were crawling all over the vehicles and hosing them with venom.

Two APCs were drenched instantly and when the occupants ran out they were pounced on and ferociously speared. Howard gave the order to scatter but as the vehicles turned away, another was hit and its armour blistered and ruptured. Whether the driver was dead or went *kamikaze*, no-one knew. But the smitten APC tore straight into the funnelwebs and three of them shrieked as the tracks ripped their legs from their bodies.

Only three vehicles were left now – the commander's vehicle, the 2 Platoon HQ vehicle and the 1 Platoon 3 Section vehicle. Andy Shute was with 3 Section and Jimmy O'Rourke had gone with Colin Coombs as Acting Commander, 2 Platoon. They broke south, shot across Fairbairn Avenue and spun back around the oval on Morshead Drive. When they pulled up, there were no funnelwebs nearby so Howard ventured into the turret for a look.

Three hundred metres north, he saw the monsters feeding from the ravaged APCs and it was plain, even at that distance, that none of the occupants was left alive. But what grabbed Howard's attention immediately was what was happening beyond, on Mount Ainslie.

The funnelwebs from the north and the east had joined up and were advancing in a crawling black crescent that stretched for two kilometres. The refugees were massed to the west of the crescent and were floundering in panic up the eastern side of the mountain. However Howard could see they were being herded into a trap. Ascending on the western side, silhouetted by lightning, he could see a second phalanx of funnelwebs closing fast. Then the refugees saw them too and as Howard watched in horror, the mob turned back and fell over itself in a desperate bid to escape.

Soon the phalanxes of funnelwebs joined together to form a circle and the only way left for the refugees to go was up. In blind mindless dread, they trampled each other to get higher, without thinking that at the summit there would be nowhere else for them to run.

Watching the vice tighten, it occurred to Howard that the monsters that had jumped them must have been the outer flank of that western phalanx. He turned and scanned behind and sure enough, the way to the city was clear – the funnelwebs were now all ahead of them.

Looking forward again, he saw Mount Ainslie was a seething mass of humanity, surrounded at a radius of a kilometre by a tightening black ring. The catastrophe just waiting to happen was now a reality, and Howard felt himself choke on the despair that had been shadowing him all day.

O'Rourke and Shute were on either side of the commander's vehicle, awaiting orders. Howard snapped into the radio, 'Follow me,' then barked instructions to his driver to head for the city. 'Bravo' Company clattered across the Pialligo roundabout, past Molonglo Reach, past the RMC main gate, past Russell Offices, and rounded the right hander in Morshead Drive to the junction with Kings Avenue. Howard was relieved. All they had to do now was cross Lake Burley Griffin on Kings Avenue Bridge, cover the kilometre of Kings Avenue itself to

Capital Hill . . . and they'd be there, at the one place Howard had realised he could defend – Parliament House.

It was an unusual building. The intention had been that to symbolise Australian democratic equality, the Commonwealth's law-makers should not look down on their constituents. So the architects had not built onto the hill, but into it. Accordingly the front and rear quadrants of the roof were grassy slopes which could be ascended on foot to what appeared to be the hill's natural apex, directly beneath the 81-metre flag mast.

A kind observer might interpret the design as satisfying the intention. One less kind might say the building resembled a feudal stronghold behind whose earthworks robber barons might barricade themselves against malcontent serfs. Either way, the building was a natural fastness, and it was that which had inspired Pat Howard to select it as a bolt hole.

The three APCs arrived at the roundabout and without slowing swung left onto Kings Avenue. O'Rourke was in the last vehicle and as they raced for the bridge he was watching to the rear from his turret. So it was he who first saw the funnelwebs break from the trees behind the Australian-American War Memorial, and flood into Sir Thomas Blamey Square.

Within seconds there were eight or ten of them, oblivious to the receding APCs, and cavorting almost playfully in the rain. O'Rourke had never seen them behave like that before. But it occurred to him that perhaps this was how they acted when their bellies were full.

O'Rourke snapped into the radio, 'Funnys at six o'clock, sir!'

Howard looked back as Shute popped his head up, and what happened next, they all saw at once. Three of the monsters, apparently alerted, reared back and moved their heads about, as if trying to detect something. Then the first of them caught a scent, and turned, and looked straight at the APCs.

As the funnelweb's eyes fell upon him, O'Rourke knew again the fear that he'd known at Menangle. Those eyes lanced straight into him and for a moment he was paralysed like an insect that was pinned to a board. The eyes exuded a power that was pure evil, and in the depths of his being, O'Rourke somehow knew that it was not an evil born of this world.

They were crossing the Kings Avenue Bridge when the funnelwebs started after them, and within seconds the monsters were gaining at 60km/h. Howard gave the order for the vehicles to accelerate but the funnelwebs continued to close. O'Rourke knew he had to delay them, but his machine-guns were empty – then recent events provided inspiration.

Contrary to regulations, O'Rourke knew Colin Coombs carried whisky on the vehicle. He ducked down and a moment later reappeared with an unopened half bottle of Bushmills. He uncapped the bottle and tipped out the contents. The APC was also carrying petrol in jerry cans. O'Rourke unstrapped one, flipped it open, filled the bottle and quickly recapped it. Then he tore a strip of scrim from the scarf around his neck, soaked it in petrol and knotted it around the neck of the bottle.

Looking up, he saw the funnelwebs were still gaining – in ten seconds they'd made almost twenty metres. He heaved the slopping jerry can into the road where it crashed and ruptured, and gushed petrol from verge to verge. Then with his lighter he set fire to the soaking scrim, and with all of his strength hurled the Molotov back at the funnelwebs.

The flaring bottle arced through the darkness then shattered on the road and exploded into a towering conflagration. The funnelwebs stopped dead and hung back, apparently mesmerised by the flames. And by the time the fire dampened and the monsters ventured round it, the APCs were already hammering up the exit ramp to Parliament Drive.

Howard's intention had been to barricade themselves in but there was no time for that now. Their only hope was to take the high ground, so the APCs skirted the forecourt and headed for the apex of the roof. The grassy slopes on either side of the Great Verandah narrowed to a few metres where they levelled and ran onto the crest of the hilltop. It was there that Howard halted and after a quick appreciation deployed his vehicles.

The 1 and 2 Platoon vehicles he put across the front slopes to block the approaches with a crossfire from their Brownings. The commander's vehicle he put at the back of the roof to cover the rear. Then, as the surviving twenty-nine infantrymen debussed to take up fire positions, the first of the funnelwebs crossed Parliament Drive and entered the main forecourt.

Howard knew the monsters could spurt venom up to twenty metres. He guessed it was a hundred to the base of the slopes but barely twenty vertically down the face of the Great Verandah. So he spaced his last five flamethrowers along the rim of the parapet and with the remaining soldiers behind their personal weapons, they waited for the funnelwebs to attack.

In the hiatus, Howard listened through the rain but there was no sound of helicopters. Two Black Hawks could easily have lifted them to safety but as yet there was no sign of them. He'd radioed from Fairbairn to call in an air evacuation and had been told he would get one as soon as priorities allowed. Now he radioed again – for the third time in ten minutes – but for the third time all he could raise on the Battle Group Command Net was interference.

Five funnelwebs entered the forecourt and milled about. They knew there were humans there but they couldn't see them. Then one of them found the right grassy slope, and Howard bellowed, 'Shoot!'

The parapet exploded in gunfire. The five funnelwebs were cut to shreds but the noise attracted others and soon a mob of twenty was coming on. The machine-guns fired continuously killing eight or ten more of them, but the rest made it into the forecourt, hosing venom.

Several spurts hit the facade without effect but others soaked the grassy slopes and the turf boiled and spattered in smoking clods. Then two monsters went crazy and ran straight at the verandah, spurting wildly. The flame-throwers opened up but just a little late and the venom doused two riflemen who never knew what hit them. In an instant the funnelwebs were an inferno but in the light of their flames, the soldiers caught first sight of something they hadn't seen before.

The monsters were all soiled with some kind of debris. Then the grim realisation passed through the company what the debris was – heads, torsos, torn limbs – human body parts – spiked on and clogged in the funnelwebs' putrid black hairs. At the summit of Mount Ainslie, after gorging themselves sick, the monsters had frolicked in the remains of their ill-fated victims.

For one soldier, it was the end. Corporal Alan Thomas, 1 Section, 2 Platoon, was behind a .30 cal. at the left end of the Great Verandah. Despite his insubordination at Alfred Park, Colin Coombs had covered for him because even though his emotions could get the better of him, Alan Thomas had the heart of a lion.

But now, having seen things no human being ever should, at the sight of this unspeakable obscenity, Thomas cracked. He grabbed up his machine-gun and ran off down the slope, cursing the funnelwebs and spraying fire indiscriminately all around him. He caught two monsters napping and hosed their undersides with bullets, but when he ran into the mob he was surrounded and speared through the head.

The funnelwebs were around behind them now and Colin Coombs opened up from the commander's vehicle with the .50 cal. As Howard turned to look, the monsters scuttled back to safety, but over the bark of the machine-gun he thought that he heard something else.

He looked up into the southern sky and, sure enough, there was a Black Hawk approaching. Seconds later the aircraft was hovering above them, and in its downdraught the soldiers were yelping like children. Howard's relief was tempered by the knowledge that one Black Hawk could carry twenty men at most. But still it was a start and O'Rourke was already pulling back the younger men to get them loaded.

Colin Coombs and the commander's vehicle driver had advanced to halfway down the rear grassy slope and were forcing the funnelwebs back further with a continuous fusillade. Behind its cover, the pilot dropped to hover a metre above the rear slope and O'Rourke immediately sent down a stream of men to begin clambering aboard.

Andy Shute took over the Browning on the left flank, releasing the private gunner to board the helicopter. Relishing a go at the Funnys with the big calibre weapon, Shute let rip and 'Yahoo'd' when the bullets dropped two of them cold. But unnerved by the helicopter most of the funnelwebs were hanging back now, so Shute applied the safety and looked around to check things out.

That was when he saw the figure on the Senate roof – a civilian, grimy and blood smeared, and trying desperately to attract his attention. Shute couldn't believe it. In the midst of the bloody melee, it was like a scene from an old silent comedy. But then Shute saw the civilian had attracted the interest of a funnelweb, and he stopped smiling.

The monster had got into the courtyard between the Central Zone and the Senate building and was looking for a way up the walls. Shute re-aimed the Browning at the monster's craning head, and with a two-second squeeze on the trigger, the problem was gone.

The civilian had been unaware of the danger. But when he realised what Shute had done, he waved his thanks. Shute signalled to the civilian to wait. Then he ducked into the APC and in seconds was back out with what he needed. The cartridge-propelled grappling hook was overkill but it was all that was on hand. Shute coiled the trail rope so that it wouldn't snag, then anchored the launcher into the APC's track and pulled the lanyard.

The cartridge thumped and the grappling hook shot straight through the Senate skylight, shattering the glass and showering it down into the chamber. Shute teased the rope until the hook snagged in the skylight framework, then he drew it tight, tied it off around a pillar and waved to the civilian to come over.

The civilian seemed reluctant but saw that if he was going to live he had no option. So he grasped the rope, swung his legs up and carefully began to monkey climb across.

Jack Fitzgerald could have died several times that afternoon. When earlier he'd been trapped in the ministerial suites, he'd discovered power had not only been cut to the lift, but to the airconditioning too. Given that the windows didn't open he'd calculated that he had two days air at most – if the sun beating on the armoured glass windows didn't bake him alive first.

Focussed by that thought, it came to him that there may be a way out through the defunct airconditioning ducts. He rushed through the suites again, checking every room, but the vents were recessed and only a few centimetres wide. However that idea led to another and he searched every inch of the area for any other possible openings. And eventually he found one, right back where he'd started, on the wall immediately next to the lift.

It was a maintenance panel, and when Fitzgerald prised it off he found a lever which operated the lift doors manually. Soon he had them open and was clambering through an inspection hatch onto the lift roof. There he found a ladder bolted to the lift shaft wall, leading all the way up to the machinery room. Excited, he climbed up quickly and soon emerged from the murk into the sunlight on the Senate rooftop.

His relief was short lived. The Parliament House was deserted, and half a dozen circuits of the parapet failed to reveal any way down. After an hour, in desperation, he climbed back down inside the lift shaft and tried opening the doors to other floors. But it was hopeless, so he climbed back up again, and sat alone on the Senate roof, and waited.

Hours passed. And as hope waned, the events that had led him there filled his thoughts. He thought of Colleen, and of Kieren, and of how but for the error of a drunk his life would have been so different. He thought of Bill Reid, and of how he had stood by him in his personal battle, and then of all the other battles that it seemed he had been fighting all his life. And he thought of Helen, whom he had known so briefly and yet who had led him from the void back into the living world. Helen – where was she? Would he ever see her again? And the question that plagued him most – why had she left there without him?

The rain came, and then darkness, and he huddled in the machinery room, hoping beyond hope that a helicopter would overfly and see him. But none did. Later, he watched in horror as a departing plane crashed onto thousands of refugees at the airport. And soon afterwards, he shuddered as an unearthly screaming arose from the blackness, and went on and on and on until it very nearly drove him mad. Because he guessed what was the cause of it, and knew eventually that his turn would come.

Now, miraculously, the soldiers had arrived, and for the second time that day Jack Fitzgerald had the men of 'Bravo' Company to thank for his life. But he was only halfway along the rope, and suspended above the chasm, when disaster struck.

Given the gravity of things, the pilot had gamely loaded twenty-two men into his aircraft, leaving only Howard, O'Rourke, Shute and Coombs to cover their departure. Crammed to the gunnels, the big helicopter rose slowly, turning on the axis of its rotor. The pilot planned to take the men to the Brindabella Ranges then return for their commander and NCOs, but as it turned out, he would take them less than ten metres.

In the commotion no-one saw the three funnelwebs approaching from the south-east, until two of them reared back and spurted venom at the ascending Black Hawk. The deadly streams arced up and crossed above the aircraft, then dropped onto the rotor blades and atomised into the teeming rain. For a moment, there was no effect, and Coombs and O'Rourke who were directly beneath could not believe they hadn't been touched. But a second later, the Black Hawk's rotor disintegrated, and the NCOs ran for their lives as the stricken helicopter fell out of the sky.

It missed them by a body length and, as strange things can happen, their lives were saved by freakish chance. The Black Hawk exploded, killing all its passengers and crew, but Coombs and O'Rourke were blown halfway down the rear grassy slope and staggered to their feet, shaken but unhurt.

Pat Howard had been manning the .50 cal. on the 2 Platoon vehicle to the right of the Great Verandah. And as he watched the remnants of his company fry, he realised the funnelwebs responsible must have passed him on that side of the building. There was no way he could have seen them because they had skirted Capital Hill in dead ground. But Howard didn't know that – he thought he must have missed them – and that was one burden too many for him ever to carry.

On the other side of the fire, O'Rourke and Coombs were in trouble. The three funnelwebs had moved in and cut them off at the base of the slope. As the monsters edged closer, the soldiers, without so much as a pistol between them, had three choices: burn, get eaten, or jump the last eight metres to the ground. So the two men were already edging slowly towards the wall, when the 2 Platoon APC exploded out of the flames and shot straight at them.

Coombs and O'Rourke threw themselves aside as the vehicle hurtled past them at the funnelwebs. The first one didn't know what hit it – the APC smashed through its legs then backed up over it, bursting its body like a balloon. The other funnelwebs recovered quickly and were already rearing back to spurt venom. But the APC stopped dead, Pat Howard leapt up into the turret and before anything else could happen, he decapitated another funnelweb with the .50 cal.

If fortune had favoured the brave, he would have gotten away with it. Because he was already re-aiming when the last of the funnelwebs spurted. The venom hit the armour like a rapier pointed lance and before Howard could evade it, the searing liquid had splashed up all over him.

Howard cried out as he tumbled from the turret and flailed on the ground. The funnelweb must have sensed that the danger was past because it advanced and stood over him, watching him writhing and wailing. It all happened so fast that O'Rourke and Coombs had barely taken it in. But when the monster moved in closer and nudged Howard with its fangs, tormenting him and causing him to scream, something unexpected happened.

Colin Coombs, the hard arse from the caves of Coober Pedy, went apeshit. He grabbed up a broken shaft that had been part of the Black Hawk's undercarriage, then bellowing, 'You bad bastard! You don't do that to *my* fucking officer!', he ran at the funnelweb, yelling and hacking at it wildly.

The giant spider actually recoiled – Coombs was dwarfed but he attacked so ferociously that for a moment it looked as if the monster might run off. But then from nowhere it flicked its head and speared Coombs on its fangs, and as he screamed out in fury, it lifted him and started shaking him violently.

However for the funnelweb, it was a mistake. Because despite being speared, Coombs intensified his attack with the savagery of a man possessed. Screaming, 'Fuck your eyes! Fuck your eyes!', he slashed and hacked and stabbed, ripping the monster's eyes and gouging them from their sockets. Until the funnelweb's head had been reduced to a mushy pulp, and Coombs and the spider were a meld of torn flesh and bloody humour.

Finally Coombs screamed, 'I killed 'em, Jimmy! I killed its eyes! I killed all its evil fucking eyes!' And as the monster scurried off with its nemesis still impaled, Colin Coombs, the hard arse from the caves of Coober Pedy, was laughing.

Jimmy O'Rourke stood in the firelight, gazing after the funnelweb. He hadn't moved.

And it was that, and not the action of Colin Coombs, which had been unexpected. O'Rourke had known, as in a fire-fight, that the only way to win the advantage and save his commander was to go forward, as Coombs had done. And perhaps he would have – had, in the last moment, the funnelweb not looked up, and glared at him.

O'Rourke had turned to stone. Somewhere in his mind, he'd screamed at himself to get going, but his legs wouldn't work. He'd tried desperately to break out of it by moving his arms, his fingers, even the lids of his eyes. But the harder he had tried the more ensnared he became, until as surely as if he'd been bound up in spider's silk, O'Rourke was paralysed.

Now he was so racked with self-reproach that he was trembling. He had committed the unforgivable, the unthinkable offence – he had frozen in the face of the enemy. He was overwhelmed by a suffocating wave of self-loathing. Never had he felt so bad as he did at this moment. Nevertheless his reflexes and his training took over, and on autopilot he ran to Pat Howard and checked him out.

Howard was alive, but he was barely conscious and shivering uncontrollably. The side of his head and face were raw flesh and through the shoulder of his dissolved tunic, O'Rourke saw bone. O'Rourke pulled off his own tunic and carefully wrapped it around his commander to keep off the rain. Then from behind there was a metallic screeching and O'Rourke turned to see the commander's vehicle crash through the dampening fire.

The APC slewed up and Andy Shute jumped out of the driver's seat, shouting excitedly, 'Sir, the Funnys have gone . . . they just mooched off. If we run for it, we can make it out to the south.' Then he saw Pat Howard and took in his injuries, and averting his eyes, looked around, and inquired, 'Where's Coombsie?'

O'Rourke said only, 'He's dead.' Then making a supreme effort to pull himself together, he snapped, 'C'mon, let's get the boss aboard.'

Shute jumped down, went to the back of the APC and dropped the ramp. Then he went to O'Rourke and they carefully carried their commander to the vehicle. When they arrived, O'Rourke saw the inside was stacked. Shute had raided the 1 Platoon vehicle of everything – food, petrol, ammunition, and serviceable weapons. And in amongst it all, there was a civilian. O'Rourke recognised him but thought at first that his eyes must be playing tricks on him. Then peering more closely, he realised, incredibly, that he was right.

'Christ, where did you spring from, Doc – I thought we got rid of you this morning.'

Fitzgerald grinned exhaustedly, and replied, 'So did I, Mister O'Rourke,' then added, 'Good to see you.'

O'Rourke nodded, 'And you, Doc. Can you do something for the OC – he copped a faceful of venom.'

Fitzgerald hadn't recognised Howard. But as O'Rourke and Shute laid him out, Fitzgerald saw that he was lucky to be alive. He said, 'I'm not a medical doctor,

Mister O'Rourke, but I've got some first aid. If you've got a kit, I'll do what I can.'

Andy Shute produced a first aid kit and as Fitzgerald delved into it for morphine, O'Rourke and Shute regarded each other. Then after a moment, Shute asked disbelievingly, 'Is this it then, sir . . . is this all that's left?'

O'Rourke looked away, and said, 'This is it.' And there was an empty silence.

Eventually, Shute asked, 'So what now?'

O'Rourke replied, 'Pilot said the Funnys won't go high, so we head for the hills – Brindabellas are the closest.'

Alarmed, Fitzgerald interjected, 'Forget the Brindabellas – they're going to nuke the Brindabellas.'

O'Rourke and Shute gaped at Fitzgerald, and O'Rourke repeated, 'Nuke them?'

Fitzgerald moved away from Howard who had fallen into a drugged sleep, and confirmed, 'To stop the funnelwebs getting through to the western plains – they're going to do it.'

O'Rourke and Shute looked astounded.

Then Fitzgerald said, 'But it's true the funnelwebs won't go above eight hundred and fifty metres. So the safest place to be is in the mountains, but as far from the Brindabella Ranges as possible.'

Looking again at each other, O'Rourke and Shute had the same thought. But it was O'Rourke who said the word – 'Kosciusko.'

With renewed urgency, the NCOs went to the 2 Platoon APC and cannibalised it too of everything useful. And by the time they had finished, the commander's vehicle was like a quartermaster's clearance sale. Over the top of it all they made the most comfortable bed they could, and with Fitzgerald watching Howard, Shute in the driver's seat and O'Rourke in the turret on the .50 cal., they headed off.

They went west on Adelaide Avenue then south on Yamba Drive, and as they passed through Woden there was no sign of either people or funnelwebs. Within an hour they hit the Monaro Highway south of Tuggeranong and there they stopped to refuel and check the vehicle. As Shute buried himself in the engine, O'Rourke drifted off for a smoke. The storm had passed, the sky was crystal clear and the only sounds were the stirring of the trees and the song of a cricket.

O'Rourke was feeling like death. No matter how he looked at it, he could not reconcile himself to his faint-heartedness. It was something he had never expected, something he couldn't understand, and at that moment he had no idea how to deal with it. All he could think about was what a joke he was. There he'd been worrying about the arachnophobes and in the end the only member of the company who had faltered was himself. He felt a fraud. He felt worthless. He felt he'd let his men down. But worst of all by far, he felt that he had failed his commander.

He took a small book from his breast pocket. It was a diary he had retrieved when it had fallen from his OC's tunic as he'd lifted him into the vehicle at Parliament House. O'Rourke had no wish to intrude but for some reason, he felt that he should read it. So he leafed through, and found nothing unexpected, until he came to the last entry. It had been written that morning, as they had stood watching the funnelwebs gathering on the slopes to the east of Lake George.

Howard had written,

> *'Despite everything I have believed in and fought for in my life, I am confronted with the proposition that Nietzsche was right –*

The Earth has a skin, the skin has a disease, and the disease is called man.

Finally it is not the funnelwebs that are the pestilence, but ourselves.'

O'Rourke stared at the entry for a long time. Then he closed the book and stood in silence, empty, and alone.

Eventually, he looked north, and listened. There was no trace of the awful wailing that had earlier filled the air – either they were too far from Mount Ainslie now or the refugees were all dead or taken. He shuddered as he put the thought from his mind and, turning, pulled out his maps of the Snowy Mountains.

As soon as Shute had finished they set off again, and minutes later they were racing in a tunnel of headlights through black and deserted country. With the clatter of the tracks, there was no conversation and each man became lost in his own thoughts.

One prayed for the souls of the innocents he had killed and one wondered with concern about his lover. And one brooded darkly on how a single incident of cowardice could make the honour and achievement of a lifetime count as if for nothing.

13

Richard Bartlett punched the End button on his digital mobile and dropped the device into his attache case. The news was good. His bank had confirmed that another large deposit, the second in thirty-six hours, had been credited to his private numbered account in Vienna. But this deposit was for considerably more than the $US50 million lodged earlier. It was, in fact, for ten times more – $US500 million – and the depositor was an anonymous company registered in the Bahamas. Through a tortuous and untraceable network of international holding entities, that company was ultimately the instrument of a consortium of governments led by the United States, the others being Russia, China, Japan, and their junior partner, Indonesia. The US State Department, with its experience of expediting secret alliances, had set it up.

For the Americans, the deal with Bartlett was routine except that on this occasion it had been struck with the leader of a Western democracy rather than with a Third World dictator. However the circumstances had presented an unusually good opportunity and the USA had not become the leader of world capitalism by allowing such opportunities to pass it by.

The arrangement was simple. Bartlett would clear

the way domestically for the Americans to execute Operation Hot Ditch, which would achieve three ends. First, it would confine the funnelwebs to the Australian eastern seaboard. Second, it would in time eradicate them from the effects of starvation. And third, from radioactive material permeating down through the water table, it would render the Australian east coast permanently uninhabitable. From the consortium's point of view, this third outcome was eminently desirable. The eastern coastal plain was Australia's most populous region and denied it, Australian national independence would be economically and politically untenable. And that state of affairs would be highly conducive to the consortium's ultimate ambition, which was to turn the empty inland of Australia into one vast open cut mine.

In return, the remnants of the Australian Commonwealth would receive 'appropriate payments' and the 'protection' of its northern hemisphere allies. And, covertly, there would be a gratuity of $US1 billion paid to the Prime Minister, half up front, half on settlement.

In plain English, Bartlett had sold his country, lock, stock and barrel, for a bribe. And a very handsome bribe it was. Nevertheless by the mores of his new income bracket, he felt that he had probably undersold himself. Film producers and computer moguls were multi-billionaires these days, and Bartlett had just parted with an entire continent. That the continent had not been his to sell did not concern him. But then, it wouldn't have.

Bartlett hit keys on a computer terminal and called up the latest reports from ASIO. The multi-force naval blockade that had seemed so ominous only a few hours ago was already dispersing. The Russians, the Chinese and the Indonesians were mollified now that they had been brought in for a share of the spoils. The Americans had concluded that military confrontation would have been expensive and the outcome uncertain. This way, it was win-win for everybody, and especially for those key decision makers of the consortium's member governments who were already enjoying their own 'personal gratuities'.

Bartlett hit other keys and an encrypted e-mail from Dennis Carson popped up. After decoding, it informed the Prime Minister that preparations for the execution of Hot Ditch were progressing smoothly, that zero hour was set for 5.45 the following morning, and that all other 'business of the day' had been completed.

Bartlett hit Exit and the message was replaced by swimming fish. Irritated, he switched off the video display, and sat back in his chair to chew things over.

Carson's remark about 'other business of the day' was a reference to Bartlett's special directives, which had included the disposal of Jack Fitzgerald. Fitzgerald had at first promised to be an asset. But when the gamble of using him to lend authority to Hot Ditch had backfired, Bartlett had been forced to have him eliminated.

He thought what a fool Fitzgerald had been – passing up the chance of achieving such heights in his profession, and all for the sake of indulging himself in adolescent moralising. Bartlett had sensed that Fitzgerald had had an 'attitude' at Holsworthy, and on the principle of 'keep your friends close but your enemies closer', he'd decided to embrace him into the fold. It had been the right move. Because Fitzgerald had immediately betrayed himself as a loose cannon, and Bartlett had been able to stomp on him before any damage was done.

The Prime Minister looked at his watch and was surprised to find it was already after midnight. His dinner at the Victorian Parliament House had gone on for far too long, but his announcement that Melbourne would now be the Federal Capital had been rapturously received. More significantly, it had bought him the State of Victoria's unreserved co-operation.

Bartlett smiled to himself. He had relished the 'old money' of the Victorian Liberal Party fawning all over him – those same old farts that so recently had cast him carelessly aside. Now what the fools failed to understand, preoccupied as they were with petty provincial rivalries, was that it was entirely academic which city wore the mantle of the Australian capital. Because Australia, as a nation, in any meaningful sense, was finished.

However there was a far greater return to be made on the carcass than there ever had been on the living organism, which was perhaps why Richard Bartlett was sleeping so well these days.

The Fairchild Republic A-10 Thunderbolt could not be described as an elegant aircraft. With brutally square lines, a twin fin tail configuration and externally mounted oversized engines, it has the look of a plane that might have been drawn by a five year old.

However in the role for which it was designed, the A-10 is singularly effective. That role is killing tanks, and the means it employs is one of the most potent pieces of weaponry in the contemporary tactical arsenal. It is a gun, or to be more precise, a cannon – a rotary cannon based on the principle of the Gatling gun first used to such murderous effect in the American Civil War. However the similarity between R.G. Gatling's 1862 original and the weapon equipping the A-10 ends there. In comparison to the 350 shots the Gatling gun could fire in a minute, the General Electric Avenger 30 mm seven-barrelled rotary cannon has a firing rate of 2,100 or 4,200 rounds per minute, depending on requirements. At the higher rate, that translates into seventy armour-piercing cannon shells, each three centimetres in diameter, slamming into the hull of an enemy tank every second. And that makes the Avenger the most powerful gun ever to fly.

But for the authors of Operation Hot Ditch, it was less the A-10's potency as a tank killer that was of interest than the material of which its ammunition was made. In the germination of their plan, mindful of what had happened with the neutron bomb, Christian Phelps and his American colleagues had taken the view that thermonuclear detonations alone would not produce sufficiently high levels of ground radiation to guarantee an effective barrier against the funnelwebs. What was needed was something far more radioactive – something that would not be dispersed by wind and rain yet could be quickly and easily emplaced over 120 kilometres.

A dozen ideas were considered and rejected and for a time it had seemed there was no way to make it work. But a staff member at Annapolis, Lieutenant Commander John Kristen, a nuclear physics PhD and a brilliant computer analyst, came up with the answer. Depleted uranium – uranium purged of its radioactive isotopes – was first used as a material for anti-tank ammunition during the Gulf War. And despite being attributed by some as the cause of the mysterious Gulf War Syndrome, its use in that role is unrelated to its radioactive properties.

Uranium is the heaviest of metals. Which means that the kinetic energy delivered by uranium cannon shells of any given calibre translates into the maximum destructive impact physically possible. In simple terms, uranium ammo packs a greater punch than any other kind – enough to penetrate even the hardest armour plating yet devised. However, depleted or not, uranium is still uranium, and its latent atomic instability remains a potential source of far greater power.

Kristen's idea was to have A-10s stitch the ground with their depleted uranium shells. If the shells were then bombarded with high intensity neutrons from thermonuclear explosions, the uranium would be re-activated and produce levels of radioactivity far in excess of anything survivable. He calculated that each shell would create a killing sphere twenty metres across – that is, any living organism that should come within ten metres of the shell would die instantly. From the mass of each shell, the muzzle velocity of the Avenger, and ground density figures from the CSIRO's geological database, he then calculated that the shells would penetrate the earth to a depth of three metres. That would leave a segment of each killing sphere above ground with a lateral diameter of 19 metres. However if the A-10s were to fly at 630 km/h firing at 2,100 rounds per minute, the ground would be stitched at intervals of one shell every five metres, meaning that every point on the surface along the line of the stitching would lie within at least three overlapping killing spheres.

It was the most devastating overkill. But that was not the reason why Kristen had thought his idea would be rejected. It was because the most potent isotope of uranium, U-238, has a half life of 4.5 billion years, meaning that without a trillion dollar clean-up, the Hot Ditch would, for all practical purposes, be there forever. So it was with considerable surprise that Kristen received word of his idea's acceptance in a jubilant phone call from the President of the United States personally.

The Thunderbolts of the Air National Guard crossed the Queensland coast near the sleeping sugar town of Mackay at a little after 2am. The five thousand mile flight from their training base in South Korea had taken almost thirteen hours, relieved only by two routine rendezvous for in-flight refuelling. Once inland however, the formation caught a tailwind and covered the remaining nine hundred miles to the target in only two hours.

Reaching the Blue Mountains, the A-10s banked over the Wombeyan Caves and dropped back into a staggered single file. Seconds later, they were bearing down on the black outline of Mount McAlister. Then as the first aircraft overflew it, the pilot pressed his trigger button, and the night was filled with the drone of rotary cannon fire.

With its magazine holding 1,174 rounds, it took only half a minute for the first A-10 to exhaust its ammunition. The last ten rounds were white phosphorus, which made a fifty-metre marker of brilliant light. As the first A-10 peeled away the next lined up on the marker, and the pilot put the first of his shells bang into its flaring point.

And so it continued, each aircraft in turn, until after twelve minutes, twenty-one of the twenty-four Avenger magazines were empty. No backups were needed – the stitching had gone to plan. So the Thunderbolts climbed back to their cruising altitude where they rendezvoused and reformed before stealing away like thieves into the blackness of the southern sky.

High in the Snowy Mountains, the distant rumble of turbofans rolled in across the alpine meadows. It was the first aerial activity Jimmy O'Rourke had heard since Canberra and it sent shivers through him. Fitzgerald had told them the details of Hot Ditch and O'Rourke guessed that whatever the jets were up to, it meant the missiles would be coming soon.

O'Rourke cut a bizarre figure in his NBC suit,

crouched below the skyline at the crest of a precipitous ridge. He was returning from a solo figure-8 patrol. And now, beneath him on the floor of a deep gully, he could see Shute and Fitzgerald stripped to their waists and shovelling for their lives. The commander's vehicle was already covered with earth-filled sandbags and the dirt being thrown on top of them would give camouflage and extra shielding from radiation.

Scanning the skyline in the pre-dawn incandescence, O'Rourke was satisfied that there was no-one else in the vicinity. Lower down, the town of Jindabyne had been turned into a stronghold – when the APC had approached, it had come under intense small arms fire. It wasn't clear if the occupants were locals or bandits, but when the missiles came it would amount to the same thing. Radiation-crazed zombies would be marauding around the countryside and O'Rourke didn't want any of them knocking on the APC's door.

So they'd left the road and driven across country to the slopes of Mount Kosciusko where they'd found this concealed narrow gully. At a hundred and sixty kilometres from the closest detonation, it would give excellent protection from blast and heat. In regard to fallout, their best chance was to sit it out inside the APC for two weeks, by which time, according to doctrine, any fallout should have decayed to safe levels.

By the time O'Rourke got back, the APC had virtually disappeared. Where it had been there was an earthen mound with alpine scrub and stunted bushes growing out of it. The only give-away was the open battle door which when closed would be concealed by clumps of shrubbery.

O'Rourke wrestled out of the cumbersome and chafing NBC suit. Then he stripped and quickly defecated before jumping into the little creek that ran through the gully. It would be his last bath for two weeks so he tried to make the most of it before climbing out and redressing in his underclothes.

Entering through the battle door, O'Rourke found the APC surprisingly roomy. Shute and Fitzgerald had stowed almost everything under the vehicle and made meagre but adequate sleeping spaces for each of them. The most comfortable place was occupied by Pat Howard. He'd been drifting in and out of consciousness ever since they'd left Canberra but thankfully seemed at last to have fallen asleep. O'Rourke asked, 'All done?' and when Shute and Fitzgerald nodded, he slammed the battle door behind him, and locked it.

Around and beneath the sleeping spaces there were cartons of rations, tins of fresh water and first aid supplies. They had buried most of the weapons but had kept four Steyrs and a Minimi in case of trouble. There were also four NBC suits in case they had to go out. The driver's position had been partitioned off to make a latrine, not for the sake of modesty but rather to contain the worst of the fumes. Because despite the bucket being charged with chemicals, over a period of a fortnight, fumes there were going to be.

The only light source was a tiny map-reading lamp rigged to the vehicle's auxiliary battery, which also powered the little pump circulating air from outside through a filter. Shute had disconnected the main battery to save it for restarting the engine. He guessed the auxiliary might last a week, and after that they would have to take turns on the hand-powered dynamo.

The most ingenious thing Shute had done was to rig up an over-the-horizon periscope. The M113 is fitted with a number of periscopic instruments – Shute had cannibalised them and some optical fibre from a field telephone to cobble the simple device together. It worked like a *camera obscura* – light gathered by a lens mounted up on the gully ridge travelled down the optic fibre, which entered the vehicle through a tiny sealed hole in the turret. A second lens then focussed and projected the light down onto a piece of white paper.

O'Rourke gazed in fascination at the image on the makeshift viewing screen. The north-eastern horizon was lightening and he could see across the mountains for miles. Amazed, he enthused, 'Andy, you're a fucking genius. You should have been in the Engineers.'

Without thinking, Shute quipped back, 'If I'd been in the Engineers, sir, I'd probably be dead by now.'

The reality of their situation crashing in on him, O'Rourke looked up. Two skull faces were watching him from out of the gloom. For an instant he was unnerved, sure they must be able to see the guilt that was consuming him. Then he realised their haunted eyes meant only that they were struggling as much as he was to stay together.

O'Rourke looked past them to the figure lying beyond. Howard was still sleeping and as O'Rourke sat there watching him, it came to him that this was his source of strength. For as long as Howard lived, O'Rourke would be there to protect him, that or to die in the attempt. A second incidence of failure would not occur. Not because O'Rourke had overcome his chronic arachnophobia – he had resigned himself to the certainty that he never would. Rather it was because he now knew from personal experience that to live with such failure was so much harder than facing up to death.

Perversely comforted, O'Rourke looked back down at the paper screen, and calmly awaited whatever the future might hold.

Three thousand miles away, a sleek black leviathan passed in silence through the Pacific depths. The Ohio Class SSBN *Montana* was approaching co-ordinates at which she would hover and, for the one and only time, perform the sole task for which she had been designed.

It was ironic that of all US ballistic missile submarines the *Montana* should have been chosen for this mission, as it was she that had created the funnelweb problem in the first place. The irony had been lost on COMSUBPAC (Commander Submarines, Pacific) whose only concern had been to get the job done without any hitches. So he had chosen the *Montana,* which with her crack crew, her brand new captain and her reinstated Trident II missiles, was the gun sub of the US Pacific fleet.

However at that moment, the mood in the *Montana* was tense. Minutes before, the submerged boat's radio room had received an encoded Emergency Action Message via Extreme Low Frequency underwater radio transmission. Following correct procedure, the radio room had informed the officer of the deck, who had put the boat on Alert 1 and called the captain to the conn. The captain's first order had been to the executive officer, to 'Man battle stations – missile.' And the executive officer, in turn, had ordered the chief of the watch to sound the general alarm.

Seconds later, with the crew racing to their posts, the *Montana's* four senior officers assembled. As the captain entered, the executive officer said, 'Captain, the EAM received is a properly formatted message. Permission to authenticate?'

Fail-safe required that all senior officers should concur with each assessment, so the captain asked crisply, 'Mister Deeds, do you concur?'

Mister Deeds answered, 'Yes, Captain, I concur.'

The captain then asked, 'Mister Brann, do you concur?'

Mister Brann replied, 'I concur, Captain.'

Accordingly, the captain said to the executive officer, 'You have permission to authenticate.'

The executive officer replied, 'Authenticate. Aye, aye, sir,' and went immediately to a safe close at hand. Inside he found the top secret launch validation codes which had been placed there only minutes before the submarine had sailed. If the codes in the safe matched the codes contained in the EAM, then the EAM would be validated as a legitimate order from the President.

All four officers scrutinised the codes. They matched.

Mister Deeds said, 'Captain, the message authenticates.'

Mister Brann said, 'I agree, Captain, the message authenticates.'

The executive officer said, 'Captain, I concur.'

The captain said, 'I concur that it is an authentic message – executive officer, break out the launch keys.'

The executive officer said, 'Break out the launch keys. Aye, aye, sir,' and the four men dispersed.

In the high country, the land was awakening. As dawn touched the peaks and began creeping into the valleys, from the stillness there arose the buzzing of flies. Then the butterflies fluttered, the dragonflies darted, and soon every insect that flew was dancing in the sunlight.

Somewhere in a windowless room, Richard Bartlett gazed at a bank of TV monitors. The images were from a variety of viewpoints but their subjects were all the same – the one hundred and twenty kilometres of land between Mount McAlister and the Brindabella Ranges.

There were perhaps forty others in the room – senior military, foreign observers, security personnel – but only two were of any interest to the Prime Minister. On his right, Christian Phelps was also glued to the video displays, and appeared nervous. On Bartlett's left was a man who seemed to be there permanently these days but who by contrast with Brigadier Phelps betrayed no emotion. Dennis Carson had in fact been absorbed in quiet conversation on his mobile phone. But now, with the appointed time approaching, he put the phone away and turned his attention to the monitor screens.

For an American submarine to launch its missiles, separate keys must be turned simultaneously in different locations, to prevent any individual officer from acting alone. The keys are retrieved from separate safes by three junior officers who will only pass them to their superiors in the moments immediately preceding launch.

As the keys were being retrieved, the captain returned to the conn and announced over the PA, 'This is the captain. Set condition 1 SQ,' thereby bringing the boat to its highest state of readiness. What he did not announce, which caused every bowel aboard to tighten, was that what was happening was an exercise – because it was not.

The EAM was live. Not only was it live but the target co-ordinates it contained were entirely unexpected, and inexplicable. Nevertheless the message had been validated, and in the *Montana*, that was all that mattered.

Seated in the weapons conn, the non-commissioned officer assigned as launcher had already set the submarine's missiles to condition 1 SQ. Standing opposite him, in communication with the captain by intercom, the weapons officer now instructed, 'Stand by for fire order.'

The launcher repeated, 'Stand by for fire order. Aye, aye, sir,' and waited.

Then the weapons officer relayed, 'The fire order will be . . . twelve through fifteen.'

The launcher repeated, 'The fire order will be twelve through fifteen,' then immediately said into his own intercom, 'Verify twelve through fifteen.'

The response was immediate, and the launcher said, 'Fire order verified, sir,' and the weapons officer said curtly, 'Very well.'

In the conn, the chief of the watch said, 'Officer of the deck, the dive is in 1 SQ,' signifying that all was ready for the launch.

The officer of the deck relayed to the captain, 'Dive is in 1 SQ, sir,' and the captain replied, 'Very well.'

Then the captain said into the intercom, 'Weapons conn, the print-outs have been validated.'

Recognising that it was the voice of the captain that had confirmed validation, the weapons officer said to the launcher, 'Hold all tubes with the exception of twelve through fifteen.'

The launcher repeated, 'Hold all tubes with the exception of twelve through fifteen – aye, aye, sir,' and he went to work on the illuminated missile console in front of him.

Of the vertical column of buttons numbered 1 through 24, each designated HOLD, the launcher pressed buttons 1 through 11, and 16 through 24, the designation of each pressed changing to MANUAL HOLD. When he had finished, the launcher said, 'Manual hold imposed on all tubes with the exception of tubes twelve through fifteen.'

Then the weapons officer said, 'Launcher, select normal launch depth – pressurise tubes twelve through fifteen to normal launch depth.'

The launcher complied, then confirmed, 'Normal launch depth selected – tubes twelve through fifteen pressurised to normal launch depth.'

In the conn, the captain registered the snapped confirmations of readiness from all participating stations. Then he looked at the bank of digital clocks on the bulkhead in front of him, focussing on one designated, Eastern Standard Time + One Hour [Daylight Saving]. It read 05.44.47, and as the seconds clicked past 50, the executive officer announced, 'Zero minus ten seconds.'

The captain and the weapons officer simultaneously turned their separate launch keys in their separate fail-safe locks, and the executive officer intoned, 'Five – four – three – two – one – mark!'

Then with no trace of hesitation, and an almost pleasurable inner release, the captain said, 'Weapons conn – you have permission to fire.'

The executive officer confirmed, 'Initiate fire.'

The weapons officer relayed, 'Initiate fire.'

And the launcher pressed the button marked 12.

In the Brindabella Ranges, the ground had come to life with crawling insects, which had brought out lizards, amphibians, marsupials, rodents and birds. Wallabies grazed on eucalypts, platypuses swam in the creeks, and wombats that had foraged through the night were returning to their burrows.

The ocean erupted.

A column of foam spewed one hundred metres into the air.

Then within it – a flash – and from out of it, a missile erupted and soared deafeningly into the sky.

Then another, and another, and another followed after it as the launcher pressed buttons 12 through 15.

Until four silver needles were ascending over the ocean atop pillars of thunderous flame and solid smoke.

The Tridents arced out of the atmosphere and into orbit, where their motors shut down, their nose shrouds detached, and when their gyros had finely pitched their attitudes, their MIRV buses separated.

Each MIRV bus was a tiny orbiting spacecraft, with a miniature propulsion unit and 'smart' stellar guidance system. And each carried four x 475kt thermonuclear warheads, independently targeted, and encased in individual re-entry vehicles.

Following instructions fed into them on board the *Montana*, the MIRV buses slid silently into line. Then seemingly in slow motion but in fact at thousands of kilometres per hour, they started to traverse the Earth to their distant objective.

Richard Bartlett was disconcerted. In front of him were images of an idyllic landscape which disembodied voices were confirming was about to be obliterated. The stimuli seemed unrelated, like a radio in another room heard over a muted telecast. In that moment, even to Bartlett, the destruction of such a place seemed an anathema. But there was nothing he could do now – the missiles could not be recalled – what would happen had gone beyond all human authority. And thus relieved of responsibility,

Bartlett comforted himself with the rationalisation that he was just another innocent swept along in the current of events.

Jack Fitzgerald stood over Jimmy O'Rourke, looking down at the periscope screen. The sun was fully up now and the land was shimmering gold in the heat.

There was a cry, and they turned to Pat Howard. He was sweating profusely and appeared in the throes of a nightmare. Andy Shute moistened his lips and he quietened. But the fear from the nightmare remained in Howard's face, and the men watching him sensed that somehow he knew what was happening.

The MIRV buses manoeuvred into their final positions. Then, at the appointed moment, the re-entry vehicles launched, and plummeted earthward.

When they plunged into the atmosphere, their heat shields glowed white hot, leaving trails of ionised plasma that appeared as the thunderbolts of Thor. Then – at fifteen hundred metres altitude – the first warhead exploded.

A hundred and sixty kilometres away, Jimmy O'Rourke and Jack Fitzgerald spun their eyes from the searing flash.

Three hundred milliseconds later, within two kilometres of the airburst, everything above ground was scalding vapour.

Instantaneously, three metres down, the depleted uranium cannon shells were subjected to an intense rain of neutrons. They glowed red, then orange, then white, then blue, then liquefied and infused into the rock. And from there the deadly radiance of their reactivated isotopes pierced up through the cauldron of boiling silica that had once been the ground.

The second warhead detonated, then the third, then the fourth . . . and a curtain of thermonuclear fire rose into the stratosphere. From space it appeared as if a giant's cutting torch was incising the Earth. And as pictures from reconnaissance satellites were relayed into the windowless room, the observers could only gaze incredulously at what they had done.

When the last warhead exploded, the ground bubbled and spat for a hundred and twenty kilometres. Millions of tonnes of earth that had been thrown into the upper atmosphere would totally obscure the sun for days. And nothing was left alive on either side of the fiery curtain for well over thirty kilometres.

Fitzgerald, Shute and O'Rourke gazed together at the screen as the eerie nuclear phosphorescence gave way to nuclear night. For a long time they stood there . . . until after the screen had gone black . . . until, in the blackness, a voice whispered, 'I am become death – the destroyer of worlds.'

The three men looked at each other, and realising that none of them had spoken, they turned and looked across at Pat Howard.

Howard was still, his eyes open, staring at nothing.

O'Rourke went to him, and when he found that he was dead, he closed Howard's eyes and covered his face with a blanket.

With good instinct, Andy Shute drew water for a brew. Fitzgerald considered saying something, but thought better of it and instead went on through into the driver's section. And there, beyond the curtain, he tried to close his ears against the desolate sound of Jimmy O'Rourke sobbing.

The following dawn.

The sky was a dirty brown haze.

The silica of the Hot Ditch had cooled and solidified into a black glass scar three hundred metres wide.

There was no breath of wind. Everything was still, and deathly silent.

In the windowless room, the atmosphere was stale. People had slept there and the place stank of junk food and body odour. Christian Phelps was awoken with news that the funnelwebs were on the move. Nervously he barked for the place to be cleaned up and by the time Richard Bartlett and Dennis Carson arrived, it had been. But with the smell hardly improved, they sat down in a climate of tension to await developments.

They waited an hour. Then on one of the screens, there was movement. A shadow emerged and approached through the lightening haze. The remote cameras zoomed in as the shadow loomed closer until finally its form was distinct – and the room held its breath as the mob of mutant funnelwebs advanced to the edge of the Hot Ditch, and stopped.

Their leader stepped forward.

The day before, the light had returned, and he and his followers had been drawn by it. Now, as he prowled cautiously at the rim of this place, he could again feel the weight of its energy. At first, it was just a throbbing, like something ominous approaching from the distance. But then the pain came – a searing pain that lanced into him like white hot needles, bringing agonising but strangely pleasurable feelings, of power, and of awesome aggression. The feelings pulsed through him like a thousand drums beating, growing and growing until he felt that he would explode. It was then at the very core of him that something unhooked . . . and a deluge of acrid force erupted and flowed in him like lava.

The leader darted and froze, he reared back and trembled, he spun and leapt and quivered in a crazed dance. And the force incinerated his pain as it cauterised his every nerve, and overwhelmed him with urges that were black, and irresistible.

Looking on, the others became excited. And then they heard the drumbeats, and one by one the pain came to them too. They darted and froze, they reared back and trembled, they spun and leapt and quivered in a crazed dance. And when the acrid force erupted in each and every one of them, the gathering at the wellspring of the light was visited by pandemonium.

In the windowless room, the observers stood involuntarily as the first funnelweb emitted a scream. Then, with its venom pulsing, it reared back into a fearsome stance of attack, and sprang down from the rim onto the black glassy skin of the Hot Ditch.

There was a gasp, and people ran out as all the funnelwebs started screaming. And with their venom pulsing, they too reared back and sprang. Until soon they were dropping into the Hot Ditch by their hundreds, and advancing across its breadth in a loathsome, unstoppable tide.

They quaked wildly in the force from the wellspring. But soon their pain numbed and was overtaken by triumphant euphoria.

Before long, they had reached the other side. And as the leader set their path into the emptiness beyond, they knew that the supremacy for which they had striven was finally theirs.

No blood remained in Christian Phelps' face. On the screens, so many funnelwebs were crossing the Hot Ditch that they appeared as a solid mass. Richard Bartlett looked at Phelps without expression. Then he stood, and silently walked out.

Dennis Carson drifted off, followed by the others, leaving Phelps to face failure alone. And there he stood, unblinking, until long after the screens were blank and the windowless room was left in darkness.

Phelps knew it was only time now before the funnelwebs overran the entire continent. And in the way that things worked, he knew also that he would be blamed. He'd lost his career, his professional credibility, and his country. It was time to go.

He would return to England – to Oxford, where he had been so successful as a Rhodes scholar. There, none of this would matter and with his qualifications he would certainly find a 'chair'. That was it – he'd go to ground, and through his contacts in the Masons, he would spirit himself away to a new life.

Christian Phelps turned to leave but stopped when he saw the figure in the doorway. Despite the fact that it was in silhouette, he recognised the figure immediately and so knew that a plea for mercy would be pointless. But Phelps was still a soldier, and he was not going to just stand there and take it.

He flew across the room and lunged viciously at the figure. But before he got close, three silenced shots thumped into his chest and he was dead even before he hit the floor.

As they zipped Phelps into a body bag, Dennis Carson stepped forward and took the pistol from the killer's hand. It had been an unnecessary action and even more unnecessary for the Prime Minister to pull the trigger personally. However he had insisted, and now even Carson was discomfited by the manic pleasure that glowed in Richard Bartlett's eyes. Which only confirmed to the spy master something he had for some time suspected – that the authority he served was fast descending into irredeemable psychopathy.

14

Jack Fitzgerald had been overly optimistic when he'd estimated that forty million sheep would keep the funnelwebs in New South Wales for months. It was barely six weeks before they crossed into Victoria, and within nine they were well inside Queensland and South Australia.

By then, the Commonwealth Government along with half the populations of Melbourne and Adelaide had gone to Tasmania, which across two hundred kilometres of Bass Strait was judged to be the only place in Australia safe from the funnelwebs. Initially the Tasmanians had tried to contain the massive influx within a refugee camp on the site of the old horror penal colony at Port Arthur. But huge numbers broke out and spread into the country-side, and the island became peppered with tent towns reminiscent of the Victorian gold rush.

With the failure of Hot Ditch, the people of Brisbane and the Gold Coast migrated north, and for a month the Pacific Highway between Bundaberg and Mackay was a re-run of the Hume Highway a few weeks earlier. The army garrison at Townsville mutinied and turned the town into a citadel which successfully repelled the refugees. With the vast distances beyond, only those with real money could get any further, the ironic outcome being that the far north towns of Cairns and Cooktown enjoyed their biggest economic booms since the nineteenth century. It didn't last. Merciless exploitation quickly led to anarchy, and the far north self-destructed from greed long before the funnelwebs got there.

On April 1, Western Australia's secessionists had their day when the state made a Unilateral Declaration of Independence from the Australian Commonwealth. The new nation of Westralia was proclaimed and the second act of the fledgling Perth parliament (after extinguishing native title) was to apply for recognition by the United Nations. However the UN put the application on hold when within twenty-four hours of UDI, Westralia was invaded by Indonesia. Jakarta had been smarting from the insulting pittance it was to receive in the consortium. Now, grabbing a long-awaited opportunity, they landed simultaneously at Fremantle, at Albany and at Broome. They proclaimed that Indonesia had always had greater moral claim to Terra Australis than had imperial Britain, and therefore that the Australian Commonwealth of States, as sanctioned by Britain in 1901, was illegitimate. Accordingly, they declared that part of the continent formerly known as Western Australia was henceforth to be the Indonesian province of Arafura. And so ended the annals of the shortest-lived nation in history.

The Americans, the Russians, the Chinese and the Japanese were not concerned. Sooner or later they would embark on their own Australian adventure and then, as they chose, they would swot the Indonesians like flies. However with the funnelwebs still rampaging, it was not yet a viable proposition. So for the time being the superpowers put Australia on hold, and returned to jostling for profits throughout the rest of the New World Order.

Thus unhindered in the months that followed, the funnel-webs ranged freely throughout the continent, and by the time the southern winter came the number of people in the eastern states was down to under a million. However the monsters never did go above eight hundred and fifty metres, and the high country of the Great Dividing Range became the last haven of humanity east of the Nullarbor.

In the Snowy Mountains, the snow came early that year, which despite its discomfort proved a blessing. The packs of feral dogs that had terrorised the mountains froze to death. And the snow covered the unburied corpses of the thousands of dead – victims of radiation, starvation, and the stone-age lawlessness into which the remnants of Australian society had descended.

The snow also restricted the operations of the marauding brigands who preyed ruthlessly on nascent mountain settlements. But one community was luckier than most. Occupying what had formerly been the ski village of Thredbo, the hundred or so families that had settled there were blessed with guardian angels.

In May, the village had been attacked by brigands on three consecutive nights. On the first night, they had plundered supplies and raped the women. Then on the second night, when the men of the village had resisted, five of them had been summarily hanged. However on the third night, no sooner had the brigands appeared in the streets than from the surrounding mountains had come the vengeful bark of machine-guns. And in under a minute, the brigands were all dead in the snow.

The soldiers had come down to check out the

bodies, and they had seemed to understand the funnelweb tattoos on the brigands' foreheads. The villagers had been full of gratitude and although half starved themselves, had shown the soldiers as much hospitality as they could. But then later, when the village headman had pleaded with the soldiers to stay, they had declined, and at first light had headed back up into the mountains.

But ever since, the soldiers had been visitors. And they always left loaded with everything the villagers could spare. In return the soldiers watched over the village, and the word had spread throughout the mountains that any brigand foolish enough to attack Thredbo would be buried there.

Early one freezing morning, a lone figure strode over the snowfields seventy minutes and four kilometres out of Thredbo. Sinewy and lean, he loped easily and was unslowed by the twenty kilo pack on his back. At his side, startling black against the snow, he carried a Minimi light machine-gun. The weapon seemed a part of him and fitted well with his appearance, which was bearded and wind burned, with hawk eyes that were everywhere at once.

Jack Fitzgerald was unrecognisable as the urbane academic he had once been. As he crested a long rise and paused briefly to catch his breath, he took in the vast white landscape and pondered on how much his life had changed.

Two weeks bailed up inside the APC had been only the beginning. In the event they had been forced to go outside after only two days because despite being in a body bag, Pat Howard's decomposing corpse had become a health threat. So they'd donned their NBC suits and had emerged into rain-filled darkness to bury him.

As they'd laid Howard to rest and Jimmy O'Rourke had said a prayer, it had struck Fitzgerald what an otherworldly spectacle they made – space-suited aliens burying their commander in a radioactive storm. But there was nobody there to see them, and as it thankfully turned out, no-one came anywhere near them for the entire two weeks of their quarantine.

When finally they emerged, the skies were clear blue and their geiger counters showed radiation down to safe levels. The prevailing winds had carried most of the fall-out away from the mountains and the little that had reached there had decayed or been dispersed by the rain. What they did not know was that the lower-lying coastal region was an irradiated, defoliated desert, whose ground water was so poisonous that it would be uninhabitable by humans for centuries. However what was deadly to humans was innoxious to funnelwebs, and the monsters had already spread along the eastern seaboard for hundreds of kilometres.

When they peeled off their NBC suits, they were shocked – in the daylight they looked emaciated, like inmates of a concentration camp. But after a week of hot food and much vigorous exercise, their fitness was returning and Jack Fitzgerald's transformation had begun.

Shute trained Fitzgerald on firearms and in a month he could strip and reassemble every one of them blindfold. Shooting practice was impossible as it would have given away their position, but they figured that sooner or later Fitzgerald would get more than he cared for. And so it turned out – on a sub-zero night in May, at Thredbo. For two nights running they'd heard gunfire from the valley and decided they should go down and take a look. Then when they saw the corpses still hanging from the gibbets, none of them even considered whether or not they should intervene. They killed eleven that night, three by Fitzgerald with a Steyr at two hundred metres. And because of that action, their existence became considerably more tolerable.

Fresh food and human contact bolstered their spirits and their days settled in to a harsh but manageable routine. They dug out the APC and Andy Shute nursed it like a baby, keeping it in readiness for an unforseen emergency. But fuel was gold so they fetched and carried on foot, and slept in the humpy they'd constructed from turf before the snow came. The other commodity they used sparingly was ammunition. When what they had was gone, there would be no more. So all three of them became adept in the making of bows and arrows and proficient in the skills of archery.

At night around the fire, they would sometimes talk about what they would do when the snow melted. An early plan was to drive to Melbourne and find a boat that would get them to Tasmania. But the more that they thought about it, the less enthusiastic O'Rourke and Shute became. First, they would have to run a gauntlet of funnelwebs. Then if they got to Melbourne, what were their chances of finding a seaworthy boat? And if they did reach Tasmania, what would life there be like? By now the place would be a throwback to the Middle Ages – polluted, disease ridden, and ravaged by casual violence. What was left of the army would be engaged in internal security and as O'Rourke and Shute had no taste for what they'd seen at Majura Road, they would almost certainly be cashiered and thrown onto the street.

There was no reason to believe that two ex-soldiers would be any more welcome than any other refugees, and if history was anything to go by, less so. The vagabond ronin of medieval Japan had been ignominiously cashiered soldiers, as had many Wild West outlaws and bootleggers of the Roaring Twenties.

What would they do? Join the mobs of dispossessed that infested Hobart's waterfront? Sign up as henchmen for some bully boy gang boss? Or fight their way across the inland to grab a hectare in the arsehole of nowhere? As the winter solstice passed and spring approached, such discussions became markedly less frequent.

What became more frequent were the nights Andy Shute spent away. O'Rourke and Fitzgerald knew he had a woman in Thredbo – in the circumstances the lure of female company was irresistible. They knew that sooner or later Shute would move permanently to the village, and once that happened the likelihood of their staying in the mountains would be multiplied.

O'Rourke seemed increasingly disinclined to leave anyway. As the months passed, he became more reclusive and sometimes he and the others barely spoke for days. There was no antagonism, rather it was that their lives had become so well ordered that there seemed little need to talk.

Beyond that, Shute and Fitzgerald both knew that O'Rourke had changed. Since the night they'd been in Canberra, something had been preoccupying him that neither of them could fully explain. Shute put it down to O'Rourke's sense of responsibility for the loss of the company. Logically there was nothing he could have done, but Shute knew well how the burden of those deaths must still be laying upon him.

Fitzgerald thought it was something else. He'd seen the look in O'Rourke's eyes that night as he'd carried Pat Howard into the APC, and he'd sensed then that something had happened that had turned O'Rourke's world upside down. But as is often the way with men, it was never actually spoken of, and with each of them respectful of the others' privacy, they kept their own counsel.

For Jimmy O'Rourke, the pain of his burden did not lessen. But with the passing of time it became more familiar, and with familiarity, easier to bear. He was certainly not happy. But as weeks passed into months, he was quietly surprised that this life increasingly suited him. There were no people up here. And where there were no people, there were no relationships. And where there were no relationships, there were no lies, no betrayals, and no failures.

O'Rourke settled into his own routine – protective night patrols of the high ground around Thredbo, day reconnaissance patrols further afield, and the rest of his time occupied with logistics and keeping an ordered camp. Going to the village he increasingly found good reason for leaving to the others, until eventually it was understood that it was something he just didn't do. It suited Shute of course, and Fitzgerald looked forward to a home-cooked meal and an evening of conversation.

But for O'Rourke, all he needed he found in solitude. A spectral figure in the landscape, he would become a legend in the mountains, eulogised in story and song as, 'The Kosciusko Ghost'. And as things would turn out, he would enjoy many a long hour in his own company, until the day would finally come for him to face death at the roadside – alone, in that freezing wet ditch.

Jack Fitzgerald was also changed. He was no longer the man who had been lost to himself as he grieved for a dead wife and son. But in his depths, he knew that he had not become someone else. Rather he had reverted to someone that he might have been had he not been transplanted and raised in refined civilisation.

As a child, ranging through the Wicklow Mountains, he had been attuned to his land and to his place in it in the way of a native. And as a native, he was developing the instincts and sensibilities and spiritual insights that are the gift of indigenes. That development had stopped when he had been displaced. And through his years of growing up in a city in a distant land, his intuitions had dulled and given way to a cerebral world-view.

Now, in the aftermath of the funnelwebs, the native in Jack Fitzgerald had reawoken. And in these mountains, the man who had been a child in those other mountains long ago, had been reborn.

In the process, as he had wished, his ghosts had left him. Except for one. Helen Parkes still inhabited his dreams. So much so that the man he now was had decided that if his life was to have meaning, then he must pay heed to his inner voice.

Word had reached Thredbo that notices had been seen on the Monaro Highway at Bombala, saying that the Royal New Zealand Navy was making humanitarian patrols off the New South Wales coast. The notices had been erected by the NZ Special Air Service, and announced that anyone wishing to be evacuated to New Zealand should go to the coastal town of Eden and present themselves to the landing parties on specified dates. The irony had been noted by some that the often vilified Kiwis should in the end be the only nation doing something selfless to help the last Australians.

So it was that earlier that morning, Jack Fitzgerald had bade an emotional farewell to Jimmy O'Rourke and Andy Shute, and left the Kosciusko camp for the last time. It was a hundred and sixty kilometres to Eden and barring mishap, Fitzgerald planned to be there to meet the next New Zealand patrol in nine days time.

Happily it was high ground most of the way but beyond Bombala he would start to descend to the coast.

Then, sooner or later, he would come upon funnelwebs. However between what he had learned and what he had become, he was confident he had the skill as well as the physical and mental strength to prevail.

Once he arrived in New Zealand, he had no idea what he would do or even what kind of place it might be now. What he did know is that whatever it took, he would somehow find a way to continue his quest to return to America, and find Helen.

Retying his pack, Fitzgerald heard an unfamiliar rumbling. Looking up, he saw a giant USAF C-17A Globemaster flying low over the horizon. He'd seen few aircraft since he'd been up here and then only as vapour trails too high to even be heard. Those had been U-2 spy planes, keeping an eye on the consortium's investment. But this was a heavy transport, and for it to be flying at such low altitude and so far from any possible base seemed odd.

Seconds later, the Globemaster was only a distant speck. Fitzgerald adjusted his load then picked up his Minimi and checked the safety, checked the magazine, and closed the bipod. Then with the sun in his face and the wind at his back, Jack Fitzgerald set his course and strode on, until eventually his figure merged into the vastness of the frozen wilderness.

Richard Bartlett gazed down over the wasteland beneath him, his features set firmly in an expression of stately determination. Then somebody called, 'Cut,' and turning from the window, Bartlett asked, 'Was that all right?'

The director said, 'Perfect, thank you, Mister Bartlett – we'll call that an interview,' and the TV crew packed up their gear and went for a drink.

The accommodation in the Globemaster was too spartan for Bartlett's liking, but it presented a good image for his purposes. With a retinue of press and public servants, Bartlett was flying from Hobart to Washington to have personal talks with the US President. And he was taking the opportunity en route to stage some self-serving publicity.

Bartlett had resigned as Prime Minister a month earlier, passing the reins of power to his loyal cohort and friend, Dennis Carson. What was left of Australia was still under martial law so that had not been a problem, and Bartlett was set to enjoy the pleasures of retirement whilst retaining influence through his special relationship with the new head of government.

Now in the role of Prime Minister's personal envoy, he was on his way to reassure the Americans of Australia's continued good faith. Despite Hot Ditch being ineffective, the terms of their deal would stand, and the message from Dennis Carson was that Australia's abiding fealty was guaranteed. It meant, of course, that the second half of Bartlett's gratuity would have to go to Carson. But half of a billion dollars was better than none of it and Bartlett, ever the pragmatist, took the view that it was all he needed . . . for the time being.

Now that everything was settled, he was delighted to get out of Hobart. What had arguably been the most pleasant of all Australia's state capitals had deteriorated into something like wartime Saigon or the Los Angeles of *Blade Runner*. After so many miserable months bailed up in fortified buildings, Bartlett couldn't wait to sample the delights and sophistication of Washington. And when his mission was over, he would continue on to Europe and satiate himself with the pleasures of its capitals.

As he contemplated the delights that awaited him,

he answered by rote the questions of the reporter now interviewing him. It was a well-trodden litany of clichés: 'The spirit of the Australian people will thrive in exile and their determination to win back their land will be redoubled . . . the fact that Australia is an island continent is safeguarding the world against the funnelwebs and in the end it will mean they have nowhere to hide . . . Australians must be patient until a solution is found and meantime vigorously retain their identity and their faith in God . . . Australia has lost the first battle with the funnelwebs but in the end she will win the war . . . blah, blah, blah.'

Bartlett broke off the interview when he was informed that they were about to overfly Sydney. The plane was at low altitude on his personal instructions, so the cameramen could get good pictures for their networks all around the world.

And they were not disappointed. Laid out below was a vision of the Day of Judgement. The city was still black from the flash of the neutron bomb. The high rise buildings were draped with the remnants of spiders' webs, with great silken strands drifting eerily in the wind from the rooftops. The streets were littered with car wrecks and strewn with shattered glass, and the skeletons of countless dead still lay unburied wherever they had fallen.

The mosque at Lakemba was a burnt-out shell. The Lane Cove River valley, once so lushly forested, was reduced to a forest of charcoal. And the Parramatta River – the fountainhead of the harbour – was a poisoned, rat-infested soak of putrid mud.

Vermin aside, the suburbs appeared deserted, perhaps abandoned by the funnelwebs for the rich pickings of the western plains. Or perhaps with the coming of winter, they had returned underground, to the shelter of the sewers and the railway tunnels from which they had come.

Even Bartlett was lost for words. And as the Globemaster flew low around the perimeter of the city, the only sounds in the aircraft were the clicking of cameras and the whirring of videos.

Until they reached the CBD, and flew out over the harbour, when someone let out an involuntary cry. Because directly beneath them was the most extraordinary thing any of them had ever seen. It was a spider's web, funnel-shaped, perfectly woven and formed, but of such vast proportions that it defied all imagination. At its open end, it was two hundred metres across, and supported by the arched steel superstructure of the Sydney Harbour Bridge. Then narrowing as it trailed back across Sydney Cove to Bennelong Point, it disappeared inside one of the shattered, gaping shells of the Opera House.

In the Globemaster there was a flurry of excitement and the news gatherers pleaded for another fly past so they could get better shots. Bartlett sent the request forward to the pilot, and soon the aircraft was circling to return for a second look.

As cameras were set up in every window, the pilot dropped his flaps, and like a great sea bird the Globemaster yawed in across the harbour only metres from the water. Still wafting in the slipstream, the web loomed up in front of them and every camera began shooting furiously . . . which was how what happened next would come to be seen by half of the world's population.

A vision of horror preternatural in scale erupted from out of the Opera House – a female monster funnelweb standing fully ten metres in height. In a reflex response the pilot jerked on his stick, banking the massive transport like a fighter plane. And not a second too soon because the funnelweb was rearing back, and an instant later spat a piercing stream of venom straight at the aircraft.

The pilot jerked the stick back and the Globemaster wallowed, avoiding the venom stream by inches. Then the pilot rammed the throttles open and wrenched hard on the flaps, and the four mighty turbofans urged the grudging airframe to pick up speed.

Again the funnelweb shot venom and the pilot had to evade, but this time so violently that the Globemaster stood on its wingtip. Not designed for such manoeuvres the big plane shuddered in protest, as in the cabin all the passengers and their equipment were tossed around like toys.

Struggling to regain control, the pilot overcorrected and the Globemaster began to stall. But then wrestling to get the nose down he flew slam-bang through the spider's web, ripping it from its anchorages and draping it like a veil across the Quay.

With great skill the pilot recovered and under full power pulled into a laboured climb. But below, trembling with fury, the female funnelweb screamed, and shot a parting jet of venom at the receding aircraft.

In slow motion the stream arced upwards but the Globemaster had made good height and the venom streaked past just underneath it. But then curving back down again, the stream broke up and dispersed, and showered over the entire centre superstructure of the Sydney Harbour Bridge.

Instantly, the girders began to smoke. Then they started bubbling and melting just like butter in a pan. First the transverse members, then the vertical pillars, then the arch itself distorted, and the bridge began to buckle and twist. And when finally the span broke, the structure totally disintegrated and crashed into the water in a cacophony of hissing steam and tortured steel.

The funnelweb watched as the Globemaster

climbed high over her head. And when finally it banked to the east and headed out to sea, she turned back and descended into the cavity that housed her nest.

The several hundred sheep cadavers still hanging around the walls would feed her for weeks. But the flying intruder had ripped out her resting place and in so doing had torn her egg sacs from their stalls, and ruptured them.

She would need to find a mate and start the process all over again. So she wolfed down the tasty morsels of her wriggling aborted offspring before clambering out into what had been the Opera House forecourt. Then casually, in the knowledge that she had no enemies to endanger her, she stalked off across the charred, dead city over which she now reigned supreme.

High over the Pacific, the injured aboard the Globemaster were tended as the other passengers excitedly relived their experience. Videographers replayed their tapes as producers from two US networks tried to steamroller the communications officer into transmitting their pictures ahead. In the end, they only backed off when the pilot threatened to have them placed under arrest.

By the time the pilot returned to the cockpit, things were calming down. The flight engineer reported they'd been lucky – no serious damage had been sustained. The flaps had retracted successfully and the intake of spider's silk had apparently had no adverse effect on the engines. The web material they had collected was adding a small amount of drag, but in an aircraft of that size their loss of speed would be negligible and they should make their first refuelling rendezvous on schedule. Relieved, the pilot dropped into his seat and ordered a strong black coffee to calm his nerves for the long flight ahead.

In the rear, Richard Bartlett was doing the rounds

of the injured, dispensing sympathy and platitudes and quotable dictums with equal fluency. Suddenly he felt nauseous, and turned to an aide to ask for some water. But the words never passed his lips. Because as he opened his mouth to speak, the weight of an elephant was already bearing down on his chest.

Richard Bartlett collapsed, eyes bulging, gulping for air. He flailed and thrashed, trying desperately to cry out, but the only sound that came was a sickening rattle from his throat.

A doctor pushed through the onlookers and found Richard Bartlett had died from a massive coronary. And as word of what had happened passed quickly through the aircraft, there was much sadness at the passing of the 'chief'. It was well known that he had cited health reasons for his resignation, brought on by the stress of battling the funnelwebs. Now, people postulated, with his release from that stress, Bartlett's mind must have relaxed and allowed his body to give up too. The attack by the giant funnelweb must have been the last straw, and the hero had finally fallen victim to the evil he had so bravely withstood. How fortunate, it was agreed, Australia was to have had such a son, and how important his inspiration would be in the fight ahead. The reporters and camera crews began to interrogate everyone who had ever known Richard Bartlett, as their producers recommenced their assault on the hapless communications officer.

One reporter, however, stayed out of it. It had been her interview that Richard Bartlett had broken off immediately prior to the funnelweb attack. But now, she sat by herself at the rear of the aircraft, trying to sleep.

Helen Parkes had no interest in writing the story of Richard Bartlett's death, because she had already written it. Alone in her hotel room the previous evening, she had paced up and down, going over and over it in her mind. Even through heavily curtained windows she had been distracted by the gunfights in the bars and brothels of Hobart's waterfront. So unable to concentrate, she had sat at her computer and written the scenario for Richard Bartlett's death – partly as a means of planning it, but mostly as a kind of mental preparation.

She had killed before – twice – in the cottage at Lake Bathurst. But that had been in the heat of the moment and not premeditated murder. Her training at Langley and the intensive crammer she had recently undergone there had furnished her with the technical skills. But the mental strength needed to carry out an assassination was something she'd had to find within herself.

Now it was done, and thankfully earlier than she had thought would be possible. Her plan had been to wait until Bartlett was moving around the aircraft, when she could jostle him without arousing suspicion. But as luck would have it, the attack by the giant funnelweb had provided a better opportunity. With everyone distracted, she had twisted the end of her fully functional microphone and exposed the needle of the syringe concealed inside. Then with debris crashing painfully into him, Bartlett hadn't even registered the tiny jab in the small of his back.

The delayed action nerve agent had not taken effect for ten minutes, by which time Helen had removed the concealed syringe and disposed of it in the toilet. Then in the pandemonium, she had moved right away from Bartlett and very visibly helped out with the injured to establish an alibi.

As it was, no alibi would be necessary. In the circumstances, Bartlett's death aroused no suspicion at all and on arrival in Los Angeles, his body would be taken into the care of the Company.

Helen Parkes had been recruited by the CIA during her graduating year at Columbia. She had been a prize candidate – intellectually brilliant, politically non-aligned, and emotionally malleable. The senior tutor who acted as a talent scout for Langley had picked her early, but had waited for the right opportunity to make his approach. It came when Helen had kicked out her faithless lover and had been at her most emotionally vulnerable. Subsequently the Company had provided a surrogate family, and she had committed herself to it, and to her training, with unrestrained enthusiasm.

On graduation, Helen's controllers decided she would be most useful in New York, where her breeding and contacts gave her access to the highest levels of society. The CIA was as interested in matters domestic as much as foreign, and over the next few years Helen sourced much valuable intelligence on big business and government. Her overt career as a journalist had originally been her cover, but her success in it had been largely self-earned. Which was why she had been hired quite legitimately to report the funnelweb story, thereby saving her controllers the trouble of inserting at least one of the new agents they would be needing in Australia.

Her affair with Fitzgerald had certainly been an expediency, giving her access to information at a high level. But the day she had met him, she had genuinely fallen in love with him, and her passion for him on the two occasions they had slept together had been completely real.

It had been devastating for her to leave Canberra without him. When the sealed, encrypted order had been delivered to her by Commander Swan, she had known it probably meant Fitzgerald was to be left behind. Given his antagonism to the way things had been handled, she knew why. Also because the message had been typewritten rather than faxed or computer printed, she suspected the order had originated locally. And although she had no idea who her local controller was, it seemed likely in the circumstances that it was someone inside Parliament House.

She was right. The CIA had an asset, through whom all her orders and information had been channelled, at the very top of the Australian government's bureaucracy. He had been recruited by the Americans as a double agent during his time as a military intelligence officer in Vietnam, and getting him into place as the director of ASIO had been one of the firm's more notable coups of the post-Cold War period.

Now to top that, Dennis Carson was installed as Australian Prime Minister. And for as long as Australia was under martial law, he would not have to face an election. It was not surprising then that Tasmania was crawling with 'criminals' and 'dissidents', to ensure that unrest there would remain unabatedly on the boil.

Ironically, it was Carson personally who had initiated the order to kill Richard Bartlett – ironic because Carson was the only person in the world that Bartlett had trusted. Once Bartlett had served his purpose, the last thing the Americans wanted was a greedy psychotic on the loose with their secrets – and Carson's masters were in no doubt that sooner or later, Bartlett would put the bite on them for more money. His penchant for whoring was also a concern. Carson had himself obtained information from Bartlett through an agent famous for her talents around the fleshpots of Fyshwick. Bartlett was simply too much of a risk. So now Carson, who had ordered so many deaths for the former prime minister, had himself ordered Bartlett's own. It was a Machiavellian twist that Richard Bartlett, under other circumstances, would have appreciated.

There was one detail, however, that Carson had not shared with his masters. Bartlett had always made personal calls on his digital mobile phone precisely because digital mobiles are secure. However Carson had devised a way around that. The day that Bartlett had bought the phone, an ASIO agent had bought an identical one. Then overnight the double phone had been fitted with a bug, and the next day Carson had had the phones switched. Subsequently, whenever Richard Bartlett made a call, ASIO would receive and record it. That way, Carson had not only known about the payment of Bartlett's 'gratuity', but also, from the dial tones, the phone number of his bank in Vienna and the PIN he used to make telephone transactions.

Bartlett had thought it a measure of the esteem in which Carson held him that the new Prime Minister had insisted on taking him to his plane personally. But no sooner had the Globemaster left the tarmac, rendering Bartlett incommunicado, than Carson had phoned Vienna and transferred Bartlett's five hundred and fifty million dollars into a numbered account of his own. And mindful of the fact that he couldn't trust *anyone*, he made the call from a phone which is in fact the most secure of all – a pay phone, in the concourse of the terminal at Hobart Airport.

Helen Parkes knew none of these things, as she gazed out through the window of the Globemaster across the darkening ocean. What she did know was that her final act as an agent of her government had also cast her as an agent of revenge for Jack Fitzgerald, whom Bartlett had not only left to die but had denied something he would have treasured even more than life. Unconsciously Helen stroked her swelling abdomen, and wondered if the baby growing inside her would take after its father. She hoped so, because albeit briefly she had loved Jack Fitzgerald. And now, with a different view of the world and a new knowledge of her own strength, she would reject her secret life and try to raise Fitzgerald's child with all the love that she herself had never known.

The sun had dropped low, and Helen thought the threads of spider's silk trailing from the wings were like filaments of the purest gold. She was reminded of Jack's story of Arachne, and found herself hoping that he had not died in too much pain. But as tears welled in her eyes, she put the thought from her mind and turned her attention to her laptop, and her final dispatch.

Outside in the slipstream, the threads trailing behind the aircraft floated away for nearly a kilometre. But some of the silk had gathered in a clag around the aircraft's rear fuselage.

At the heart of the clag there was a football sized nodule which had been torn from the nest of the giant funnelweb. In the nodule, something was moving . . . and not just one thing, but many . . . in a pulsing, writhing mass of life.

The nodule was an egg sac containing over a hundred gestating monster funnelweb spiders. Assisted by a freshening tailwind, the Globemaster picked up speed, and flew on into the darkness towards the United States of America.

Beverley Harper
Edge of the Rain

The blood scent was fresh. Hunger ached in her belly...the lioness slid forward as close as she dared. The little boy seconds away from death was two, maybe three years old. He was lost in the vast, heat-soaked sand that was the Kalahari desert.

Toddler Alex Theron is miraculously rescued by a passing clan of Kalahari Bushmen. Over the ensuing years the desert draws him back, for it hides a beautiful secret...diamonds.

But nothing comes easily from within this turbulent continent and before Alex can even hope to realise his dreams he will lose his mind to love and fight a bitter enemy who will stop at nothing to destroy him...

From the author of *Storms Over Africa* comes a novel of courage and an unforgettable journey into the beating heart of Africa.

'A superbly told story which will appeal to almost every audience'
Alan Gold, AUSTRALIAN BOOKSELLER & PUBLISHER

JR Carroll
The Clan

'The best Australian crime novel of recent years...powerful, exhilarating, gritty'
AUSTRALIAN BOOK REVIEW

THE KILLING
An unarmed teenage ram-raider is gunned down by police in a back alley...

THE FAMILY
The Beatties, one of Melbourne's most notoriously lawless clans stretching back to the sixties. Now their youngest is dead, and Melbourne holds its breath, waiting for the payback it knows is coming.

THE JOB
But someone is planning the biggest hold-up in Australia's history, and no-one, not even the Beattie family, is allowed to get in the way...

'A major achievement'
SYDNEY MORNING HERALD